UNETHICAL

A PSYCHOLOGICAL THRILLER

Marla L. Anderson

Wolfheart Press
Alpine, California

To my mother, Ramona, who showed me how it's done.

CONTENTS

Acknowledgements

When I started writing this novel, my thoughts were on aging and dementia, and the possibility of restoring an ailing body and mind. It never occurred to me that this book might end up being launched in the middle of a global pandemic during which humanity's welfare depended upon the rapid development of a vaccine.

The scientific community rose to meet that challenge in heroic fashion and record time for which I will be forever amazed and grateful. I have the utmost respect and admiration for these men and woman who have dedicated their lives to the pursuit of knowledge for the betterment of mankind.

A special thank-you goes to my science advisers, Doctors Terrell and Barbara Johnson, both of whom are experts in their fields and definitely know their way around a lab.

Another big thank-you goes to fellow writers Catherine, David, Jan, and Marijke for their continued support and helpful suggestions all along the way.

And a final thank-you to Ryan Anderson at Higher Images Paintings who helped me design the cover for this book and without complaint put up with countless changes.

Prologue

He'd been up all night in anticipation of this moment, desperate to know he'd made the right choice. In the dim alcove of his private lab, Dr. Adrian Kessler inserted the prepared specimen into his electron microscope. The enlarged image revealed spider webs of twisted white filaments throughout the gray matter confirming his diagnosis of Alzheimer's Disease.

This hair-thin slice of brain tissue came from Gladys Johnson, a woman of high intelligence until AD destroyed her mind and made her a resident at his facility. He had specifically selected her as a test subject because of that prior intellect, thinking a positive result in her could be dramatic. And it had been, briefly. For a few days, she'd been back... focused and present, able to converse with him and her family, cognizant of time and place. But then she began to fade again, and he knew that meant her organs would soon fail and she would be dead within weeks. As repeatedly proven in the mice, the only way to examine any regenerated neuron cells at that point was to harvest the brain immediately. But this wasn't a mouse this time. It was a human being.

Ethics dictated he let nature take its course. Science demanded he preserve the evidence. Faced with a wicked choice between following the rules or making a giant leap forward in his research, he had erred on the side of science.

Adjusting the controls, he further magnified the image, bringing an individual cell into focus. His eyes widened. There was the evidence he sought, a neuron cell suspended between death and rebirth—its synapses partially reconnected, cell body structures partially restored to normality. The word *Eureka!* screamed in his mind, but he only smiled in celebration. He was not alone.

Outside this alcove was the brightly lit area of the lab

where two of his research assistants walked silently across the polished tiles in their fabric-booted feet, speaking in hushed tones lest they disturb him. Without alerting them to his excitement, he moved the field of view to other neuron cells, some fully restored, others frozen in process. Still more showed signs of deterioration, confirming he had acted wisely to harvest the brain when he did. Here was indisputable evidence that his method of delivering CRISPR re-engineered stem cells directly into the hippocampus could resurrect dead neuron cells in a diseased human brain.

He wanted to yell out in triumph but remained silent. No one must know he was conducting unauthorized experiments on human test subjects. Not yet. Not before he obtained FDA approval for clinical trials. His treatment still needed more testing in the animal labs to qualify. To date, only a handful of mice had survived for more than a few months, and he still didn't know why.

Sometimes, he worried that hidden factors in the biochemical equation might be beyond his ability to detect with the tools currently available to medical science. What he needed was to determine which expression of DNA made the ultimate difference, but the exact path AD took to destroy a mind differed nearly as much as the affected individuals themselves. Such was the nature of a disease that attacked the essence of personality.

Dr. Alois Alzheimer reported the first case in 1906 after his postmortem exam of a woman in her fifties. By the end, she no longer recognized her own reflection, and patted the faces of others thinking they were her own. She literally lost herself. In examining her brain, Dr. Alzheimer noted an 'unusual disease of the cerebral cortex' marked by abnormal clumps and tangled bundles of fibers. Research had since identified those clumps as amyloid plaques, and the fibers as neurofibrillary or tau tangles, but to this day no one knew why they formed. Were they merely symptoms of the disease or the cause?

One thing certain, AD was an eventual death sentence, and before the end, it dragged its victims into a bleak state of existence where they were unable to express coherent thought, recall the past, or consider the future. He imagined that mental blankness must be like floating in a shore-less sea, trying desperately to remember something... anything. The image gave him nightmares of being lost and alone in dark, endless waters.

What are we but memory and knowledge amassed over time? he often pondered. *If all that vanishes, what's left?*

He wished his patients could tell him while they still lived, but it was only by examining what remained of their damaged brains under a microscope that he had any chance of learning the answer. This tissue sample confirmed he'd acted wisely to preserve evidence of cellular renewal at the first sign of regression.

He still had two more human test subjects who remained alive. They too showed marked improvement in cognition and he was keeping a close eye on them, hoping for better results, but if they followed the same downward path, he would not hesitate to act.

Never again would he wait patiently for a test subject to die slowly and allow his work to be destroyed.

CHAPTER ONE

Obligations

Josephine Rinaldi stood outside her father's bedroom door—something that had turned into a nightly ritual—listening for sounds of movement and hoping not to hear any. She leaned against the wall. It would take a while before she could assume it was safe to leave. The light at the end of the hall beckoned, but there was no point in her going back to bed only to be woken again by him wandering through the old house, searching for something he couldn't name. The diagnosis was Alzheimer's Disease.

How did this become my life? But she knew the answer. This was the price of being a dutiful daughter. Of her promise to fulfill her mother's dying wish.

Eyes closed, with her head resting on the wall, she almost fell asleep, but then the old schoolhouse clock next to her chimed, making her jump. She glared at it as if it had intentionally spooked her, then sighed at the hour—two am. She wanted to be at work by eight to prepare for the litigation meeting. She did the math—six hours, minus one to get herself ready and supervise her father if he woke before his caregiver arrived, minus another to allow for traffic—that left four if she fell asleep right here on her feet. Her body demanded seven on average, a requirement she hadn't met in... *what? A week? A month?* She'd lost count.

Maybe I'm getting it, too. That would be one way to erase the past, it occurred to her with a bitter note. *Stop it*, she scolded herself, then automatically heard the words drilled into her by a therapist. *It wasn't your fault. You were just a child.*

No matter how many times she repeated that declaration, it never fully registered. Maybe because the sentiment had never been voiced by the one person she needed to hear it from and probably never would.

When all remained quiet, she headed back to her bedroom. Halfway down the hall she paused at the bedroom door between her father's room and her own, placed her palm on the dark wood and whispered, "Good night, Tommy." She seldom went inside. This simple gesture alone hurt enough.

As she dropped her hand, a low creak stopped her cold, pulling icy fingers down her back.

Don't be stupid, she told herself. She shook off the eeriness of the moment, then continued down the hall to her own room, closed her door, crawled under the covers, and turned off the light. But as she lay there, the creaking sound nagged and her eyes refused to close, blinking at what she couldn't see. *Stop it, you're being ridiculous.* Time ticked by. She couldn't stop it. Finally, she had to face that there would be no sleep for her until she proved just how ridiculous she was being. Annoyed, she sat up and turned her bedside lamp back on.

She imagined walking down the dark hall, opening her brother's door, and finding the overhead light inside the room not working. *That would be the end of me right there,* she thought, and though probably unnecessary, grabbed the flashlight from her drawer.

Leaving the lights off for fear of re-awakening her father, she tiptoed down the hall like a stealthy burglar with her flashlight throwing strange shadows on the walls. She hesitated at the closed door. Come on, this isn't some stupid low-budget horror movie. At worst, there's a mouse or a rat in there. Not much liking those possibilities either, she took a deep breath, turned the knob and inched the door open.

Her flashlight cut through the silent darkness. Nothing scurried, chittered, or jumped out at her. She flipped on the wall switch. The overhead light lit up the room, dispelling any notion of lingering spirits. She let out the breath she didn't realize she'd been holding and experienced an odd combination of relief and disappointment. What wouldn't she give to see her brother again, even if it were only his ghost?

Although neater than he had ever kept it in life, Tommy's bedroom looked basically the same, thanks to twenty years of a mother's loving maintenance. With their mother's passing and her father's illness, it was up to Jo to decide what was to become of Tommy's shrine. So far, she hadn't touched it. His roller hockey sticks still made an 'X' above the bed. Medals and ribbons hung next to a lettered jacket framed on the wall. His high school, Little League and Pop Warner trophies filled the shelves next to hardbound and paperback novels about wizards and warriors, kings and dragons. A surfboard decorated with brilliant blue waves stood on end in the corner. She stared at it and not for the first time wondered if it was the same one he'd ridden that day. Had one of Tommy's friends returned it to his grief-stricken parents?—"Hey, thought you'd like to have this."

Could anyone be that clueless?

She shook her head, then poked about, sweeping her flashlight beam across the floor, nudging the empty trashcan with her foot, and ruffling the bed-skirt to see if any scurrying, scrabbling, or other noise resulted. It didn't.

"See? There's nothing in here."

Speaking aloud felt almost sacrilegious but confirmed the only ghost present was the one in her head. One that wouldn't go away, ever.

This was Tommy's room. He'd slept here, dreamt here, planned his future here. She remembered him sitting on the orange-and-brown plaid bedspread reading his favorite books aloud to her. That last year, his senior year in high school, he'd been sharing "The Lord of the Rings" with her one chapter a night. She'd been 10 years old then, totally enraptured, not only by the story, but by his voice. To this day the trilogy remained unfinished. She'd never been able to bring herself to read the rest on her own.

She recalled Tommy saying, "Someday, I want to be a writer like Tolkien."

"I thought you wanted to be a lawyer like Dad," she'd said.

"I don't have to be just one thing, do I?"

Back then, her brother believed he could do and be anything he wanted, and so had she. An athlete and scholar, he'd graduated first in his class. The only downside for her about the breadth of his accomplishments back then was that he'd gotten into the college of his choice and planned to leave soon. Something she'd dreaded. She'd relied on his counsel, trusted him completely, and did whatever it took to earn his trust in return, even when it meant keeping secrets. When he said, "Don't tell Mom and Dad," there was no question. She told them nothing—and that's what got him killed.

Jo sat down hard on the bed as the old guilt grabbed hold, trying to drown her in a familiar hopeless regret, that dark place where she might have taken up permanent residence after Tommy died if her parents hadn't intervened.

It wasn't your fault..., automatically sounded again in her head.

The therapist labeled her with "Situational Depression," then gave her the mantra and a prescription for Zoloft. The mantra she couldn't avoid, drilled into her ad nauseam, but the pills got flushed down the toilet. She'd been too afraid to take them, a fear born of the secret she kept to this day, that sometimes Tommy and his friends took drugs, sometimes before going out on the water.

"It's so cool, Josie. Floating out there high is like being in another world."

What if these were the same kind he took? she had worried, so only pretended to swallow them. Then she'd put on a smile and answered everyone's concerned inquiries with, "I'm fine, really." But she wasn't fine, not really, not then, not even now after all these years.

She lay down and buried her face in Tommy's pillow, wanting to feel close to him again, but it smelled only of laundry soap. Like her, it had been too long without him.

A hand squeezed her shoulder. "Better not let Tommy catch you in here," her father said.

Startled, Jo realized all at once not only whose bedroom she was in, but that sunlight was streaming in through the windows. She bolted upright. "What time is it?"

His speckled silver and gray hair askew, her father looked at his bare wrist and frowned. "Where's my watch?"

"Who knows? Probably in the flour bin again."

He turned his scowl on her. "That's absurd."

"Agreed." She noticed he was fully dressed, a surprise, and that no item of clothing matched, which wasn't. She scrambled to her feet and hurried out into the hallway to look at the clock. Its hands pointed to 7:20. Leaning over the mahogany railing, she called downstairs. "Teresa?" No answer. *Dammit, she's late again.*

"Dad, I need to get ready. Would you please wait in your bedroom until Teresa gets here?"

"Who?"

"Your caregiver. She comes every morning, stays until I get home. Remember?"

"If I forgot half what I know, I'd still know more than you ever will."

Jo grimaced at the familiar insult but said nothing as she guided him back to his bedroom and turned on the morning news, hoping to keep him occupied long enough for her to shower and dress. When he seemed content, she ran back down the hall, grabbed what she needed and jumped in the shower. She finished in record time, threw on her clothes, then checked on him again... still watching television, and still no sign of Teresa.

She hurried back to put on her make-up and fix her hair, then examined the finished product in the mirrored doors of her closet. Her dark shoulder-length hair lay smooth, the make-up softened the freckles over her nose, and the pale-pink lipstick complemented the rose-colored blouse under her navy-blue pantsuit. She decided the overall effect was professional enough to make her look like she belonged where she was headed. Now she just needed to get there, but first back to her father's room. He still sat staring at the TV, wearing a blank look on his face as if waiting for someone's redirection. Looked like that someone had to be her.

"Come on, Dad. Let's go downstairs and get you some breakfast."

They took the steps one at a time, arm-in-arm. He refused to use a walker or cane even though his balance couldn't be trusted. Once down the stairs, she took him into the kitchen and chose something quick to fix—instant oatmeal with raisins. A minute-and-a-half out of the microwave later, she set the bowl and a creamer of milk on the round wood table in the nook. The windows overlooked a small green yard and the San Diego skyline beyond.

"Come eat," she said while pointing at the bowl and his chair. Instead, he stood in the middle of the room scowling at his bare wrist, which reminded her to check the flour canister. Sure enough, there inside, the tip of a flour-encrusted sock poked up, and inside the sock she found not only his gold watch but his wedding ring. She slipped the watch into her pocket and put the ring on her thumb before taking the sock over to the sink to rinse off. Under the running water, it returned to its former black, and the flour formed a puddle of thick white goop, slowly sliding toward the drain. A metaphor for her life, it occurred to her. Her father—the esteemed Thomas Lorenzo Rinaldi, Harvard graduate cum laude, professor of law—was gradually losing his mind and if this situation continued much longer, so would she.

Startling her from behind, he stabbed his forefinger into the puddle and popped it into his mouth before she could stop him.

"Ugh, that's disgusting," he said, making a face and waggling the licked finger at her. "You should take cooking lessons. Now my Amanda, there's a woman who knows her way around a kitchen."

Jo dropped the sock, washed his hand and dried it, then steered him back to the kitchen table.

"You need to eat before your breakfast gets cold."

He sat down but pointed at the dark mottled clouds above the city skyline. "Looks like rain." As if the clouds heard him, drops spattered the windows.

"Well, we definitely need it," Jo said. It was mid-January and a dry winter so far.

Wondering what was keeping Teresa, she checked her cell phone messages and found one. [Sorry so late. Car not start. Be there soon.]. Jo turned on the small television above the food preparation island, hoping to catch a traffic report, but they were talking about a political debate. As usual, the two parties sharply divided. One demanded prison reform, the other opposed increased regulations. After working as a paralegal for a public defender, Jo leaned on the side of reform.

"It's always so empty without flowers," her father said out of nowhere.

"What?" She turned to see him frowning at the table before him. "Oh. Sorry. I didn't have time."

"Amanda always makes time. She loves flowers."

The memory made Jo smile. "True. She used to say they were little miracles you could hold in your hand. She especially loved her roses." As soon as the past tense slipped from her mouth, she regretted it.

He blinked, his mouth working soundlessly, then his face darkened, and he threw his spoon on the floor. "You think I've forgotten she's gone?"

"No, I... I didn't mean..."

"It's not your place to remind me."

"I know. I'm sorry. Forget what I said, it doesn't matter."

"No, it doesn't. It doesn't at all." He glared at her for a moment, then sighed as if losing energy for the exchange. He turned back to his oatmeal, poking at it with his finger. "That's odd. Amanda knows I prefer fresh fruit. She must have run out."

Jo turned away lest emotion take over. It was a now familiar pattern. Once his anger passed, he quickly returned to a strange, muddled world of mixed realities. She took a breath, got another spoon for him from the drawer and wiped off his finger. She stood over him until he started eating. Once satisfied he would continue doing so, she looked at the clock on the microwave, her worry growing.

"Dawson's going to kill me if I'm late again."

Her father looked up from his breakfast. "What? Who's going to kill you?"

She instantly regretted speaking aloud. "No one. Sorry. I just need to get to my litigation meeting."

"Litigation? I should get ready then." He started pushing away from the table.

"No, no, you just need to eat your breakfast and wait here for Teresa."

"Who?"

"Teresa, Dad. She'll stay with you until I get back."

"Why? Has she got the hots for me? Amanda won't like that."

Explaining the who and why of Teresa had become a daily ritual. Sometimes, Jo wasn't sure if he really didn't remember or was just trying to make her crazy. Speaking of which made her remember the watch and gold wedding band she'd rescued from the flour canister. She pulled the watch from her pocket and held it out along with her thumb displaying his wedding ring. "I found these in the flour again," she said, intending to tell him she would keep them safe, but he snatched the ring off her thumb.

Looking at it, he smiled, his face breaking into a thousand spider-web lines.

"When your mother dropped this, everybody scrambled after it. They said we looked like a football team in the middle of a fumble."

"Yes, I know, Dad." Jo felt a pang at her impatience, but the wedding story had been told and retold more times than she could count. She reached for the ring, but he balled his hand into a fist and pulled it tight to his chest.

"I want my watch, too," he demanded. "It belongs to me."

The last thing she needed was to get into a power struggle. She had neither the heart nor time for it, so she handed the watch over to him. "Fine. But keep them on you. Not in a sock buried in the flour."

He scowled at her.

"Your breakfast is getting cold," she reminded him again, and he looked back at the bowl as if seeing it for the first time. Her own gaze turned to the built-in desk beneath the television. There, hidden behind the telephone was the brochure she'd brought home days ago and was still trying to get up the courage to show him. She had practically memorized the text: 'Seeking residential participants with Alzheimer's Disease, neurological disorders, or non-diagnosed dementia... Residents receive specialized care in a secure park-like environment.' She recalled the list of symptoms that so perfectly described her father. 'Ten things to look for...' and 'Important questions to ask your health provider...'

Making sure her father wasn't watching, she took out the brochure to look again at the photos of contented elderly men and women with their uniformed caregivers. On the back was the Institute's founder, Dr. Adrian Kessler, posed in a way that projected just the right combination of sincerity and professionalism. In his white coat and wire-rimmed glasses, he looked polished and confident, yet unpretentious and caring.

Her father's personal physician, Dr. Wayne Peterson, said Alzheimer's promised a slow certain death, but if anyone were likely to find a cure in the foreseeable future, it would most likely be this man. To top it off, Dr. Kessler and his Institute were clients of the law firm where she worked and thanks to a personal request from her boss, Matthew Dawson, they were holding a room open for her father, but not forever. If she procrastinated much longer, it might be too late.

Speaking of which... Jo glanced at the time again. She knew when those clouds started dumping, traffic would back up. One thing Southern California drivers couldn't handle was rain. She felt a rush of relief when she heard the key in the lock and the front door open.

"Hola!" Teresa called out, "Good morning."

"Hello," Jo called back.

Teresa was apologizing as she came in, putting away her purse and coat in the living room closet, saying something about car trouble, but Jo wasn't listening. "Dad, I have to run. Teresa's here if you need anything, okay?"

"Stop talking to me as if I were a child. Go play lawyer if you must. I'll be perfectly fine."

She gave him a peck on the cheek. "Bye, Teresa," she yelled as she hurried out the side door into the attached garage. She sidled past her father's aging black Mercedes—she'd hidden the keys from him months ago—and got into her silver Toyota.

Out on the road, the dark clouds let loose, pelting her windshield, and turning the asphalt into a slick black mirror. She waited on the signal-controlled on-ramp only to squeeze into bumper-to-bumper traffic. Recognizing the hopelessness of making the meeting on time, she called her direct office line.

"Jo-Rinaldi's-office-this-is-Beverly-may-I-help-you?" her secretary delivered in a single breath.

"Bev, It's me. I'm stuck in traffic."

"Oh boy. You know he's not going to be happy."

"I know, I know. I'll get there as soon as I can."

CHAPTER TWO

Rained Out

S oon turned out to be another thirty minutes, making Jo ten minutes late for the meeting. When the elevator doors opened to the twentieth floor, she sprinted— raincoat, briefcase, purse and all—straight to the main conference room. Hearing voices within, she took a breath then quietly edged the door open. Silence fell like a guillotine as every head in the room turned in her direction.

"Excuse me," she said and side-stepped her way around the conference table to an open chair. All eyes watched as she unloaded and took a seat. "Sorry."

Silver-haired Matthew Dawson, positioned at the table's head as appropriate for the firm's senior litigation partner, focused his cool blue stare on her.

"Traffic?" he asked.

She smiled and nodded. "There was an accident. Rain always seems to make a mess of things."

He nodded back with pursed lips, then let his gaze sweep past the other attorneys and paralegals as if to say they too had traversed the freeways this morning yet managed to be on time. Jo tried not to blink or blush red hot. None of them had to tag-team an unpredictable old man.

"Now that we're all finally here, let's review our caseloads," he said.

He introduced each pending matter, requested a status update and strategy evaluation, putting the assigned attorney on the spot. Of the eleven present—eight men and three women—more than half of them were younger than Jo, but all of them senior to her in length of employment. Success as a paralegal combined with an unexpected divorce had spurred her to earn the degree of Juris Doctor, but at age thirty, Jo was a relative latecomer. Even with high ranking in her graduating class, she knew she was lucky to have gotten a junior associate position here.

She recalled how impressed she'd been by the firm's

lobby with its long winding staircase and dark wood-pan-
eled ceiling soaring above. A young woman who could have
graced the cover of Vogue had greeted her from behind a
brass-trimmed receptionist desk and directed her to take a
seat in the rich leather upholstered waiting area where Ar-
chitectural Digest and Wall Street Business Journals lay on
polished glass-topped tables. Every detail imparted an image of prestige, responsibility, and success. Yes, Jo had
definitely been impressed. Still was, actually. Her father?
Hardly. When she'd gushed about obtaining a coveted position with Holt, Lewis, Dawson & Card, one of the biggest
law firms in town, he'd curled his lips in disgust.

"Oh no, not Holt's group. Why would you want to work
there? The place is a factory. You'll just be another cog, doing nothing but grunt work. Waste of a law degree, if you
ask me. Might as well have stayed a paralegal."

So much for sharing in her glory. She didn't know why
she'd expected otherwise. Her father seldom found anything she did of note. His disdainful remarks about her
employer had grown less frequent, but only because he seldom remembered she had one anymore. As strained as their
relationship had been, one thing she had always counted on
was his keen intellect. He had been a rock in her life, jagged
and unyielding, but reliably solid. Now that rock was sinking.

"Ms. Rinaldi?" Dawson's voice was sharp.

Jo came to the present with a start. "Pardon?"

"I asked how the Slader case was coming along."

"Oh, yes, sorry. I'm drafting the complaint now and
should have it ready for you tomorrow."

"Good. After that, I want you working on another personal injury matter that came in yesterday—"

The intercom buzzed. "I have an emergency call from Teresa Hernandez for Ms. Rinaldi," the firm operator
announced.

Jo's stomach did a somersault. With her cell phone on silent for the meeting, she realized Teresa had no choice but
to call the main office number. The others in the room
cleared their throats and adjusted the angles of their pens
and tablets. Only Carl met her gaze with a sympathetic

grimace.

Dawson sighed. "Put the call through to her office. She'll take it there," he replied to the operator then looked at Jo. "We'll talk later."

She nodded and quickly gathered her things. Offering repeated apologies, she sidestepped past the others in their seats. Once out the door, she ran down the hall and up the stairwell.

"What's wrong now?" Bev asked as Jo dashed past into her office.

"My father again." Jo dropped her things on her desk and grabbed the telephone receiver. "Yes, I'm here."

"Ms. Josephine? Is Teresa. Your father, he is gone. I go upstairs for just one minute and he disappear. I look and look. I walk down the street. I walk up the street. I knock on doors, but I no find him anywhere."

"Did he say anything, anything at all?"

"Oh si. We talk and talk. About the food, the weather. He talk about Tommy and your mother. He tell me again how they meet..." she gave a short laugh. "You know how he like to talk."

"Yes, I know, but did he say anything unusual?"

"No, no. He just happy, talking about old times, playing with his keys."

"Keys? Teresa, did you look in the garage? Is his car there?"

Teresa moaned softly. "Un momento." The phone clunked and Jo could hear Teresa's footsteps hurrying away, then moments later returning. "Ms. Josephine, I am so sorry. The car, she is gone. I did not think."

"Okay, okay." Jo's thoughts whirled. "Just stay there and call me on my cell phone right away if you hear anything."

Bev stood beside her. "Please tell me he didn't take the car."

"He took the car," Jo said as she hung up the phone and turned on her cell.

"But I thought you hid his keys."

"He must have had another set somewhere." Jo grabbed her coat and slipped it on. "I need to go find him."

"You can't keep running off like this."

"I know, but what choice do I have?"

"You can finally put him in that institute like we've been talking about, like Dawson personally arranged for you, remember?"

"Yes, I know, and you're right, but... my dad will never agree to it. You have no idea what he's like."

"I know what Dawson's like, and if you keep this up, you're not going to have a job here anymore."

Jo looked up, stung by Bev's words. With her marriage sunk along with the hope of starting a family, only her law career remained afloat. The last thing she wanted was to put that at risk, but right now, it was her father who was in the immediate danger. Jo turned toward the door, only to find Bev blocking her way, standing there with her arms crossed.

"Here's an idea. Why don't you call the police? Let them look for him," Bev said.

"No, I... I couldn't humiliate him like that."

Bev rolled her eyes. "Seriously? You're worried about humiliating *him*?"

"His pride is about all he has left," Jo said, hoping to gain sympathy, but Bev's mouth remained twisted firmly downward. "Besides, I have a good idea where he went. While I'm gone, you can start working on my draft of the Slader complaint."

Bev neither moved nor uncross her arms. Face to face, Jo couldn't help noticing the other woman's attire was even more abbreviated than usual. Bev's sleeveless red dress dipped low enough to display her formidable cleavage, and its skirt rose high enough to expose the tiny green dragon tattooed on her left thigh. Plus, she was wearing the big hair today, her burgundy red locks fluffed a good two inches out from the norm. Jo recognized the signs.

"New man in your life?" Jo asked.

Bev dropped her arms. "Why? Did he say something?"

"Who?"

"Our new P.I.—the one I've been throwing business at, making sure he can't ignore me."

"Well, I don't see how anyone could, not in that dress."

"Thanks." Bev tucked her hair behind one jeweled ear as Jo slipped past.

"I need you to correct my typos. That should keep you busy. Call me if any questions come up." Jo was already moving down the hall.

Bev trotted after her. "And what if Dawson comes up?"

"Stall."

"Seems like that's turned into my main job description," Bev said, still following her.

"That's only because you're so good at it."

"Remember that next time I ask for a raise. You also need to remember I have my limits." Bev came to a stop and placed her hands on her hips. "And so do you."

Jo gave her a backhanded wave and kept going.

CHAPTER THREE

The Old Man and the Sea Wall

ere it is only nine-thirty and the day's already ruined. Gets an idea in his head and off he goes without a thought for anyone else. Assuming he even remembers there is anyone else.

It was hard to know what to blame more—his mental deterioration or his inherently disagreeable nature. The combination grew more challenging each day.

The cold of the unheated garage worked through Jo's thin raincoat, making her shiver. She wondered if he'd thought to wear a jacket. She pictured him out there somewhere, lost and alone, shivering in the cold, or worse, dry and cozy behind the driver's wheel. She should have sold his old Mercedes, not just hidden the keys. The clicks of her heels echoed hollowly off the surrounding cement as she hurried down the rows of parked cars, searching for her own. Not seeing it, she paused and turned in place, pressing the button on her remote. Nothing.

But I always park on G-2. Oh wait, I was late this morning. Now she remembered driving around and around, looking for an open spot until ending up on the bottom level. Annoyed more than ever, she half-ran back to the elevator. Its doors were closing.

"Hold it!" she yelled, and a man's hand shot out and pressed the doors back. She slowed to a brisk walk trying to identify who was in there, but a scuffed leather Aussie hat shadowed the man's face, further obscured by the turned-up collar on his long mud-spotted trench coat, which looked like it belonged to a range-rider—or a flasher. She hesitated several feet away, recalling tales of elevator attacks, recently reinforced by an office memo cautioning female employees against going into the garage alone after dark. When in doubt, stay out. She almost backed away, but then her gaze dropped to the man's shoes—a soft gray. Her father had a pair just like them. Her father, who was out there somewhere.

To hell with this guy. Besides, it's the middle of the day.

She got in.

"You sure about that?" he asked, cocking his head to one side to peer at her from beneath his hat. "Did you think I looked dangerous?"

"Not as dangerous as me." She gripped her heavy briefcase in her left hand, keys in her right with the ends stuck out between her fingers like brass knuckles. She mentally ran through her old kickboxing moves and thought of the mace buried in her briefcase—in retrospect, a stupid place to keep it. She squared her shoulders and looked him in the eye.

He chuckled, then released the doors. "Don't worry, I haven't attacked anyone in years."

She gave him a squinted frown, and punched G-5 for the bottom level, but the elevator rose instead.

"Dammit," she cursed as the doors opened to the lobby.

"Sorry to disappoint you," he said, stepping out, "but I'm in a bit of a hurry right now." He gave her a wink. "Maybe next time."

Her mouth fell open as the doors closed in her face.

Things she could have said then rushed to mind. "Don't flatter yourself," she called out—too late and lame at that. The nerve. She punched G-5 again and simmered all the way down.

Long after she found her car, she was still mumbling insults she wished she'd thought of sooner. She took a deep breath, trying to purge the incident from her mind. She had more important things to worry about. She considered the places her father might go—their old house in Mission Beach, the Children's Pool in La Jolla, her mother's grave in Singing Hills. She decided to check the beach house first—it was closest.

Fifteen minutes later, she was cruising past Belmont Park along Mission Beach. Her family had spent many of her early childhood summers here, and her father spoke of those times now as if it were mere days ago. The swooping white arches of the old wooden rollercoaster towered overhead. Its red and white banners rippled and snapped in the offshore wind. The ominous steel gray sky threatened a downpour but was releasing little more than mist at the moment. During their summers here, she'd frequented the Park with the historic Giant Dipper coaster almost daily and her father would tell anyone who would listen its history. Built in 1925, it had been a popular tourist attraction up through the seventies. By then the coaster fell into disrepair and the park turned into a disreputable haunt for sailors looking for more than family entertainment. Deemed a hazard, city officials closed the coaster and surrounding park. Abandoned by tourists and looked at with skepticism by potential developers, the place became a refuge for the homeless and the subject of heated debate. For years, the old coaster loomed like a discarded skeleton while people dithered over what to do with it. Some insisted the coaster was too historical to tear down, others argued it was too costly to repair. Finally, the Save The Coaster Committee succeeded in having it designated as a national landmark and secured funding. Two million dollars later, the Giant Dipper reopened in 1990 to much fanfare and became a favorite attraction ever since.

Her father had been one of those pushing for restoration, arguing that reopening the coaster would bring in business and raise property values. He'd been right, as usual. Their old summer house, facing the Bay a mere mile away, was now easily worth ten times what her parents had paid for it. Too bad they'd sold it. Officially, the reason her father gave was that it was too expensive to maintain, but Jo knew the real reason was to distance what remained of their family from the ocean that had claimed Tommy.

The new owners rented the house out as a vacation home in the summer and student housing in the winter, no doubt raking in a bundle. If her father had kept it, she might have enough income now to pay for skilled home nursing care. Instead, Jo made do with Teresa. Their housekeeper had been a good interim solution when all her father needed was someone to prepare his food and keep him company, but it wasn't working anymore. He was growing too unpredictable.

While he still experienced periods of remarkable clarity,

they were less frequent, of shorter duration, and often while angry. Dr. Peterson theorized the rush of adrenaline might be stimulating his short-term memory function, unusual since most Alzheimer's patients became even more confused when agitated. But whatever the explanation, anger seemed to ground her father in the present. Knowing that, sometimes Jo intentionally aggravated him just to have a conversation that made sense. It wasn't an enjoyable way to interact, but it worked, and frankly, wasn't all that much different from what she'd experienced her entire life with him. He had a long history of short-tempered outbursts. What was new were the strange, illogical behaviors.

Some were only mildly annoying, like hiding his watch and wedding ring in the flour. Others were downright dangerous. Last week he walked into a neighbor's house and demanded they vacate the premises. Fortunately, the neighbors recognized him and called her rather than the police. More and more often, she found herself hurrying home to extricate him from some predicament Teresa couldn't handle. This was the third time in as many weeks that Jo had been forced to leave work. She was turning into an office joke.

Even worse were the nights. He constantly worried about losing things, and after dark it became an obsession. He wandered about the house, flipping on lights, hunting through drawers. Last night she'd woken in the early hours to find him rummaging through her bedroom closet. Jo felt as worn and chewed at the edges as an old dog blanket.

Oh Mom, why did you make me promise not to put him in a home?

She thought again about the Kessler Institute. It's not a home, she argued with herself. It's a medical research facility. Maybe they can help him. Plus, she could afford it since their research participants received room, board and care at no charge over what private insurance or Medi-Care would pay. She wished money weren't a factor, but she had to be practical. Her father had spent most of his savings on her mother's cancer treatments, and Jo's entire paycheck would be swallowed whole by one of those private memory care facilities.

Having no luck spotting his car at Belmont Park, she drove on to their old house, and pulled into its visitor parking spot off the alley. Though relieved to find the space open since parking was always scarce, she realized it meant her father probably wasn't here. Then again, he could have parked somewhere else. She got out and walked over to Bayside Lane, a cement walkway open only to foot traffic and cyclists. Beyond the walk lay the sandy beach fronting the bay. A pair of teenaged girls in thong bikinis glided past her on skates, oblivious to the chilly breeze and dark clouds overhead. Joggers trotted along the water's edge. To her right, a man stood, bag in hand, curbing his dachshund, waiting for it to finish its business on the narrow strip of grass in front of the wooden two-story bungalow where she'd spent her childhood summers. No sign of her father. The house was still painted white with green trim. Being mid-winter now, students were probably renting it. She pushed open the gate in the picket fence, walked across the brick patio to the screened front door and knocked. The inner door cracked open and an eye peered out at her.

"I'm sorry to bother you, but I'm looking for someone." She held out her cell phone displaying a recent photo of her father. "He's about six-foot tall, white hair, metal-rimmed glasses."

The door opened, revealing a young man with disheveled sun-bleached hair. He rubbed a hand over his face like he'd been asleep. He looked closer at the image, then nodded and his expression soured as if he'd discovered a nasty taste in his mouth. "Yeah, that's the guy. Here about a half hour ago, pounding on the door like he wanted to go through it. When I answered he started yelling, 'Get the hell out of my house!' Scared the crap out of me. Thought I was going to have to call the cops, but then he just stopped all of a sudden and stared at me like I'd grown another head or something and took off. Figured he was some nutcase."

Jo listened, her heart sinking with each word. Her father, the nutcase.

"I'm sorry. He's harmless, really. Just confused. Would you call me if you see him again?" She held out one of her business cards.

He opened the screen door, took the card, and squinted at it. "You're his lawyer?"

"Daughter."

"Bummer." He slipped the card into his pocket. "I'll keep a look-out."

"Thanks."

Jo hurried back along the bay front, scanning the walk in both directions again, but since she'd seen no sign of him or his car, she wasted little time at it. He'd undoubtedly driven off again. To the seawall, probably. That was where he'd proposed to her mother, another story he liked to tell over and over. No doubt, he would go up the winding roads hugging the coast. If she took the freeway, maybe she could beat him there. She hurried to her car, whipped it out of the space and down the boulevard. She glared at the sauntering pedestrians barring her way in the crosswalks and gunned through the yellow lights.

Finally, she was headed north in the fast lane. The mist thickened to a shower then turned into a downpour. The wipers pummeled the windshield but couldn't keep the glass clear and the white lane markers melted into the wet asphalt, forcing her to slow. When the rain lightened, she sped up again, whipping past more cautious drivers, knowing they must be shaking their heads at her, just as she would be at them if circumstances were reversed.

A sudden gust shoved her car from the side and her cell phone simultaneously rang out like an alarm, startling her into stomping on the brake. The car went sliding into the next lane. Horns blared. The anti-lock mechanism took over, pumping the brakes until the tires gripped the road again despite her over-reaction, and she swerved back into her lane.

Stupid, stupid, she told herself, relieved she hadn't spun out. Her phone was still ringing. She recognized the caller, so blew out a breath, and hit the answer button. "Hello, Bev."

"Dawson's called here twice. I told him you went to the law library to do some research, but I'm not sure he believed me. Any luck finding your dad?"

"Still looking. I'll call you when I have an update." Jo

clicked off before Bev could object. She saw her exit and cut across to the offramp for La Jolla, 'The Jewel' in Spanish. A sunny day illuminating its sapphire-colored ocean and emerald green cliffs must have inspired the name, but today the rain had washed those jewels to a gray paste, and mud-brown water rushed over the curbs.

She drove north past the curving La Jolla Shores up to the Children's Pool and hunted for an open parking space near the overlook, but even on this rain-soaked mid-week morning, all of them were full. She didn't see her father's Mercedes anywhere, but that didn't prove he wasn't here. It would only take a moment to be certain, so she double-parked, leaving the motor running and the wipers slapping furiously. Bowing her head against the wind and rain, she ran over to the metal tube railing.

The ocean roared at high tide, stirred to a white-capped frenzy. The cement seawall below her curved outward like a protective arm guarding the small beach from angry waves. Though originally designed for children, harbor seals and sea lions had confiscated the cove in recent years and posted signs warned the public against getting too close to them. She could see their dark sleek bodies lying on the sand and rocks, safe from the pounding waves. A handful of people huddled on the dry end of the walk atop the seawall below her. Among them, a pair of teenaged boys laughed and dared each other further out onto the walk until a wave hit the wall, spraying white foam high over their heads, and they scurried back.

Despite the obvious danger, one lone figure stood braced against the railing at the far end of the seawall's arm. His white hair whipped in the wind, forming a stark contrast to the dark sea surging behind him. Jo inhaled sharply.

"Dad!" she called out, knowing even as she did, the ocean would never allow her voice to be heard above its own.

Forgetting her double-parked car and its running engine, Jo rushed down the steps flanking the cliff to where people stood watching the waves break against the wall. The wet path ahead glistened from repeated washings, keeping anyone from venturing out... all but her very confused, clueless father. She gripped the cold wet rail, moving ahead as quickly as she dared on the slick stones and cement, a surface far better navigated in sneakers than dress shoes.

A wave smashed against the wall in front of her, spewing white foam over the walk and her heeled shoes. The two laughing teenagers ahead spun and dashed past her to take cover again. When the ocean sucked the wave back, she hurried to get past the curved mid-point where storm-driven waves had been known to sweep the unwary away.

People behind her yelled, "Hey, be careful out there!"

She ignored their warnings and kept moving. Another wave smacked the wall behind her, and she caught the spray on her back.

"Dad!" she called out again. The sea lions below blinked up. She was only a few yards away from him and closing fast, but he still failed to respond, so she changed tactics.

"Thomas!"

He turned around. "Amanda?"

She played along, "Yes, Thomas, it's me. You need to come home now. It's dangerous out here." She walked toward him and reached out her hand.

His face took on a frightened look, and he backed up against the end of the rail. "No, you're not Amanda."

She halted. "Dad, it's okay. It's me."

He twisted away, then dropped and thrust his head and upper body under the railing. Nothing barred him now from diving headfirst into the churning water and sharp rocks below.

"No!" Jo lunged for him. Her fingers hooked his belt and pulled hard just as a high wave hit the wall and washed over their feet. Her smooth-soled shoes slipped out from under her and she fell onto her back, sliding forward, under the rail, screaming.

"Josephine, for heaven's sake!" her father yelled in her face, gripping her by her shoulders. Her legs hung in the air, but he held on as she pulled herself back onto the walkway and got onto her feet.

"What are you doing out here?" he demanded.

"I didn't know where you were," she gasped, trying to get her breath back. "I've been searching for you and—"

"You're soaking wet."

"You're right. I am. So can we please go now?"

"I should think so." Looking at her in disgust, he took her hand, and led her back along the walkway as if she were the one lost.

The waves kept coming, but they dodged the biggest of them and stayed on their feet. The teens watched them, wearing amazed smiles.

"You guys all right?" one asked.

"Oh sure, just peachy," Jo said. "Thanks for all the help, by the way."

When they reached her car, a black-and-white with its red and blue lights flashing sat behind it and a police officer stood writing up a ticket.

"Oh, I'm so sorry," she said as she hurried toward him. "It was an emergency, really."

"Yes, ma'am," he said with no inflection in his voice. His gaze lit briefly upon her, then moved to her disheveled father. "Are you in need of medical attention?"

"What's it to you?" Thomas snapped.

Jo hurried to intervene. "No, we're fine, thank you. We just need to dry off." She laughed nervously.

The officer scowled at them both for a moment, assessing the situation, then finished writing the ticket, and handed it to her. "You need to move your vehicle, or I'll have it towed."

"Yes. I understand. Right away." Hurrying, she extracted towels and a blanket from the trunk, wrapped the blanket around her father, got him inside, then ran around to the driver's door. She sat on a towel and turned the heater up full blast. The ticket got stuffed in the glove compartment to be dealt with later.

"Okay, let's get you home," she said and put the car in reverse. "We can look for your car tomorrow."

To her surprise, he placed a hand over hers on the steering wheel. "Let's stay a while. I know how much you love it here."

She knew immediately that she was not the one he saw beside him. Struck by the emotion in his voice, she didn't correct him. A car was backing out several spaces ahead, so she shifted into drive and took the open spot. For a long time they sat there in silence, letting the heater warm and dry them as they listened to the rain pelt the car roof and watched the waves melt into crawling white froth on the sands below. She thought the stormy ocean scene looked lonely and dangerous, but her father wore a serene expression as if he saw something quite different. Her gaze fell to his hands in his lap and she noticed his ring was missing again.

"Where's your wedding ring, Dad?"

He stared at his left hand for a long moment. "I must have put it away. Somewhere. It's so hard to keep track." He let go of the blanket and pushed a damp forelock of silver from his eyes. "I wish to God things would stay where they belong."

With no words of comfort to offer, she let the silence take over until she couldn't stand it any longer. "Feeling better? You warm enough now? Are you ready to go home?" she asked, but he didn't answer. "Dad?

He turned to her. Wrapped in the wool blanket like an aging washer woman, she thought he had never looked so old and vulnerable as he did in this moment.

He squinted at her. "You're Josie, not Amanda. Not Amanda," he repeated as if she might dispute it, then grimaced. "My brain keeps playing tricks on me. My mind's going."

"Don't say that."

"One moment everything's clear, but the next..." he sighed and shook his head. "I couldn't remember how I got here, where I left my car... if I even had one. I don't know what I would have done if you hadn't come."

Jo nodded, unable to speak. She knew how much that admission must have cost him. In a rare moment of calm clarity, he was asking for help. She felt hot tears on her cheeks.

He lifted his gaze to her face and frowned. "Oh, for Pete's sake, don't cry about it. I would have remembered eventually. Stop crying. I hate that."

She swiped the tears away, knowing her weakness obligated him to be strong. "I've been meaning to talk to you about something." She caught her breath again, fearing the emotion that might escape with it, but steeled herself and reached for her briefcase in the back seat. She pulled out the Kessler Institute brochure and handed it to him. Her next words came with effort. "I think we should look into this place for you."

He carefully unfolded the brochure, skimming the text, and ended up staring at the photograph on the back. "Who is he?"

"Dr. Adrian Kessler. A neurologist. He specializes in treating people like you. My boss recommended him and so does Dr. Peterson."

"You've been talking to my doctor behind my back? I could sue the shorts off him."

"I'm sure he didn't break any rules. I just asked him what he thought about the Kessler Institute. It's unusual in that they operate a memory care residence on the lower floors and conduct medical research on the upper ones. They run clinical studies there that you could be part of. It's an impressive place, and I was hoping you'd like to see it." She stopped, having already said more than she'd intended. The look on her father's face was stone-like. She both feared and needed the growing anger she saw there. It could keep him clear-headed long enough to finish this conversation.

"So, you've been conspiring to put me away, have you? No surprise. You always were secretive. If it weren't for your mother keeping me informed, I would have thought you were flunking out or taking drugs."

Jo steeled herself, knowing any defense she offered would be quickly sliced, diced, and discarded. The outcome of arguments with her father had always been a forgone conclusion, which was why she'd learned early on to avoid them. In fact, she'd been a straight-A student, and hadn't even smelled pot until college, but tried to be as unobtrusive as possible around him to make her life simpler.

"So, are we just going to sit here all day? Don't you have a job to go to?"

"Yes, I do"—Jo stopped herself from adding, *assuming I haven't been fired yet for running after you*—"but right now, this is more important."

"I won't be locked up and forgotten."

"That's never been my intention."

The muscles in his face twitched beneath his papery skin.

"Suppose I should have expected this. People get old. It's not pretty. It's not convenient. Of course, you'd choose avoidance."

"I'm trying to get you some help. That's the opposite of avoidance."

"Gets you off the hook, though, doesn't it?"

"I'm not a doctor. The people at this Institute are experts. They know how to deal with the problems you're having."

"What about your problems? You're not exactly a model of success. Divorced, childless, starting over. At your age."

She fought back from taking the bait. *He's just trying to change the subject.* "We were talking about the Kessler Institute."

"Sounds like a prison."

"No. It's a nationally acclaimed medical research facility founded by a respected neurologist. You're judging it without even seeing it."

"Fine, let's go see it then."

"Now?"

"You'll just keep bringing it up otherwise."

Jo hesitated. Her shoes and skirt were still wet, her hair sticky with salt water, her father drenched. Under normal circumstances she would drive home, change clothing, phone ahead, make an appointment—but there was nothing normal about this. He was having a calm, lucid moment and had given consent. There was no telling when or if it would happen again.

Go, she told herself, *go right now.*

"Okay, if that's what you want, then that's what we'll do." She kept talking as she shifted into reverse and backed onto the street. "Wait till you see it. I was super impressed. It's very modern but doesn't feel the least bit clinical. I'm sure you'll like it."

"I'm sure I won't."

Jo shut up and drove. Anything more she said to sell Kessler and his Institute would only make her father more determined to hate them both.

CHAPTER FOUR

A Day Tour

The Kessler Institute for Geriatric Research sprawled across three lush acres of prime North County real estate. Wide shade trees and landscaped gardens softened the stepped six-story glass and granite structure. Vines of bougainvillea, flowering in orange and red hues, entwined the surrounding wrought-iron fence. Jo had called to let them know she and her father were on their way, and now the same voice spoke to her through the box at the gate. When it opened, she drove down a long curving driveway of interlocking pavers, past a wide parking area up to the front entrance. The rain slowed to widely spaced droplets, and the dark clouded ceiling cracked open to reveal blue sky beyond. Strips of sunshine reflected off the pansies along the driveway, heightening their pinks and purples to a day-glow intensity. Jo took the suddenly radiant scenery as a good omen. She glanced at her father.

"Beautiful, isn't it?"

"Dress it up all you like. Doesn't change anything."

He was still in a dark, angry mood, recalcitrant and argumentative. When he was like this, no sunlight could pierce his world, but at least it was grounded in reality and she knew what to expect. She parked in an open visitor spot and guided him into the lobby. Jo's hair no longer dripped, but her shoes squelched, and her father still wore a blanket.

"You must be the Rinaldis," said a young woman at the front desk. She had deep ebony skin and dozens of long layered braids gathered in a ponytail. "Uh oh, looks like you got caught in the rain. We have hot coffee over there. Maybe it will help." She gestured toward a table nearby, then handed Jo a clipboard of forms. "Please fill these out and I'll let our Director know you're here."

Jo took the clipboard and steered her father over to a curved purple sofa. She was glad to see it covered in a shiny faux-patent leather that should resist their damp clothing.

She set the clipboard down on the coffee table—a red lac-quered kidney-shape that balanced on three chrome legs—then went to fix coffee for them both. Walking back, she noticed the undulating shapes and bold primary colors of the furnishings were echoed in a huge carved area rug and the framed art on the walls.

"Is that a Miro?" Jo asked, indicating one of the wall art pieces as she handed him a cup.

"Museum posters," he said, dismissively. He sipped the coffee and glared around the room.

"Yes, but still a Miro, right?" she asked as she sat down and picked up the clipboard.

"Looks like it," he said. "Never been a fan."

"No? I thought he was supposed to be one of the greats in modern art." Knowing her father had minored in art history as an undergraduate, she hoped to keep him engaged while she filled in the blanks.

"Oh yes, a so-called pioneer in dream imagery and psy-chic automatism—the creative license to the unconscious mind. Feh...I've seen Kindergartners do better." He looked around. "You sure this is a medical facility? Looks like we're in some kind of psychedelic time warp or an Austin Power's remake."

This was how conversations with him used to be. She hoped it would last. "Retro is in, they say."

"Just means regurgitating something that wasn't all that great to begin with."

"Can't say I care for it all that much myself," said a man now standing before them. Jo looked up at medical whites, sandy blond hair, and horn-rimmed glasses. He had a strong-boned face, but a waistline surrendering to middle age. Her initial impression that he must be a doctor, de-moted to orderly when she noticed his worn-out sneakers.

"You can thank some specialists in interior design psy-chology for it. I didn't offer my opinion, not that they asked."

"And why should they?" her father asked.

"Why indeed? What do neurologists know about interior design?" He flashed an engaging smile and Jo caught her breath.

"Dr. Kessler." She jumped to her feet. "I'm sorry. I didn't recognize you. I didn't think that you, I mean, that you would take the time to—" She made herself shut up. Why was it that persons in authority reduced her to a simpering idiot?

"You must be Thomas Rinaldi," Kessler said, looking down at her father. "We've been saving a place for you for some time now."

"Never asked you to," her father snapped and pushed himself up to look him in the eye.

Jo interrupted before he said more. "Yes, thank you. I'm sorry it took us so long. I've heard wonderful things about your program here."

Kessler was looking past her. She turned to see a woman with upswept blonde hair, dressed in a dark business suit not unlike the one Jo was wearing, approaching them with her hand outstretched.

"Hello. I'm Suzanne Sutton, the Administrative Director here. I see you've already met Dr. Kessler."

"We're not signing anything," Thomas told them forcefully.

Mrs. Sutton smiled at Dr. Kessler. "Mr. Rinaldi is a retired law professor."

"Torts," Thomas said, "Medical malpractice mostly."

"Good to know." Dr. Kessler's eyebrows rose along with the corners of his mouth. "Guess we'd better watch ourselves."

"Rinaldi's an old Sicilian name," Thomas continued. "My ancestors were used to taking matters into their own hands."

"Dad, please." Warmth rushed to Jo's face.

Kessler's beatific smile remained. "Again, good to know. I must excuse myself, but I leave you in good hands. Mrs. Sutton will arrange a meeting with me after your tour—assuming you're still interested."

"Thank you," Jo said again, before her father could offer another rude remark. She watched the doctor leave, amazed she had met the famous researcher so casually.

"Shall we?" Mrs. Sutton said. As she led the way, she kept up a well-rehearsed patter, guiding them through a series of common areas designed for dining and recreation. Groups of elderly people engaged in a variety of activities: crafts, games, exercise, and group-led conversations. "We emphasize mental and physical stimulation and encourage independent living as much as possible."

"I see a lot of wheelchairs and walkers," Jo commented.

"Yes, most of our participants require some form of ambulatory assistance."

"How many of these people actually live here?"

"Oh, all of them. We believe consistency of care is vital. The trouble with most clinical trials is that there is no way to be certain what outside influences might affect the results. By restricting participation to in-house residents, we eliminate the unknowns by monitoring intake, screening visitors, and preventing unwanted intrusion."

"Told you it was a prison," Thomas grumbled.

Mrs. Sutton's mouth smiled, but not her eyes. "On the contrary. We welcome visitors and family, and our residents are free to roam the property. Residents exercise a great deal of personal freedom yet feel safe living in a secure environment with the best medical care available. As you've seen, we offer a variety of activities—plus educational courses and local entertainment, along with bussed excursions around the city, but of course no one is obligated to participate. It's totally up to you."

Thomas scowled even more.

Mrs. Sutton took them up to the third floor, where she showed them a nicely furnished shared living space next to a dedicated nurse's station, then on down a hallway to a door marked 312. She used her keycard to open the door.

"This is the unit reserved for you."

Inside was a seating area and bedroom with a built-in closet and private bathroom equipped with a handicap-accessible shower. Large windows on the far walls framed an ocean view, lending the space an airy feel. Jo could see the accommodations were well planned, both for esthetics and efficiency. Thomas stood in the doorway without entering.

"Come look, Dad, it's nice. Kind of homey."

"I have a home."

"I'm sorry," Jo whispered to Mrs. Sutton. "He's not very keen on this."

Mrs. Sutton nodded and lowered her voice. "He'll adjust. They all do."

"Stop whispering over there," he barked. "I'm old, not deaf."

"Sorry," Jo said automatically, and ended the conversation.

Mrs. Sutton continued the tour, leading them back out past the nurse's station to the elevators again and up to the next level. "The lower floors are for ambulatory residents like your father. When a patient becomes ill or bedridden, we move them up here to be closer to the examination rooms and surgical facilities."

This floor looked more like a traditional hospital setting, though rooms were personalized with pictures and knick-knacks. The staff in their pastel-printed uniforms smiled and said hello as they passed. Sutton showed them examination rooms and a surgical theater. All the monitors, medical equipment, and computers looked new and Jo said as much.

Mrs. Sutton nodded. "We pride ourselves on being state-of-the-art."

On the fifth floor, there were no residential apartments. Instead, white-coated personnel in facemasks bustled through the hallways, appearing, and disappearing through heavy stainless-steel doors.

"These are the research labs," Mrs. Sutton explained. "Our goal is to find the underlying causes of aging and brain disorders like Alzheimer's in order to prevent and even reverse the disease, rather than merely treat its symptoms as so many others are doing."

Jo peered through a meshed glass window. Inside she saw rows of test tubes, microscopes, and computer stations. Mrs. Sutton placed a restraining hand lightly on Jo's arm. "I'm afraid this is a restricted area."

"Oh, of course." Jo backed away from the door. "I've read a little about what you're doing here, identifying chemicals in the brain, using genetic engineering, that CRISPR thing, right?"

"Yes, the field of neurological medicine has made significant advances. Dr. Kessler believes it possible to recreate the chemistry of a healthy brain in a malfunctioning one. It's all very exciting, but not really my area of expertise. Dr. Kessler can explain it far better than I can. Shall we see if he can speak with you now?"

"That would be great," Jo replied before her father objected.

He squinted at her and grunted in disapproval. "Bloody waste of time."

Jo smirked at his use of the word 'bloody'. Every once in a while, he revealed the influence of his British-born mother.

Sutton stepped away and used her cell phone. After conversing briefly, she returned. "Good news. We've caught the doctor during a free moment."

She waved for them to follow. They rode the elevator to the sixth floor where she led them down a long hallway of administrative offices and around the corner to a tall wooden door. She knocked first, then peered inside, before opening it wide for them to enter.

"He's on the phone," she whispered, "but you can go in and have a seat. He'll be with you shortly." She waved them inside, then closed the door.

Behind an imposing desk of smoked glass held aloft by crossed walnut legs, Dr. Kessler sat in a tall executive chair with a telephone receiver pressed to his ear, but with his eyes on them. "Yes, yes," he was saying, "but that's not my concern. Do I need to remind you we have a long-standing agreement? I need at least three more by the end of the week." He waved them to sit in the pair of large brown leather chairs in front of his desk. "Perhaps I should talk to your superior." He covered the mouthpiece. "This should only take a minute."

Jo looked around at the enormous expanse, realizing that Kessler's office occupied the entire west end of this floor. Deep tinting on a curved wall of ceiling-high windows denied the sun's glare without diminishing a one-hundred-and-eighty-degree view of magnificent Southern California coastline.

"Yes? Good. I'll expect their arrival no later than Friday." Kessler hung up and sighed. "My apologies." He stood and wheeled his chair around the desk to sit beside them. He smiled briefly at Jo but turned his full attention on her father. "So, Thomas, tell me. What do you think of our place here?"

"Not sure what to think. You've got too much equipment for a retirement home, but it doesn't exactly look like a hospital either."

Kessler smiled in pleasant surprise. "That's very astute of you. And you're right, seeing as it's neither of those. What I've built here is an in-patient medical research facility. As one of our residents, you would become an integral part of it."

"A human guinea pig, you mean," Thomas said.

"We prefer the term residential participant."

"Window dressing."

"Dad, please."

"No, no, your father is right to be cautious. What we ask isn't always an easy thing. For someone looking to spend their waning years in restful decline until the inevitable end, this is not the place. On the other hand, if you have a strong will and a determination to fight this disease, we can be an unprecedented ally. But I admit our program isn't for the timid."

Thomas leaned forward aggressively. "I'm no coward, sir. But I don't see any point in prolonging the inevitable, nor subjecting myself to torture simply to fulfill your personal ambition."

"Dad!"

Kessler's eyes widened and tracked back and forth between the pair of them, then settled on her. "Ms. Rinaldi, may I speak with your father in private?"

"Oh. I'm sorry," she said, thinking she'd spoken out of turn. "You want me to wait outside?"

"Yes, please. If you don't mind."

"No, um, of course not." She stood abruptly, berating herself for butting in.

She quickly exited and closed the door. Just outside she found a windowed seating area furnished with curved couches similar to those down in the lobby, but upholstered in a soft suede. Confident her skirt was dry enough now not to leave a mark, she sat on the end closest to Kessler's door, straining to hear what new insults her father might sling. Unfortunately, the thick wood proved an effective barrier.

I shouldn't be eavesdropping, anyway. I'm sure Dr. Kessler knows how to handle difficult patients.

Still, everyone has their limits. If her father proved too obnoxious, Kessler might tell him good riddance. While waiting for final judgment, she pawed through a stack of magazines on the table to distract herself. They were all pretty much what one expected to find in a doctor's office specializing in geriatric medicine—*Journal of American Medicine, Longevity Magazine, Retirement Living*—but then she came across a publication that seemed completely out of place. *The Prison Journal.* The title jarred her, especially in light of her father's comments. She picked it up and skimmed the article titles: "The High Cost of Caring for Aging Inmates," "Prison Reform and Its Impact on Privatization." She then saw the next publication underneath, an inch-thick *Journal of Correctional Healthcare.* She picked up the heavy magazine and flipped through over a hundred pages, all dealing with medical care for the incarcerated. *Weird, why would Dr. Kessler have these here?*

The magazines reminded her of the current debates going on in Congress on prison reform legislation. *Maybe he's involved in that somehow, helping establish guidelines. Or this could be related to some required public service, like the way law firms do pro bono work. Is that a thing in the medical community? And why do I care?*

Deciding she didn't, she set the boring prison magazines aside. Her gaze came to rest on a far more inviting copy of *Retirement Living* showing a silver-haired couple standing next to an RV with a rushing waterfall in the distance. Their frozen smiles of shared bliss tugged at her and she picked up the magazine to look closer. This is how things should have been. Her father wasn't supposed to be a widower. She wasn't supposed to be divorced. He wasn't supposed to be degenerating into dementia. She wasn't supposed to resent him for it.

Dr. Kessler's door popped open. She tossed the magazine aside and stood. Kessler came toward her, wearing a smile, but it hardened as he noticed the stack of prison magazines on the sofa next to where she had been sitting. "Now where did those come from?" He grabbed the offending pile and dropped them all into a wastebasket nearby. His smile came back. "Good news. Thomas has decided to give us a chance."

"Really?" She looked past him to see her father still seated inside Kessler's office. His chin hung low on his chest with his hands gripped into fists on his lap. She walked toward him. "Dad?" She crouched down to look him in the face. "Are you okay?"

"No, I'm not. Obviously." His eyes flicked to her, then back to his white-knuckled fists. In that brief glance, she recognized a silent rage she hadn't seen since the day he'd told her that her mother's cancer was terminal.

The doctor walked past and leaned back against his desk to face them. "We can enroll Thomas immediately. We'll provide whatever he needs for tonight and you can drop off his personal items in the morning. Just see Mrs. Sutton before you leave to sign the admittance forms. We already have his medical records on file from Dr. Peterson, but of course we'll want to do a complete neurological work-up of our own."

"He's already been through a lot of tests," Jo said, trying to slow things down, feeling overwhelmed by the rapidity of all this.

"Yes, Dr. Peterson was very thorough, but we have our own system here and I'm sure you'll want us to take every precaution. Once our initial assessment is complete, we'll assign Thomas to one of our study groups."

"So that's when he'll get experimental medication you're testing?"

"Yes, unless, of course, he's assigned to a control group, in which case he'll receive a placebo."

That gave Jo pause. "What about his prescription from Dr. Peterson? Will he keep taking it?"

"Donepezil?"

She nodded.

"I'm sure Dr. Peterson explained it only provides temporary symptomatic improvement."

"Still, it's better than a placebo, right?"

"Not in this case. Our goal is to treat the underlying cause of the disease, not mask its symptoms." Jo wanted to interrupt, but he kept talking. "Something else to consider is the psychological benefit of participating in research like ours. Depression and hopelessness can be as destructive as the disease itself. With us, your father will play a vital role in fighting a disease well on its way to becoming a national epidemic."

"Yes, I suppose, but—"

"Are you aware that by age seventy, a person has a twenty percent chance of contracting Alzheimer's? At eighty, the likelihood goes up to fifty percent. We're talking millions and millions of people. It's only with the help of courageous volunteers like yourselves that we have any chance of finding a cure."

Jo blinked wondering if he was exaggerating those odds and she didn't feel courageous. On the contrary. "I just want to be sure he's getting what he needs."

"As do I, of course, but sadly what he needs isn't available, at least not in the public domain. Any truly effective treatment will only come out of a study like ours."

"And you believe you have an effective treatment?"

"Well..." Dr. Kessler smiled. "Let's just say I've seen some amazing results and I'm optimistic."

"Okay. And he'll get this treatment of yours assuming he's in the right group?"

"More than likely, yes."

"Or he could get sugar pills."

Kessler shrugged and nodded. "Possibly, but even if that were the case, his residential status here would put him first in line to receive the treatment once we prove its effectiveness."

"Well, I guess that's something." Jo chewed her lower lip and looked at her father again, hoping to see whether he was truly on board with this. He was frowning, staring down at his fists. She wanted to do the right thing, but the choices were far from clear. Was enrolling him in an experimental study like this right for him? Or was she merely looking for a way out of her own predicament?

"Dad, are you sure this is what you want?"

"What I want?" He snapped his words at her. "What choice do I have? I'm turning into a drooling vegetable, an imbecile who'll be crapping my own pants."

She scowled at Kessler, realizing how ruthless he must have been in their private discussion. She clasped her father's hand. "You don't need to worry about any of that. I promised Mom I'd take care of you, and I will."

He pulled his hand away. "No. I won't have it." He glared at her as if she were the enemy. "I won't be humiliated like that, not in front of you of all people. I want some dignity, some purpose to all of this. If science can't stop what's happening to me, then at least let someone learn from it. Apparently, I've nothing else left to contribute, so give me that much, will you?"

She sucked in a breath, not trusting herself to speak, and nodded.

At that, her father let out a long sigh. Slowly, he unclenched his hands and laid them flat on his thighs. He'd held on to his anger for a long while, grounding himself in the present, but he was clearly exhausted by the effort. She watched as his face gradually relaxed and his eyes unfocused, a pattern familiar to her once he grew too tired to fight it any longer. When he smiled as if seeing something far beyond the walls, Jo knew he had left this world behind. She almost wished she could share that vision, however deluded it might be. Sadly, all she could see was her last living relative and the illness destroying him.

She saw the doctor staring at him, too, observing the change. The intensity in Kessler's face rivaled that of a young boy watching a bug under a microscope.

CHAPTER FIVE

The Slader Case

T he next morning, Jo beat the morning rush and made it into the office early. She intended to use the quiet time to get some concentrated work done. She felt energized, ready to tackle her back-load of assignments after enjoying her first night of uninterrupted sleep in weeks, months maybe. The stack of files filling the length of her credenza would take days stretching into the late-night hours to address, but the prospect no longer daunted her. Today there would be no interruptions, no frantic calls from Teresa. Her father was in the care of trained professionals. Only the teeniest tinge of guilt marred her relief and she reminded herself it had been her father's choice.

First assignment in line was the Slader complaint she'd given Bev to polish yesterday. She checked her email for an updated version, but it wasn't there. No doubt Bev had counted on Jo being late as usual and having the morning to finish up. Deciding not to wait, Jo went out and sat in her secretary's chair, got Bev's terminal up and running, opened the word processing program and located the Slader file. It looked like Bev had already corrected her rushed typing errors. The complaint was little more than a form filled in with the names of the parties, and specifics of the place and date of the accident, but she read every word and was soon lost in the work, focused on sentence structure and word choice... *As a proximate result of the negligence, carelessness, and unlawfulness of defendants, and each of them, and the resulting collision, as herein alleged, plaintiff sustained personal injuries as set forth in the attached medical reports, all of which injuries have caused and continue to cause plaintiff great mental, physical, and nervous pain and suffering—'*

A man's voice interrupted. "Morning, Sweetheart, your boss around?"

Nonplussed, Jo looked up at a dark-haired man peering over the top of the cubicle. "My boss?"

"Yeah, I assume you're filling in for Beverly?"

"No, she'll be here at eight o'clock."

He looked at his watch. "Guess I got a little ahead of myself. I wanted to catch her first thing. I've got an update for her boss on the Slader case."

"You can give it to me. I'm working on the complaint now."

"Don't bother. It'll never get filed."

She frowned at him. "Why would you say that?"

"Turns out the guy's got a bad habit of staging accidents."

"You're kidding."

"Nope. Wanted in three states."

"Wow." Jo's mind raced. "Does Dawson know?"

"Not yet. Beverly said her boss could use some extra points with him, and she's been great about steering business my way, so I'd like to return the favor." He waved a manila envelope in the air. "Got copies of warrants and driver's licenses under his various aliases here."

"Let me see." Jo reached for the envelope.

He pulled it back behind the cubicle wall. "Sorry, can't be giving this to just anybody." He paused, squinting his eyes. "Hey, don't I know you?"

"Obviously, not."

"Sure, I do." He smirked at her. "You're the dangerous one."

She scowled at him. "The what?"

He popped a leather hat low over his eyes. "Remember me now?"

And, of course, she did. "Oh yes. Mr. Obnoxious from the elevator. Clearly you haven't changed. Now if you'll please hand over that report."

"Sorry, no can do. Like I said, I'm saving this for Beverly's boss."

"Who would be me."

He smiled crookedly. "No, I'm talking about Joe Rinaldi."

"The name's Josephine." She held her hand out again.

"Seriously?"

"Do I look like I'm joking?"

"No, I have to say you definitely do not." He removed his hat but still wore an amused expression. "So you're Joe Rinaldi. Not exactly what I was expecting." He extended the envelope and Jo grabbed it.

"Perhaps my secretary and I need to have a chat."

His half-smile faded. "Hey, don't blame her. She's not the one who called you a..." He grimaced and shook his head. "Never mind."

"What?"

He crinkled his nose. "Forget it. You don't want to know."

"Oh, but I insist."

"Okay, fine, but you're not going to like it. 'A real son of a bitch.' I probably misheard the 'son of' part."

Jo glared at him.

"Said you wouldn't like it. Anyway, my bill's inside." He gestured with his hat. "Appreciate it if you would send it in as soon as possible. I got bills to pay."

"Certainly. Assuming I judge your work worthy of compensation, of course."

He stiffened. "Look, I'm sorry if I offended you, but you insisted. I didn't mean anything by it."

"I'm not interested in what you meant."

"Hey, I apologized, didn't I?"

"That wasn't an apology, that was sucking up."

He narrowed his eyes and put his hat back on. "I was wrong. You're exactly what I expected."

As he strode away, Jo had an urge to fling the envelope at the back of his head. Instead, she retreated to her office and tore it open. Inside she found everything he'd claimed—arrest warrants, driver's licenses—indisputable proof of their client's long nefarious criminal career. She shook her head, thankful that she hadn't yet filed that complaint with Dawson's name on it. If the defense lawyers had learned this information before they had, this firm would have ended up a laughingstock, and she quite likely looking for another job.

An invoice clipped to the documents listed a phone number and P.O. Box for Scott Benson, Private Investigator. Three hundred dollars—a bargain. He'd saved her job, saved the firm. Perhaps she was the one who needed to apologize.

Jo picked up the phone receiver and punched in the tele-phone number on the invoice. After the third ring, his recording answered.

"Scott here. Don't waste my time and I won't waste yours."

The abrupt message took her aback, and she almost for-got what she'd intended to say.

"Um. Hi. This is Jo, Josephine Rinaldi. I've reviewed your report and will have Accounting cut you a check. You should receive it in the next day or two." She started to hang up, then added, "Good work, by the way, and, uh, thank you." Grimacing, she replaced the receiver.

CHAPTER SIX

A New Deadline

Deep in concentration, Kessler sat bent over a lab bench examining the best electron micrographs of the brain tissue samples he'd collected, pausing only occasionally to scrawl notes on a pad. The writing would be illegible to anyone but himself, but that suited him fine. He didn't want any of his conclusions shared as yet. An insistent vibration in his pocket gradually registered in his awareness and he pulled out his cell phone to read the caller's name—Suzanne Sutton, the woman he'd had an affair with, and still relied on to run this place. Though reluctant to tear himself away from the work, he knew he needed to answer.

"Yes?"

"I'm sorry to disturb you, but Reginald Howell is here and insists on seeing you. I tried to get him to make an appointment, but— well, you know how he is." She sounded agitated, unusual for her, except whenever Howell showed up.

Rubbing his eyebrow, Kessler mentally ran through a list of excuses, before giving in. Howell essentially held the purse-strings for this Institute, which made keeping him happy a top priority.

"Very well," Kessler said with a deep sigh. "Have him wait in my office."

He rubbed the back of his stiff neck as he stood and squinted against the glare of fluorescent lights reflecting off the white walls and steel countertops. Sensing the slow approach of another headache, he popped a couple ibuprofen in his mouth to ward it off, swallowing them dry.

Normally, he exited through the back of the lab and used his private elevator, but he didn't want Howell seeing him emerge from behind the bookcase in his office, so he walked out the front doors into the outer hall and rode one of the main elevators up to the sixth floor. He kept few precious secrets from Howell, but his hidden lift was one of them. Kessler forced his face to take the shape of pleasant surprise as he entered his office. Howell already sat in one of the wide leather visitor chairs. The man's sizeable girth filled every inch.

"Reginald," Kessler said as he closed the door behind him. "I wasn't expecting you."

Howell swiveled the chair to face him but stayed seated. "Doc, you and I need to talk." His southern twang both doubled the length of his vowels and cut consonants off. "Sit down, sit down," he said. He held his ten-gallon hat off the side of the chair in his left hand and patted the empty visitor chair with his right, thus circumventing Kessler from taking the superior position behind his desk.

Kessler kept his smile steady, not an easy task considering how much he disliked this man and the condescending way he spoke to him as if Kessler were the junior partner in their joint enterprise. "Very well," he conceded and lowered himself into the chair.

Howell watched him with his copper penny eyes, and smirked, an expression that pursed his mouth into the same round shape as his face.

"So what's on your mind?" Kessler asked, hoping to hurry this along.

"Seems there's been a slight misunderstandin' 'tween you and the interests I represent."

"Oh? I'm sorry to hear that, but I'm sure we can rectify any miscommunication."

"I hope so, I truly do. Problem is, my clients were under the distinct impression you'd have some concrete results by now. As you know, a whole lot of money's been goin' into this here operation, and, so far, nothin's been comin' out."

"That is the inherent nature of medical research. I made it clear from the beginning that it's a long road with a heavy investment up front."

"Oh I understand, I do, but it's been goin' on so long now, that investment's gettin' a might too heavy and we're startin' to run out of road. Won't be long before we all go flyin' off the end if you get my meanin'."

"I'm not sure I do."

"Point is, Doc, your sponsors are under a microscope of their own now and they need somethin' positive to turn public opinion around. Now, as I recall, last time we met, you said you were gettin' close to a cure for this here Alzheimer's Disease."

"Yes, I believe I'm on the right track."

"Good, good. That's what I was hopin' you'd say. What we need is for you to publish your findin's, the sooner the better."

"Publish?" A disbelieving smile formed on Kessler's face. "It's still far too early."

"And why's that, when you say you got it all figured out?"

"I said no such thing. We're still in the preliminary testing stages."

Howell glared at him, and when he spoke again his good ol' boy accent vanished. "You told me a year ago that you were on the FDA's expedited schedule."

Perceiving the abrupt change in both Howell's demeanor and diction, Kessler licked his lips and adjusted his glasses. "Well, yes, but...." but only for a neurotransmitter drug formula which hadn't panned out, not for the unapproved stem cell therapy showing genuine promise. "You must understand what I'm doing here is an extremely complicated process which takes considerable time."

Howell's eyes narrowed further. "Time's something we're running out of, Doc. We need results and we need them now. That's the way we do business."

"I'm not making widgets here. We're talking about medical research. If you understood all the steps required, the painstaking methods involved—"

"Oh, I know all about your methods, and the pain they cause your patients, and up to now, I've looked the other way... even cleaned up when needed."

"Excuse me?" Kessler pressed his left eye to counter a nervous tick.

"Is that why you've started drinking? Trying to forget all the patients you've been killing, or is it still just about the dead wife?"

"How... how dare you?" Kessler felt simultaneously outraged and stripped naked.

Howell made a sound of disgust. "Drop the pretense. I know exactly what goes on here and what you've been up to. Remember, I was the one who took care of those lawsuits for you."

Kessler scowled. "We settled out of court. Suzanne worked with our attorneys."

"For all the good it was doing. Those people never would have settled if I hadn't made them see reason. And let's not forget your wife's untimely demise, real mess you made there."

Kessler's eye twitched as memories of that night flooded back... his wife Ellen unexpectedly walking in on him and Suzanne, Ellen screaming threats as they tried to cover their nakedness, the ensuing tussle, the violent fall, the blood on the tile.

"Thanks to me it ended up looking like the accident you wanted everyone to believe it was." Howell pursed his mouth again into a smug pink rose.

Ellen's death had been accidental, a fluke really, but the ugly circumstances could have ended his career. He remembered Suzanne making a call. Then some seriously silent men came and cleared it all away. He never knew who they were, hadn't wanted to know. He still didn't, but now it seemed there was no way to avoid it. He was looking at the man who'd sent them.

"I resent what you're insinuating. Ellen's death was an accident, just a sad, tragic accident, unforeseen and unplanned." Kessler kept his tone level, despite a rising rage.

"May so, but hard to prove, especially with step-by-step photos showing a staged car crash, showing exactly how it was all done."

Kessler stared at Howell in shock, realizing he was being blackmailed. "What exactly do you want?"

"Like I said, Doc, some good publicity. We need you to tell the world you found a cure, assuming you really have one of course, and thank your sponsors for making it all possible."

"And if I refuse?"

"Then I'll have to take our business elsewhere, and who knows where those photos will end up. No more money, no more Institute, plenty of jail time. Clear enough?"

Kessler had always disliked Howell but hadn't fully despised him until this moment. When the federal government cut off funding for fetal stem cell research and the major pharmaceutical companies he went to all rejected him down, Kessler had turned to a most unlikely source of revenue, the private prison industry. He'd spent years as their consultant advising them on how to deal with their growing population of aging prisoners and saw a way to profit from a partnership. If they would fund his facility, he would take their most difficult inmates—those displaying symptoms of dementia—off their hands. It was a double win for his investors, saving them the expense of increased care and supervision for these difficult inmates, plus they could write off the money as a charitable donation. It was also a double win for him, keeping his Institute financially afloat and well-supplied with test subjects. The only downside had been having to deal with their liaison, Reginald Howell. Five years ago, Kessler had been desperate enough to sign a deal with the devil. Now it felt like he had.

Howell rested his elbows on the chair's armrests and pyramided his fingers. "Now, bearing all that in mind, Doc, I have just one question for you. Do you believe in this here cure of yours or not?"

"Yes, I do, but—" Kessler hesitated, knowing the truth wouldn't save him and he had no believable lie. In reassuring Howell about his progress in finding a cure, he'd stretched the facts and now they were snapping back on him.

"Go on," Howell said.

Kessler clasped his hands together and leaned forward. Perhaps honesty was the best choice now. "What I may have failed to make clear is that the expedited schedule I mentioned was for a drug designed to mitigate dementia symptoms. It's not a cure, was never intended to be, and, regretfully, it hasn't done as well in the clinical phase as we'd hoped."

Howell's face turned florid. "So, you don't have a cure? It was all a lie?"

Kessler raised his hands defensively. "No, no, it's what I'm working on now, an injected stem cell therapy that regenerates neurons. I have everyone working overtime to get it approved for clinical testing."

"How soon will that be?"

"I'd estimate as early as the end of next year," Kessler said, once again stretching the truth.

Howell stared at him for a long, cold moment. When he spoke, his voice was soft but sinister. "Next year's gonna be one year too late."

"Please try to understand."

"You're the one who doesn't understand. This administration's coming down hard on us. We're talking increased regulations, public scrutiny, Senate investigations. As things stand now, you're a liability my clients can't afford. Think how this little arrangement of ours is going to look. Us providing you with senile test subjects, most of whom happen to be dead now. Don't think I haven't been keeping track. Imagine how the press will paint it. We need something to justify it all. So have you got the goods or not? Cause if you don't, I'm pulling the plug right now."

Kessler removed his glasses to put a finger on his eye to stop it from twitching. "I assure you I'm on the edge of something truly ground-breaking."

"Then what's the problem?" Howell opened his hands wide.

"Getting FDA approval takes time. I don't have enough data yet."

"Then get it. Do whatever it takes. Cut through the red tape, round off them corners, just get it done."

Kessler replaced his glasses and looked at Howell. "You do realize we're talking human lives here."

Howell laughed hard and short. "Hasn't seemed to bother you so far. But if you want to take the high road, that's even more reason to hurry things along. You say people are dyin' from this disease every day, so how can you sit there whinin' at me about jumpin' through regulatory hoops?" As Howell's twang returned, his volume rose to match that of an evangelistic preacher. "You know how this world works, boy. You want somethin' to happen, you gotta *make* it happen."

Kessler bristled at the word 'boy' but clamped down on reacting to it. *Make it happen, cut through red tape, round corners...* what Howell really meant was falsify records, something that was illegal and dangerous. And also doable. With modern computers, years of painstaking experimentation could be fictionalized in a matter of hours. He wouldn't be the first to create a history of work where none existed, but careers had come to a screeching halt with federal indictments for less.

"So can you deliver the goods or not?" Howell asked.

Kessler saw Howell sizing him up, his future hanging in the balance, supported only by the hand of this one man, a man with no heart or vision, just greed and a keen cold talent for knowing where one's jugular lay. This was the real enemy, not the FDA. He had to appease him. The only reason he hesitated was the knowledge that leapfrogging over intermediary steps could easily result in bad science, leaving him with a pile of unreliable data that could neither be verified nor duplicated. On the other hand, risking it all might actually work. Perhaps this was just the push he'd been waiting for. The question was, if he succeeded, could he trust his own genius to sort it out later?

"Yes," he said, reaching a new resolve. His eye stopped twitching. "I can."

CHAPTER SEVEN

Warning Signs

Over the next few weeks, Jo whittled her in-box down to a reasonable height and re-routed the many files lined up on her credenza like soldiers waiting for orders. Her billable hours skyrocketed. Dawson had not only thanked her for saving the firm from embarrassment in the Slader case, he'd started acknowledging her when they passed in the halls.

"It's after five," Bev announced, standing in Jo's doorway. "How about coming out with the girls for a drink?"

"I wish, but after I finish up here, I need to visit my father. Raincheck?"

Bev sighed. "Sure, but promise me you'll take the rest of the night off."

Jo nodded. "I promise. See you tomorrow."

An hour later, desk cleared, Jo grabbed her purse and headed out the door, briefcase free, only to find Carl Freedman, a fellow associate only a few months senior to her, blocking her way.

"Oh thank god you're still here," he said.

Jo narrowed her eyes suspiciously, seeing the thick file in his hands. She liked Carl, known for his bubbly personality and non-stop storytelling, but this didn't bode well.

"I was just leaving."

"Yeah, sorry, I really hate to ask, but I'm absolutely desperate, trapped between two opposing forces—both immovable—our killer boss and my killer boyfriend. I promised to meet Alan's parents tonight and I can't reschedule because they're from out of town. Can you imagine what Alan would say if I even tried? I was getting ready to leave to meet them at the restaurant, when Dawson shows up totally unannounced and hands me this huge contract." Carl held up the thick file as proof without pausing. Jo marveled at his ability to leave no space for interruption. "He needs a summary of it first thing tomorrow—can you believe it? And

I have zero time, obviously, but I couldn't say no, not that he gave me a chance to anyway, not that I would dare, but how can I be in two places at once? It's impossible. So can you help me out, please, just this once?" He put the file down on her desk and pressed his palms together. "Please, please, please."

Posed as he was, tow-headed Carl, with his round face already resembling an overgrown infant, only needed a set of wings to make the perfect lawn ornament. "I promise to return the favor, I swear."

Jo let out a long breath, only now realizing she'd been holding it. "Wow. Okay, fine. So where do I meet Alan's parents?" she asked, keeping a straight face.

"What? No. I—" Carl stopped. "Very funny. You going to help me or not?"

"I shouldn't, but..."

"So you will? Oh, thank you, thank you so much."

"You definitely owe me."

"Yes, absolutely. Whatever you need. Just not tonight and this has to be just between you and me, okay? Dawson can't know." Carl thrust the file into her hands.

"Oh great. So I do all the work and you get all the credit. You really do owe me."

"I know, I know, sorry, You're the best. I'll pay you back, I promise. Love you." Carl scooted down the hall, sending air kisses as he ran off.

Shaking her head, Jo returned to her office, grabbed her briefcase, and stuffed the thick file inside. Despite her promise to Bev, looked like it would be another late night.

As she drove toward the Kessler Institute, she was already thinking up ways for Carl to pay her back. Maybe she could ask him to visit her father in her stead once in a while. Carl had been one of his students back in the day, so it wasn't totally inappropriate. She felt a trace of guilt at the idea, but these visits weren't fun. Her father's side of the conversation ranged anywhere from the semi-rational to the totally bizarre, and much of it contentious. She especially hated it when he mistook her for her mother.

Tonight, when Jo walked into his room, he was sitting in a chair by the window.

"I'm talking about that man down the hall," he said to her as soon as she entered, as if they'd been in the middle of a conversation. "You know the one. What's his name again... Danny, Donny...?"

"You mean David?"

He snapped his fingers. "That's the one. Tells everyone he's a hundred and three. Liar. He's not a day over ninety— just wants everyone to think he looks young for his age. And that Shirl or Cheryl or whatever her name is, she claims she's only sixty-five. If she's not sliding down the far-side of seventy, I'll dance naked on the tables." When he chuckled, Jo laughed too. "Yeah, you'd get a kick out of that, wouldn't you, old girl? You always did appreciate me in the altogether. Must be why I married you in the first place."

Jo grimaced but resisted setting him straight.

"Some people can't handle getting old," he continued as she sat down in the chair next to him. "As if lying about it changes one day. I'm what, sixty-eight now?"

"Sixty-nine." She said with a note of sadness, thinking it was far too soon for him to be this far gone.

"Nine? You sure?"

Jo nodded.

"Ah well, who can keep track? The point is to live each day, not worry how they add up."

"Sounds like a good philosophy."

A long silence followed while her father stared blankly at the wall and Jo tried to think of something to say. "Well, I'm glad you're meeting new people here and making friends."

His head swiveled toward her, and his eyes narrowed abruptly. "This isn't preschool."

"No, of course not."

"What business is it of yours anyway?" He looked around the room. "Where's Amanda? You've scared her away."

"No one's scared anyone."

"She was just here." His face twisted with anger. "I won't have strangers coming in here frightening my wife."

"Dad, it's me, your daughter, Josephine. I came to see you."

"Josephine." He blinked at her as if she were slowly coming into focus. "So this is what we've come down to, isn't it? The obligatory visit."

"Don't be unpleasant. Remember, it was your choice to stay here. We can always make other arrangements if you're not happy."

"Happy?" he replied with a sneer. "How can anyone be happy about devolving like this? I'm turning into a foolish imitation of myself, a drooling idiot."

"Dad, don't."

He sighed and the energy seemed to drain out of him. He leaned back in his chair and closed his eyes.

"Are you feeling okay?" she asked.

"Hmmm?" He opened his eyes again and looked over at her. "Just a little tired, dear. You're right, I work too hard. You're always right."

Jo hated to see him slip back into his fantasy, but only the rush of anger-fueled adrenaline seemed to ground him. Hardly a pleasant way to interact and ultimately unsustainable. This disease was robbing them both. Neither could give or receive comfort from the other, especially when he didn't even know who she was half the time. His rapid decline in the last few weeks reinforced her fear that he might have ended up in the placebo group. She felt her responsibility for his care like a weight on her chest and sometimes couldn't seem to pull enough air into her lungs. "I should go and let you rest."

He grabbed her sleeve. "This place. It's not right here."

"What do you mean?"

"People are disappearing."

Jo sucked in a breath, trying to come up with a reasonable response to what appeared to be a growing paranoia. "Okay, okay. I'll look into it, but I'm sure everything's fine. The doctors here only want to help you."

He scowled and his mouth worked as if he couldn't form the words. A tear welled in his eye and tracked down one cheek. "No, it hurts, Josie, it hurts so much. I want to go home, please."

"Oh, Dad..." She squatted down to look in his face. "I thought this is what you wanted. To be part of this study, but I agree you shouldn't be in pain. I'll go talk to them."

"No, don't. It's too dangerous. Stay away." He looked around as if fearing someone might be listening. "Go now. Don't worry about your mother. I'll protect her," he said and shooed her away. His hand fell back into his lap and he turned to stare at some distant place beyond the wall.

The rapidity of his decline appalled her. No doubt what she feared might happen had come to pass. He'd ended up in the placebo group, receiving no medication at all. Dr. Kessler had promised that even as part of the control group, he'd be in the best position to receive treatment once approved, but at this rate even a miracle cure would come too late. But above all, he shouldn't suffer. On her way out, she stopped at the nurse's station where a young brunette sat making entries on her computer. Her name tag read Donna.

"Could I speak to the physician in charge?" Jo asked her.

"After six pm, we only have the nursing staff on duty with a doctor on call for emergencies." Donna smiled, but her eyes had a hard, tired look about them. "I can page him for you if it's necessary. Is it?"

Jo doubted her worries constituted an emergency in anyone's view but her own. "No. I suppose not. I'd really rather talk to Dr. Kessler anyway."

"In that case, you'll need to talk to Mrs. Sutton. She schedules all his appointments." Jo nodded her understanding and Donna pressed a button at her station, unlocking the elevator.

When the doors opened, Jo entered and selected the ground floor, the only one that worked without a keycard. Mrs. Sutton had explained the necessity for such tight security, but Jo still thought it extreme. As she rode the elevator down, another idea occurred to her. If there was anything she recognized, it was the look of someone who lived for their job. Her father had worn that look for as long as she could remember, and Dr. Kessler wore it as well. Chances were, he was still here. Making a daytime appointment meant she'd have to miss work, and who knew how long it would take to get one. Meanwhile, her father was slipping away. She was here now, and Kessler probably was too. Maybe she could meet with him right now.

In the lobby, a security guard sat behind the receptionist area, arms folded, staring at a series of monitors. Jo walked up to him. "Excuse me. Is Suzanne Sutton in? I wanted to ask her if Dr. Kessler might be available to meet with me."

The man turned to look at her. "She's out on an errand right now, but should be back soon. You can wait for her in her office if you like." He pointed to the open door beside a large, framed mirror.

From inside Suzanne's office, Jo looked back out into the lobby through the window that matched the mirror on the other side. Jo had thought it odd the Administrator would have her office on the lobby floor rather than up with Kessler and the rest of the clerical staff until she'd seen this one-way view. The woman was like a guard dog, keeping watch on everyone's comings and goings. When Jo signed her father's admittance documents in here that first night, she had noticed this view of the lobby. She'd also noticed boxed displays hanging on the walls but hadn't examined their contents. She walked over now and saw they contained enameled gold and silver badges depicting pistols in raised relief and underlined with the words: expert, sharpshooter, or marksman.

Oh great, she's not just a guard dog, she's a guard dog with a gun fetish.

From her impression of the woman, Jo doubted Suzanne Sutton would spontaneously grant permission for her to see Dr. Kessler tonight. No, her knee-jerk reaction would be to insist she make an appointment, days or even weeks in advance, even when she only needed a few moments of his time. She was here now and wanted to deal with this now. She should be able to just hop on that elevator and go knock on his door, but doing so required a coded keycard She recalled seeing Suzanne put her card in her upper right desk drawer, before accompanying her out of the building that night.

I wonder if she leaves it there whenever she goes out.

Jo moved behind the desk, quietly slid open the drawer and there it was. Her heart quickened. She struggled for a moment between breaking the rules and her need to act. Her father was clearly getting worse. The sooner she spoke to Dr. Kessler, the better. True, he might not be thrilled by her showing up unannounced, but what was the worst that could happen? He'd either talk to her or he wouldn't. Right?

"Oh, for heaven's sake, show a little backbone."

She snatched the card and when the guard wasn't looking, headed for the elevator. She swiped Sutton's card through the control panel and pressed the button for the sixth floor. It lit. As the elevator rose, she pulled out her business card, cleared her throat, and mentally rehearsed what to say.

Be professional, and no matter what, don't cry.

Jo exited on the sixth floor and rounded the corner, then hesitated at hearing loud voices. Ahead, Kessler's office door stood ajar. From the timbre and energy of the exchange, this was not a friendly discussion.

"You can't do that!"

She recognized the voice as Kessler's.

"We can and we will." The other voice she didn't recognize, a male baritone with a distinct southern accent. "I gave you fair warnin' and we're well within our rights."

"What about your ethics?"

"You fraud, you're the last one to talk to me about ethics. This do-gooder act of yours may fool everyone else, but we both know the truth."

Kessler's door slammed shut and she could no longer hear what was being said. She stood frozen with the words 'fraud' and 'ethics' and 'truth' echoing in her ears.

I should leave, she thought, but then the image of her father begging to go home prodded her forward and she did something even more out of character than borrowing Sutton's keycard. She pressed her ear against the heavy wooden door. She heard the two men arguing inside, their voices heated and angry, but could grasp only a few words here and there. Something about more testing, breaking the law, and running out of time. Jo yelped when the door swung open, and she found herself face-to-face with a short, heavy-set man carrying a large-brimmed hat. Behind him, Dr. Kessler stared at her in surprise.

"I'm... I'm terribly sorry," she said. "I didn't mean to intrude."

"The hell, you didn't." The short round man eyed her then pushed past and strode away.

Kessler pointed a finger as if trying to jump-start his memory. "You're, you're um..."

"Josephine Rinaldi," she said, and extended her business card. "My father is your patient, Thomas Rinaldi, Room 312."

"Oh yes." Kessler took the card, read it, frowned, then looked back at her. "And what brings you to my door at this hour?"

"I was hoping to talk to you. My father's quite upset and isn't doing well."

Kessler sighed. "Patients often exhibit a worsening of symptoms when introduced to an unfamiliar environment. Once he gets used to his surroundings, he should stabilize."

"I'm worried it's more than that, that he's only getting the placebo."

"I made it very clear that this is a blind study."

"Yes, you did, but now I'm wondering if he'd be better off back on his regular medication."

"You may as well sign his death warrant."

Jo's mouth opened and her eyes widened.

"You do realize he has a terminal illness."

"Yes, of course, I understand that, but it seemed like his prior medications were helping, so wouldn't it be better if he—"

"No, it wouldn't," Kessler snapped. "Those medications merely interfere."

"You mean with your study?"

The doctor exhaled a long breath. "I don't mean to be short with you, but frankly I find your questioning me like this now perplexing, especially considering the fact that Matthew Dawson personally asked me to include your father in our program as a favor to you. You went on the tour, listened to the requirements, signed the admission papers. It's all in writing which I trust you read, though by what you're saying now, it seems you may not have. If I gave your father or any other patient here preferential treatment, the results of our study would be invalid."

Her mind struggled for a moment over his accusation that she'd missed something in the papers she'd signed. "I'm not asking for special treatment, but I'm thinking it might be better for my father if he withdrew for now. Perhaps he could return when you're further along."

"This isn't a revolving door. He's either in or out. Trust me, he's better off in. What I'm offering may be his only chance." Kessler's volume rose a notch. "Everyone's so damned impatient. I need more time. Why can't people understand that?"

Surprised, Jo took a breath. "I'm sorry. I'm not trying to pressure you. I'm just worried about my dad."

Kessler's scowl softened. He took a step closer and laid a hand on her shoulder. "Of course you are. I understand how difficult this is, but you made the right decision to bring him here. Your father is exactly where he needs to be."

Jo smelled alcohol on his breath and stepped back, letting his hand drop away. "Obviously, I came at a bad time. That man who was here just now. It sounded like he was threatening you."

Kessler froze for a moment. "A difference of opinion is all. Nothing to worry about." He waved dismissively.

She didn't find his reassurance believable. "It sounded pretty heated to me. It might be a good idea for you to call Matthew Dawson to discuss it. As your attorney, he'd want to know."

"I keep Matthew fully informed."

Though not convinced, Jo decided not to press the matter further. She didn't come up here to offer legal counsel. She came to talk about her father. "I'm sorry for barging in on you like this. It's just that I'm worried about my father and wanted to see you as soon as possible."

"No, I understand, and I don't want you to worry. I'll be sure to look in on him tonight and go over his chart to see if anything needs adjusting."

"Thank you. I would appreciate that."

"No problem. And I in turn appreciate your input. We must all remain vigilant in this fight. Alzheimer's is a cruel and deadly foe. It destroys hope, empties the mind, and leaves nothing but an empty shell. That's why I'm so determined to defeat it."

The doctor's choice of words made him sound like a superhero in a comic book. It occurred to her that maybe something wasn't quite reality-based there, but she brushed the thought aside. "Well, I hope you win then."

"As do I. You can trust us to take good care of your father. Feel free to consult me anytime," Kessler said as he ushered her out the door.

Jo allowed herself to find comfort in his promises and as she retreated, she questioned her right to question him. *Dr. Kessler is a world class neurologist. What do I know about treating Alzheimer's? Zero.* She stepped into the elevator, comparing what he'd said with the bits and pieces of the angry argument she'd overheard. That man had called Kessler a fraud. Could there be anything to it?

No, that's ridiculous, she told herself. *Peterson and Dawson both recommended him. Besides, not only is Kessler Dawson's client, he's his personal friend. He has to have been thoroughly vetted. Right? Unless there's something neither Peterson nor Dawson knows about.*

Jo thought of the Slader case, how Dawson had nearly gone to court on behalf of a known felon. It happened once, could it happen again? She visualized that man storming out of Kessler's office, the icy look in his eyes when he saw her there.

Upon returning to the ground floor, Jo found Sutton's office empty. Relieved not to confront her, Jo quietly returned the card to its drawer, then left the building. As Jo drove home, she replayed the night's events in her mind. Kessler's comments about what she'd agreed to in her dad's admission papers worried her. Once home, she put a kettle on to boil and rummaged through the household file drawer searching for the folder containing those papers. She found it just as the kettle whistled for attention. She fixed herself a hot cup of chamomile and carried the folder and her briefcase upstairs to her bedroom, a sanctuary where she could block out the world to either focus or unwind. On this occasion it would be the former. She had work to do.

The appliquéd squares on her quilt worked well for organizing papers. 'A' is for *Appellate*, 'B' is for *Brief*, 'C' is for *Complaint*, 'D' is for *Defendant, 'E' is for Equitable. Each* square contained a letter of the alphabet and a corresponding legal term illustrated with embroidered images of law books, scales, and courthouse scenes. She smiled at the detailed handiwork of her mother, a young bride working in secret during long lonely evenings while her husband studied for the bar exams. She remembered the story of how he'd reacted when presented with this quilt in honor of passing the bar.

"Your father said, 'What the heck am I supposed to do with this?' I told him if he couldn't think of anything, maybe he should sleep on it."

Mom always knew how to handle him. Guess I could take a lesson there.

Although at first glance, her father hadn't appreciated the quilt, he soon discovered how to put it to use—exactly as she was doing now. She sat cross-legged on her bed with the quilt spread before her, ready to organize whichever task she chose. So which to tackle first? Her father's admission papers or Carl's assignment? She was already tired, and Carl's report for Dawson was due first thing tomorrow. She'd made a promise. Reluctantly, she set aside her father's admission forms and opened the legal file.

Carl's assignment was to summarize the key points of a client contract and cite any escape clauses. The document entitled 'Affiliation and Patent License Contract,' appeared to be a standard partnership agreement with a bundle of attachments labeled A, B, C, etc. She placed the attachments on their appropriate squares, then leaned back against her pillowed bolster to sip her tea and read.

The two named parties were The ACC Services Foundation, and Bio-Med, Inc., a privately held medical research company. "Under the terms herein, any and all profits resulting from any and all pharmaceuticals, medical treatments or biotech devices developed by BioMed pursuant to the trial studies as referenced in said attachments, will be divided as follows..."

Her eyes drooped. She hadn't counted on the dry language putting her to sleep and wished now that she'd fixed herself a cup of high-octane coffee instead of a soothing herbal tea. She took a breath and refocused. Jo had always thought of medical research as being funded by government grants, huge pharmaceutical companies, and charities. So who was this ACC, anyway? Couldn't be a charitable foundation if it was sharing in the profits. That would be tax fraud. *Hmmm, possible loophole?* She wrote IRS with a question mark, then read on. The Foundation would underwrite all costs of research, development and licensing, including funding the operation of Bio Med's residential memory care facility. *Wait, what?* She sat up and read those words again—*residential memory care facility.* She skipped to the last page, looking for named officers, but the empty signature lines were underscored only by 'President of ACC Services Foundation' and 'President of Bio-Med, Inc.'

No, it can't be the same person. Then again, how many of Dawson's clients own and operate a memory care facility? She only knew of one. This meant Kessler's Institute wasn't a non-profit as she had assumed. *So much for the altruistic superhero act.* The thought brought her up short. *We all have to make a living. Why should he be any different? It's not like I work for free.* She shook her head, annoyed by her own naivety.

She looked at the attachments spread out before her, listing ongoing projects and clinical trials. Could the trial in which her father was participating be among them? Her excitement died when she read the coded designations: A-123, A-124, B-214, etc., meaningless to anyone outside the studies themselves. None of this would help her figure out what medication her father was or wasn't receiving. Her best move might be to call her father's old physician, Dr. Peterson. Maybe he could find out for her.

But knowing the answer to that wouldn't reveal why that man questioned Dr. Kessler's ethics and called him a fraud. The look he gave her had been chilling, and Kessler's evasive answers left her uneasy. She couldn't shake the feeling he was hiding something. And yet, she'd ended up accepting his reassurances, telling herself he was the expert, not her, and walked away even though the tension in her gut remained. Seeing this contract only tightened it. To learn if that gut reaction had any basis in fact meant she'd have to investigate, not her forte, so that meant she would have to hire someone. Bev's new P.I. Scott Benson jumped into her mind, along with contrasting images, one winking, the other glaring. Both annoying. She shook her head. *There must be someone else I can call.*

Still, he did do an outstanding job uncovering Slader's criminal history and, just as importantly, he'd kept it quiet. Slader never suspected they were on to him until the police showed up. Discretion here was every bit as crucial. She couldn't risk offending Kessler while her father was still in his care, nor did she want Dawson to know she was investigating his prized client without his permission.

Maybe Scott Benson was exactly the person she needed. Disliking him was irrelevant. What mattered was getting to the truth, discreetly.

CHAPTER EIGHT

Freed from Restraint

After first getting rid of Howell and then that annoying woman from Dawson's law firm, Dr. Kessler's chronic headache returned. He rummaged through the bottom drawer of his desk and pulled out a bottle of ibuprofen plus a sleek silver flask with his initials engraved in large elaborate script on the front, a gift from his late wife. He'd thought it an odd choice at the time, unreflective of his personal habits. He hadn't much use for it until recently, but now he was glad he'd hung on to it. He tossed two of the bitter white painkillers into his mouth, unscrewed the lid and took a swig of the expensive bourbon within to wash them down. Liquid fire seared his chest, a soothing heat he'd learned to appreciate of late. He relaxed into the sensation as he walked over to the wall of windows to take in the night view of the restless ocean below.

Its dark rolling waters reminded him of the old nightmares that used to haunt him, ones where he floated lost and alone in an endless black sea with no memory of who he was or where he'd been. He recalled thinking if there were nothing left to remember, there could be nothing left to hope for, but now he felt nothing. As he watched the waves rolling in, one after the other, he noted the change in himself, but felt no urge to identify the cause. The absence of fear was a relief. Now if he could just be rid of these damned headaches. When the warmth in his chest faded, he drank again.

Claiming she needed to make a run to the bank, Suzanne Sutton hid in her car. Once certain Howell had left the building and driven away, she returned to her office. Her policy was to never go home for the night until Adrian did. She still thought of him as Adrian and always would, but was careful to address him as Dr. Kessler in front of other people. She tried to keep things professional, but it was a continual struggle. She remembered how it used to be when he'd shared his dreams and his bed with her. How she grieved for that lost intimacy.

Addressing Adrian as Doctor Kessler and keeping her hands to herself was a daily torture, but not seeing him at all would be worse. He once promised to love her forever, promised to make a life with her. So many broken promises, all because his wife came home one day too early.

The image of Ellen lying on the cold white bathroom tile, eyes fixed, as a pool of red billowed from beneath her head, jumped unbidden into Suzanne's mind. She squeezed her eyes shut and shook her head to make it go away.

They'd had no intention of harming Ellen, but intention made no difference. She was dead and the circumstances of that fact would have destroyed Adrian's reputation and career, something Suzanne couldn't permit. In a panic, she had called the one person she knew with the wherewithal to cover it up and enough skin in the game to want to, Reginald Howell. Soon a pair of grim-faced men had arrived, and the next morning the police found Ellen's crumpled car down the side of a cliff with her body inside it.

To avoid suspicion, Suzanne and Adrian agreed to put their relationship on hold, and she would have found employment elsewhere if he hadn't begged her to stay. He just needed time, he'd said, to get over the shock and the guilt. That was nearly a year ago, but instead of bringing them back together, time seemed to be pushing them farther apart.

Not that she was ready to give up. She hoped reducing Adrian's stress would help facilitate their reunion. Step one was getting rid of Reginald Howell. His continued presence was a constant reminder of that awful night, not simply because it had happened, but because he brought it up whenever she balked at fulfilling his requests. She often visualized shooting Howell with the revolver she kept in her desk, a favorite fantasy. In lieu of murder, she had their attorneys working on a way to break their contract, while she worked to find alternate sources of funding. She looked forward to the day she could say good riddance, but until then, she had to keep Howell happy no matter how much he repulsed her. It was her job to protect Adrian and preserve this Institute. It was Adrian's job to cure Alzheimer's. Together they would make history.

Suzanne glanced at her watch again, worried at the late hour, especially in light of changes she'd seen in his behavior of late. He used to be friendly, asking after the staff, wishing them well, and often thanked them for their work. Now, he walked by them without a word. She feared he was pushing himself too hard and jeopardizing his physical and emotional health. She'd tried several times to ask if something was bothering him, or if he needed her to hire more help, but he dismissed her questions abruptly, even to the point of being rude. The last time they'd spoken in private, she'd left his office in tears and he hadn't even seemed to notice.

She rose from her desk and went out to look at the security monitors. The camera outside of Adrian's office showed only a closed door. Patience gone, she headed for the elevator. At Adrian's door, she knocked and waited. When no answer came, she knocked again, then heard a cry followed by a loud thump. She burst into the room. He lay on his back, arms covering his face, shoulders heaving.

"Adrian!" She rushed to his side and when he lowered his arm, she expected to see anguish, but realized he was laughing. Then the smell of alcohol hit her. "Oh dear."

"Oh dear, oh dear," he mocked and snorted again in laughter.

"All right, come on, get up." She helped him to his feet, but he wavered dangerously. "On second thought, you'd better sit." She grabbed his desk chair and wheeled it under him.

He fell into the chair making it spin accidentally, then he did it again on purpose, again and again, laughing as he did.

She didn't laugh. "Stop that. You're not a child anymore."

He slammed both feet on the floor, stopping the spin, and looked up at her. "You're right. Time's chasing me now. And it wants to squash me like an ant. Turns out, that's all I am, Suzie, a tiny insignificant ant." He pinched two fingers together in front of her nose.

"That's nonsense." She scowled at him, confused both by his inebriation and self-deprecation. This was all so out of character. "You're not the least bit insignificant. You're a brilliant scientist and the leader of this Institute. Didn't you tell me just the other day how well your research is going?"

He waved his hand as if shooing flies. "Doesn't matter now. It's too late."

She lowered to her knees and looked him in the face. "What are you talking about?"

"Howell wants me to tell the world I have a cure, but I can't, not yet. I don't have it. Don't tell him. He mustn't know. And he's given me an impossible deadline. I'd have to create years of research nearly overnight."

"Well, you can't do that, obviously."

"Actually, I could." Kessler scoffed. "Howell says I have a higher moral obligation. Imagine that coming from him. But I admit, it's hard to disagree. Do you remember Gladys Johnson? She couldn't speak, could barely swallow, but that idiot husband of hers wanted us to employ every means possible to prolong her life. That meant putting her on a feeding tube and even with that, I estimated she had two, maybe three months left at most. So I took a chance. I injected her with my genetically altered stem cells, like the ones we've been testing in the animal labs, and she rallied. It took a few weeks, but then suddenly she was back. She could talk. She knew where she was, who she was. It was remarkable, miraculous even. Her husband was thrilled, but before long I saw signs of regression and knew if I didn't get her brain out immediately, any evidence of cellular renewal would be lost." He paused and tilted his head as if listening to some inner voice. "'Physician, do no harm.' I always tried to live up to that, but..."

Suzanne listened as he confirmed her suspicions about those three late-stage Alzheimer's patients, all of whom seemed to recover miraculously, only to die days later. He had explained the deaths away to the satisfaction of the authorities, but not to their families, whose unanswered questions led to the lawsuits. When the families refused to settle, and Mrs. Johnson's husband threatened to go to the press, Reginald Howell intervened. A week later, the suits ended, and she received signed nondisclosure agreements.

"They would have died anyway," she said.

"Yes, eventually." His eyes searched the room as if he no longer saw her. "It's something with their gene expression— just like in the mice, but mice don't necessarily react the way humans do. There are just too many variables. I realized the only way to solve the puzzle in my lifetime was to work backwards, do the last step first. If I succeeded, even with just one person, just one, I could reverse engineer it. I keep trying, but..." He shook his head and fell silent.

Alarms buzzed in her head. "You've been testing this on more people?"

He looked back at her. "Only the terminal ones. Ones with no close family. I learned my lesson there. Trouble is, limiting myself to only the most advanced cases diminishes the chances of success. There's only so much damage that can be overcome. No, if I have any hope of meeting Howell's deadline, I'll need healthier subjects."

"But it might kill them."

He nodded. "True, but they'll die eventually, anyway."

She thought about that for a moment. *A few may die sooner so that many more can be saved later.* It sounded reasonable, felt wrong. Could she live with the cold logic of it?

"Do I shock you?" he asked, as if reading her mind.

"No, I... I think I understand."

"Of course you do. You always did. Not like my Ellen." He said the name of his dead wife with a bitter note. "I could never have trusted her with this."

Her stomach clutched, remembering that awful night again.

"I can't do this alone." He laid his hand on hers and leaned close, inches from her face. "I need your help, I need to know you're with me now, more than ever."

Her heart soared at his touch and the prospect of being 'with' him again. The last of her trepidation fled. "Yes, of course, whatever you need. You know you can count on me."

"Good girl." He squeezed her hand. "We'll find the answer together, I promise."

His eyes stared into hers but seemed focused on some distant vision. She hoped he was seeing the same one she was. With her by his side, he would save millions. He was her hero, and she was his... what? She tried to fill in the blank, but decided it wasn't needed. She was just his, and that was enough. She returned his unblinking stare, willing him to close the small gap between them. Instead, he leaned back and released her hand. She felt the loss like a blow.

"There's someone else worrying me besides Howell." He stood to search the top of his desk. "Her card's here somewhere. Here it is. Josephine Rinaldi. She's that attorney with Dawson's firm."

"Yes, I remember her." Suzanne looked at her empty hands, already resenting the reason—dark haired, slender, attractive, about ten years her junior. He handed her the card.

"She came up here tonight trying to get special treatment for her father."

She came up here? Jealousy stirred as she looked at the card, along with outrage that their security system had been circumvented. *How did she do that?*

"Unfortunately, she overheard Howell and me arguing and was asking a lot of questions. Could be a problem. Shame seeing as her father's a prime candidate. A successful result in someone of that caliber would be especially dramatic, but if his daughter's going to cause trouble, maybe I'm better off without him."

"No, if you want him, you should have him." Suzanne tucked the card into her pocket, glad to have a target. "Just leave her to me."

CHAPTER NINE

Repercussions

Early the next morning, Jo slipped into Carl's empty office to drop off the file with her report, then texted him: [It's on your desk. You can bill 3 hours.] As she walked back to her office, she received two hearts and a kissy face emoji in response. Next, she sent a message to Scott Benson. Within the hour he was sitting in one of her visitor chairs.

"What I am about to tell you must stay between us. Can I count on that, Mr. Benson?"

He nodded. "Absolutely."

"Very well." Jo related the events of the previous night, voiced her concerns and suspicions, and finally her desire to find out what might be going on behind the scenes at the Kessler Institute. Scott listened intently, sitting with one elbow propped to hold his chin and a forefinger pressed against his lips. When she couldn't think of anything else to add, she waited for a reaction. To her annoyance, he just kept staring at her. "Did I put you to sleep?"

He dropped his hand and straightened. "Hardly."

"Then perhaps you think I'm making too much of this."

"Not necessarily. You say this guy called Dr. Kessler a fraud and accused him of being unethical, plus there was talk of a deadline?"

"Yes. Well, at least I think that's what he said. I couldn't hear all that well, but it was enough to make me think of the Slader situation."

"Well, we sure wouldn't want anything like that happening again. So, yeah, I think it's worth looking into."

"Good. This should give you a place to start," she said, handing over a file containing everything she knew about the Kessler Institute plus a copy of the contract Carl had thrust upon her last night. The original document, along with her report, would make its way to Dawson, for which

Carl would take full credit with no mention of her involvement. Just as well, considering what she was doing now.

Scott thumbed through the file, then looked back at her. "This will help. I'll see what else I can find out." He rose from the chair.

"You're to bill me directly and communicate solely with me on this. Understood?"

Scott's mouth lifted on one side. "So, I take it you haven't mentioned this to Dawson?"

"No, there's no reason to involve him until I have more information." Jo's face warmed. "I'm hoping you'll put my fears to rest and that will be the end of it." She bristled at his knowing smile. "If that's a problem for you, just say so."

"No, not for me. Could be for you, though, if Dawson got wind of it."

"Which is why I'm counting on your discretion. I need this done quickly and quietly. Are we agreed?"

"Sure. No problem."

"Good."

"Have to say, you've got guts."

She eyed him, uncertain whether he meant that as a compliment or a criticism. "I look forward to your report, Mr. Benson."

"Scott," he corrected. His head tilted and one eyebrow raised. "Seeing as we're in this together now."

For a moment, she thought he was flirting. She pushed the idea aside, certain his type would be far more attracted to flashy women like Bev, not conservative, well-worn divorcees like herself. "Scott, then. Call me as soon as you learn anything—I don't care what time it is."

"You got it." He raised the file to his forehead in salute. "I'll be in touch."

Jo watched him exit, then saw him pause at her secretary's desk. Bev leaned toward him, undoubtedly providing a splendid view of her ample cleavage. Without conscious thought, Jo's hand flew to her phone, buzzing Bev's desk. Scott tapped Bev on the nose with a forefinger and left. A moment later, Bev stood in Jo's doorway in all her glory—red puffed hair, a blouse barely big enough to pass law office inspection and a bright yellow miniskirt.

"You rang?" she asked.

Jo thought fast to come up with something. "Yes, I, um.... I wanted to tell you I've just hired Mr. Benson to do some research for me... on a personal matter." Jo paused, feeling her nose itch. She grabbed a tissue, catching a sneeze just in time.

"Bless you." Bev scowled at her. "This isn't about your ex, is it?"

"No, of course not. You know I have nothing to do with Ethan anymore."

"New boyfriend?" Bev suggested with a hopeful look on her face. "Doing a background check?"

"No, no, nothing like that." Jo cleared her throat, noticing it felt scratchy.

"Too bad. Thought maybe you were finally getting back in the game. So, what's it about then?"

"Something personal, like I said."

"Seriously?" Bev frowned and crossed her arms. "I cover your back, you cover mine, remember?"

Jo sighed. "Fine. Come inside and shut the door."

Her green eyes lit with curiosity, Bev closed the door and filled the same chair Scott vacated moments before. "Okay, so what gives?"

"Don't make a big deal out of this because it isn't. It's just that I'm a little worried about something I overheard last night, something involving Dr. Kessler."

Bev's mouth opened into a perfect 'O' of astonishment. "You're investigating Dr. Kessler? Dawson's prize client?"

Jo felt another itch and pinched her nose to stop herself from sneezing again. "It's not like I'm billing it to the office."

"Oh good. I'm sure he'll be perfectly fine with it then."

"Okay, so he wouldn't, which is why I'm doing this quietly."

Bev shook her head. "I swear, Jo, sometimes you are your own worst enemy. Just when things were calming down around here, and you've got Dawson eating out of your hand, you go and do this. Why not just run naked through the hallways while you're at it?"

"I haven't lost my mind. My dad's not doing well, Bev. He's gotten a lot worse since he's been there, and when I went to talk to Dr. Kessler about it last night, I heard something I wasn't supposed to. Maybe it's nothing, but I need to make sure, and I'm trusting you not to say anything until I do."

"Obviously, I won't say anything—how could you even ask me that?" Bev frowned at her, clearly offended. "I just hope you know what you're doing. If you're so worried about your dad, wouldn't it be better to just move him somewhere else?"

"That would probably offend Dawson just as much. I'm hoping this will put my fears at rest and it won't come to that." Jo stopped herself from going into the traumatic consequences of relocating an already befuddled senior.

"Well, I'm glad you hired Scott to do it."

"Because you want to date him?"

"No, because he knows his stuff. Not that I'd mind, though. I mean look at him. He's hot, unattached, not gay—pretty rare these days."

"So you think he's interested?" Jo asked, uncertain she wanted to hear the answer.

"Hard to tell. I mean he's friendly and all, but so far that's it." She let out a long sigh. "Maybe he's shy."

Jo sputtered a laugh. "I doubt that."

"Well, I've done just about everything but strip for him and so far, he just smiles and runs off. Could be I'm not his type, but I was kinda hoping for shy."

"Sorry," Jo said, understanding the disappointment that came with a one-way attraction. "Maybe he's not as unattached or straight as he seems. Like Ethan. Nobody knew until everyone did, including him."

"True." Bev shrugged. "Did you ever tell your dad?"

"God, no. I'd never hear the end of it."

Bev laughed, and Jo promptly sneezed again.

Bev handed her another tissue. "You're not getting sick on me, are you? Lot of people are out with the flu."

"No, I don't have time for that." Jo glanced at the stack of files on her desk.

"You sure? You look a little pale."

"I'm fine, really. And I'd better get back to work."

"Yeah, me too."

Jo watched her get up. "Bev. Thank you. I mean it. You really are a good friend."

"Best you'll ever have."

As the day wore on, Jo found it took more and more effort to concentrate. She still had medical records to review in an auto accident, a brief to cite check, a set of interrogatories to prepare in a slip-and-fall, plus a pile of depositions to summarize. All pretty mundane stuff, but each of them requiring a mental alertness she couldn't seem to muster. Maybe part of it was because the work wasn't any more interesting than what she'd done as a paralegal. Her associate pay was better, but little else had changed. She hated to admit that her father might have been right about her being a cog in the wheels. A rapping on her door interrupted her wandering thoughts.

"Yes?" she called out.

The door opened. Matthew Dawson peered in, entered, and closed it behind him with a soft click. He stood with his feet planted apart and his hands clasped behind his back, looking down on her from his six-foot tall advantage with those cool blue eyes of his. He wasn't smiling. She stared mutely up at him like a rabbit frozen in headlights.

"Ms. Rinaldi, something disturbing has come to my attention," he stated in a ponderous tone. "I just received a complaint about you from a client. I wonder if you know who that might be."

Jo blinked, trying to make her brain function. She had almost zero client contact. All her assignments came via partners in the firm. Most clients didn't even know she worked on their cases until the bill arrived, itemizing her hours. "I'm not sure. Is someone questioning how much time I spent?"

Dawson shook his head, his frown deepening. "No, this isn't about one of your assigned cases. This client is one of the most prestigious this firm has ever represented and you, young lady, have offended him."

Alarms rang in Jo's brain and her face prickled with heat. She was now quite certain she knew to whom Dawson was referring. "You don't mean Dr. Kessler?"

"That's exactly who I mean. I was told that last night you handed him your business card then demanded preferential treatment for your father in violation of FDA clinical testing procedures and that when Dr. Kessler refused to comply, you threatened to break your father's agreement with the clinic. His administrator, Suzanne Sutton, called me just now to ask if this firm will be able to represent them should you decide to file a lawsuit."

"What?!" Jo couldn't believe how much her words had been twisted and taken out of context. "No, I was just asking about my father's condition. I never said anything about suing anybody. I don't know why she would think that."

"If this is a simple misunderstanding, I'm happy to hear it," Dawson replied, although he didn't look any happier. "I would hope you only meant to treat him with the highest respect and express your gratitude that he allowed your father to enroll in his program, which if you might recall resulted from a personal request on my part. People have been on his waiting list for years trying to get in there. I would also hope you had no intention of damaging this firm's reputation—or mine."

"No, of course not. I'm so sorry. I never meant anything like this to happen."

"I wouldn't think so."

"What can I do to fix this?"

"You can start by writing a letter of apology. And don't bother Dr. Kessler again without an appointment."

Jo swallowed hard and nodded. "I understand."

"I want to see the draft of your letter before it goes out."

"Okay. I'll send it as soon as it's ready."

Dawson was still frowning. "Today, Rinaldi."

"I'll do it right now. Again, I'm so sorry."

Dawson nodded, then left her office and closed the door.

As the shock wore off, it sank in just how close she'd come to disaster. Then she flashed on her meeting with Scott Benson this morning. She immediately called his number, annoyed to only get his abrupt voice mail message. She waited for the beep and left a message of her own.

"This is Josephine Rinaldi. I need you to cancel the assignment I gave you this morning. I'll pay for any time you've already spent, but you need to stop working on it immediately. I repeat, stop immediately."

Jo hung up, frustrated that she hadn't been able to talk to him. Just to be safe, she followed up with a text: [Assignment canceled. Stop work immediately.]. *There, that should take care of it.* She moved aside the file she'd been working on and turned to drafting the obligatory letter of apology Dawson had demanded.

Dear Dr. Kessler, It has been brought to my attention that... she began, choosing language that sounded both professional and suitably conciliatory. She finished with *Sincerely Yours*, then forwarded the letter to Dawson for approval. It came back within minutes, marked-up in red. She grimaced at the new groveling tone. Now she sounded like a simpering fool pleading for his royal forgiveness. She wanted to reject it—knew she didn't dare. Swallowing her pride, she accepted the changes and signed the letter.

Ugh. The things I have to do.

CHAPTER TEN

The Senator and the Lobbyist

Two men strode through the halls of the United States Senate, one in front of the other. Though dressed in nearly identical dark gray suits, they made a comically mismatched pair. Randall Pike, the far taller of the two, was fit and slender with thick brown hair touched gray at the temples. He moved in long confident strides, acknowledging colleagues with an enthusiastic flash of white teeth, or a slap on the shoulder. He seemed oblivious to his squat middle-aged companion, who was talking non-stop and following so closely that he threatened to un-shoe him.

"We need mo' time," Reginald Howell was saying, slightly out of breath and with a distinct southern twang. His coat-wings flapped like a distressed bird, revealing dark sweat stains under his armpits. "Now I know you can swing that much for us."

Pike shushed him, thankful no one was within earshot. He passed his clerk sitting outside his office and waved for them not to be disturbed. Howell followed him in. Once he closed his office door, Pike spun to face the tenacious lobbyist who had been dogging his footsteps since he'd exited the committee hearing chamber.

"You could try being a little more discreet. You want everyone to know our business?"

"Pssh. Nobody was listening. Not that it matters. I never name names."

"I can't help you, anyway. Not after that last investigative news report came out. Videos of prison guards abusing inmates. Documents itemizing how you're ripping off the American taxpayer and making huge profits. You should read the emails I'm getting."

Howell made a raspberry sound. "If I didn't know better, I might think that was the sound of moral indignation I was hearin'."

"Don't get sarcastic with me, Howell." Pike tore at the knot of his burgundy-red tie until it came loose. Howell's persistence combined with the same slow speaking style that Pike had spent years erasing from his own mannerisms deeply annoyed him, especially when he knew it was mostly an affectation Howell adopted and dispensed with as it suited him. Pike wished he could be rid of the man, but Howell was a powerful political influencer and represented one of his major benefactors, the ACC, otherwise known as the American Civic Corporation. Pike took a deep breath and changed his tone. "You know if I could help you, I would, but it would be political suicide right now. Your people are splashed all over the headlines."

"It's all just fake news, hoaxes drummed up by bleeding-heart liberals. You know that."

"Do I? Even if it were, it makes no difference. What matters is what my constituents believe, and they don't like you. What am I supposed to do about that?"

"I get it, I do, which is exactly why we're undergoin' a full public relations makeover. Launchin' a counterstrike with testimonials from rehabilitated prisoners, and a brand-new spokesman. Can't say who it is just yet, but think along the lines of Charlton Heston and the National Rifle Association."

"Wonderful," Pike said with zero enthusiasm. "Some old has-been expounding on the virtues of privatization."

"Now, don't be so quick to judge. He's going to make an announcement that'll put us right up there with Mother Teresa and Jonas Salk. We'll be getting checks in the mail."

"Are you trying to be funny?"

"Never been mo' serious in my life. I'm tellin' you, public opinion's gonna flip one-eighty, and when it does, we won't be forgettin' our friends who stuck with us. Keep that in mind, Senator, specially seein' as how you're aimin' for higher places."

Pike automatically averted his gaze. It had long been driven into him the importance of appearing modest and unassuming whenever anyone mentioned his aspirations to the Presidency. "I value your support, you know that, but I can't see how you're going to turn public opinion around anytime soon and I'm not risking my reputation until you do."

"Then I'll explain, but you've got to keep this just between us. Agreed?" When Pike nodded, Howell's good-old-boy demeanor vanished and he spoke in a low serious tone. "Okay. As I've told you before, we've been investing in other business models with the goal of improving our image and financial base, but what I haven't shared until now is exactly how. We're backing a neurologist who's working on a cure for Alzheimer's."

"Alzheimer's?" Pike screwed his face into a puzzled frown. "That's a stretch. What do your people know about medical research?"

"Not a blessed thing, but that's the beauty of it. We farm it all out and still make a killing. So to speak." Howell smirked sardonically.

Pike didn't know much about Alzheimer's except that it only affected old people, which meant it lacked both sex appeal and star power. "Why Alzheimer's? Why not cancer, or something to do with children? Nobody cares about the elderly."

"I think Baby Boomers would disagree, and unlike their children and grandchildren, they vote. Boomers make up most of your constituency and they'll continue to do so for another decade or two. It's the graying of America." Howell gestured at Pike's silvered sideburns, though at age 43, they didn't give him Boomer status. "They've seen this disease ravage their parents and they're scared to death of going out the same way, plus they've got money, lots of it, which means the payoff for owning a cure will be astronomical."

"Okay, but how does that fit in with me? My committee's working on prison reform, not medical research."

"Yes, and if those bills make it to the floor, it'll expose us to increased regulations and government oversight. If our inner workings come to light, it would be bad. Not just for us but for you... personally."

"I doubt that. I'm on the other side of the fence here."

"Except you keep sticking your arm through it with an open palm. Some could argue you've taken money in exchange for turning a blind eye, and people have died as a result."

"Died? What are you talking about?"

"Inmates used as test subjects."

Pike scowled. "Test subjects? Are you saying they're being used as human guinea pigs?"

"Now don't get all riled up. Using prison populations for medical research has a long history."

"A long dark history. Just how many are we talking about?"

"Oh, quite a few, I'd say. The elderly inmate population has increased by more than 500 percent and you can't believe how much it costs to care for someone with dementia—like nine times standard. The government per diem doesn't begin to cover it. So I came up with this arrangement about five years ago. Our doc takes problematic inmates off our hands and in return we fund his facility, then write it all off as a charitable donation. Pure genius. Thanks to me, and you."

"Christ," Pike said, appalled. "You know very well that I had nothing to do with it."

"Try telling that to the press. You and I are tied together like a gordian knot."

"You're blackmailing me now?"

"Such an ugly word. Think of it as one friend helping out another. I've been protecting your interests for a long time. All I'm asking now is for you to stall that legislation in committee a little while longer. The last thing we need right now is more regulations that could lead to states blocking future contracts with us or forcing closure of our facilities... possibly even ones we own outright. We can't afford that. And neither can you."

Pike chewed his lip, struggling to come to terms with all of this. "Just for argument's sake, let's say I do as you ask, delay things for a few more months. What good will it do?"

"It'll give us more time, which is all we really need. Won't be long before our Doc announces his cure for Alzheimer's. When we take credit, our stock will skyrocket. People will see we're on the right side of things, and that will flip public opinion on its head. After that, those regs will end up dying in committee on their own."

Pike rubbed his mouth, considering. If Howell wasn't exaggerating, Pike might well regret failing to intervene. Howell's people consistently donated large sums of soft money for his campaigns, and he didn't want to see his biggest resource dry up. And then there was this matter of inmates being subjected to questionable research practices. Should it be proven they'd been harmed, or worse, died as a result, and his name was attached to it, his political career would be over.

If a mere delay could prevent such a calamity, it might be worth sticking his neck out a cautious inch or two. As a three-time incumbent, he was well-skilled at subtle manipulation. He could easily sway his colleagues to agree to a more in-depth analysis of the costs involved—even make them think it was their idea. Delays seldom raised eyebrows. It was his job to be thorough, and when it came to enacting legislation, a snail-like pace was the expected norm.

"I suppose I can buy you a few months, but that's the best I can offer."

"Good man." Howell smacked the desktop in emphasis. "You won't regret it, and we won't forget it."

"You really think this Alzheimer's thing will pay off?"

"Already is just by giving us a huge tax deduction. And it'll earn us a fortune in good-will. Folks will see we're helping people, not just locking them up."

"What about your dead guinea pigs?"

"I wouldn't mention that if I was you."

CHAPTER ELEVEN

Down Time

Three days later, Jo hadn't heard back from Scott Benson, but she was too ill to care. She lay in bed, immersed in a miserable self-pity, surrounded by wadded up tissues. She'd come down with whatever virus was going around the office. Her throat felt scalded with acid and every muscle ached. Just lifting her stone-heavy head from the pillow took all the willpower she could muster. When the front doorbell chimed downstairs, she cursed at whoever had the audacity to disturb her suffering.

"Go away," she moaned.

It chimed again. After three more times, it fell silent.

"Thank God," she whimpered and pulled the quilt over her head.

A rattling noise ended her relief abruptly—*What was that?* She listened hard then recognized the sound of her refrigerator door opening. *Someone's in the house!* But she'd locked the doors—she was sure of it. Nobody had a key, not even Teresa anymore. Her heart pounded and the rush of fear-born adrenaline gave her the strength to move. She threw her covers aside, wrapped a robe around herself, then crept barefoot down the hall. More noises came from the kitchen—the swish of drawers opening and closing and the rattling of metal pots. She moved silently down the carpeted stairs and carefully placed a naked foot on the cold tile, preparing to sprint to the front door and escape.

"Oh, good. You're awake," a man's voice greeted her.

Jo yelped, threw herself forward, slipped, and went down.

"Whoa, you okay?"

Hands reached for her and in a confused panic, she pummeled at them blindly.

"Hey, hey, calm down. It's just me."

She blearily focused on the face in front of her. Scott Benson?

"You!" She sat up. "Are you nuts?"

"Probably." He was laughing now. "Sorry I scared you, but you wouldn't answer the door."

"That's no excuse for breaking into someone's home."

"I didn't break anything, I promise. Come on, let me help you up."

She slapped his hand away. He took a step back as she got to her feet, then pointed a thumb over his shoulder toward the kitchen. "You hungry?"

"What?" Jo couldn't believe this conversation was taking place.

"I think you'd better come sit down. You look awful."

"Gee thanks," she said trying for sarcasm, but since her dizziness had returned she couldn't put any energy into it and her reply sounded sincere instead. She found him steadying her, guiding her into the kitchen. She noticed all the cupboard doors stood open, revealing their contents.

"I see you've been snooping."

"Comes with the job. How else am I supposed to figure things out?"

He pulled out a chair for her at the table, and she sank into it heavily. Then a steaming bowl appeared in front of her, with a spoon.

She grabbed the spoon from his hand and waved it in his face. "You had no business coming in here like that."

"Had to. Beverley's worried about you. If you'd answer your cell phone, it would have saved us all a lot of trouble. She's going to want a full report when I get back, so I'm not leaving until you eat. It's chicken soup. It'll help, trust me."

Steaming broth tickled her nostrils with a salty aroma, and her mouth watered in response, annoying her all the more. "Fine, but then you have to go."

She sipped a spoonful of the broth cautiously, not sure her stomach could deal with the large chunks of chicken, chopped carrots and wide flat noodles. Rosemary, thyme, and flavors sharp and unfamiliar burst on her tongue. She hadn't realized how long it had been since she had anything to eat. She took another spoonful, then another. "This is good," she admitted, even though she'd wanted to hate it.

"Can't beat homemade."

"Bev cooked for me?"

"No, I did."

She stopped eating and scowled up at him. "Why on earth would you bother, and why would Bev send you of all people?"

His half-grin faltered, and she had the fleeting impression that he was hurt, but his expression quickly neutralized. "I have information about Kessler. You said to call—day or night, but seeing as you stopped answering your phone, here I am."

"Didn't you get my message?"

"You mean that panicked one—'assignment canceled, stop work immediately?' Sure, I got it. You think my phone's bugged, or yours?"

"No, I... I was just being careful."

"I noticed. When clients get that careful, I get curious. You got a PC or laptop around here?"

"Why?" Jo asked, even while pointing at her laptop on the built-in kitchen desk.

"Perfect." He retrieved her laptop, turned it on and whipped out a thumb-sized flash drive from his pocket. "I recorded this for you last night. Meet Dr. Kessler's partners."

On the screen, an actor who had starred in a number of action-packed thrillers smiled out at her.

"Movie magic can make most anything seem real," he said as Scott turned up the volume. "It can even make honest hardworking citizens appear to be villains, but it's time to look at the facts. State and federal prisons were once perilously overcrowded, plagued with violence, riots and suicides, until privatization came to the rescue with modern new facilities where inmates are housed under humane conditions, and participate in life-changing re-entry programs."

Corresponding images played along with the narration.

"Thanks to privatization, they can now earn high school degrees, receive vocational training, cognitive-behavioral therapy, substance abuse treatment, and faith-based services to reduce recidivism. Our employees are thoroughly trained professionals who make a difference in the lives of these inmates, and the community they serve every day.

This is what prison reform looks like and we're doing it without government interference, because we know the right things to do. Our purpose is to serve the American people and today I am announcing we are furthering that service by working to eliminate one of the most heartbreaking diseases of our time.

"Alzheimer's is rapidly rising as a leading cause of death and will soon outrank AIDS and cancer. Thanks to our financial backing, great strides are being made in developing a cure for this dreaded disease, a cure that will soon be made available to the public. For more information, please visit our website at www dot ACC Services Foundation dot org. Thank-you and God bless."

Jo frowned at the screen as it returned to a monotone blue. *Kessler's working with private prisons?* An unlikely pairing, but then she remembered those correctional-facility magazines on the table in the waiting room outside his office. "The ACC Foundation was the partner named in that contract. Who or what exactly is the ACC?"

"The American Civic Corporation runs private prisons and holding facilities for detainees all across the country. We're talking big money."

"Why would they be backing medical research?"

"To improve their image, I'd guess. The media's been pretty hard on privatization lately. Anyway, this clears up who's been paying your father's bills."

Jo bristled. "It's not about the money," she said even though it had played a large part in her decision-making.

Scott raised a palm. "Just passing on information here."

Jo swallowed her guilt, realizing she was doing it again, acting as if she were in the defendant's chair. "I thought I told you to stop working on this."

"Yeah, you did. So who's pressuring you?"

"No one. It was my decision."

He raised an eyebrow. "You don't really expect me to believe that."

She sighed. "Dawson got a complaint about me from the client, so I needed to end it."

"That's your decision, of course, but as long as I'm here, mind if I ask you a couple questions?"

She shrugged permission. "Like what?"

"Any of these names ring a bell—Lawrence Marks, Gladys Johnson, Evelyn Rubio?"

"No, should they?"

"They were Kessler's patients. Causes of death were listed as complications from dementia. But the funny thing is, their families claimed Kessler murdered them."

Jo inhaled at the accusation, and her father's anguished face jumped into her mind. She remembered the sound of his ragged voice, begging to come home, but even as her fear soared, denial worked even harder. "I would have heard about anything like that. You're talking front page news."

"Yeah, if it had made it that far, but it was hushed up. The families were paid off, and these files were sealed." He pulled out a set of three files and laid them on the table in front of her."

She placed a hand on them. "If they're sealed, how did you get your hands on them? How did you even find out?"

"The usual. I did some research."

Jo felt her headache returning. "Could you be more explicit?"

"Sure. Started out at the courthouse looking for anything naming Kessler or Bio-Med, Inc. or known associates. I found three cases: Rubio, Johnson, and Marks, like I said—titles only of course since the files were sealed. So I started doing cross-checks, looking for anything else under the same names till I found a match—Gladys Johnson—from when her husband filed for power of attorney. Got his name and address. He's moved since then but wasn't too hard to track him down. The hard part was getting him to talk to me. All off the record, but he finally told me how his wife and these other two patients died under some really weird circumstances. One day they all seemed to be doing great and the next, they were all dead. He couldn't get the authorities to investigate but convinced the other families to go in on a lawsuit. Ended up settling out of court."

Jo shrugged, unimpressed. "Doctors get sued all the time, and their insurers settle because it's less expensive. Doesn't mean Kessler did anything wrong."

Scott nodded. "Yeah, I might have thought that too, except Mr. Johnson said the families were told to take the money in a way that didn't give them a choice."

Jo smiled in disbelief. "Come on. You want me to believe Kessler is murdering his patients, then using mafia tactics on their relatives?"

"I know how it sounds, but it took a lot to get this man to talk to me and only after I swore up, down and sideways not a word of it would ever come back to haunt him. He said he had his children and grandchildren to think of."

"You actually believe there's something to this?"

Scott shrugged. "Hard to say. I just know if I had someone in there, I'd sure as hell want to find out."

Jo resisted the temptation to let guilt overrule logic. "There could be a thousand explanations. This man you talked to was grieving, maybe not thinking straight. He could easily have jumped to the wrong conclusions."

Scott smiled and leaned back. "Last week, you were hellbent on investigating Kessler and now you're bending over backwards to give him the benefit of the doubt. What gives?"

"I was upset. My father isn't getting better, but people with Alzheimer's don't get better. That's something I have to accept."

"So you want to ignore everything I've told you?"

She scowled at him. "I'm not ignoring anything. Kessler has an excellent reputation—he's a renowned specialist. People wait for years to get into his study. My father's incredibly lucky to be part of it." The words soured in her mouth even as she spoke them.

Scott opened one of the files he'd set on the table in front of her. "Before you decide just how lucky he is, maybe you should take a closer look."

She skimmed the first page of a redacted complaint. Much of the language had been blacked out, but the names of the parties and their attorneys remained. The attorney for the defense was Matthew Dawson, no surprise. "Okay. So, what exactly am I supposed to see?"

"For starters, ask yourself why Dawson would go out of his way to get your father into that clinic?"

"Maybe because he's trying to help me and happens to know someone who can. This isn't some diabolical conspiracy."

"And yet, they complained just because you asked a few questions. Kessler's your father's treating physician. You damned well ought to be able to ask questions without fear of reprisal."

Jo couldn't argue with that.

"Look at the autopsy reports." He waited as she flipped to them, "You'll see they all say the same thing. Each of these three patients had their brains removed."

Jo recoiled. Still, she could justify that too. "They were enrolled in a study for Alzheimer's—so of course Kessler would want to examine their brains postmortem."

"Yeah, except the examiner couldn't be certain they died before their brains were removed or because of it. At best, he had to be hovering over them, waiting for them to flatline."

"These are coroner reports, not private autopsies? So the police were involved?"

"Yes, Mr. Johnson called them when he saw his dearly beloved with stitches across her forehead. I keep envisioning something out of Frankenstein, but it must have been more subtle than that, because it wasn't until the funeral home commented on it that anyone noticed. Then one thing led to another and the coroner did autopsies."

"Why didn't it get any press then?"

"Like I said. It was hushed up. The coroner's findings were inconclusive, and Kessler produced a signed donor release, so the police dropped the case, but the families weren't buying it. Mr. Johnson said his wife had been doing so well he was planning to bring her home again, but when he went to tell her that, she was dead. Same thing with the other two, all within days of each other. It didn't smell right, so the families got together and sued, until they were scared off."

"Scared off, or paid off?"

"Both, it seems. I called all of them, but Johnson was the only one who would talk to me."

"Why should we believe this guy?"

"Just a gut feeling, to be honest." Scott leaned forward with his elbows on the table. "Look, I know the last thing you want to hear is that there may be a genuine problem, and you've never met this Mr. Johnson, so you've only got my take on this, but my instinct's telling me something's off enough to make me want to keep digging. So now you need to ask, what's your gut telling you? If you really trust those people with your father's life, fine then, just tell me to back off."

Jo wanted to tell him exactly that, to take the easy way out of this, but her gut, as he called it, said she'd be doing it for herself, not for her father. If something terrible happened to him, could she live with that? She already knew the answer, and it didn't make her happy.

"If you keep digging, what would that involve?" she asked.

Scott took a deep breath. "Well, I've pretty much exhausted my outside resources, so the only way left to figure out what's going on in that facility is from the inside."

Jo knew she was addled by fever. Maybe that was why he seemed to be making less and less sense. "You want to break in?"

"No." He laughed. "They've been advertising for help. I'll just apply for a job. That will give me the chance to check things out, assuming they hire me."

"Right." Her eyes drooped as she tried to make sense of that, wondering what could possibly qualify him for employment in a medical research facility, but she didn't have energy enough left to ask. It did however occur to her that she'd be footing the bill. "Sounds expensive."

"Not really. If they pay me a salary, all you'll have to cover is my overtime, if you get my drift."

She didn't but attributed her increasing slowness to the muddled state of her flu-filled head. "Yeah, okay... I guess." The bowl in front of her was empty. Had she really eaten it all? The licked spoon in her hand and full stomach testified she had. As she stared at the empty bowl, it seemed to elongate and in the polished depths of the spoon she saw a distorted image of herself.

"You still with me?" he asked.

His voice grounded her again, but she feared it was only temporary. "I better get back to bed," she said and squinted around at the room which seemed to be moving strangely. "I'm not sure what things are doing."

She was surprised to find Scott already behind her, helping her to her feet. Time seemed to be jumping erratically. She was going up the stairs, his strong arms supporting her. And then she was falling into bed as the quilt whipped over and tucked in around her. She felt a cool palm on her forehead.

"You're burning up."

His words sounded distant. She didn't even attempt to reply. Why bother, when it was all funerals and autopsies, doctors with bloody hands and angry old men screaming garbled accusations? She couldn't make any sense of it. She gave up trying and closed her eyes.

When she opened them again, the room was dark except for the soft glow of the night lamp on her bureau. Its small yellow bulb cast just enough light to see that she was not alone. A man sat in the chair in the corner. Her flash of alarm dissipated with recognition. Scott's chin lay low on his chest which rose and fell with the slow rhythm of sleep. His partially unbuttoned shirt and rolled-up sleeves revealed a bare chest and thick forearms, and his shoes were off. He must have been here a long time. She felt both amazed and touched that Scott had stayed to watch over her. She shivered, realizing her sheets and pajamas were cold and damp. Her fever must have broken. She slipped from the bed and retreated into her bathroom to change. When she emerged, Scott was on his feet, shoes on, shirt buttoned, in the middle of unrolling his sleeves.

She froze in place, stiff with discomfort. It had been a long time since she'd had a man in her bedroom, and her thoughts were straying to places she didn't want them to go.

"Feeling better?" he asked.

"Yes, thank you." She walked over and straightened the bedding. "Can't believe I passed out like that."

"No worries," he said as he buttoned his cuffs. "Got a little warm in here, but that's good for a fever."

She picked up one of the decorative pillows from her bed and held it in front of her chest like a shield. "Yes, well, I'm sorry you were uncomfortable. I appreciate your concern, but you needn't have bothered. I shouldn't keep you any longer."

He nodded with his mouth turned downward. "Yeah, sure." He turned back to the chair to retrieve his coat. "Do you know what you want to do about Kessler?"

"No, I need to think about it with a clearer head. Pretty sure my fever made things sound a lot worse than they are. There's probably nothing to worry about."

"Nothing, huh?" He shook his head. "Okaaay." He headed toward the door.

Still clutching the pillow, she followed him out, saying the things she knew she should. "Thanks for coming over and for the soup. I hope I didn't expose you to anything. I can't believe I missed another day of work." She heard her nervous laugh and knew her words were coming too fast. "I should be able to get into the office tomorrow, so at least I won't miss the entire week. Fridays usually end up shorter anyway, so if I have to leave early, should be no big deal."

Scott hesitated in the doorway. "Um. Actually... this is Friday."

"No, it's Thursday. You came here this afternoon, with soup. I remember it clearly."

"Yeah, but that was yesterday."

Jo stared at him. His expression remained steady and guileless, filled with concern. "Wait. Are you telling me I slept away an entire day and night?"

"Well, no. I mean you weren't asleep the whole time. But you know that, right?"

Jo scowled.

"Oh Geez." He looked genuinely dismayed. "You really don't remember? I mean about you and me... how we...?" He fell silent.

"How we what?"

"Well, it's just you were freezing and I wanted to help, so we..."—he shrugged—"you know." He rubbed a hand over his head. "Damn, I can't believe you don't remember."

Jo gaped in horror. "You don't mean that... that you and I... that we..."

His sad puppy dog look twisted into a lopsided grin. "Gotcha."

"You jerk!" She wanted to slap him, but merely dug her nails into the pillow.

"Sorry, sorry." He held up his hands in surrender. "Just trying to make a point. What I did there just now was a quick demonstration of how easy it is to confuse someone, especially when they're in a stressful situation. And I can't think of easier prey than an old man with dementia and his worried daughter."

Jo blinked at him. "That's no excuse."

"You're right, it isn't, and you have every right to be angry. I'm glad you are. Never let anyone gaslight you like that. Not me, not Kessler and not Dawson."

Anger seethed inside her. "I think you'd better leave."

"On my way." He trotted down the stairs and opened the front door, but just before exiting he looked back up at her. "Don't be a victim, Josephine. You're better than that," he said, then closed the door behind him.

Jo flung the pillow, but it only bounced harmlessly off the door. "Damn you."

She dropped onto the top stair and sat with her head in her hands. She wanted to deny Scott's accusations, but they stung with truth. Fear was guiding her, fear that she was over-reacting, fear that she might lose her job. It would be insanity to defy Dawson, to secretly investigate his most valuable client. If he found out, he'd fire her for cause. Not a firm in town would touch her after that.

She tried to think of a way around taking that risk. Maybe she didn't need to deceive Dawson to get to the truth. If Kessler was doing something unethical, Dawson should be grateful to have someone bring it to his attention. But seeing how he'd reacted when she merely tried to talk to Kessler, she doubted he'd listen. No, Scott was right. To find out if there was anything to this, she'd have to investigate on her own. Or rather, she'd have to let Scott Benson investigate, someone she'd initially written off as a sarcastic jerk and so far, her opinion of him hadn't changed. She recognized his investigative talent, but how dare he humiliate her like that? And who was he to lecture her? She knew her rights. She wasn't anyone's victim.

She stared at her balled fists, anger turned inwards, and in that moment, knew that she truly was a victim, a victim of her own fear and self-doubt—the result of growing up intimidated by her own father and longing for his approval. And now, in his absence, she'd fallen into the same pattern with the next highest authority figures in her life, Dawson and Dr. Kessler, letting them impress and intimidate her with their lofty reputations. In believing them superior to herself, she had sought out their approval, needed it even. A false premise. What wasn't false, however, was the fact they wielded power over her and standing up to them would have consequences.

The prospect of losing her job sent a stab of dread through her. To safeguard her career all she needed to do was follow orders, question nothing, and be the good little girl she'd been taught to be—all at the mere cost of her self-respect, and possibly what remained of her father's life. She felt a surge of self-loathing that she ever even considered it. She pulled out her cell phone and texted Scott Benson.

[Keep digging.]

CHAPTER TWELVE

Undercover

Waiting in the Institute's lobby, Scott rocked on his toes and heels while the dark eyes of the receptionist kept glancing at him. Clearly his refusal to take a seat disturbed her, but he had too much nervous energy to plant himself in a chair. He smiled and gave her a wink to ingratiate himself, knowing receptionists could be a good source of information. She smiled back and shook her head as she looked away. *Yeah, she's interested. And cute,* he decided, but he had no intention of following up. This was business, and he already had his sights set on someone else.

While he waited, he took in his surroundings. The black-framed artwork and primary-colored furniture reminded him of an old 70s club scene, especially with the piped-in instrumental version of Donna Summers' *Last Dance* currently playing in the background. The air smelled of vanilla with a touch of antiseptic

"Mr. Benson?" A tall sturdy blonde in a dark business suit approached him. "I'm Mrs. Sutton, Head of Administration. Welcome."

Mid to late forties, he concluded, and attractive enough, despite thick ankles and sand-colored hair upswept so tightly that it seemed to lift her face with it. Her voice and handshake matched the exterior, self-confident and stiff.

She handed him a manila envelope. "Our employee guidelines, and the forms you need to fill out and return to me by the end of the day. Your immediate supervisor can answer any questions. Please follow me." She guided him toward the elevators. "We've been short-handed, so I'm sure they'll want to put you to work right away. I hope you're ready for some long hours. Dr. Kessler is really pushing for results."

"Huh. I didn't think results were something you could push."

She scowled at him. "That's not what I meant."

He thought she objected a bit too forcefully. "Sorry. Guess I misunderstood."

"You certainly did." She picked up speed, her heels clicking like a wound clock on the tile. "That wasn't at all what I meant."

Maybe not, he thought, *but it sure got a rise out of you.* To test her more, he gestured back at the bold furniture and artwork. "Unusual look for a research facility. All it needs is a disco ball."

She gave him a tight smile. "Most of our residents were in their prime during the seventies and eighties, and bright colors promote mental stimulation."

"I get it. A little nostalgia to make them feel at home, and a kaleidoscope to get their brains fired up. Do they get to take acid trips, too?"

The sour expression on her face proved he was making a bad impression, as intended. Pushing people's buttons, getting under their skins, were tools of the trade. Nothing like irritation revealed a person's character and motivations faster. He was learning just how far he could push her, not very. He figured she wouldn't fire him without cause, but now that he'd annoyed her, she'd be looking for one. Inside the elevator, she took an extra moment to select a floor, but her body blocked the control panel so he couldn't see why.

"You'll be working in the animal labs," she said, "below ground level."

"So much for an ocean view."

As the elevator descended, he thought how funny it was, the way things circle back... not funny ha ha, but funny weird. He'd spent summers working in the university labs where his father taught, and he told the interviewer here he wanted to get back to that. Nothing could be further from the truth, but here he was, about to don a lab coat again. His mouth twisted as unpleasant memories tried to crawl up from the grave where he'd buried them.

"When's payday?" he asked, more to distract himself than to annoy her, but it did both.

"Every other Friday." She wore a frown, which only encouraged him to irritate her further.

"So, how long have you worked here?"

"Nearly fifteen years," she replied, pride evident in her voice and carriage.

"Wow. You must be making a pretty penny by now."

She sighed and looked away. When the elevator stopped, she marched ahead of him out the door, down the hall and through a pair of double doors into a windowless room filled with tables and computer stations. There she introduced him to Dennis Ackerman, a forty-something man shaped like an S-curve with black-rimmed glasses and thinning hair. As they shook hands, Scott noted the man's pasty complexion and flaccid grip. He doubted Dennis had seen the sun in months.

"He's all yours," Mrs. Sutton said, then exited the room without so much as a good luck.

As the sharp clicks of her heels faded, Scott stage whispered to Dennis, "Think she likes me."

"Really?" Dennis squinted and pushed his glasses higher on his nose. "What makes you say that?"

Scott's grin faltered. He didn't run across this type often but recognized the symptoms. The man had absolutely no sense of humor. "I was kidding."

"Oh. We tend to take things pretty seriously around here."

"I'm getting that impression." Scott let his attention roam the room, taking in steel desks and computer equipment. White melamine boards scribbled with lists and formulas covered three of the walls. The fourth held charts and colored cellular diagrams. "Does working in a place without any windows ever get to you?"

"Not at all. Windows create unwanted glare on monitors. And we have full control of lighting in the animal labs this way. If it bothers you, you can take your breaks in the employee lounge on the first floor. Your workstation's over there." Dennis pointed to a desk devoid of personal items. "Decorate it however you like, within reason, of course."

"Great." Scott flipped the envelope Sutton had given him sideways, so that it flew onto the naked desktop, spun and came to rest in the center. Dennis stared at the envelope as if he had never witnessed such a stunt before. "I assume the labs are through there?" Scott pointed at another pair of double doors opposite of the ones he'd come through.

Dennis's attention switched back to him. "Yes, but you'll need to wait here until someone comes to get you for training. Also, be sure to wear your nametag. It should be in your envelope along with your employee forms. You can get started on filling them out while you're waiting." Dennis gave him a curt nod and turned back to his screen.

So much for small talk. Scott followed Dennis's suggestion and sat at his assigned desk to open his envelope. He found a keycard along with his nametag and a stack of forms. He started filling in the blanks... all bogus information. He didn't want them contacting anyone he knew.

Minutes later, a young man with dark stand-up hair and a ring in his left eyebrow popped through the lab doors. Scott made out the name on the man's tag, Jacob Petrovich.

"Meet your new tech," Dennis said and pointed at Scott.

"About time they hired someone," Jacob said, then turned to Scott. "Welcome to the dungeon. Hope you work out better than the last guy."

"That sounds ominous."

"Guess we'll find out. Grab a coat." He waited for Scott to slip on a lab coat and pin his nametag on, then led him through the doors and down a long hallway of meshed windows.

"So what's your background?" Jacob asked.

"Summers at a university lab."

Jacob nodded. "Hope you're not squeamish about needles."

"No, not really," Scott lied.

"Good. The last tech we had kept fainting. Got to be a running joke—go pick Andy off the floor."

Scott tamped down a squirming discomfort. Jacob took him into a large room lined with cages, all of them filled with long-tailed rodents climbing under and over each other, running inside wheels, or snoozing in blissful oblivion. Some planted tiny clawed feet against the glass as Scott walked by, noses wriggling, watching him with their bulging little eyes.

"Do they bite?"

"They're mice," Jacob said, with a shrug, as if that explained everything. "And be careful with them. They're expensive."

"Since when are mice expensive?"

"When they're PDAPPs—transgenic mouse models of Alzheimer's disease. Like their human counterparts, they develop amyloid plaques in the brain and experience memory loss as they age." He pointed at the cages. "1 through 5 are the control group. They're limited to food, water, and vitamins. Group 2, cages 6 through 15, get tacrine added to their diet; and the group 3, cages 16 through 20, get a generic version of donepezil." When he got to the last row, he rubbed his hands together and grinned. "Now this is where things get interesting—Group 4, cages 21 through 25. These guys get the house special, injections of genetically altered neural stem cells."

"Fetal?"

Jacob stiffened. "You got a problem with that?"

Scott raised empty palms. "No, but I just thought the government stopped funding it. Am I wrong?"

"No." Jacob took a breath. "They have, but we're privately funded. Discarding fetal tissue is the real tragedy, but some people just can't see the logic in that."

Scott hesitated, not sure why Jacob was so riled up. "I didn't see anyone picketing outside."

Jacob looked confused for a moment. Then he laughed and shook his head. "No, my problem is a lot closer to home. Actually, it's *in* my home. My mother thinks God speaks through the Pope's mouth. Ever since he took a stand against embryonic stem cell research, she's been lighting candles for my soul."

"Huh. I never would have guessed someone named Petrovich would have Catholic roots."

"Only half. My father's Jewish. I grew up going to Synagogue on Saturdays and Mass on Sundays, with Hebrew school and Catechism sandwiched in-between. If that doesn't screw you up, nothing will. Now I'm a born-again atheist."

"Sounds like an oxymoron."

"Exactly. Which means it confuses people enough to shut them up."

Scott laughed. He was starting to like this guy. "So I should confuse people enough so they don't worry about what I do."

"Yeah, but only on your own time. In here, you'll be cleaning cages."

"And for this I went to college?"

"Yep, you've finally made it—Head Rodent Poop Engineer. Congratulations. I'll get you your official mouse ears later. Bad news, though. In between cleaning, you'll have to do a bit of science."

"Okay, so where do I start?"

"With our newest arrivals." Jacob pointed to a cage behind him. "We're starting another batch. Allow me to demonstrate." He retrieved a tray loaded with syringes. "These come prepped for us by the boys and girls in the sterile labs upstairs."

Jacob lifted the cage's lid, plucked a mouse up by the tail, and flipped it over to expose a number on its belly. "Make sure you write down the ID. You don't want to accidentally inject the same one twice." Jacob checked off the number on a list next to the cage and wrote the date and time. "Hand me that tape over there."

Scott saw a roll of blue painter's tape and tossed it to him.

He watched as Jacob taped the mouse onto the steel countertop, picked up a syringe and aimed it at the back of the mouse's neck. "See where it's shaved? X marks the spot."

Scott peered closer and sure enough, there was a small black 'x' near the naked base of the mouse's skull.

"Insert the needle in the center of the 'x' up to the red line, but no further," Jacob said.

Scott's stomach flipped as he watched the needle slide in. He remembered again why he'd stopped working in his father's lab.

Jacob pressed the plunger down smoothly until the syringe emptied. He freed the injected mouse and dropped it into an empty cage, then looked at Scott. "Your turn."

"Right." Scott set his expression into stone and faced the cage. He was going to have to stick his hand in there. Any squeamish hesitation might get him fired. He lifted the lid and tried to zero in on a tail. They looked like worms, worms that wouldn't hold still. "Damn," he muttered under his breath.

"Problem?" Jacob asked.

"Nope. No problem," Scott made a grab for something long and whip-like. To his own amazement, when he pulled back, a mouse hung from his fingers. "Got it."

"Great. Now note its number and tape it down."

Scott followed Jacob's directions. Before he knew it, he was aiming a needle at the tiny 'x' on the back of the mouse's neck. He tried hard not to grimace as he felt the resistance of skin and flesh.

"Steady. Just up to the red line on the needle, good, now inject." Jacob watched closely as Scott emptied the syringe. "Little shaky there, but you'll get the hang of it. Do another one."

Scott dropped the mouse in the cage with the other injected mouse, then snatched up his next victim. Jacob watched closely as he checked off the mouse's number and taped it down.

"This is the fourth group we've started this week," Jacob said.

"Oh yeah? How'd the others do?" He forced a nonchalant tone as he aimed the needle.

"Mixed," Jacob said, nodding in approval as Scott delivered the syringe's payload. "Better. Cage 23 is still in good shape. We'll see how long that lasts." He gestured at the cages as he spoke. "In number 25, about half have started going around in circles and falling over. Cage 21 fared the worst. Within twenty-four hours, they were all on their backs, feet twitching. Doubt the folks in the sterile labs will try that formula again."

Scott looked at the cages Jacob indicated. He saw mice chasing their own tails or tipping sideways like drunks. He didn't see any on their backs with their legs in the air, but only because the cage marked 21 was empty. "What do you do with them when they go belly up?"

"We send them to the labs upstairs to be made into tissue samples for analysis. They're looking for changes in plaque formations, tangles and cell structure, and any evidence of side effects."

"So what's killing them?"

"Jury's still out. Could be a lot of things. Tissue rejection's likely. Sometimes the body's immune system is its own worst enemy."

"I thought the brain was an immune-privileged organ."

"Yeah, but you can't keep cells from traveling. Xeno-transplants—cells from a genetically different source—usually need some form of immunosuppression. I'm guessing the ones doing better had that added to their injections."

"Why don't they do it for all of them then?"

"Because it creates other problems. Human transplant recipients have to take medication for the rest of their lives which can have lots of nasty little side effects."

"Such as?"

"Loss of appetite, vomiting, diarrhea, hair sprouting out of your ears; you know, fun stuff like that. Not to mention having to undergo regular blood tests to make sure your liver and kidneys aren't failing. When your immune system's knocked out, any infectious disease that comes along could kill you."

"So it's a case of curing one disease only to die of another.

"Yeah, sometimes it's not much of a trade-off. That's why Kessler is keeping us all hopping down here. He wants the holy grail. A universal treatment that's easily distributable, and close to painless."

Scott grimaced as he emptied another syringe and the trapped mouse squeaked in protest. "They don't seem to think it's so painless."

"Yeah, poor little mousie." Jacob petted its furry little head with a finger. "But it's all for a good cause."

Scott freed the mouse and deposited it in the cage with the others. "So I take it you think Kessler's on the right track."

"Yeah, I do. Come take a look over here." Jacob led him to two small cages, each housing a single mouse. "Meet Fred and Wilma." One of them was running like mad in a wheel. The other lay curled up on its side, half-buried in sawdust, snoozing peacefully.

"Something unusual about them?"

"Very. They're old, really old, about equivalent to a human centenarian. Before we treated them, they had Alzheimer's-like symptoms. Now they act like pups. No immune suppressants, no side-effects, no deterioration. Problem is, we haven't been able to duplicate the results consistently. We often observe short-term improvement, but then most of them either revert to their prior state of dementia or die from complications. All except for a select few so far, like Fred and Wilma here."

"I'm guessing they must carry some genetic trait the others don't."

"Yeah, but what? Kessler hasn't been able to pinpoint it... yet."

"Sounds like you work pretty closely with him."

"Nah, not really. I'm just a lowly lab tech." Jacob wore a frown that expressed genuine displeasure. "He used to come down here to check on Fred and Wilma pretty regularly, and we'd talk, but I haven't seen him in a while. He's locked in his private lab pretty much full time now and anybody who wants to see him has to get past Mrs. Sutton."

"That woman who's in charge of personnel?"

"She's a lot more than that, supervises everything here but the lab work itself. I take it you met her?"

"She introduced me to Dennis."

"Figures. She keeps close tabs."

"Seemed a little stiff."

"Stiff? Ha. That's being generous. People around here call her 'the frigid iron maiden.' Ice cold metal on the outside but on the inside..."—Jacob patted his heart—"filled with spikes. Actually, that's one of the nicer things she's called. Not to her face, of course."

"So you don't like her?"

"I never said that. Tell anyone I did, I'll call you a liar." Jacob waggled his finger and adopted a fairly accurate Billy Crystal impression of an elderly Jew. "But between you and me, should she drop dead, I wouldn't grieve."

Scott laughed in appreciation.

"Just don't irritate her," Jacob finished in his own voice.

"Pretty sure I already have."

"Too bad. Should have talked to me first. I know how to keep her buttered side up."

"Oh?" Scott's left eyebrow shot up.

"Ugh, no. Don't give me nightmares." Jacob twisted his face in disgust. "No, the way to the ice queen's heart is to praise Kessler. Just tell her what a genius he is, and how much you admire his greatness, the more effusive the better. Then she'll think you're a fine addition to her little kingdom."

"I'll keep that in mind."

"Hope so. I don't want to have to train another replacement."

"She wields that much power?"

"You bet. But enough office gossip, we have work to do." Jacob pointed to the tray filled with syringes. "When you're done there, I'll show you how to log in and make your entries."

An hour and dozens of newly injected mice later, Scott sat before a terminal back in the data entry room with Jacob peering over his shoulder. Scott tapped a key to clear the screensaver and a colorful diagram of research and administrative departments appeared.

"We're Lab LL4," Jacob instructed.

Scott clicked and a password protected window popped up. Jacob reached around and slowly tapped keys with his forefinger.

Scott read each one aloud, "4, P, L, A, Y, 4, M, E. Really?" He laughed.

"Hey, it's easy to remember seeing as my girlfriend keeps reminding me. You'll set up your own file with your own password, but right now we're working my shift."

"And you don't care if I know your password?"

"Nope. Use it all you like, then I'll get all the credit. I can use the extra income."

"So our pay is linked to our entries?"

"Yep. One of the ice queen's internal security systems. Entries have to match up with your scheduled shift. If you need to work extra hours, be sure you clear it with security, or the system won't let you in," Jacob said.

"So I wouldn't even be able to log on?"

"You wouldn't even be able to get into the lab here. Your card only allows access to your own floor and only during your scheduled hours."

"We need a card?"

"Should be in your envelope. Don't worry, you'll soon get the hang of this place. Dennis should have explained already, but guess he forgot. He's a decent scientist, but to be honest, kind of a doofus. If you've got questions, you're better off asking me."

"Why all the security?"

"Couple reasons. The AD residents are at high risk of going AWOL. Plus, and maybe even more important, what we do here is cutting-edge stuff. We don't want spies in here, or wackos. Science scares some people. There are plenty out there who think like my mother. Fortunately, she doesn't know how to use a shotgun."

Scott smiled at Jacob's humor, but at the same time realized his plan to infiltrate this facility wasn't going to be as easy as he'd hoped. He had expected a job on the inside to give him free run of the place, not limit him to pre-approved hours on a pre-approved floor. He eyed Jacob's eyebrow ring and spiked hair, thinking he must chafe at such restrictions.

"So, you never go anywhere in this building besides the lobby and this lab dungeon?"

"Well... I wouldn't say never." A smile inched up one side of Jacob's mouth.

The smirk renewed Scott's hope. Clearly, Jacob knew a way around the system.

CHAPTER THIRTEEN

Confrontation

W earing a mask so as not to infect anyone else, Jo returned to work, not fully recovered, but determined not to get any further behind. The winter bug that knocked her down had continued to claim new victims, one of whom was Beverly, which meant Jo had the added handicap of working with a temp to whom she had to explain everything at least twice. Meanwhile, she worried about her father. She hadn't seen him since falling ill since the Kessler Institute barred visitation by anyone who displayed viral symptoms, a reasonable precaution. Until the last of her sniffles and a lingering cough vanished, she was restricted to checking on him by phone.

The last thing she wanted to do was pass whatever made her sick on to her father, but trying to monitor his care over the phone was proving an exercise in frustration. Half the time, the floor nurse said he was asleep, in therapy, or otherwise unavailable. Using the bathroom, she guessed. Whenever she did reach him, he was so agitated and confused, she could make little sense of what he was trying to tell her. All he seemed to do was cry and beg to come home. The nurses said he was okay or "doing as well as can be expected." Their reassurances sounded hollow.

She'd sent that text to Scott Benson giving him the go-ahead to 'keep digging', but never heard back from him. She wondered if she ever would. After their awkward last encounter maybe it was just as well. Maybe she should hire someone else, or simply accept that this is how things were and there wasn't anything to be done about it.

Getting her father enrolled in Kessler's study was supposed to have been a huge relief. Instead, it had turned into a nightmare of uncertainty. The only way she could see out of this quagmire was to move her father out of there, something she'd been hoping to avoid. It would add to his confusion and most certainly offend Dawson. But at least then she could wash her hands of the place. Whatever was going on in that place wouldn't be her problem any longer. On the list of lousy choices, moving her father out seemed the best of the lot.

Decision made, she shoved her legal files aside and started calling every agency, care facility and Alzheimer's support group within a fifty-mile radius. The most highly recommended facilities exceeded her budget, as did even most of the less desirable ones, but she vowed she would find some way to swing it. Unfortunately, all of them had waiting lists so the best she could do was add her father's name and hope something would open up soon, but that could take weeks or months even, and she didn't have the luxury of waiting. Her only interim solution was to bring him home. The local chapter of the Alzheimer's Association recommended several in-home caregiver services, and after checking their references and interviewing families over the phone, she settled on one with consistently positive reviews. They assured her they could provide care twenty-four seven. With their help she arranged for delivery of a hospital bed and all the necessary equipment.

The downstairs guest room transformed over the next few days into a hospital-like setting. By the time it was done, she let go of the last of her wishful thinking—that a miracle cure might happen. A fantasy, for now at least. Maybe someday. As things were, the best she could do was to make sure her father suffered as little as possible as he approached the end of his life.

She called the Kessler Institute. "I'd like to meet with Suzanne Sutton as soon as possible."

The receptionist put her on hold, then came back. "The soonest she can see you today would be at 5 pm. Does that work for you?"

"Yes, thank you. I'll see her then."

During the tour, Kessler's Administrative Director had impressed her as a business-like professional, despite her glowing descriptions of Dr. Kessler and the facility. But that was to be expected. It was her job to put a positive light on it all. Jo would explain to her that she had made other arrangements for her father's care and Mrs. Sutton would handle the paperwork for his release. Jo would bring him home tonight, and that would be the end of this mess. Oh wait, she'd forgotten to call off Scott Benson, assuming he'd ever followed up. She dialed his number and got his abrupt voice mail message about not wasting time, so she kept it short.

"This is Josephine Rinaldi. I don't know if you've kept digging as I requested, but if you have, you can stop now. I've come up with an alternate solution. Send me an invoice for time spent. Thank you." She hung up, satisfied both with the message and her decision. It was time to leave for her appointment with Suzanne Sutton.

Jo arrived at the Kessler Institute shortly before five pm. The sun hovered low over the ocean turning the building into a dark silhouette and flooding the lobby with orange light. The same receptionist she'd first met, the one with the big smile and long braids, saw her coming and picked up the phone. "I'll let Mrs. Sutton know you've arrived."

High heels clicking down the hall soon announced Mrs. Sutton's approach and Jo followed her into her office.

"Please have a seat." Mrs. Sutton smiled warmly and walked around her maple desk to sit in her own chair. "So how can I help you today?"

"I've reconsidered my father's situation and have decided to bring him home."

"Home?"

"Yes, I have everything arranged, and would like him discharged tonight."

She stared at Jo, the smile still frozen on her lips. "Discharged?"

Jo sighed, annoyed by Mrs. Sutton echoing her like a parrot. "Yes, as I said, I have everything ready."

"If I may ask. Why would you remove him from the one program that offers him any hope?"

Jo frowned in discomfort. "Well, to be honest, I'm not convinced there is any. He's only gotten worse since he's been here and he's clearly unhappy."

Mrs. Sutton continued to smile. "People in his condition frequently complain about their caretakers. I assure you that won't change. Except that it would be about you, instead."

"This seems more extreme than that. He's frightened and keeps begging to come home."

"My dear, what you're describing is a symptom of the disease. Dementia can cause strange ideas that have little or no connection to reality."

Jo grimaced, annoyed be lectured. "Yes, I understand that, but it doesn't change the fact that he's miserable staying here. If I can make him happier by caring for him at home, then that's what I need to do."

Sutton pyramided her fingertips. "That's just guilt talking, not a sound basis for decision making. I would ask you to take a step back and reconsider. We all want what's in your father's best interest."

"You needn't worry. He'll have caregivers round the clock."

"Caregivers." Suzanne frowned and shook her head slowly. "Here, your father is surrounded by skilled nurses and doctors who specialize in neurological disease. Why in the world would you trade that for a lowly caregiver?"

For a moment, Jo had no answer. Mrs. Sutton made her decision sound vapid and thoughtless, as if she were acting on a whim. But she wasn't. She had good reason to be worried, as evidenced by her father's rapid physical and mental decline, plus the argument she had overheard, and what Scott Benson had told her. She had good reason to fear something very wrong was going on in this place, and she didn't want her father to stay here even one more day. She felt in her bones that he would be better off somewhere else, anywhere else, even if it meant being stuck at home with her and a *lowly* caregiver, which was merely a temporary solution anyway, only until an opening came up at a facility she trusted far more than this one, not that she needed to explain any of that to this woman. She took another breath, determined to remain polite.

"I appreciate your concern, but my father's care is my responsibility, and my decision is made. Please make whatever arrangements necessary to have him released."

"I'm sorry to hear that." She picked up her phone. "Letisha, would you please bring me the admittance file for Thomas Rinaldi?"

They waited for the file without speaking. The receptionist walked in, handed over a file and left. Mrs. Sutton
thumbed through the contents, bent back a page then
flipped it around for Jo to see. "This is the agreement you
signed upon admittance. Please read paragraph six. Aloud,
if you please."

"I don't see why that's necessary."

"Indulge me. Please."

Jo scowled but took the file in her hands and read, "The
undersigned consents to any and all medical treatments said
attending physician considers necessary or advisable, and
further agrees that all results and findings stemming from
said treatments shall be the sole property of said Institute."
She paused, not understanding the point Mrs. Sutton was
trying to make. "Okay, so?"

"Keep reading."

Jo frowned but returned her attention to the document.
The next line made her eyes widen. "What? No, this isn't
right. I would never have intentionally signed this."

"And yet that is your signature, is it not?"

"I don't care if it is. A physician can't have power of attorney over a patient. It's a complete conflict of interest.
This will never hold up in court."

"Oh dear. Are you threatening us with a lawsuit?"

"Not what I had in mind, but if that's what it takes."

"I see. Then it seems I'd better contact our attorney." She
picked up the phone again. "Letisha, please get Matthew
Dawson on the line for me."

Jo's mouth went dry. "Wait."

Suzanne regarded her with half a smile. "Yes?"

"Would you just... please, just wait."

"Hold that call," Suzanne said, then replaced the receiver.
"Why don't I just step outside and give you a moment to
think."

Jo nodded, feeling ill.

Sutton stood and walked out of the office.

Stunned, Jo remained seated, staring blankly ahead while
her mind raced. *She's blackmailing me. But why? I thought
they had a long list of people waiting to get in here. Why is she*

so determined to hang onto my father? What the hell is going on?

Jo couldn't fathom Mrs. Sutton's motivation, but her threat was clear enough. Jo looked at the form releasing power of attorney for her father. She didn't remember seeing it before, let alone signing it. She squinted at the scrawled signature. *Is that even mine?* She pulled out her cell phone and took a picture. Even if she had signed it, she hadn't meant to. She was convinced it would be thrown out by a judge, but there was no telling how long that might take—anywhere from twenty-four hours for an emergency injunction to years if she had to go through a full-blown lawsuit. Either way, it would most certainly cost her her job, and she'd be going up against Dawson as opposing counsel with the whole law firm backing him up. They could afford to stretch legal proceedings out for years. She couldn't. By then, she'd be bankrupt and whatever Kessler had in mind for her father would be a foregone conclusion.

The smart choice was to walk away. Her father's life was nearing the end no matter what she did, while hers stretched ahead with a career just getting off the ground. And what if Sutton was right, that this really was the only hope for him, and her idea of taking him home was just a guilty conscience getting the better of her? She thought of her father's anguished pleas. Of course, she felt guilty. Who wouldn't? But, no, it was more than that. This was about what Scott had told her added to her own suspicions, which only seemed further confirmed by this Administrator's aggressive reaction to a perfectly reasonable request.

Here she'd thought she'd figured a way out of a no-win situation but had only dug herself in deeper. She chewed her lower lip and pulled her fingers in consternation, weighing her options, or rather lack of them. She felt like a cornered animal.

Through the office's one-way view into the lobby, she could see Mrs. Sutton talking to Letisha at the receptionist desk. Sutton said something and Letisha shook her head and smiled. No doubt Jo was the subject of conversation. Seeing their smug expressions, Jo's resentment built with each smirk and sideways glance in her direction. A cold anger slowly filled her, remembering the last time she'd felt like this, intimidated by a bully. It was during divorce negotiations with her ex's attorney who cowered her into making one concession after another. If she'd fought harder then, she might not be saddled now with student loans. Instead, she'd caved...all for the sake of peace.

Not this time.

She shoved herself up from the chair and marched out the door. Mrs. Sutton turned to her.

"I've made my decision. I'm taking my father home. Tonight."

Mrs. Sutton sighed. "Please be reasonable, Ms. Rinaldi."

"You're the one who's not being reasonable, and you know it. You can sign his release papers or not. Your choice. Either way I am going up to my father's room now to pack his things and then we're leaving." Jo turned away and walked to the elevator.

When the doors opened, Jo stepped inside and punched the button for the third floor. It didn't light. She peered out the door and saw Sutton and the receptionist looking back at her.

"I need you to unlock this elevator," Jo told them. She knew the receptionist had a button she could push from her desk, and Sutton had a keycard, but neither of them made a move. "Either unlock it or give me a card."

"I'm sorry, but that's not going to happen," Mrs. Sutton replied. Her face and voice matched in coldness.

Jo strode toward her. "I want that card."

Mrs. Sutton raised her arm into the air and called out, "Security!"

A large bulky man in black with a silver badge on his chest and a pistol at his hip popped to attention from behind a half-circle of video monitors. Jo stopped short.

"Please remove this woman from the building," Mrs. Sutton instructed him.

The guard's eyes focused on Jo. He moved toward her, all height and muscle. The closer he got, the bigger he looked. Jo couldn't believe this was happening. He stopped inches before her and gestured toward the front entrance. "I've been asked to escort you out, Ma'am. I hope you intend to cooperate."

"I'm not leaving here without my father." She kept her voice firm as she looked up at the man's face. "If you interfere, I will call the police."

The guard looked back at her, unimpressed. "This is private property, Ma'am. If you won't leave of your own accord, I'll be forced to remove you."

"You don't understand. My father wants to go home. You can't keep a patient here against his will."

"Please, Ma'am." His hand reached out and enclosed her upper arm. It didn't hurt, but she knew it could quickly escalate to pain. "You need to leave."

Jo's body started trembling, a combination of fear and outrage. "Take your hand off me." Rage outweighed fear and she tried to pull free. The grip tightened. "Ow! You're hurting me!"

"I'm sorry, Ma'am, but you've left me no choice." He pushed her toward the entrance, shoved her outside and closed the door in her face.

Jo stood on the other side of the glass, gaping in disbelief. Mrs. Sutton and the security guard stared back wearing determined expressions. Jo had no doubt if she tried to reenter, they would repeat their previous performance, probably with even less gentleness.

She backed away, then found herself running to her car. Before she reached it, the tears had come.

CHAPTER FOURTEEN

Consequences

W*ho to call? Who can help? Is this a civil matter, a criminal one?* Jo sat in her car and scanned the contacts on her phone, trying to think, looking at the list of friends, relatives, attorneys, and government offices, while her thoughts raced to make sense of what had just happened. *Maybe this is all just a misunderstanding. Maybe Sutton thinks I'm a kook. But that guard actually put his hands on me. It was outrageous. It was criminal. I'm calling the police,* she decided, but it wasn't exactly a 911, so she looked up the non-emergency number and thought about what to say. *I'll explain they're holding my father against his will and the guard physically removed me. They'll have questions, I'll have to answer. Yes, he did willingly enroll, and yes, I did sign the admission papers, and no, I don't have any evidence of injury, and yes, I'm aware it's private property and they have the right to deny entry, but... but what? The police will conclude this is a civil matter and they have no jurisdiction.* It rang once and she clicked off before anyone answered.

Battling this out in court would take time. Meanwhile, her father would be subject to their whims. Jo envisioned pleading her case, trying to convince a skeptical judge that her father was better off at home with her than under the care of the famous Dr. Kessler. The image dissolved into a judge ruling against her, putting her right back where she'd started. No, it would be worse. She will have openly declared war. The memory of Suzanne Sutton's stony face rose in Jo's mind and it didn't seem farfetched that she might take it out on her father. There had to be some way to avoid a protracted struggle. She needed to extricate her father quickly and safely, but how? Who could influence these people? Who could fix this fast?

Only one person came to mind, the very one she most dreaded asking, but the only one who had any chance of straightening this out. Dawson, of course—her boss and legal counsel to Kessler. It was Dawson who had gotten her father in there, and now it seemed he was the only one who could get him out. There was no other option. She would have to go see him and plead her case.

Thankfully, Dawson was still in the office when she called and he agreed to meet with her before leaving for the night. By the time she got there, the sky's red and purple streaks were darkening and the sun had sunk well below the horizon. Jo knocked on the open door of Dawson's corner office on the 23rd floor. He was on the phone but waved her inside. Lit-up skyscrapers framed him through the windows. The tall downtown buildings looked like dark jutting mirrors dotted with light.

As she waited for him to finish his call, she compared his office to Dr. Kessler's, both of them located in windowed corners offering stunning views. Kessler's office had a light airy feel, breezy as the ocean it overlooked, yet cutting-edge modern with its clean technology openly displayed. Kessler's office was exactly what one would expect of a modern-day medical researcher at the top of his field. Exactly. In contrast, Dawson's office hid its modernity in dark wood, hunter-green carpet and printed fabrics. The room felt rooted in tradition and old-world values in a way that perfectly suited its occupant. It was exactly what one expected for a successful lawyer. Exactly.

While the two offices, each set into corners with sweeping vistas, starkly contrasted each other, at their core they were the same, projecting an image that spoke of money and power.

Dawson replaced the receiver and smiled at her.

"I'm glad you're here," he said. "I've been wanting to talk to you."

"You have?" Jo asked, hoping for something positive.

"Yes, I was thinking about our near fiasco in that personal injury matter last month. What was the name?"

"Slader."

"Right. That incident revealed a disturbing short-coming in our client screening. I'd like to put you in charge of revising our protocol for conducting background checks so nothing like that ever gets past us again."

"I'd be happy to," Jo said, truly pleased. This was just the lead-in she needed. "In fact, this fits in exactly with what I wanted to talk to you about."

"Oh?" Dawson's amiable smile remained.

"I'm afraid it's about Dr. Kessler." Jo paused for Dawson's reaction, but he seemed frozen, so she continued on. "I know what an important client he is to you, which is why I wanted to talk to you directly. I'm concerned about some of the language in his admittance documents and have reason to believe it may be putting him at risk." Jo then described as simply and unemotionally as possible the events of the afternoon, how she had requested to remove her father from the Institute, been shown a power of attorney form she didn't recall signing, then was physically evicted from the premises. Dawson listened without interruption. "... so that's why I came to you," she ended.

"I see. Well, I'm glad you did," he said. "We certainly want to make sure our clients understand the law and follow it. But before we go into the specifics of all that, I'm a bit confused as to why you've decided to have your father discharged, seeing as how much trouble we went to getting him admitted in the first place. What's prompted this sudden change of heart? Did something untoward occur you haven't mentioned?

"Well, he's gotten worse, a lot worse, since he's been there, and I'm not sure what they're giving him. They're very secretive about it."

"I'm not sure secretive is a fair term considering he enrolled in a blind study. Isn't that the nature of the beast?"

"Yes, you're right, it is, but..." Jo hesitated, fearing to reveal the extent of her suspicions lest she reveal her unauthorized investigation, "...but why I wanted to remove him isn't the point. The point is that it's not their decision to make. That's what concerns me. What's truly worrisome is the existence of a clause in their admission forms giving them power of attorney over their enrollees. I admit I'm no expert on medical law, but it has to be a glaring conflict of interest. Even if it isn't, which I doubt, they can't just slip in a clause like that without full disclosure. Frankly, I'm not even sure if that's my signature. If they pull this on someone else, they might call the authorities. I figured you'd want to intervene before they get themselves into real trouble."

Dawson peered at her over a pyramid of his fingers, the same way Suzanne Sutton had earlier. "Do you have a copy of that document?"

"Yes, I took a photo and printed it out." She handed him a page showing the offending clause in highlighted yellow.

He read for a moment. "Hmmm.... does seem a bit irregular." He looked up again and gave her a reassuring smile. "Let me contact Dr. Kessler and see what can be done."

"Thank you." Jo felt as if a great weight lifted off her. Tears of gratitude stung her eyes. Embarrassed, she wiped them away. "I'm sorry. I haven't been getting much sleep worrying about my dad. And then getting evicted like that. I really appreciate your help."

"Of course. And after you've been ill recently, too. All this stress must be taking its toll. Why don't you go home, get some rest...take the morning off, and let me handle this." Dawson stood and guided her from his office. "By the time you come in tomorrow afternoon, I should have things resolved."

Jo thanked him all the way out the door.

Taking Dawson's advice, Jo left a text with Bev that she wouldn't be in until after lunch, silenced her cell phone and turned off her alarm before she crawled into bed that night. Despite her exhaustion from all the drama, she worried over the day's events for a long while before finally giving into a long-delayed need for sleep. Once she finally did, she slept hard and deep until the sharp jangling of the landline startled her into an upright position. Though her brain remained locked in a half-dream state, she snatched up the receiver.

"Hello?"

"Where the hell are you and why aren't you answering your phone?" It was Bev's voice, but the question made no sense.

"I am answering."

"I'm talking about your cell phone. You know, that thing you never turn off, ever. What is going on?"

"Nothing. I'm fine. Dawson told me to take the morning off, so I did. Everything's fine."

"Oh really? Then why is the firm posse here packing up your office?"

The words 'posse' and 'packing' pierced through Jo's fog. "What! Why?"

"All I know is there are people in your office clearing out your files and I got a memo on my desk saying I'm being reassigned. I'm not even supposed to talk to you."

"That's ridiculous. Go see Dawson. He'll straighten it out."

"Dawson signed the memo. You better get in here fast. Uh oh, someone's coming. I have to go."

The phone clicked.

"Bev? Bev?"

The dial tone buzzed in Jo's ear.

Thirty minutes later, Jo pulled into the office building's underground parking lot. She'd thrown on the first suit she could lay her hands on, run a quick brush through her hair and jumped in her car. Other than the taste from the breath mint she found in her glove compartment, her mouth felt filmed with sleep. *Terminated?* It had to be a joke, a mistake, a monumental miscommunication. As she exited the garage elevator into the lobby, she saw Carl Friedman, the research associate she'd so recently saved from loss of face with Dawson. Carl saw her too and the tragic look on his face told her this was no joke. At his feet sat a cardboard box with a potted plant on top. Jo recognized the plant. She walked toward Carl and he held out an envelope.

"I was asked to give you this."

Jo ripped it open. Inside was a payroll check and two typed lines on the firm letterhead. "By the terms of your employment at will with Holt, Lewis, Dawson and Card, you are hereby notified that your services are no longer required. Two weeks' severance pay is enclosed." Dawson's signature appeared at the bottom.

"I don't understand. I just talked to him last night."

"I'm sorry, Jo. Seemed like you worked harder than anybody."

"I did. Is Dawson in his office? I want to see him."

"I don't think you can." Carl glanced sideways at a guard standing a few feet away. "You've been listed as a security risk."

"What? No, this is crazy. I bet Dawson doesn't even know about this. Somebody's rubber stamped his signature."

Carl let go a long sad exhalation. "Trust me, he knows. He's the one who sent me down here with your stuff—guess he figured it would be easier coming from me."

It took Jo a long, stunned moment to digest that information. "So I'm just supposed to take my things and leave? Is that it?"

"I guess so." Carl shrugged.

"No, no way. I'm not leaving here until I get an explanation. Not after what he said to me last night. Dawson has to look me in the face and explain himself." She started for the main elevators but suddenly the security guard was in front of her. He was every bit as big as the guard at the Institute. Did all security guards come in size extra-large?

"I'm sorry, Ms. Rinaldi, but you're not allowed upstairs."

This was beginning to look like a rerun. Jo raised her palms and looked directly into his dark eyes. "I'm not going to cause any trouble, I promise. I just need to speak with Matthew Dawson."

The guard shook his head. "Sorry, I can't let you get in that elevator."

"All right, then you can ask him to come down."

"Won't do any good. He already left me clear instructions. You're to take your personal effects and leave the premises. Those were his exact words."

Personal effects. It sounded like she'd been declared dead on arrival.

Carl picked up the box and balanced her plant on top. "You want me to carry these to your car for you?"

She looked from Carl's sympathetic face to the guard's stoic one and knew neither of them would help her confront Dawson. Part of her knew it would be useless, anyway. Between the words in the letter and those quoted by both Carl and the guard, Dawson had made his wishes known. He wanted her out. He wanted her gone. The only misunderstanding was hers.

She grabbed the box from Carl's arms and wordlessly turned away before she lost control. She didn't want to cry, not in front of them. She bit her lip and concentrated on her rage as she marched away, head high.

Fired. Fired? She kept repeating the word in her mind, unable to believe it could apply to her. She'd never been fired in her entire life. How could he just fire her like that? Dawson had seemed so sympathetic last night. Said he would help. Told her to go home, get some rest. As if he cared. What a fool she'd been. Not only wasn't he going to help get her father out of Kessler's Institute, he'd fired her just for asking. That had to be what this was about.

She found herself standing next to her car without remembering the elevator ride down or the walk it took to get from there to here. She'd been moving like an automaton, distracted by her whirling thoughts. Only one repeating question remained.

What do I do now?

CHAPTER FIFTEEN

Blind Date

It only took a short time for Scott to settle into the routine of looking after his furry little pharmaceutical pincushions. He was almost getting used to taping them down and sticking them with needles. Repetition hardened one to most anything. The thin skin of revulsion was thickening again. He remembered growing that callous before doing this same kind of work. He didn't like the fact that he was growing it again, and he found himself mentally rehashing ancient arguments with his father over the decision he'd made years ago.

"You're looking a little down in the mouth." Jacob's voice pulled Scott out of his funk.

"Hey." Scott glanced up at the clock. "What are you doing here? Your shift doesn't start for another hour."

"Just dropping stuff off. Got a hot date with my dulce senorita." Jacob bobbed his eyebrows. "But I need to ask you a favor first."

"Oh?" Scott hoped this was the opportunity he'd been waiting for. He knew Jacob regularly rendezvoused with his girlfriend somewhere in the building, and it definitely wasn't down here in the dungeon. He needed to learn how Jacob was circumventing the building's security system. "What's up?"

"I hate to ask, but I promised Maggie I'd find a blind date for her roommate tonight. They want to go dancing. Can I twist your arm?"

"I don't know. If she can't get her own date, she must be a real dog."

"She's not, I swear. Besides, any woman's prettier than you."

Scott laughed. "True, but I'm not completely desperate."

"Come on, she's great. A tall redhead. A surgical nurse. She works with the terminal patients on the fourth floor. You'll like her, I swear."

"Oh yeah? Is she here now?"

"Yeah. The plan is for the girls to go home and get ready and we'll pick them up from there. So we good?"

"Depends. How about a sneak peek?"

Jacob scowled at him. "Not cool, man."

"Then count me out. I've been burned before."

"Geez." Jacob rolled his eyes and exhaled in annoyance then promptly left the room.

Scott turned back to entering the data on his latest task of injecting mice, wondering if he'd just blown it. After a few minutes, Jacob returned, carrying two dark blue long-sleeved overalls, a pair of mops and a bucket. He held out one of the overalls to him.

"What's this?" Scott asked.

"Your ticket for a sneak peek like you asked."

Scott noted a nametag on the shirt. "Harold Lloyd?"

"That would be you," Jacob said as he climbed into the other set of overalls. His tag read Steven Sanders. He handed Scott a mop and bucket. "Think of it as a promotion."

Scott traded his lab coat for the overalls and followed Jacob out a side exit and through the back halls. After a few twists and turns through the halls they entered a service elevator with shipping blankets draped down the walls. Jacob pulled a card from his back pocket, inserted it into the control panel, and punched number 4. It lit up.

"How did you get a card keyed for the fourth floor?"

"I didn't. I've got Steven's card and he cleans *every* floor," Jacob tapped his borrowed nametag. "Don't you go telling on me."

"Your secret's safe with me," Scott replied with a raised hand. "Assuming it's all for a good cause, of course."

"Best there is. True love, or close enough anyway. Maggie and I have a secret little hideaway up here, real private."

"What, like in a closet?" Scott joked, then saw the sheepish look on Jacob's face and knew he'd hit the mark. "How romantic."

"Yeah, I know, but she's got a roommate and I've got my mother, so we've learned to improvise."

Scott smiled, reflecting on stupider stunts he'd pulled in his twenties. The elevator opened to a long hallway papered with green vines and punctuated with doorways on either side. Jacob held a finger to his lips. As they walked along the industrial tiled floor past the open doors. Scott glanced inside. In the first, an elderly woman lay on a bed with her eyes closed. A halo of white hair encircled her wizened face. Her bone-thin arms crossed over her chest, corpse-like. He would have thought her dead, if those arms weren't rising and lowering ever so slightly with each shallow breath. In the next room, a balding man slumped in a chair by the window and returned Scott's glance with a watery stare. The man raised his hand a few inches and his hanging lower lip quivered as he mumbled something below Scott's hearing. In the next, a woman stood unmoving in the middle of the room, head tilted downward, her face hidden behind a sheet of silver hair. Each room held a similar still-life rendered in shades of gray: one steel-framed hospital bed, one ladder-back chair, one chest of drawers, and one aged human being.

"Damned depressing around here," Scott said as he followed Jacob through a door marked 'Staff Only.'

"Yeah, they're all in the advanced stages on this floor," Jacob replied. "Not many laughs in the terminal wing."

Scott puzzled at that. These people looked sad, lonely, and depressed... but on death's door? He hadn't noticed anyone hooked to an I.V. "Terminal? You sure?"

Jacob nodded. "Sure, I'm sure. This is where Maggie's roommate works, so she should know."

Ambulatory patients in a terminal wing didn't make sense. Maybe Jacob had it wrong. Somebody obviously did.

Voices and footsteps were coming their way. Jacob put a finger to his lips and pulled Scott into an empty room. The footsteps and voices grew louder. He waved excitedly for Scott to peek through the hinged crack to see a tall red-haired nurse walking by beside a bulky orderly pushing a patient in a wheelchair.

"That's her, that's Jessica, Maggie's roommate," Jacob whispered once they'd passed. "Nice, huh?"

"Where are they going?"

"I don't know. What difference does it make?"

"Let's find out." Scott picked up the scrub pail and mop and went to follow them.

"Wait!" Jacob came flying after him. "If we get caught, we get fired."

"We're just janitors. Who's going to notice? Start mopping."

Scott pushed his mop down the floor of the hall keeping a safe distance as he worked his way behind the two walking ahead with their patient. He watched as they wheeled him through a heavy set of steel doors. Scott scooted up to the meshed window only to see a second set of windowed doors beyond. He put his hand on the outer door to push it open and Jacob stopped him.

"Are you crazy?"

"I didn't get to see her face. I need to see what she looks like."

Jacob threw up his hands and took a step back. "If you get caught, I don't know you."

"Got it." Scott slipped through the doors and sidled up to the next set of windows. He saw the woman Jacob wanted him to go out with, tall and slender with blue eyes and red hair—nothing to complain about. She and the orderly lifted their patient out of his chair and laid him face down on an examination table, then strapped his head and body in place. Another white-coated man, who must have been waiting inside, approached. When he turned toward the patient, Scott saw his face. It was Dr. Kessler, but what really caught Scott's attention was the long syringe in the doctor's hand. Scott cringed when Kessler stabbed the needle deep into the base of the man's skull and the man cried out.

"Holy shit!" Jacob hissed in his ear.

Scott jumped, finding Jacob standing behind him. He pushed Jacob back out through the exterior doors.

Jacob shook his head angrily, grabbed his pail and mop, then stalked back down the long hall toward the service elevator. Scott followed him with his own mop and pail. He could see Jacob struggling internally, seething with anger and confusion, but remained silent, waiting him out as they rode the elevator back down to their basement floor, returned the pilfered janitor equipment, and re-entered their mouse-filled lab—all without exchanging a word. Jacob stood tugging at his chin, his eyes flickering back and forth, while Scott watched and waited. Finally, their eyes met.

"Ready to talk about it?" Scott asked.

"No." Jacob shook his head. "No. I don't know what that was and neither do you. We don't know what we saw."

"Don't we?"

"No. We have no information... no idea what that was. Could have been anything."

"Right."

Jacob grimaced. "Damn it."

"He's experimenting on them, isn't he? Same as what we're doing down here to these mice."

Jacob glared at him. "We don't know that."

"Okay. So how do we figure it out?"

"We don't. It's none of our business. We should just forget what we saw."

"Think you can live with that?"

"Yes. Maybe. I don't know..." Jacob groaned, wiped his hands down his face, then stared up at the ceiling.

"That nurse, you know her. Can't you just ask?"

"No, I can't ask her. She'll know I was spying."

"What about Maggie? Would she know?

"I don't know. Maybe. I don't think so. She would have told me. She knows what I do down here. We talk about it all the time. All she does is monitor vital signs, change bedding, and do some filing."

Scott's eyebrows rose. "Patient records?"

"Yeah, I guess." Jacob paused.

"Think she'd let us take a look at that man's file?"

Jacob frowned. "I'm not getting her in trouble. And neither are you."

"No one else needs to know." Scott fell silent, letting Jacob work it out.

"I should go," he said. "Maggie's expecting me."

"Right. Wouldn't want to disappoint her. That would be rude."

"You know what would be even ruder? Spying on her friend then refusing to go out with her."

"Who said I was refusing? It'll give me a chance to ask her some hard questions without having to corner her in the parking lot."

"You wouldn't."

Scott shrugged. "I'm not turning a blind eye to this. Not until I get an explanation."

Jacob rubbed his forehead and sighed again. "Okay, look, I'll make a deal with you. I'll get that man's records from Maggie, but only if you promise to go out with us tonight without turning it into an inquisition."

Scott sighed deeply in a show of reluctance, but inside he celebrated the win. "Okay, fine."

"Good."

Scott held up a finger. "On one more condition. I want another patient's files too. His name is Thomas Rinaldi."

"What? Why?"

"He's the father of a friend of mine. I want to know if Kessler is doing the same thing to him."

The muscles worked under Jacob's face before he nodded. "Okay, fine. But after that, we're done. I don't want to hear anything more about this. Okay?"

"Okay."

"Good. It's settled then." Jacob started to walk away, then turned back. "And no sneaking around here. Promise me."

"Sure. No sneaking." Somehow Scott felt zero guilt about lying to him. Jacob wasn't his client.

CHAPTER SIXTEEN

Scott's Report

Scott turned up as promised to be a blind date for Maggie's co-worker and roommate, Jessica, a nice enough young woman but rather vapid in his view. In contrast, Jacob's girlfriend, Marguerite, aka Maggie, turned out to be a little spitfire with dark eyes, and curly hair out to there. Throughout the night, she flashed Scott spiteful looks and snubbed Jacob's advances. Whatever points Jacob had hoped to score by snagging a date for her roommate had obviously been nullified by the fact that she'd been coerced into obtaining medical records for Scott. After a tedious night of making small talk with Jessica over burgers then dancing with her in a crowded nightclub, Scott finally had a chance to look at what he'd come for, pages and pages of medical records, one set of which belonged to Josephine's father. All sent to his phone.

Most of it looked like standard care stuff, until he came across matching handwritten lists of dates and times with no descriptions. The last entries were for this afternoon, which correlated with what he and Jacob had witnessed. If so, that meant it was the fourth injection that man had received in as many weeks. The list in Rinaldi's file showed the same number. Most of the mice died after five injections and nearly all of them by the seventh. These lists wouldn't convince anyone else of wrongdoing, but it convinced him. Then he came across a redlined note in Rinaldi's file barring all visitors, including family members. He immediately called Josephine. It took her a while to answer.

"It's three in the morning," she mumbled.

"We need to talk. I have to stop for supplies first, but I'll be there within the hour. Make us some coffee." He clicked off and started the engine.

"What? Why? What's going on?" Jo asked then realized he'd already hung up. "Unbelievable."

Reluctantly, almost painfully, she pushed herself out of bed, wondering what could be so damned urgent but couldn't be shared over the phone.

Counting on that promised delay, she took a shower to wake up, threw on some sweats, went downstairs and started coffee. Before the pot was half full, a knock came. She started for the door, then thought better of it, and instead, she crossed her arms and waited. The knock came again.

After a long pause, her cell phone buzzed in her pocket.

"Yes?" she answered.

"You going to let me in?" Scott asked.

"I was waiting to see how you got in here the last time."

He exhaled. "Just open the door, will you?"

"Fine." She hung up and opened the front door.

"Thanks," he said as he entered, whipping off that same long coat and hat that he'd worn when they'd first crossed paths in the parking lot elevator. He unceremoniously dumped them on the sofa along with a shopping bag.

"So what's this about?" she asked.

"Coffee first." He strode past her into the kitchen as if he lived there, going straight to the correct cupboards to retrieve two coffee mugs and cream and sugar from their hiding places. He filled the mugs with the freshly brewed coffee and added cream and sugar to one, which he handed to her. "Drink up. I want you wide awake for this."

She took the mug and frowned at the caramel-colored liquid. "And just how the hell do you know the way I like my coffee?"

"Beverly must have mentioned it." He took a gulp of his black brew, then sat at the kitchen table in the chair her father had always sat in. "Come. Sit. I have something you need to hear."

She frowned at being ordered around in her own home but was too tired to argue. She sat across from him and took a tentative sip. It was perfect, dammit. "Okay, so what gives?"

"I believe Kessler is running illegal experiments on his patients, including your father, injecting their brains with re-engineered stem cells at the base of their necks."

She paused from sipping and stared at him. "What makes you think that?"

"I witnessed it, plus I found this list of dates in your father's file." Scott held up his cell phone displaying a page of times and dates.

"You actually saw him do this?"

He nodded in confirmation. "Not to your father. Another patient. But the lists are identical."

She wasn't sure whether this was good news or bad. Her main fear had been that he was part of the control group and not being treated at all.

"I'm sure Kessler knows what he's doing," she said. "Maybe this is a good thing."

"Not if the results are anything like what we're seeing in the mice. Ninety-eight percent end up twitching uncontrollably and going into shock. That's when they send them to the sterile labs so their brains can be made into samples for analysis. So far, only a handful have survived for more than a few weeks, and no one knows why."

"Now you're scaring me."

"I mean to."

"I don't understand. If it's so dangerous, why did Kessler let you see him do it?"

"He didn't know I was there."

"So you were spying on him?"

Scott nodded again.

"And how did you get my father's file?"

"I persuaded a nurse to get it for me."

Jo wondered just what that persuasion had entailed. Not that it was any of her business. Then again maybe it was. She was paying him for all of this, wasn't she? And that brought up another issue. She no longer had a paycheck coming in. "I sent you a message to stop working on this."

"Yes, you did, but I already had this in the works and wanted to see it through. So now that you have this information, what do you want to do?"

She sunk back in her chair. "I... I'm not sure. I already tried to get him released, but they wouldn't even let me see him."

"Why didn't you tell me?"

"I thought I could take care of it." She fell silent, reluctant to share the extent of her humiliation.

"You still have power of attorney for him, don't you?"

There was no avoiding the truth. "I thought so, but Mrs. Sutton claims I signed that over to them."

"Is that even legal?"

"No, I don't think it is, which is why I went to Dawson..." She trailed off in embarrassment.

"And?" Scott prompted when she fell silent again.

"He fired me the next day—this morning, or rather, yesterday morning, seeing as it's already tomorrow." She scowled, trying to scold him for the ungodly hour, but Scott stared back at her so intensely, she had to look away. She couldn't understand how she could have been so stupid and felt certain he was wondering the same.

Scott nodded. "I know but I wish you'd called and told me when it happened."

"I should have, but—wait, you knew? Did Bev tell you?"

"No. There's a note in your father's file, written by Suzanne Sutton. It says you're banned from the Institute and were fired from your law firm for making threats against Dr. Kessler."

She banged her mug down on the table. "I never threatened anyone. That woman is insane. All I did was ask Kessler a few questions, and it got blown all out of proportion. Like I'm some sort of menace. Do you know that Dawson wouldn't even see me? All I got from him was a memo. Fired, just like that, for no reason." She shook her head and took a breath.

"I'm sorry about the job, but we need to focus on your dad right now."

"Yes, yes, I know. I was planning to go down to court in the morning to get an emergency injunction, but with Dawson as opposing counsel, it could be an uphill battle."

Scott grabbed her wrist. "Josephine, wake up!"

Startled, she pulled her wrist free. "I am awake."

"No, you're not. If you were, you'd realize they're using your father as a guinea pig and keeping you away while they do it. He might not be alive by the time you get that order."

His words were like ice water in her face. "But what else can I do?"

"We go get him. Now."

"What? You mean like bust him out?"

"Exactly."

She almost laughed. "That's insane. I wouldn't have the first idea how to do something like that."

"I know. That's why you've got me."

CHAPTER SEVENTEEN

The Escape

*J*ailbreak. The silly word kept inserting itself in Jo's thoughts as she hunkered down in the passenger seat of Scott's car, hiding like a criminal in the dark of the too early morning. He'd parked in front of the building and gone around back to the employee entrance, leaving her here to wait for his signal. She wore a pale baby-blue sweater over pink scrubs decorated with frolicking blue puppies. She glared at their happy faces and lolling red tongues remembering the smirk on Scott's face when he'd presented them.

"You'll be needing a disguise," he'd said as he pulled the scrubs out of the bag he'd brought.

"So you just assumed I'd go along with this."

"Well, I figured getting banned from the Institute and fired from your job should be enough to persuade you."

It annoyed her thoroughly that he'd known about both and pretended ignorance to wheedle a confession out of her.

"Asshole," she said aloud.

Her ponytail poked the back of her head, annoying her even more, and the drugstore reading glasses distorted her vision, forcing her to peer over them. She doubted the ponytail, scrubs and red-framed glasses were much of a disguise and imagined how easily Suzanne Sutton might recognize her. She glanced at the time on her cell phone again. *Why is he taking so long?* As her impatience grew, so did her incredulousness at what she'd agreed to do. *This is kidnapping, right? Sort of. God, I hope Dad recognizes me.*

She kept glancing at her cell phone expecting it to ring. Instead, a high-pitched wailing alarm went off outside. She opened the car door and the screech rose to an earsplitting crescendo. It took half a second to realize it was the building's fire alarm. She watched people emerge from the exits. The crowd of personnel and patients grew steadily as staff directed them to the north end of the parking lot. Those who could walk or wheel themselves along did so, while those who could do neither were pushed along in wheel-chairs or on gurneys. Finally, her phone buzzed with a text from Scott.

[Your Dad's coming out in a wheelchair. Go get him.]

She took a steadying breath, got out and made her way toward the escapees flowing from the building in rumbling rivers of discontent to pool at the far end of the parking lot. One strident female voice rose above the rest.

"Move along, people! Quickly now," Mrs. Sutton ordered, clapping her hands and waving them forward.

Jo ducked her head and tried to blend in as she searched for her father, scanning outlines of heads, dismissing those with hair too long, the wrong color, or missing altogether. Finally, she spotted him in a wheelchair as Scott had prom-ised, lined up with over a dozen others. She worked her way over and stood behind him.

Okay. Now I just need to get him over to Scott's car on the other side of the parking lot without anyone noticing. She tried to look casual as she rested her hands on the handles of his wheelchair and peered about, searching for a clear path, but only someone on two feet could sidestep through this tight crowd without bringing attention to themselves. *Be patient, once we're given the all clear, I can hang back then peel off.*

A yellow firetruck and a black-and-white police car wheeled into the parking lot with their lights flashing. Mrs. Sutton trotted toward the emergency vehicles as they came to a stop. Jo sighed with relief to see the woman hurrying in the opposite direction, the farther away the better, but at that precise moment her father chose to throw his arms into the air and yell out.

"Hey! Hey, you! Over here. Help! I need help!"

Jo put a hand on his shoulder. "Shhh. It's okay. You're all right."

"Get your hands off me. I'm not all right. Help! Help!"

Heads turned—patients, nurses, and orderlies alike—all frowning and looking at her expectantly, as if to say, *You're a professional. Deal with the problem.* From across the lot, Sutton turned in her direction.

"I need to move him," she announced. Ducking her head down, she shoved his chair forward, forcing people to clear a path. Astonished, they jumped aside for the crazy nurse with her even crazier patient. "Sorry, excuse us please, let us through, sorry," she apologized as she forced her way through while Thomas kept yelling for help. At last, she broke free and pushed his chair full speed across the parking lot. Thomas gasped and finally stopped yelling. He gripped the arms of his chair as she bumped him over the rough asphalt, and he twisted to see the face of his abductor.

"It's all right, Dad. It's me, Josie. I'm taking you home."

"Nurse!" a man called out from behind them. Glancing back, she recognized the security guard who had evicted her. "Where are you going with that patient?"

"Just trying to distract him," she yelled back. To her right, she locked eyes with Suzanne Sutton from across the parking lot.

Oh shit, game's up.

"Stop her!" Suzanne yelled.

Even with a good head start, Jo doubted she could outrun the guard even if she weren't pushing a loaded wheelchair, but with no alternative she kept going as fast as she could. Then Scott's car squealed to a stop in front of her and he leaped out.

"Get in, get in," Scott said as he lifted her father and stuffed him into the backseat like a sack of flour. Jo got inside and held her breath as Scott raced back to the driver's side just in time to slam his door shut in the security guard's face and floor the accelerator. They peeled out past Mrs. Sutton running towards them waving her arms in the air, screaming, "Stop!"

Thomas stuck his hand out the back window, middle finger raised high as they sailed away out onto the open road. Jo laughed from the surging adrenaline rush of a close call. Scott grinned back in a shared moment of triumph. For the next few minutes it appeared they had gotten away clean, but soon the sound of a police siren and flashing lights in the rearview mirror said otherwise. Her heart that had started to slow sped up again. "Oh no."

"Get out your IDs and let me do the talking," Scott said as he pulled the car over, then rolled down his window and waited.

The black-and-white pulled in behind them, lights flashing. A tall sandy-haired officer in mirrored sunglasses exited his vehicle, approached alongside them with one hand on the driver's door, then leaned down. His brown eyes peered over the sunglasses and swept over them, then focused on the driver.

"Scott."

"Frank. How are you?"

"Fine, thanks. You?"

"No complaints."

The two men nodded, waiting each other out.

Finally, Officer Frank sighed. "Okay. Mind telling me why that lady back there says you're kidnapping one of her patients?"

"No idea. We're just taking him home." Scott handed over Jo's valid driver's license, along with her father's expired one, both bearing the same address. "Father and daughter."

Officer Frank looked from one face to the other and back at the licenses. "Okay. So then why is that administrator so hopping mad?"

"It's a contractual dispute, a civil matter," Jo said. Scott scowled at her, clearly wanting her to remain silent, but she ignored him. "Not your jurisdiction."

Frank narrowed his eyes. "What are you, a lawyer or something?"

"Yes, as a matter of fact."

Frank made a rude noise, then looked back at Scott. "And I suppose you're working for her?"

Scott nodded, looking sheepish now.

Frank frowned at Jo. "Well, you're right, little lawyer lady, interpreting contracts is not my area of expertise, but making sure no one's being coerced is." Frank examined the licenses again, then spoke to her father. "Sir, are you Mr. Thomas Rinaldi?"

"Professor," Thomas corrected.

"Okay, Professor, do you want to go back to that clinic where you were staying, or do you want to go home with your daughter here?"

Jo held her breath. Her father stared blankly.

"Sir?" Frank prompted. "Can you understand what I am asking you?"

Thomas blinked a few more times before answering. "Home. I want to go home."

Officer Frank nodded. "All right, home it is then." He handed back the licenses and addressed Scott. "Just so you know, setting false alarms is a misdemeanor that can earn a person up to a year in jail."

"I'll keep that in mind," Scott replied.

Officer Frank made a sound of disgust and shook his head. "Next time you call, it better include a six-pack."

"You got it. Thanks, Frank."

Jo watched as the officer returned to his vehicle, turned off its lights, and did a U-turn. Scott pulled back onto the road and accelerated to just below the speed limit.

She sat quietly for a few moments, absorbing what had just happened. "So that was a friend of yours. Huh, how did we get so lucky?"

Scott smirked. "I gave him a heads-up. Figured we could use a friendly ear if we had to talk our way out of this."

Jo's mind tripped over itself trying to figure out how all the pieces of this puzzle of a man fit together, but she was too tired to press him for more information, so merely said, "Good move." and let it alone. For now.

CHAPTER EIGHTEEN

Home Again

J o set her father up in the downstairs guest room, already outfitted with a hospital bed, wheelchair, and walker in anticipation of bringing him home before. The attached bathroom housed medical supplies and sported recently installed handrails.

Things went pretty much as expected over the next few weeks, with the nurses and caregivers she'd already arranged for coming and going. When awake Thomas remained confused about time and place, and the identities of people surrounding him, but most of the time, he slept so soundly he had to be prodded awake just to eat and use the toilet. Jo hadn't known it was possible for anyone to sleep that much outside of a coma. Getting him up and dressed to make a trip to the doctor would have proven a monumental task, so his old physician Dr. Peterson agreed to make weekly house calls before going into the office.

"His vitals still look good," Peterson told her again this morning. "I don't see any red flags. I'm giving you another refill for Donepezil and his blood pressure medication."

"What about the way he sleeps all the time? Is that normal?"

"Well, the elderly do tend to sleep a lot," Peterson said in that reassuring tone doctors save for the slow to comprehend. "I wouldn't worry too much."

Right. The doctor and her father were close to the same age, and worry had become her norm. She had no proof he had received any unauthorized injections, only suspicion, and no idea what effect they might ultimately have on him if he had.

She said goodbye to Dr. Peterson and checked on her father again—asleep as usual. Meanwhile, Teresa was vacuuming in the living room. Jo waved for her attention. "Don't clean his bathroom. The nurses are taking care of it. I'm just going upstairs for a few minutes."

"Okay," Teresa said with a smile and nod.

Jo smiled back, hiding a guilty thought. *I need to let her go.* She hated to do it, but how could she not? The bills were piling up. Her father's savings was nearly depleted from un- covered medical expenses from her mother's long fight with cancer, so there was little left for his own battle with Alz- heimer's now. Insurance covered part, but only part, which meant she needed to find a job soon. Unfortunately, the search wasn't going well.

For some reason, she couldn't seem to get past the initial interview stage. She had another one scheduled for this af- ternoon and hoped things would go better but feared they wouldn't. She suspected her potential new employers were losing interest once they spoke to her prior one. If she could prove it, it could be grounds for a lawsuit, but that would hardly serve her in the short term. Worry that she was being blackballed in the legal community was pushing Jo's stress level to an all-time high, and repeated phone calls from Su- zanne Sutton threatening legal action against her for absconding with their patient weren't helping any. Jo had lost count of the number of times she'd hung up on the woman. Jo finally stopped answering and let all her calls go to voice mail.

The only calls she looked forward to were from Carl, Bev and Scott, friends who stuck with her and showed genuine concern. "How are you doing? How's your dad? Is there an- ything you need?"

She appreciated their support, but her answers remained consistent. "I'm fine. He's okay. No, not really, but thanks."

She was too proud to tell them she was freaking out, her dad was nearly a vegetable, and what she desperately needed was her career back. She finished getting ready for her interview, keeping close track of the time, and planned to leave as soon as the nurse arrived. Jo thought of her schedule like standing dominoes, each event carefully posi- tioned to enable the next. One "oops" and it all went to hell. When she heard the toilet flushing in the downstairs' bath- room, it sounded like one of them falling over. The guest bath was littered with medical supplies—a bedpan on the floor, tubes hanging over the shower rod, a menagerie of prescription bottles filling the counter—none of which she wanted disturbed.

Dammit, Teresa, I told you not to clean in there.

Jo abandoned her make-up and hurried downstairs. To her surprise, she saw Teresa still in the living room.

"Were you in the guest bath just now?" Jo asked.

Teresa shook her head. "No. You tell me no clean it."

Uh oh. Jo hurried into the made-over guest room. The hospital bed lay empty, its blue-striped comforter thrown aside.

"Dad!"

The bathroom door opened, and Thomas stuck his head out. "Why are you yelling?"

"What are you doing?"

"Peeing. Didn't know I needed permission. Someone sure made a mess in here. There's stuff all over the place. I'm going upstairs."

"What? No." Jo moved to block him. "It's not safe."

"Don't be ridiculous. I need a shower and change of clothes, which I'll do in the privacy of my own bedroom, thank you very much." To her shock, he walked around her. She followed him closely, ready to catch him.

"Will you stop breathing down my neck?"

She ignored his complaint and followed him up the carpeted stairs, one step behind. When he reached the top, he paused to catch his breath.

"How did I get so out of shape?" he grumbled, then walked ahead to his bedroom. When she went to follow him inside, he turned an angry face on her. "For heaven's sake, you're like a lost puppy. Go find something useful to do." Then he shut the door in her face.

Jo stood there flabbergasted. With one hand poised on the knob, she pressed her ear against the door. She heard the shower come on, the normal sounds of drawers and closet doors opening and closing. No crashes, no thumps.

"Is okay?" Teresa asked.

She turned to see Teresa halfway up the stairs, a puzzled look on her face, no doubt mirroring her own. "I'm not sure." Jo hesitated, uncertain what to do, torn between making it to her interview on time and staying here to ensure her father's safety. The uncertainty lasted only a second. No way was she leaving. "Could you come up here, please? I need to make a call. If you hear any loud noises, yell."

Teresa nodded and stood by the door while Jo went to retrieve her cell phone. She called the firm that was going to interview her, asking if she could reschedule.

"Certainly, just call us back when you're ready," she was told.

Yeah, sure, probably just blew that one.

The next call was to Dr. Peterson. To get him on the phone quickly, she claimed it was an emergency. "I don't know what's going on, but all of a sudden, he's up out of bed, walking around, acting like his old self. I don't know what to make of it. Can you come back?"

There was a long pause. "I know how stressful this has been for you."

"I'm not hallucinating. He went up the stairs on his own. He's in his old bedroom, taking a shower—by himself."

There was another long pause on the other end. "Is a nurse due there soon?"

"Yes, yes, any minute."

"Good. Have her call me as soon as she arrives."

"His name is William," Jo corrected, annoyed by his assumption. She also sensed that Peterson wanted confirmation of Jo's claims. "Just get here." She hung up, irritated, and went back to relieve Teresa. She positioned herself at her father's bedroom door again, listening.

Ten minutes later, Thomas emerged in sweats and sneakers. His mouth twisted in annoyance upon seeing her there. "I thought I told you to go find something useful to do."

"Dad, I don't think you realize how sick you've been."

He brushed past her heading for the stairs. "I'm fine, a little weak—but that's probably because I'm famished." As he made his way down the steps Jo held her breath. She followed him into the kitchen and watched in amazement as he made himself a thick peanut butter sandwich and wolfed it down with a tall glass of milk.

"You say I've been ill?"

She nodded, lost for words.

"Well, whoever's been taking care of me hasn't done a very good job of it." He slapped his non-existent stomach. "Nothing but skin and bones. I have a lot of work to do to get back in shape. Think I'll start by going for a walk."

"A walk? Outside?"

"Of course, outside. Must you question everything?" He swallowed the last bite, emptied the glass, then headed for the front door. That's when he saw Teresa in the living room. "Who the hell are you?"

She spun around clasping a fringed green sofa pillow to her chest, staring at him open mouthed.

"This is Teresa, Dad, our housekeeper, plus she fills in for me if I need to go out before the nurse gets here," Jo said.

"You hired a nurse for me?"

"I had to. You were practically comatose."

He frowned, his eyes sweeping the room. "I need some air," he said. He aimed for the front door, but moved shakily.

Jo rushed to his side and grabbed his arm.

"I'm all right," he said even though he clearly wasn't. He took a breath then seemed to find his equilibrium again. Still, he made no objection when she didn't let go. Together, they walked out the front door and down the brick steps out onto the sidewalk. Gradually, his feet found a slow rhythm, and Jo's death-grip on his arm lightened.

"You say I've been ill. For how long?" he asked.

"A while. I'm not exactly sure where to begin. Do you re-member that Dr. Peterson diagnosed you with Alzheimer's?"

"Yes, of course, but that was long before your mother passed."

"Right." Jo realized just how aware he was. "Well, a few months ago you enrolled in an in-house drug study at the Kessler Research Institute. It seemed like a good fit at the time, but you weren't doing well there, so I brought you back home. Do you remember any of that?"

Thomas shook his head, "It's all a blur. I do remember Peterson saying I had Alzheimer's and being mad as hell about it."

Jo laughed. "Yes, you were."

"What day is it?" he asked.

"Wednesday."

"Aren't you supposed to be at work?"

"They let me go. Apparently I asked too many questions."

"That hardly seems fair. What were you concerned about?"

"One of our clients—Dr. Kessler. I was afraid he was using you as a guinea pig."

"Kessler..." Thomas stopped walking and put his hand to the back of his neck.

"Scott says it was something experimental, something not approved for use on people."

"Who's Scott?"

"Scott Benson, an investigator I hired. They wouldn't release you or even let me see you, so he helped me kidnap you."

"I wouldn't be throwing that term around lightly."

"I'm not."

"Are you in trouble then?"

"I don't think so, but it was a close call."

"This isn't some kind of joke, is it? If so, I find it in bad taste."

"No, it's the truth. You can ask Dr. Peterson when he comes. I called him while you were in the shower and asked him to come over."

"He's making a house call? How much is that going to cost me?" Thomas came to a stop, out of breath. "Maybe we should turn around." As they made their way back, he kept grumbling. "I can't believe how weak I am. You've let me completely fall apart. What were you thinking?"

Anger surged in Jo. What did it take to earn a little appreciation? "Maybe one of these days, I'll tell you exactly what I was thinking."

He scowled, but she made no apology for her sharp tone. Once back in the house, he rested for a few moments then returned to the kitchen, fixing himself another sandwich. Seeing him eating with such enthusiasm was unnerving. The doorbell rang and Jo assumed it would be the nurse, William, but instead it was Dr. Peterson.

"You did say it was an emergency," he said in a rueful tone.

She grimaced, embarrassed now. "He's in the kitchen, having a sandwich."

He raised his eyebrows, clearly skeptical. As Peterson entered the kitchen, her father looked up from the kitchen table and smiled, then the smile faded into puzzlement.

"Hello, Thomas. Do you know who I am?" Peterson asked.

Thomas scowled at his old friend. "Wayne? When did you get so fat? I don't remember all that gray hair either."

It was true that silver streaked the doctor's hair and his waistline had thickened to a paunch, but those traits had been there for years.

Peterson laughed in surprise. "Ever the diplomat. So how are you feeling?"

"Hungry. Starved, in fact. Seems no one around here's been bothering to feed me."

"We tried," Jo answered. "You had no appetite."

Thomas shook his head. "Well, I sure have one now." He waved the remaining quarter of his third sandwich in the air before polishing it off.

"Well, a healthy appetite's always a good sign," Peterson said and sat his leather bag down upon the kitchen counter. He pulled out a laptop, stethoscope, and blood pressure cuff. "Let's see what's going on here, shall we?"

Jo excused herself to give them some privacy. The phone rang and when she answered it was the nurse she'd been expecting. When he began to apologize, she interrupted. "That's okay, I think we should cancel today. There's been a change in my father's condition. His doctor is here now. I'll call back when I know what's going on." When he hung up, she dialed Scott.

He picked up on the first ring. "Hey, Josephine. I was thinking about you and—"

"You're not going to believe this. My father's awake, on his feet, eating, conversing... I mean coherently. He even took a shower all by himself, then went for a walk. Outside. His doctor's here now, but I thought you might want to come over and see for yourself." When only silence followed, Jo thought the connection had broken. "Hello?"

"Yeah, yeah, I heard you. I definitely want to see him, but it's just that you caught me in the middle of something here."

"Oh. Sorry. That's okay. I just thought you might be interested."

"Course I'm interested. Oh what the hell, she can wait. I'm coming over."

The connection broke. The word 'she' hung in Jo's mind. Not that it was any of her business. She pulled her thoughts back to her father and his seemingly miraculous recovery. Up until this morning, he'd been bedridden, mumbling nonsense, relying on others to spoon-feed him and empty his bedpan. Now here he was, up walking around, making sandwiches, complaining about how lousy she'd been caring for him. She wished now that she had a video documenting everything she'd been doing for him. It never occurred to her he might get well enough to see it. She recalled his moments of clarity during angry episodes in the past, but he didn't seem angry now, just his old critical self. This sustained period of cognizance was unlike anything she'd seen since his diagnosis. She wondered what Dr. Peterson would make of it. She sat on the sofa, pulling at her fingers, her mind racing with unanswered questions and wild theories, then the doorbell rang again.

She found Scott on the porch, balanced on one foot to tug off a muddy boot. He set it next to its twin on the stoop. He dusted himself off and walked in on socked feet.

"Sorry I'm such a mess. So where's our miracle man?" he asked.

"In the kitchen being examined by Dr. Peterson. Could be a little while."

"Oh, well in that case maybe I have time to clean up. Mind if I take a quick shower?"

"Um... the guest bath's full of medical stuff," she said, making a face, hoping to discourage him.

"That's okay. I'd rather use yours anyway. I love all that girlie stuff—cute little scrubbies, scented bodywash.

Thanks," he said and without waiting for permission bounded up the stairs.

"Unbelievable," she muttered, and followed him up. She grabbed a towel and washcloth from the linen closet. He was already unbuttoning his shirt as she handed them over. "What were you doing when I called?"

"Snooping. As usual."

"How did you get so filthy?" she asked.

"Character flaw," he answered with a grin then disappeared into her bedroom.

"Ha ha. Fine, don't tell me."

In a moment, she heard the water running, and him humming to himself. She shook her head and left. As she went back down the stairs, there came a crash from the kitchen and her father's raised voice.

"How many times do I have to say it? I'm not going to the hospital."

Jo entered the room and her father turned toward her.

"Tell him, Josie. I'm perfectly fine."

Jo looked from her father's angry face to Dr. Peterson's puzzled one. She spotted a broken vase on the tile floor. She needed to de-escalate this quick. "Why don't we all just calm down and talk about this?"

"There's nothing to talk about," her father snapped. "Why won't anyone listen to me?"

"I am listening—we both are," she said. "But you need to understand that you've been ill for some time. You've trusted Dr. Peterson for years, so can't you, please, just take a deep breath and hear him out?"

Her father glared at her, and for a moment she thought he would explode again. Instead, he waved an arm in resignation. "Fine. Won't change anything though."

"Neither will breaking things," Jo replied and went to pick up the shattered vase.

"Sorry," her father said, looking aside now as if embarrassed. "Hope that wasn't one of your mother's."

Jo sighed. "No, just something I brought home from the office."

"You mean the one they fired you from? Just for asking questions? Sons of bitches. I told you not to work for them."

She frowned at him, annoyed at the way he could simultaneously take her side and criticize her in the same breath. "Yes, you did." She finished picking up the blue and white shards and disposed of them. "Let's sit down now."

They each took a seat at the kitchen table. Peterson spoke first, addressing Jo.

"On the surface, your father appears to be doing remarkably well. His vital signs are all within normal ranges. He appears fully aware of his surroundings, providing appropriate responses to questions of time and place."

"Like I said, I'm fine," Thomas interjected.

"The problem is that previously he exhibited all the signs of being in the later stages of Alzheimer's and people simply don't recover from that. Frankly, I've never seen anything like it before, which suggests the possibility of a misdiagnosis. I strongly recommend he be admitted into a hospital so we can run additional tests."

Thomas put a hand up like a stop sign. "No. I've had enough tests and doctoring for a lifetime. I just want to be left alone."

"What kind of tests?" Jo asked.

"To start with, blood work, and a dye contrast MRI."

"No. I'm not going to the hospital. Period."

Jo appraised her father's scowl and resistant body pose, something she recognized. He'd taken a stand and there would be no convincing him otherwise. "Could he do these tests on an outpatient basis?"

Peterson sighed. "Yes, but it's not what I would recommend. I honestly have no idea what's going on here and I think he should be in a hospital setting where we can monitor him."

"He's making a lot of sense, Dad."

"Poppycock, balderdash and horseshit! I'm not letting them hook me up to some infernal machine, waiting for me to flatline so they can zap me back to life and do it all over again. No. When the end comes, I'll do it only once, thank you very much, and preferably in my own home."

Her father sat glowering at them, arms crossed in front of his chest, the picture of entrenched resistance. Getting him into a hospital would take a full-scale war of wills. Not one she was willing to wage.

"Let's try it on an outpatient basis and see how it goes," Jo said.

"Very well," Peterson acquiesced unhappily. "I'll order the blood work and an MRI."

"Don't bother," Thomas barked.

Jo sighed, then half-smiled at Peterson. "I'll work on him."

Peterson looked to his patient. "I hope you'll listen to her, Thomas. Remember I'm not just your doctor, I'm your friend and I'm telling you we need to figure out what's going on here. In the meantime, I'd like to get some other opinions, if I may."

"Good idea," Thomas said. "Seeing as you're clearly out of your league."

Peterson shook his head but said nothing more. Jo walked him to the door and thanked him for coming. When she turned back, Scott was trotting down the stairs in his socked feet.

"Did you hear any of that?" she asked.

"Enough. The doc wants him in the hospital. Your dad wants no part of it."

Her father came out of the kitchen. "Who are you talking to?"

Scott held out a hand. "Scott Benson, sir."

Thomas squinted at him. "So you're the one who kidnapped me."

"I prefer the word 'rescue.'"

"Whatever you call it, I'm glad to be back in my own home." Thomas said as he shook Scott's hand. "Thank you for that."

Jo watched their interaction in disbelief. "Hey. I was there, too, you know."

Her father nodded, then rewarded her with a deep frown as he put a hand to his stomach. "Can't believe I'm still hungry. Is there anything else to eat around here besides peanut butter?"

CHAPTER NINETEEN

Suzanne and the Doctor

From her desk at the Kessler Institute, Suzanne Sutton dialed the number for Josephine Rinaldi again, and again the call went directly to voice mail. She hung up without leaving another message. There was no point—the daughter refused to talk to her. Whenever diplomacy had failed her in the past, Suzanne had no regrets about taking stronger measures, but in this case, she wasn't sure what more she could do. She'd already gotten the woman fired, and suggested bringing charges of kidnapping, but their attorney, Matthew Dawson, said there was no legal basis for it. While he agreed the daughter had made a poor decision, it wasn't a criminal one. However, he did say there was a good chance he could sway a judge to remove her as her father's conservator and was moving forward with a petition. Suzanne hoped for a favorable ruling but there was no guarantee. She needed a back-up plan and tapped her pen on the desktop, trying to think of one.

I must be overlooking something. Some way to leverage this.

She hated the idea of calling Reginald Howell. They were already far too deep in that man's debt, but if this petition failed it might be the only option. The man had deep connections and few qualms about getting his hands dirty when it came to problem solving. She couldn't see another way to ensure the outcome at this point. Her mouth twisted in preparation to deal with him again. She reached for the phone just as her intercom buzzed, so she answered it instead. "Yes?"

"I have a Doctor Peterson on the line requesting patient records."

The name sounded familiar. "I'll talk to him." When the call clicked over to her, she said. "This is Suzanne Sutton. May I help you?"

"Hi. I'm calling about a former patient of yours. Thomas Rinaldi."

Suzanne snatched up the receiver. "Have you seen him? Is he all right? Dr. Kessler's very concerned."

"In that case, it's probably best if I speak to Doctor Kessler directly. Can you connect me?"

"I... Yes, of course," Suzanne replied, remembering her place. She had no business asking about a patient's condition. "Please hold." She rang Adrian's office, mentally chanting, *pick up, pick up, pick up.*

He did.

"I have Dr. Peterson on the line calling about Thomas Rinaldi. He wants to talk to you."

"Put him through."

Suzanne connected the call but didn't hang up. Instead, she covered the mouthpiece and continued to listen in.

"Kessler here."

"Yes, hello, thank you for taking my call. I examined a recent patient of yours today. Mr. Thomas Rinaldi. You may recall that I diagnosed him with Alzheimer's before referring him to you, and he appeared to be entering advanced stages of the disease, but now... well, to be honest, now I'm not sure what to think. When I examined him today, he displayed no signs of dementia."

Suzanne's eyes flew wide and she choked back a sharp intake of breath.

Peterson continued, "I pulled my notes and his old MRI's, which clearly showed markers of the disease. I've ordered new scans, but he's not being very cooperative, and I'd really like to figure out what's going on with him. I was hoping you might have more recent images that I could see."

There was a pause.

"I'm sure we must," Kessler replied, his voice devoid of emotion. "I'll have his records pulled and forwarded to you."

"Much appreciated." Peterson hung up.

Suzanne waited for the second click. It didn't come.

"Did you get all that?"

She swallowed her guilt and answered. "Yes, I'm sorry. I know I should have hung up, but..." She left off, having no excuse.

The connection clicked off. She frowned and placed the receiver back in its cradle.

Now you've done it, you stupid cow. Did you really think you could deceive him? The inner voice scolded her, vicious as always, sounding exactly like her mother's.

I was just trying to help. He needs me.

Right. He needs your help. Who do you think you're kidding?

He said so.

He was drunk, remember?

She remembered. She also remembered him holding her hand, looking in her eyes, and saying she was the only one he could count on, and she wasn't about to let him down.

Kessler pulled out his personal file on Rinaldi, excited by what Dr. Peterson's had said. *No evidence of dementia whatsoever?* No doubt, it was merely temporary improvement like the others, but still the possibility of finally having created a patient zero curled in Kessler's chest like a coiled cobra, making his heart quicken. He needed to examine Rinaldi as soon as possible. His private notes started with his first impression of his now wayward patient:

Thomas Rinaldi, retired law professor, appears to be a perfect candidate. The man's sarcastic wit still sparks on occasion—revealing remnants of a keen intelligence. Of particular interest are episodes of marked lucidity when enraged. Explosive anger, even physical violence, are common traits of this disease, but this patient thinks more clearly in the midst of it. His referring physician speculated that the rush of adrenaline and dopamine might be stimulating brain function. I can't rule it out. Short-term memory is centralized in the hippocampus where dopamine plays a vital role, the very reason stimulants such as Ritalin are prescribed for attention deficit disorders.

Rinaldi's lucid moments differed from the common experience of most patients when overstimulated. For example, another resident, Mr. Gerard, a career military man, believed himself back in the army during his fits of rage. The staff braced whenever he started snapping orders at them like a drill sergeant. In contrast, when angered, Rinaldi became acutely aware of the reality of his situation. Curious, but then what about this disease wasn't? The fact that Rinaldi didn't fit the pattern was precisely why he'd been so determined to include him in his experiment.

Kessler searched for his handwritten list documenting the dates of injections. Based on prior experience, the optimal time for harvest was only days from now.

CHAPTER TWENTY

Jo's Day in Court

Her cell phone started ringing early the next morning... another flurry of calls from the Kessler Institute, plus one from a number Jo didn't recognize, all of which she let go to voicemail. The last message turned out to be from a physician's assistant at the University Hospital confirming labs ordered by Dr. Peterson, along with instructions on where to go and when. With her thoughts focused on how she was going to talk her father into it, Jo gave up on sleep. She got dressed and went downstairs to sit at the kitchen table with a cup of coffee and her laptop to continue her job search looking for any local openings in the legal field. She heard soft footfalls coming down the stairs and tensed, fearing catastrophe, but they remained steady.

"You're up early," her father commented as he entered the kitchen, wearing slippers and pajamas. "I thought you said they fired you."

"They did. I'm doing a job search." Jo stared at him, still not believing that he could converse in so normal a fashion. She watched him pour a cup of coffee from the pot she had just made.

"Any luck?" he asked, blowing the steam away before taking a sip.

"Not really. Most of the listings are for secretaries or paralegals. There's only one for an attorney, a research associate position downtown."

"Well, at least that one sounds marginally promising," he said, then spotted an unopened package of bear claws and made a beeline for them.

"Yeah, except I already applied for it and haven't heard back." Seeing him rip open the package of sweets, she raised her eyebrows. "Maybe you should try eating an apple, something more nutritious."

"Don't nag."

Her cell phone buzzed, vibrating alongside her laptop. Seeing Scott's name on the display, she answered and walked into the living room out of her father's hearing range. "Good morning."

"Hi. Afraid I've got some bad news," Scott said. "Beverly gave me a subpoena to serve on you. You know she's working for Dawson now, right?"

Jo sighed. "Yes, she told me. She got a raise."

"Don't be mad. She's still on your side."

"I'm not mad. Not at her, anyway. So what's this subpoena about?"

"I don't know. I was hoping you'd tell me when you open it."

"All right. See you when you get here." When she turned around, her father stood in the hall looking at her, a mug of coffee in one hand and a stack of bear claws in the other.

"Job lead?" he asked.

"No. That was Scott. He's on his way over."

"Is he now? You two sleeping together?"

"What? No. It's not like that." Heat warmed her face.

"Then why are you blushing?" He smirked and trotted up the stairs.

A half-hour later, Scott arrived and handed over a legal-sized envelope with her name and address on it. "You've been served. Sorry."

She ripped open the envelope. Inside, she found a petition for an emergency modification to the conservatorship for her father. She read the legal basis—alleged elder abuse due to denial of medical treatment. Dawson was handling the matter pro bono, representing the county. She shook her head, thinking of all the strings he must have pulled to accomplish that.

"Unbelievable." She shoved the papers at Scott to read. "Why can't they just leave us alone?"

Scott pursed his lips as he skimmed the petition. "Well, at least you don't have to hire an attorney."

She rolled her eyes at him. "I'm no expert on elder law."

"Okay. Got any friends who are?"

"Sure. Tons, but none of them can talk to me since they all work for Dawson. He has a whole family law department to back him up." Jo exhaled and crossed her arms over her chest to trap the anger inside.

"Yeah, that sucks." Scott tapped the papers atop his other hand, mulling it over. "But aren't conservatorships meant for people who are incapacitated?"

"Yes, that's exactly what they are," Jo replied, unable to keep the impatient tone from her voice.

"And you really think a judge is going to believe your father can't take care of himself?"

Jo blinked at Scott. "Oh my god, you're right." She smiled, picturing that dramatic reveal in court. "I just need to put him on the stand."

"All rise," ordered the bailiff as Judge Douglas Fordham strode into the courtroom in his black robes.

Jo stood and focused on the man who would decide her father's fate. Short and solidly built, his face was nearly as dark as his robes, bald and clean shaven, with deep intelligent eyes that sized her up in return. His gaze moved from Jo over to the plaintiff's side where Matthew Dawson stood with Suzanne Sutton. Fordham frowned at them all equally as he whipped the robe behind him and took his seat behind the bench.

"You may be seated," the bailiff announced then handed a file to the judge. "In the matter of Thomas Lorenzo Rinaldi."

Fordham flipped open the file and studied it for the time it took everyone to settle. When he looked up, he clasped his hands in front and peered down at the plaintiff's side. "Counsel?"

Dawson stood again and automatically smoothed his striped-blue tie and tugged the sleeves of his charcoal-gray jacket straight. "Matthew Dawson, Your Honor, representing the Plaintiff, the County of San Diego."

"Mr. Dawson, I see here that you're requesting an emergency modification to Mr. Rinaldi's conservatorship."

"Correct, Your Honor," Dawson answered.

Jo noted the expensive suit and tie, and the black leather shoes polished to a reflective glow. Seated next to him,

Suzanne Sutton looked his equal, dressed in a designer knit skirt and jacket, her make-up smooth and her blonde hair swept into a perfect chignon. Jo self-consciously pushed her unruly dark hair back from her face, painfully aware of the last-minute safety-pin repair to the hem on her department-store skirt.

She glanced back at the gallery, half-filled with people waiting for their cases to be called or just observing. One young man stood out to her due to his blue hair and the fact that he was scribbling madly with a stylus on a notebook tablet in his lap. She watched him, puzzled by his evident interest. He glanced up, caught her eye and smiled, then returned to his note taking.

She didn't see Dr. Kessler anywhere.

"And who is the person next to you?" the judge inquired of Dawson.

"Suzanne Sutton, representing the interested parties of the Kessler Institute for Geriatric Care and Neurological Research, and the San Diego Conservatorship Society," he replied.

Guess Kessler lets Sutton do all his dirty work, Jo concluded. She recognized the first party, of course, but had no idea who the second one was. Not that it would change her defense strategy.

"Very well. You may proceed," the judge said.

"Thank you, Your Honor. Pursuant to Probate Code Section 2651, we are petitioning the court to remove Mr. Rinaldi's current conservator for cause and replace her with the San Diego Conservatorship Society. We filed with the court a report written by an Investigator with the Office of the Public Conservator, which concludes that Mr. Rinaldi's daughter is unfit to act as her father's conservator. The investigator reported that Mr. Rinaldi was being cared for at the Kessler Institute up until the morning of November 16, when his daughter went to great lengths to remove him from said facility against his doctor's advice. To accomplish her aim, she set off a fire alarm, causing the evacuation of the facility's patients and staff. Then while impersonating an employee, she grabbed Mr. Rinaldi's wheelchair and pushed him across the parking lot to a waiting vehicle where her accomplice shoved Mr. Rinaldi inside and sped from the scene, all while ignoring Mr. Rinaldi's cries for help and without regard for his personal safety."

Jo saw Judge Fordham's eyebrows inch higher as he listened. At the end, he scowled and turned his attention to Jo. "Is this true, Ms. Rinaldi? Did you in fact abscond with your father in the manner just described?"

Jo rose to her feet. She hesitated a moment, but had to answer truthfully. "Well, yes, although I wasn't the one who set off the alarm, but—"

Dawson spread his hands wide, distracting her.

She took a breath. "What Mr. Dawson has failed to tell you is that my father begged me to come home, and I had reason to believe he was being subjected to unapproved medical treatments. When I tried to have him released into my care, I was summarily evicted and barred from re-entering the facility. I had no choice but to take extreme measures to ensure his safety."

Fordham raised his eyebrows again. "Well, that's why we're here, isn't it, to ensure your father's safety. And now that you have him in your home, how are you doing that?"

"I've arranged for in-home care under the supervision of his physician, Dr. Peterson." She opened her briefcase. "I have receipts here from his doctor and caregivers."

"Your Honor, if I may?" Dawson brandished a document of his own. "I have a signed statement here from said same Dr. Peterson, the physician who has been overseeing Mr. Rinaldi's care since his forced removal from the Kessler Institute. I ask the court to accept this statement into evidence as well." He held the document out to the bailiff.

Jo followed it with her eyes. "Objection. Your Honor, I haven't been given a chance to examine that."

Fordham waived the bailiff to deliver it into her hands. Jo read the statement, frowned in annoyance, and gave it back to the bailiff, who then placed it before the judge along with her receipts.

Dawson wore a smug half-smile. "As you will note in his statement, Dr. Peterson says that Mr. Rinaldi lay in a near vegetative state for weeks after his abduction. Dr. Peterson recommended hospitalization and additional testing, all of which Ms. Rinaldi has declined. It is our understanding that instead of following Dr. Peterson's advice, she has kept Thomas Rinaldi at home and relies almost exclusively on care from unskilled helpers. We submit that Ms. Rinaldi has endangered her father's life by removing him from the Institute against his doctor's advice and continues to do so by denying him medical treatment."

Judge Fordham's eyebrows climbed high. "Ms. Rinaldi?"

She hesitated again, trying to formulate a response that didn't make her sound like an irresponsible lunatic. "I am honoring my father's wishes. I've tried to convince him to undergo the tests Dr. Peterson has recommended, at least on an outpatient basis since he adamantly opposes being hospitalized, but—"

"Your Honor, my apologies," Dawson interrupted, "the man she's talking about has Alzheimer's related dementia and is incapable of making sound decisions. Clearly, Ms. Rinaldi is either unwilling or incapable of performing her duties as his conservator."

The judge held up a hand and turned back to Jo. "Ms. Rinaldi, based on your own testimony and these documents evidencing the seriousness of your father's condition, I am inclined to rule in favor of the plaintiffs and appoint a new conservator to oversee his care. So unless you have something further to add..."

"I do, Your Honor. While I have no objection to being removed as my father's conservator, I submit to you that you must deny their request to appoint a new conservator on the basis that he no longer requires one."

Dawson turned toward her with an incredulous smile. "Excuse me?"

Jo ignored him and continued to address the judge. "With your permission, I would like to call my father, Thomas Rinaldi, to the stand."

"He's here?" Fordham asked.

"Yes, Your Honor. He's waiting outside."

"Holy shit!" exclaimed the blue-haired man in the gallery. A buzz of whispers followed.

"Quiet!" Judge Fordham's gavel came down with a crack. "I will have quiet in this courtroom. No more outbursts, young man."

When everyone fell silent again, Judge Fordham narrowed his eyes at Jo. "This better not be some misguided prank on your part, Ms. Rinaldi."

"No, Your Honor. I wouldn't do that."

"Very well." Fordham smiled for the first time. "Bailiff, please invite Mr. Rinaldi in."

The bailiff marched down the aisle, opened the doors and called out, "Thomas Rinaldi?" A moment later he marched back in with Jo's father following him. Scott trailed behind them, gave her a nod, and took a seat at the back while the bailiff and her father continued forward to stand before the judge.

"Sir, would you please state your full name for the record?" Fordham said.

"Professor Thomas Lorenzo Rinaldi, esquire."

"And are you the father of the defendant, Josephine Rinaldi?"

Thomas looked over at Jo. "I am."

"Well, this is a pickle, isn't it? I was led to believe that you were in the advanced stages of dementia, of feeble mind and body, and in need of twenty-four-hour care. Bedridden, in fact." He turned to Dawson. "That doesn't seem to be the case, now does it?"

Mouth slightly ajar, Dawson stared at Thomas.

"Counselor?" Fordham inquired.

Dawson looked back at the judge. "I, uh, I don't quite know what to say. I promise you that when those documents were filed, I believed Mr. Rinaldi to be in the condition described."

Fordham turned back to the admittedly aged, but obviously mobile man before him. "Professor Rinaldi, thank you for joining us. So, tell me, how are you feeling?"

"A bit perplexed to be honest. I've been through quite an ordeal, and my recall of recent events is somewhat spotty. I'm still trying to put the pieces together. I do remember being subjected to some extremely painful medical procedures while in the care of Dr. Kessler. Apparently they believed I had Alzheimer's, but once I got free of that place and had a chance to recover, my physical strength and mental clarity returned. So I think you might understand why, when these same said doctors want to subject me to additional tests—to cover their asses I presume—I'm not particularly keen on the idea."

"Yes, I can see why that would be the case," Fordham said. He frowned back at Dawson. "In light of this new evidence, would your clients care to withdraw their petition?"

Suzanne Sutton pulled on Dawson's sleeve and he bent down so she could whisper in his ear. The two entered into a heated exchange of hissed conversation. Jo relished the sight of Suzanne's face turning a rosy red.

"Counsel?" Fordham asked in a stern tone as the whispering continued, then whapped the top of his bench with his hammer. "Counsel!"

Dawson straightened to face the judge. "Begging your pardon, Your Honor. In light of Mr. Rinaldi's testimony, we withdraw our petition."

Fordham brought his wooden gavel down on the bench again with another resounding whack. "Case dismissed. Court will recess for ten minutes."

Jo breathed a sigh of relief as the judge stood and walked away from the bench.

"Glad that's over with," Thomas said. "Now how about we go find some place to eat? I'm starving."

She laughed and shook her head at his bottomless appetite. She thought he ought to be getting fat, but somehow he wasn't. "Fine with me."

She took her time, gathering up her papers, tucking them back into her briefcase, relishing how her very first court appearance had resulted in victory.

"That went quite well, didn't it?" Thomas said.

"It did." She smiled thinking she was finally going to receive some praise from him.

"Did you see how I handled that judge? Been a while since I've done trial work, but clearly I haven't lost my touch. Maybe I should take it up again."

She snapped her briefcase shut with more force than required but stopped herself from snapping at him. "Maybe you should."

He followed her as she exited the courtroom. Dawson and Sutton stood in the outer hallway, arguing. They immediately quieted and stared back at them. Jo looked away and kept walking. Out of the corner of her eye, she saw her father lift a middle finger.

"Dad!" she exclaimed in a horrified whisper and tugged him forward. "That's unprofessional."

"Fuck professional. This is personal."

When they rounded the corner, Scott was waiting.

"That was fun," he said. "Did you see everyone's faces when he walked in?"

Jo thought it odd he hadn't joined them inside the courtroom and was about to mention it, but the blue-haired notetaker from the gallery jumped in front of her. A grim expression came over Scott's face and he backed away. The man in front of her wore a big lopsided grin and held his cell focused on her face, evidently recording.

"Can I get a statement?" he asked.

"No, thank you. Please, go away."

"Are you going to sue the Kessler Institute? We're talking medical malpractice, right?"

"Absolutely," Thomas answered.

Blue-hair pivoted his phone toward Thomas. "So what do you think was wrong with you then, if it wasn't Alzheimer's?"

Thomas shrugged and shook his head. "I'm really not sure."

The young man focused the cell back on Jo. "Did you think he had Alzheimer's?"

"No comment." She looked around for Scott, but he seemed to have vanished.

The man thrust a business card at them. "Check out my feed. I'm going to make you famous."

"We're really not interested," she told him, but Thomas took the card. When the elevator doors opened, she grabbed her father's arm and pulled him inside, leaving Blue-hair behind.

"Think he was serious?" Thomas asked, studying the card.

"About what?

"Me. Being famous."

Don't be ridiculous." Exiting on the ground floor, she felt her cell phone vibrate. She pulled it out and read a text from Scott.

[Getting the car now. I'll pick you up on the northwest corner.]

She showed the message to her father.

"He sure made himself scarce when that guy showed up." Thomas bobbed his bushy gray eyebrows. "It's almost like he's afraid to get his picture taken."

"He just went to get the car," she said, even though the same thought had occurred to her.

CHAPTER TWENTY-ONE

In the News

The front doorbell startled Jo awake. She looked at the numbers glowing on the clock and groaned—6:03 a.m.—barely light out. "Why do I keep getting woken up at ungodly hours?" she asked the ceiling.

She wrapped her fuzzy blue robe over her pajamas, grabbed her phone, and went downstairs. She froze at the bottom seeing the view through the living-room window. At least a dozen people stood on her lawn, plus there was a News 10 van parked out front. *What the hell?*

She hurried to the door imagining various crime scenarios, murder being the first. She recalled a screaming argument she'd once overheard between the neighbors next door, but dismissed the notion.

It's probably just a gas leak, or something.

When she opened the door, everyone on the lawn turned in her direction and moved toward her as if pre-choreographed.

At the front of them, a young man in a suit gripped a hand-held microphone and spoke into it. "James Kucher with 10 News. Are you Josephine Rinaldi?" He thrust the microphone toward her.

She thought she recognized his face. "Yes. What's going on?"

"We understand your father has had a miraculous recovery from Alzheimer's. Is he here? We'd love to interview him for our morning show."

She gaped at him, then saw a film camera pointed in her direction – ratty blue robe, hair uncombed, no make-up. She held a hand up to block her face. "I haven't given you permission to film me."

James waved the cameraman back, but kept the microphone extended. "It's all over Twitter how your father showed up as a surprise witness at his own conservancy hearing. Don't you want people to hear your side of it?"

My side? Why are there sides? She kept her hand in front of her face. "No comment."

Another news van pulled up and its door slid open spilling out more people armed with cameras and mics. Across the street, her neighbor's front door opened and the older couple who lived there emerged. She knew them, though not well. A group of four women walking by paused on the sidewalk to stare.

Jo pulled back. "I'm not interested in being interviewed. Please leave."

"I understand. How about if we give you a little time to think about it?" James said and waved his people back, but as they retreated the other camera crew rushed forward, heading for Jo.

"Oh no. No way." She closed the door in their faces.

Someone knocked. When she ignored it, they knocked again. "Go away!" she yelled.

"We just want to talk to you," someone yelled back.

"That does it." She pulled out her cell phone intending to call the police, and felt it buzz with ignored calls and unread texts. Then it rang in her hand showing a number and caller name she didn't recognize. She tapped decline and dialed the police.

"9-1-1. What is your emergency?"

"People are trespassing on my property. Can you send someone?"

"Have they threatened you?"

"No, but they won't leave."

"So you'd like an officer to come to your home?"

"Yes, please."

The dispatcher took her name and confirmed her address. "A unit is on the way."

Jo ran upstairs to change—putting on a pair of jeans, a long-sleeved top, and sneakers. She tied her hair back, washed her face and brushed her teeth. Dabbing on pink lipstick, she heard the doorbell ring and hurried downstairs again. She squinted through the peephole. Seeing a uniformed officer, she opened the door.

"Josephine Rinaldi?" he asked.

"Yes. Thank you for coming. Can you make all those people out there leave?"

"Probably not." He turned aside to point. "They're on public property."

She scowled and stepped outside to look. The reporters had left her lawn to surround a man on the sidewalk. She gasped. The man, who was smiling, talking, and waving his hands with enthusiasm while surrounded by reporters, cameras, and microphones, was her father.

"Oh my god. What is he doing?"

"Having fun, it looks like." The officer crossed his arms over his chest and watched.

Jo shook her head. "No, they're taking advantage of him. That's my father. He's not well. I need to get him inside and you need to make them all leave."

"He appears to be acting of his own free will, and, as I said, they're on a public sidewalk."

Jo thought for a moment. She still had papers stating that she was her father's conservator with guardianship over his person. The judge had dismissed the case seeking a new conservator but had said nothing about invalidating her as the current one. "Wait here, please." She ran to get the papers and showed them to the officer. "Now, can you help me?"

He looked them over but shook his head. "I don't know, Miss. Unless someone presents a danger to themselves or others, I really don't have cause to intervene. Why don't you just go talk to him?"

She frowned at all the cameras, reporters, curious neighbors, and gawking strangers, reluctant to insert herself into the middle of what looked like a circus, but her father stood in the center of it and who knew what he was saying.

"Dammit," she cursed under her breath, then marched toward the crowded sidewalk with the policeman trailing her.

"Let her through, please," the officer said.

Thomas turned and scowled at them. "What's the problem, officer? I'm just talking to some friends here."

"Your daughter called." The officer glanced over at Jo.

Thomas glared at her. "You called the police?"

"Dad, these people are not your friends, they're reporters. Talking to them isn't a good idea."

"I'm perfectly capable of deciding what is or is not a good idea."

Jo put a hand on her father's arm. "I'm just trying to protect you. You need to come inside."

Thomas pulled his arm away. "I don't need protection. Go inside and hide if you like. This has nothing to do with you."

Jo held her temper, barely, the personal dig not lost on her. "This isn't about hiding, it's about using some common sense. These people don't care about you, they're just looking for a story."

"And I have a pretty good one and the right to share it if I so choose. They came here to see me, not you, so why don't you just run along?" He turned around to face the cameras again. "So as I was saying..."

Seeing him turn his back on her filled her with a rage that overwhelmed her normal reluctance to bring attention to herself. "How dare you?!"

He looked back at her, eyes widening.

"I'm not one of your stupid little star-struck students. They might be willing to kiss your ass, but I'm the one who's been wiping it when you couldn't make it to the toilet in time. I'm the one who's been juggling work and doctors and caregivers, trying to keep you out of trouble when you wandered into other people's homes and went driving off without a license. You have no idea what I've been through just to keep you fed and clothed and safe from your own craziness. And for what? Have I ever gotten one word of thanks? No! Never. Not one. All I ever get are insults." She stopped on a screeching note, and inhaled to get her breath back, blinking away angry tears.

The reporters looked from her to him and back again, microphones aimed to catch every word.

Thomas stared at her for a long pregnant pause. "Daughter, do you have any idea how ridiculous you sound?"

She wanted to scream. Instead, she clenched her teeth and balled her hands into fists, tempted to punch him, knowing she couldn't. Neither could she walk away and accept defeat. Determined to win this showdown, she turned to the police officer, hoping he would follow her lead.

"If I understood you correctly, when someone is a danger to themselves, you can take them into custody and place a hold on them for psychiatric evaluation for up to seventy-two hours—is that correct?"

The officer glanced at the cameras. "Well, yes, but—"

"You wouldn't!" Thomas exclaimed.

"Don't test me. If you don't get back in that house right now and stop making a fool of yourself, I absolutely will."

"This is outrageous!" Thomas turned to the reporters. "I can't even stand in front of my own home and talk to you fine people out here without fear of persecution. Threatening to have me arrested. Can you believe it? My own daughter."

The police officer attempted to intervene. "Sir, I think there's been a misunderstanding."

Jo didn't let him finish. "I'm not just your daughter, I'm also your conservator. Now do as I say and go inside. You're making a scene."

"*I'm* making a scene?" He laughed. "Oh, God forbid I should be an embarrassment to you." He turned back to the others. "Forgive me, everyone, but at the risk of abuse at the hands of the authorities, not to mention my own flesh and blood, it seems I must excuse myself. Put that in your story. Good day."

Head high, he marched back into the house, and slammed the front door behind him.

Jo thanked the bemused police officer and hurried after her father, dreading the fireworks to come.

Instead of the hot explosion she expected, she got ice. He disappeared in his room upstairs without another word, locked his door and didn't come out again. When she knocked and tried to talk to him, he refused to answer.

Having gotten what they'd come for, a juicy story, the reporters abandoned the street outside, and drove away in their vans and the gathered onlookers dispersed. Relieved, Jo decided she could still make it to her afternoon interview. When the nurse showed up, Jo knocked on her father's door and announced she was leaving.

"Do you need anything?" she asked.

"Not from you," he answered.

"Okay. Well, your nurse is here, and I'll have my cell phone if there's any problem. Wish me luck."

Silence.

Jo's interview didn't go well, even in her own estimation. She was too distracted, thinking about all that had occurred that morning and worrying about what else might be happening in her absence. The attorney interviewing her frowned through most of it. She thanked him for his time and left, figuring she'd never hear from him.

Back home, Jo's day stretched into evening with no communication with her father. William, the nurse, traveled back and forth with plates of food. After dinner, William left and Jo sat downstairs, working on her laptop, extending her job search to include farther and farther distances and leaving messages with every contact she knew. If she didn't find work soon, they were going to be in serious financial trouble. She had student loans to pay, the mortgage was due next week, and unpaid medical bills sat stacked on the counter. Her father's monthly pension and what remained in their combined savings weren't nearly enough to cover it all.

Jo took a break, flipped on the six o'clock news while searching the fridge for something to eat. She froze hearing her father's voice coming from the TV. She turned to see herself and her father arguing on the sidewalk in front of their house. "Oh my god," she moaned, watching the whole ugly scene play out. With his silvered mane and oratory manner, Thomas looked and sounded like an enraged lion. She on the other hand came across as a bitter shrew.

When the film ended, her father harrumphed behind her. She hadn't realized he was standing there. He shook his head at her, set down an empty plate and walked back upstairs.

A deep sense of shame washed over her. She'd aired their personal issues in public, exactly what she'd been trying to avoid. She'd lost it in front of the whole world. She was embarrassed, of course, but still convinced that getting him away from those reporters had been the right thing to do. She thought about going up to him now and saying exactly that, but her cell phone vibrated on the counter first. She glanced at the screen prepared to deny another unsolicited call, then saw it was Scott.

"I take it you caught our performance," she answered.

"Yep. Not exactly your finest moment."

"Thanks. I really needed to hear that."

"Sorry. The real reason I'm calling is I want you to meet someone from the animal labs at the Institute."

She frowned, uncertain. "Why?"

"I'd rather explain afterwards. Any of those reporters still hanging around?"

"I don't think so. Not since this morning."

"Okay, good. We'll come in through the back just in case. Say in about an hour?"

"Yeah, sure." She hung up, disappointed at his impersonal tone. What was his story, anyway? Sometimes he flirted with her, the next he was all business. She couldn't get a clear read on him.

CHAPTER TWENTY-TWO

New Friends

When Scott showed up with a bearded young man, Jo was surprised to see two young women in tow, both dressed in short skirts and abbreviated tank tops. The man had his arm around the shorter one with dark curly hair. The other, a freckled redhead, stood tall enough to peer over her friend's head. The women looked like cartoon opposites, but their outfits gave off a similar 'party' vibe.

Scott made introductions as they entered. "Josephine, meet Jacob, his girlfriend, Maggie, and her roommate."

"Jessica." The redhead finished for him.

"Right."

Jacob—eyebrow ring, beard, torn jeans, wire-rimmed glasses, and a striped, buttoned-up shirt—nodded hello and offered a shy smile. A would-be rebel living a conformist life, she decided.

"Heeyyy!" the two women chorused in greeting, then walked past her on into the living room where they plopped side-by-side on the sofa. Jacob followed them into the room but didn't sit.

Jo turned back to Scott and mouthed, *"What the fuck?"*

"Package deal," he replied softly, then raised his voice to normal again. "So where's your dad?"

She slid the glass door shut. "Upstairs, sulking. He's been giving me the silent treatment since I put a kibosh on his big moment in the spotlight. He's also mad because I unplugged the landline. It was a nightmare, ringing non-stop. Newspapers, magazines, TV... they all want a piece of him now."

Scott frowned, his eyes glancing around the room as if expecting to find someone lurking in a corner. "Can you get him to come down?"

"Think you'll have better luck leaving me out of it."

"Okay, we'll give it a go then." He stepped toward the living room. "Hey, Jake, let's go up and see Mr. Rinaldi. The girls can wait here."

As Jacob and Scott clomped up the stairs, Jo resigned herself to hosting her uninvited guests.

"Would you like something to drink?"

"Sure. Got any beer?" Jessica asked.

"I do. And for you?" Jo looked at Maggie.

"A beer sounds great, thanks."

"Be right back." Jo retrieved two beers from the refrigerator. She forgot to ask if they wanted glasses but brought them anyway. She put the glasses and beers on the coffee table in front of them, then sat in the leather armchair next to Jessica. The tall redhead seemed all legs with her glittery skirt hiked up, while petite Maggie wore tall leather boots. The two women were obviously dressed for a night out. They popped open their cans, poured, and smiled. She smiled back, feeling plain in the steel gray pantsuit she'd worn to her job interview this afternoon. Her awkward discomfort turned slowly into resentment.

Why are these women here? Package deal might explain why Jacob's girlfriend tagged along, but what's up with this other one?

"Super nice place you have," Maggie said. Her big silver hooped earrings caught the light as she looked around. "I just love old houses like this."

Jo saw them taking in the gold-hued room with its Mission furnishings, all in her mother's signature style. Frank Lloyd Wright would have felt right at home.

"Ooh." Maggie pointed up and the other woman tipped her head back. "Is that what you call a coffered ceiling?"

"It is." Jo knew from counting them as a child that there were eighty wood-grids, each two-foot square framing three decreasingly smaller squares within. Her mother had said it was one of the main reasons she'd fallen in love with the house.

"Wow, that's so cool." Maggie said and repositioned her curly hair as she looked down again. "Have you always lived here?"

"No." Jo found herself tucking back her own hair. Maggie looked at her expectantly as if waiting for more information. "I moved back in when my mother got sick."

"Oh, I'm sorry. Is she okay now?"

"No, she died, which is why I'm still here. Taking care of my father."

"Right. Sorry, I didn't mean to pry. I was just... you know." Maggie grimaced.

"Making conversation?"

"Yeah, I guess. You don't need to explain."

"Speaking of your dad. We saw you on the news this morning," Jessica said. "Got pretty crazy, huh?"

"Don't remind me." Jo offered a raised eyebrow, hoping to appear amused rather than humiliated. She searched for somewhere else to take the conversation. "So, how did you two become roommates?"

Jessica answered. "We met in school and ended up working at the same place, so it just made sense." She poured the beer into her glass at an angle to keep the foam down. "Maggie's like a sister to me. How about you? You got any siblings?"

"No." Jo kept her answer to one word, both the truth and a lie.

"Just you, huh, and this is the house where you grew up?" Jessica asked.

"Yes, well, partly. My parents wanted to be close to where my father was teaching and thought the neighborhood would be good for me... fewer drugs I guess." *Why am I talking so much?*

Jessica laughed, a high-pitched sound Jo found annoying. "Oh right, like drugs aren't everywhere."

Her words stung, but Jo kept her expression neutral. "I wouldn't know."

"Good for you, then," Jessica said.

"Yeah. Some of us have to learn the hard way," Maggie added in a tone that suggested personal experience.

Jo changed the subject. "So, you and Jacob then?"

"Uh huh..." Maggie replied with a smile. "Almost a year now."

"I have a boyfriend, too," Jessica said. "but he's a little old for me so I'm keeping my options open. To be honest, I'm kind of liking this Scott guy." Jessica leaned toward Jo, lowering her voice as if they were confidants. "This is our second time out."

"You're on a date?" Jo asked, incredulous.

"Well, sort of." Jessica looked to her friend for an assist.

Maggie explained. "I made Jacob promise to take us all out to dinner after this."

Jessica nodded. "Scott drove his own car, so I was thinking if things go well, I just might let him take me home tonight." She smiled coyly, waiting for Jo to smile back. When it didn't happen, she said, "I know most people say you should wait till the third date, but sometimes two's enough, don't you think?"

Jo cleared her throat. "Well, personally, I think three is still a good rule. Four, five even. You can't really get to know someone that fast and opening yourself up too soon can—" Jo stopped herself. Scott was a free agent. Though clearly much younger than she was, this was a grown woman she was looking at. Personal fantasies aside, it wasn't any of her business. "Don't mind me. I'm a little old-fashioned."

"You're sweet." Jessica leaned forward and patted Jo's knee.

Jo barely stopped herself from smacking that hand away, as she imagined grabbing Jessica by her long red hair and twirling her around like a baton before slinging her out the door. "Thanks."

The two women sipped their beers and the conversation dragged. Jo tried to keep her fingers from drumming on the wide wooden arm of her chair as her jealousy grew.

Finally, she heard Scott and Jacob coming back down the stairs. Jacob rushed into the room and startled her by dropping to his knees right in front of her.

"Holy freakazoid, your dad just blew my mind," he said as his hands mimicked an explosion on either side of his head. "It's like he was never sick at all. Do you have any idea what this means?"

She looked at Scott, not sure how to answer, but Jacob didn't wait.

"Kessler's cured him. He's—"

Maggie interrupted. "You don't know that."

"Yeah, I do. You should go talk to him. You saw what he was like before."

"Hold on." Jo turned to Maggie. "You know my father?"

Jacob answered for her. "Didn't she tell you? Maggie was his day nurse. She's the one who got his medical records for you. And I was the one who set off the alarm so you and Scott could get him out."

"Jacob, shush," Maggie hissed, sliding her eyes sideways at Jessica.

"Babe, relax, we're all friends here." He turned back to Jo. "Jess and Maggie are both nurses there and I work in the lab with Scott." Jo scowled at Scott. He'd been working in the labs there? This was all news to her. Jacob went on without pause. "We use transgenic model mice that mimic a range of Alzheimer's symptoms. We inject re-engineered stem cells directly into their hippocampus. Most of them end up dying, but a few responded like your dad—"

"Jake!" Maggie yelled. "You're going to get us fired."

Jo scowled, digesting what Jacob just said. "So all of you work there and you think Kessler injected my father with this same stuff?"

"Looks like it," Jacob said, his excitement undiminished. "I'm not really sure, but whatever he did, it obviously worked."

"Has it worked for anyone else?"

Jacob's smile left his face. "I—I don't know."

Maggie put her palms out, as if to stop a truck barreling down on her. "Oh my god, Jacob. Why don't you think before opening your mouth?"

All eyes in the room turned to Maggie.

Jessica rose to her feet. "We should go."

"Not yet," Jo countered. "Maggie, are you aware of other patients who've received this same treatment?" Jo waited until Maggie lowered her hands and looked back at her. "You need to answer me."

"No, she doesn't," Jessica said.

"How many?" Jo asked, keeping her eyes glued to Maggie's.

"I don't know. Four, five... maybe more. I'm not exactly sure."

Jo looked over at Scott. "I think we'd better find out... exactly."

Scott nodded, his expression grim.

Jo cocked her head at Jessica. "Anything you'd like to add?"

"You're meddling in things you know nothing about," Jessica said, clearly indignant. She grabbed her purse and turned to Scott. "Take me home. Now."

He smiled in surprise. "What? Why me? You came here with them."

She frowned at him. "Because. Because it's the gentlemanly thing to do."

His smile turned into a smirk. "Whatever made you think I'm a gentleman?"

Jessica glared at him.

Maggie pointed a finger in Jacob's face. "I told you this was a bad idea." She stood and took Jessica by the arm. "Come on." The two women went out through the sliding glass door, leaving it open in their wake.

"Maggie?" Jacob twisted on his knees. No answer came. "Dammit!" He scrambled to his feet. "Sorry," he said to Jo and Scott, then ran after the two women, calling for them to wait up. The three disappeared into the dark with Jacob's pleas fading into the distance.

"Did we just break up a couple?" Jo asked.

Scott walked over to the door and slid it shut. "Nah. Jacob will bring her around. Not so sure about her friend though."

"You mean your date? Jessica." She waited for his reaction.

He made a face. "Not exactly a date. You hired me to investigate remember, and she's involved so I needed her here. Nice job getting Maggie to open up there, by the way. You're obviously good at being a lawyer."

"Glad you think so. Too bad nobody else does." She gestured toward her computer displaying a job search website. "Haven't been able to find anyone willing to hire me yet."

"Screw 'em then. Open your own practice."

"Oh sure. I'll just hang out a shingle and start chasing ambulances."

"Hey, don't knock it. I hear that actually works. I could help you catch them, if you like. I'm pretty fast on my feet." He did a little quick step in demonstration.

She laughed. "I'll keep that in mind."

"Seriously, though, you doing okay with all of this?" He came over and sat on the end of the sofa across from her. "Couldn't help notice you kind of lost it with those reporters today."

"Yeah." She looked aside. Her gaze landed on the stack of unpaid bills beside her computer. "Let's just say my future doesn't look all that bright at the moment. No shades required."

He half smiled at her weak attempt at humor. "Sorry to hear that, but you must have contacts... people you can call?"

"I thought so, too. It's amazing how fast people disappear when things go south."

"Yeah, I get that." He leaned forward onto his elbows and looked at the floor. "But sometimes you just have to move on, you know, make new friends, ones you can actually count on."

Jo wondered if he was still talking about her. She realized she knew next to nothing about him. "Someone like you?" she asked.

He straightened. "Yeah, sure. Me. And Beverly. She's still your friend, even if she is working for Dawson right now. And I hear that attorney Carl's been going around saying how he thinks you got a raw deal. And of course, there's your dad, though I admit he's not real happy with you at the moment."

"What did he say exactly?"

He shook his head.

"Come on, I can take it. Tell me. I insist."

"Okay, but only if you promise not to blame the messenger this time."

When she nodded, he took a breath. "Okay, I'll try to get this right. To begin with, he thinks you were out of line with him today and he's pretty steamed about it. Then he went on to say how you never listen, you just withdraw. I believe his exact words were, 'It's like talking to a clam.'"

Jo smiled at Scott's impromptu impression of her father. "A clam? Ha. Is that what he thinks? I learned early on arguing with him is useless, so I may as well shut up."

"Not exactly what you did this morning."

"No, I guess I kind of exploded."

"Yes, you did. It was quite impressive, actually. And a little scary."

"Well, he's not exactly easy to get along with. He pushes and pushes, like he's never satisfied, no matter what you do." She took a breath to tamp down her emotions again. "He seems to like you, though. Maybe that's one reason I shouldn't." She raised an eyebrow.

"Ooo... harsh. Besides, what's not to like?" Scott spread his arms wide.

"An excellent question," Thomas said as he walked into the room. "Exactly what I was wondering."

"What are you going on about now?" Jo asked.

"I've been doing a little investigating of my own."

"Sorry. Is there a problem?" Scott asked.

"Apparently. I couldn't help noticing how averse you are to the press, which seems unusual for someone in your profession. I would think you'd enjoy the publicity, but you run every time. Also, sometimes you're a little too congenial, a little too flippant, like you're putting on a show. It's an engaging one to be sure, which gullible young women like my Josie here no doubt find seductive, but it raises suspicion in someone as discerning as myself. So I decided to run a background check on you and the results are quite interesting."

He slapped a printout on the coffee table in front of Scott.

"Turns out your real name isn't Scott Benson, though you didn't stray far. It's Benjamin Scott. Your father, Hector, is a medical researcher at Washington University in St. Louis, and your mother, Julia, is a chemistry professor. You're no low-brow P.I. You have a bachelor's degree in biology and were well on your way to earning a master's, when for some mysterious reason you dropped out and enlisted in the Army. You did two tours and when you got out, you changed your name, moved here to San Diego, and started working for a private detective agency."

Scott regarded Thomas for a moment before spinning the papers around and reading. He turned them back again and looked up. His expression stayed flat. "Yeah, so?"

"If you're trying to disappear, it didn't work. There's a paper trail. Why did you change your name? And why in the world would someone with your educational background be sneaking around spying on people?"

"That's my business... literally. I'm good at it, I like it, and that's all you really need to know."

The two men stared at each other like a pair of bulls deciding whether charging the other was warranted.

Thomas was the first to blink. He harrumphed and tapped the papers again. "Extremely unusual behavior in my opinion."

Scott offered a slow, humorless smile. "Depends on your point of view."

"Is that all you have to say?" Thomas asked.

"For now."

"There's more to it then. Which means either you don't trust us enough to share the truth of the matter or feel no obligation to. And the way you keep avoiding the press tells me it's nothing to brag about."

Scott blew out a rush of air and rubbed a hand over his head. "I should be going." He stood and looked at Jo. "I'll call you later," he said, then left via the sliding door to the backyard, the same as the others. Jo watched him meld into the dark, heard the gate open and close with a metallic clink. Only then did she turn to her father.

"What the hell, Dad? He's been nothing but helpful. Why would you do that?"

"I see the way you look at him. You need to know exactly what kind of man you're dealing with. He's hiding something. I won't sit back and watch you make another mistake."

"I got a divorce—that doesn't make me an idiot." She heard the rising pitch of outrage in her voice and took a long breath. "Please, this is so not your business."

"Of course, it's my business. I'm your father."

CHAPTER TWENTY-THREE

Higher Ups

As Senator Randall Pike read his morning summary of national and global news, he noted a curious uptick of interest about medical research, spurred by a story that originated in San Diego about a man diagnosed with Alzheimer's who appeared to have experienced a total reversal of the disease after being treated at the Kessler Institute for Neurological Research. He called in his clerk Patrick, a young grad student from Yale, Pike's alma mater, and the author of the daily news summary he found on his desk each morning.

"Have you sourced this San Diego story?" Pike asked.

The young man nodded. "It started out in a feed from a social influencer, then hit the regular news."

Frowning, Pike sat back in his chair. "Is Reginald Howell still in town?"

Patrick made a face, demonstrating his familiarity with the man's unpleasant reputation. "I think so, why?"

"Get him in here. I want to talk to him."

When Howell received a call from Senator Pike's office requesting his presence, he wasted no time showing up. Being solicited by a US Senator was a rare event. He was usually the one begging for an audience, not the other way around.

As he rode a cab from his hotel to the Capitol building, he was in a buoyant mood thinking Pike must be responding to the recent industry polling reports he'd sent him. Since their ad campaigns started, phone surveys showed a marked improvement in public opinion about prison privatization, citing its rehabilitation programs and reduced recidivism numbers, and then the big reveal about backing Alzheimer's research gave their ratings a huge boost. Things were turning around. He hoped it would be enough to convince Congress to shelve the proposed regulations currently stalled in Pike's committee. Perhaps Pike was planning to tell him just that. Anticipating good news, he walked into the senator's office wearing a smile.

"Didn't you tell me your doctor was close to finding a cure for Alzheimer's?" Pike said, skipping over the social niceties.

Howell's smile froze on his face. He knew better than to stutter an unprepared answer before understanding why Pike was suddenly so interested. "Is there a problem?"

"You tell me." Pike threw the printout across his desk to land at Howell's feet.

Howell picked up the page from the floor and read a headline circled in yellow, "San Diego Man Cured of Alzheimer's" then skimmed the article looking for names, stopping on the Kessler Institute. His smile returned, and he looked back at Pike. "It's okay. This is our guy, the researcher we're backing."

"Then why haven't you taken credit? Whatever happened to publishing results in medical journals and holding press conferences? This only came to light because some blogger posted a video of a man testifying at his own conservatorship hearing."

Howell had no idea what was going on. He did, however, know that Suzanne Sutton had left a message asking him to call. A call he had yet to make. His mind raced to come up with a response that made him appear in control of the situation.

"Don't worry, I'm already on top of it. I'm flying out tomorrow to meet with Kessler to determine the best way for him to come forward."

Pike's mouth turned into a knowing smirk. "I can always tell when you've been caught with your dick in your zipper. That good ol' boy act of yours goes clean away."

Howell grimaced. "I will fix this."

"You'd better. I didn't stick my neck out for you for nothing. You said it would pay off."

"It will, it will... trust me. You're not the only one counting on it."

CHAPTER TWENTY-FOUR

Howell

Suzanne Sutton paced the floor in her office, taking measured breaths, trying to calm her nerves. Reginald Howell was due here any minute, and she had no idea how much he knew or what demands he would make on them. He'd never returned her call, but last night she received a text informing her he was taking an early flight out from D.C. to meet with Dr. Kessler. She'd called back immediately, but he didn't answer. Teaching her to know her place—his policy of telling her what she needed to know when she needed to know it.

She spun angrily on one heel to cross the length of her office again. A wisp of hair came loose from her chignon and fell across her cheek. In a rush of panic, she hurried over to her desk and pulled out a standing mirror and box of hairpins. She nailed the stray hair back in place, and checked for anything else amiss. The lines around her eyes and mouth deepened with her frown, but she still considered herself a handsome woman, not delicate or particularly feminine perhaps, but attractive enough to warrant unsolicited advances, the reason she still wore her wedding ring six years after becoming a widow. The only man she wanted to take notice of her was the one she worked for. Her icy exterior easily held most men at bay, but Howell took a perverse joy in treating it as a challenge.

Her stomach knotted when she spotted him walking into the lobby. Short, fat, with his face flushed to pink, he reminded her of a cartoon pig stuffed in a suit. She knew he could only see his own reflection in the one-way mirror through which she viewed him, but he smiled and waved in her direction. Rather than let him corner her inside her office, she hurried out to greet him.

"Reginald." She extended her right hand and he squeezed it between his clammy ones. She struggled to keep her smile intact and not pull away. "Shall we?" She gestured with other hand toward the elevators, hoping to hurry this along.

Howell patted her captured hand. "Oh yes, my dear, yes, we shall." He finally released her and waved her forward.

"Let Dr. Kessler know we're on our way," she said to the receptionist, then walked ahead. Behind her, Howell wolf-whistled softly and she bristled inside. When the elevator doors opened, she entered and turned her backside to the wall.

"Lookin' good, Suzie, lookin' good," Howell said as he followed her in. "That tight little skirt o' yours really accentuates the positive."

Looking down on him, she smiled again. "Sweet of you to notice."

"Well, now that's my forte, ain't it? Noticin' things, I mean. Like who's tellin' me the truth and who ain't." Howell kept smiling, but his eyes were cold.

Suzanne knew they were in trouble. When the elevator opened, he waited until she took the lead again. There was no whistling behind her now, just the sound of soft footfalls following her, too close and too quiet, like a predator, making the hairs on the back of her neck lift. She had to stop herself from instinctually spinning around. Kessler's door stood open, and they entered without knocking. Inside, the doctor was on his feet looking out at the ocean. When he turned to them, Suzanne sucked in her breath. Uncombed hair, wrinkled clothing, unshaven... for days it appeared. She hadn't seen him since the judge ruled against their petition on Friday. This was Monday. *Did he stay here all weekend?* She wanted to ask but refused to embarrass him in front of someone else.

Howell had no such reservation. He barked a laugh. "Looks like you got rode hard and put away wet."

Kessler ran a hand through his hair and tucked in his shirt. "I've been working is all."

"Well, it seems to have paid off. Word is you've gone and cured someone. What I'm wondering is why you didn't tell me. And why you haven't announced it."

When Kessler glanced over at Suzanne with a pleading look in his eyes, she stepped forward. "The man I assume you heard about was one of our patients, but he left us several weeks ago. We only learned of his recovery when everyone else did. As for alerting you, I left several messages."

Howell scowled at her. "You could have been more specific." He sat down in the chair and sighed. "So you lost control over one patient of yours. That's unfortunate, but hardly earth-shatterin'. You've got plenty of other patients."

Kessler removed his glasses before answering. "Yes, but we haven't seen the same result in anyone else yet."

"Yet. So is it just a matter of time?"

Kessler squeezed the bridge of his nose and stared at the floor, letting his glasses dangle from his other hand. "Possibly. The odds of success improve with each widening of test subjects so being more inclusive as I have been increases that possibility but it's still difficult to say. He may be unique in some way that's made all the difference. The injections are customized for each recipient based on their genetics which makes it nearly impossible to analyze the results in his absence."

Howell half-smiled in disbelief. "Are you saying that you cured someone but don't know how you did it?" When neither of them spoke, Howell's face reddened, and his voice rose. "How the hell is that possible?"

Kessler shoved his glasses back on. "This is your fault. You forced me to take shortcuts."

Howell snorted. "Oh no, no, this is on you. How was I supposed to know you're were feeding me a pile of horseshit? So what was your big plan, anyway, or did you even think that far ahead?"

Kessler glared back. "Don't underestimate me. My plan as you put it was to widen the field, increase my chances of hitting the right combination in at least one subject, after which I could reverse engineer it and generalize the treatment to a wider population. And I succeeded. I created my patient zero. I just need to get him back here."

"Okay." Howell tapped his hand on the rolled arm of the chair. "So what's stopping you?"

Suzanne answered. "Mainly the daughter. She's keeping him isolated."

"We have to get him back. Time is of the essence," Kessler said.

"Fine." Howell turned to Suzanne expectantly. "I'll need whatever information you have."

Prepared, Suzanne handed him a thumb drive. "It's all there—names, addresses, phone numbers, everyone coming and going from the house, including some of our own employees." She smiled bitterly at the last. "I haven't fired anyone as yet, so they're still unaware they're under surveillance. Mr. Rinaldi lives with his daughter, Josephine. She's the real problem. She's his conservator, and an attorney. She's hired a private investigator, who has a rather complicated history. He might be your best bet."

Howell enclosed the thumb drive in his fist and smiled. "Good work. I'll have this Rinaldi guy back to you by the end of the week."

Kessler nodded and exhaled in relief. "That's all I need." He turned away and stared off at the ocean as if they had already left.

"Thank you," Suzanne said to make up for Kessler's lack of cordiality, and stood to leave.

"My pleasure, Suzie Q," Howell said as he rose to join her. "You know I've always enjoyed working with you. I'm looking forward to when we can get together again so you can thank me properly." He slid a hand around her waist as he spoke, then paused to look back at Kessler who stared out the window. Howell leaned close and lowered his voice. "Is he okay?"

"He's fine," Suzanne replied stiffly, barely stuffing down her revulsion. She too looked at the doctor now turned away from them, lost somewhere in his own world. Where was the man who once would have jumped to her defense? "He has a lot on his mind."

Howell nodded but didn't look reassured. "Keep an eye on him. We have a lot riding on this."

Scott turned off his lights to go to sleep just as his cell phone rang. He grabbed it off the nightstand hoping it might be Josephine, but the screen displayed a number he didn't recognize. He would have let it go to voicemail but seeing as the phone was already in his hand, he answered. "Scott here."

"I'm callin' to make you an offer, Mr. Benson," said a man with a mild southern twang.

Crap, a telemarketer, Scott concluded. "Look, buddy, whatever it is you're selling..."

"Not sellin'— hirin'. You are a private investigator, right?"

Scott sat up. "Yeah, that's right. What's this about?"

"I'm in need of a particular service, somethin' which you are uniquely qualified to provide."

"And what would that be?"

"Access to one Thomas L. Rinaldi."

Scott laughed. "What? Are you a reporter or something?"

"Why don't we talk about how much I intend to pay you?"

Scott smiled, ready to turn him down. "It'd have to be a hell of a lot."

"Fifty thousand now, fifty thousand on delivery. Is that a lot?"

A hundred thousand dollars? That's like hit money. "Um, yeah, I'd say so." Curious, Scott decided to play along. "So what exactly do you mean by delivery?"

"Simply return him to the Kessler Institute."

"Sorry, not happening. He's not interested in going back there, believe me."

"Oh I do. But you won't take 'no' for an answer."

"You know I can trace this call."

"Don't waste your time. It's a burner. Better you should worry about what happens if you refuse. I'm told there are some very dangerous people interested in learnin' the current whereabouts of one Corporal Benjamin Scott. Be smart, soldier, take my offer. Not only will it make you a lot of money, you'll still be around to spend it."

A sinking sensation grabbed Scott's gut. "Who is this?"

"Someone who doesn't make empty threats. The only question you should be asking yourself right now is would you rather be alive with money in the bank, or dead broke—with the emphasis on dead—in which case I'll just have to hire someone else. Someone with fewer qualms. I'd prefer Mr. Rinaldi be returned unharmed, but either way, he will return." The caller paused to let that sink in. "I've deposited the money into your account—you can verify that. The other half will show up when the job's done. Agreed?"

Scott held his breath, hoping some inspired flash of brilliance would jump to mind, showing him how to escape the corner he'd been painted into. It didn't.

"Yeah, okay," Scott said, hoping he was just buying time.

"If you need muscle or an unmarked van, I can provide."

Muscle? An unmarked van? Shit! "No, uh... I have my own resources."

"Good. You've got three days," the man said, then the line went dead.

Three days. Scott pulled up his bank account on his cell phone and checked the balance. Sure enough, it showed a deposit in the amount of $50,000, more money than he'd seen in a long time, but it didn't make him glad. On the contrary. It scared the hell out of him.

CHAPTER TWENTY-FIVE

Mountain Maneuvers

Jo's packed bag sat by the front door. Scott's call propos-
ing to whisk them away to a mountain retreat came as a
surprise but also a welcome relief. The continual media
harassment was driving her crazy. A little peace and quiet
in the woods sounded wonderful, and if she were being honest with herself, so did the opportunity to spend some alone
time with Scott.

"Dad? You ready? Scott will be here any minute. Dad?"

"I'm here, I'm here," Thomas grumbled as he came down
the stairs with a ratty old suitcase. "I'm still not sure why
we're going."

Jo marveled how easily he negotiated the steps. "We discussed this already. You might be enjoying this media
circus, but I'm not."

"Fine, fine." He waved his hand to silence her as he set
his suitcase down next to hers. "All locked up?"

"Yes, I checked everything."

"Good, good." He nodded. "I'll just double-check."

She rolled her eyes as he went about the house testing
doorknobs and tugging at windows. He returned with a golf
club and jammed it in the frame of the sliding glass door
leading out to the backyard. "There. No one's getting in here
now," he declared.

"No, not unless they break the glass."

He frowned at her. "Why are we leaving again?"

She smirked back. "Bet you're wishing you'd let me put
in that security system now."

"Phhh... waste of money, and those things are always going off when you don't want them to."

The doorbell rang. Jo took a breath, made her face into
the picture of nonchalance, then opened the door. *Oh my.*
Hip-tight jeans, unbuttoned striped shirt over a white T
snug enough to show off his abs. She pulled her gaze up to
Scott's face. He raised an eyebrow.

"Ready?" he asked.

"Yes," she replied, hoping it wasn't obvious just how ready.

The drive up to the local mountains took them along a winding route of treed hills and open meadows layered in lush green hues and patches of white lying frozen in the shadows. Their destination, the old mining town of Julian, was better known these days for its apple pies than for the gold mine that gave it birth. On weekends and whenever snow fell, the place turned into a tourist trap, beloved for its quaint western décor and eclectic shops.

Scott, normally taciturn, displayed a nervous energy, entertaining them with stories about his investigative adventures—everything from locating lost pets to accused murderers. "You meet a lot of interesting people in this line of business, everyone from the scum of the earth to the upper crust. Take the guy who owns these cabins in Julian. He's a tech tycoon with a gigantic ranch in Poway. He was in the middle of a bitter divorce and custody battle when I met him. His kids are young and there was a lot of money involved, so he hired me to find dirt on his ex."

"Lovely," Jo said with heavy sarcasm.

"Yeah, I know, but he's a good guy, and she was... well, trust me, things went the way they should."

"Trust you," Thomas said from the backseat. "A difficult request seeing as you still haven't explained yourself."

Scott glanced up so their eyes met in the rearview mirror. "Well, that's kind of what I've been trying to do here, but okay, fine, what do you want to know?"

"First of all, what exactly are you hiding from?"

Scott shook his head and smiled. "What makes you think I'm—"

"Don't," Thomas said with no trace of humor.

Scott closed his mouth and drove on in silence. Jo turned her attention from the rolling hills to stare at Scott. She knew he could see her scowl in his peripheral vision.

"What is it?" she asked.

He glanced at her, twisted his mouth in resignation and said, "Okay, fine. Let's just say, I made some enemies awhile back."

"And you believe they're still holding a grudge?" Thomas said.

"Oh yeah," Scott replied in a bitter tone.

There was definitely a story there. "Do you want to talk about it?" Jo asked.

"Yes. No." He gave her a quick smile. "I will, I promise, but not right now, if you don't mind. It's such a beautiful drive. I don't want to spoil it." He looked at Thomas in the rearview mirror. "Professor, I bet you have some great stories. Did you always want to teach?"

Thomas barked a laugh. "No, I was a litigator for years and quite successful at it."

Though concerned by Scott's obvious ploy to change the subject, Jo wasn't willing to force him into an interrogation... not yet.

Her father, always quick to jump on any invitation to occupy the spotlight, rose to the occasion, regaling them with tales of his courtroom victories, then on to his career of intimidating students as a law professor.

"Nearly wet his pants, that one. Dropped out the next day. And a good thing, too. If you can't field questions in the safety of a classroom, you'll be useless in court when lives could depend on it. I made it my business to root out the weak. I take great pride in that."

Jo felt sorry for the student. Who knew what he might have achieved, given a little respect and empathetic guidance instead of scalding derision? But that wasn't her father's way. He believed in trial by fire. She knew what it was like walking over those coals and doubted she was any better for it. The old resentment threatened to raise its ugly head, but she shoved it back into the depths before Scott could witness it.

After a pleasant afternoon of meandering through the town's western-themed shops, then enjoying hearty dinners followed with fat wedges of Julian's famous apple pie, Scott finished their drive up to his friend's cabins hidden in the forested hills north of town. Tall pines, and branching oak trees sheltered three separate log cabins with wood porches. Lit wall lamps showed them the way down a twisting path of flat stones.

Scott unlocked the door to the first cabin and flipped on the overhead light. Thomas glanced around the rustic room. "Oh wonderful. Drafty log cabins in the middle of winter. No heat, no phone, no TV, no internet. This should be fun."

"Yeah, sorry, not exactly the Hilton," Scott said.

"No, it's perfect," Jo replied and meant it, even though it was cold enough inside that she kept her jacket on. She put her suitcase down on a worn wooden bench at the foot of the bed. "I love it, really."

"Good. I'll go open up the other two cabins and check back to see if you need anything."

Thomas rolled his eyes and followed Scott out.

"Try enjoying the quiet," Jo told him then closed the wood slatted door, letting its black metal latch fall into place. The cabin was definitely chilly inside, but spotlessly clean, and equipped with a fireplace of promised warmth. A Native American tapestry, striped horizontally in brown with a blue diamond in its center, hung on the wall above a knotty-pine four-poster bed covered with a patched quilt. Lace runners ran across the top of a wide bureau and dripped down the sides of two bedside tables, holding knobby white glass hurricane lamps. An interior door with a worn brass knob led to a small bathroom equipped with a mirrored medicine cabinet above a white pedestal sink and an old-fashioned pull-chain toilet. Next to the toilet perched a claw-footed tub with a circular shower curtain. The small window above the tub was dark, but should reveal the trees outside come daylight.

"All the comforts of home," she said to no one.

Returning to the main room, she noted with disappointment that the rock-surrounded fireplace was empty of wood and there was none stacked nearby. A red-handled axe leaned in the corner.

"Guess we're supposed to chop our own," she observed but couldn't picture doing that unless it were a matter of life and death, especially not in the dark, so she gave up on the idea of a fire and went to unpack her suitcase. She set her clothes in the drawers and arranged her toiletries in the bathroom. She pulled out her electric teapot, found an outlet in the wall and plugged it in, looking forward to having something hot to drink. While waiting for the water to boil, she thought about Scott, and his promise to return to check on her, wondering how to conduct herself. Wondering how he would conduct himself. Was this his idea of a romantic get-away, or not? Her father being included didn't point to it, but he had his own cabin, so maybe it did. She didn't know what to expect. Should she go outside, check on her father? Wait here for Scott to show up? Would he show up?

Feeling antsy with the need to do something, she re-zipped her jacket, intending to at least step out the door to look around when came a knock.

"It's me," Scott said. "Came to light your fire."

She grinned, unzipped her jacket, and opened the door. He held a large stack of wood in his arms.

"Oh, firewood," she said, her grin fading. She stood aside to let him enter.

"It's going to be a cold one, tonight," he said, "but once I get your fire going, it should warm up in here pretty fast." He set the wood down, got on his knees in front of the fireplace and started stacking logs inside the sooty interior. "I got your father all set up, so he should be good for the night."

"Great. I was just about to make tea,'" she said. "Would you like some?"

"If it's hot, I'm game."

By the time Scott had flames licking up the sides of the logs, she had teabags steeping in a pair of steaming mugs. Scott poked the flames higher, then stood to take the mug she offered. He sipped and nodded. "Mmmm... I'm not much of a tea drinker, but this is pretty good. Thanks."

"No, thank you. For the fire and the cabin. I really needed to get away from all that craziness. The quiet here is such a relief." She let out a nervous laugh.

"I can imagine." He turned to face her, holding her in his gaze.

The door was closed against the outside world. With no television, phone, or internet service, and her father probably already asleep, there was nothing and no one to interrupt whatever was or wasn't about to happen. The fire crackled sending out shimmering sparks. A fire of anticipation burned nearly as hot inside her as they stared at each other. *Alone at last*, the old cliché hit her, and she felt her face flush. Despite her best efforts to control her thoughts, she imagined him ravishing her like some muscled hero in a cheap romance novel, an embarrassing admission even to herself. Instead, to her chagrin, he turned away. He sat on the bench at the foot of the bed, took a deep breath as if to speak, but then just blew it out again and stared at his mug.

"You look like you have something to say," she prompted.

"Yeah." He set his mug down and planted his hands flat on either side as if bracing himself. His right knee bounced with nervous energy. "There's um, some stuff about me you should know."

She took a breath herself. She'd wanted him to open up and now it looked like she was about to get what she'd asked for, but it didn't look like good news. "Okay. What kind of stuff?"

"Stuff I'd rather not talk about, but it's better you should hear it from me."

Resigned, Jo sat next to him and waited.

Scott sighed and rubbed his forehead. "Okay. To start with, I'm an addict."

She stiffened.

"Recovered addict," he amended quickly. "I'm not using anymore, haven't for years, but—you know, once an addict, always an addict—so I have to be careful."

"I see." She pursed her lips and nodded, covering her growing inner turmoil by adopting her advocate personae. "So what and when did you last use?"

"Opioids. Years ago. Back in college. Tried to stop on my own, but I had all these druggy friends back then and I was under a lot of pressure."

"And you thought drugs were the answer?"

"No. Yes. I don't know. I didn't think of it like that. I'd been programmed early on to follow in my parents' footsteps. My father made a name for himself in bio-medical research and my mother taught chemistry, so I grew up surrounded by all these like-minded people. It was all I ever really knew and for a long time I just went along even if it felt wrong."

Jo looked away. This was sounding all too familiar.

"It wasn't that I couldn't do the work or thought it was boring, but it was never something I particularly enjoyed. And working in the animal labs at the university really got to me. I was hating what I was doing more and more and using seemed like an easy escape, harmless enough at first, but of course it escalated and one night I overdosed. My mom found me and called 911. They'd had no clue till then."

He waved a hand as if dismissing the event. "Obviously, I lived through it, but realized things had to change and I was trying to do that, trying to make new friends, change up my routine, figure out what I wanted to do with my life. But all that stuff takes time, and my father is not a patient man. He gave me an ultimatum. Either go to rehab, which he generously offered to pay for, or move out, which of course he wouldn't pay for. He figured I'd take option number one. Obviously, he didn't know me very well." Scott paused to laugh at himself. "God, I was so angry. I marched right down to the local Army recruitment center and enlisted." He shook his head. "Can't say it was the best decision I ever made, but on the plus side I've been clean ever since."

"Oh. Well, that's good then. You should be proud." She knew those were the right words to say, but the weight in her gut hadn't budged, not because she didn't believe him, but because the scowl on his face told her he wasn't finished. "I take it there's more?"

Scott let out another big sigh and nodded. "Yeah. It's about what I mentioned before, about making enemies. Something bad happened when I was over in Afghanistan. Actually, a lot of bad things happened, but there was this one time in particular." He looked around the room, rubbing his head again. She could see what a struggle it was for him to go on. "Okay, so anyway, we got a report that this village was hiding insurgents and went in. We followed procedure, cleared all the buildings. We'd been told there were only a couple dozen people living there, but it turned out to be a lot more.

"We had the men on their knees, hands behind their heads, women hanging onto kids. The men were arguing with us, women wailing, kids crying. It was chaotic, tense, and we were badly outnumbered, trying to interrogate them, figure out which were terrorists, which were just villagers caught in the middle. There are no hard lines over there, no way to know for sure."

Jo pulled images she'd seen on television to create a picture in her mind. "Sounds terrifying."

"The women there wear these long skirts, all that damned fabric..." He sounded angry. "You can't always see if they're hiding something. A shot went off, one of our guys hit the dirt and everyone started shooting. It was only seconds, but..." He stopped and stared at the floor.

"You're talking about civilian casualties," she said.

He nodded. "A lot wounded, some dead. Women and kids screaming and crying. I said, 'I'm calling it in' and the next thing I knew, I was on the ground with a rifle pointed at my head. My own lieutenant."

"Oh my god."

"I'll never forget what he said to me. 'We were told to clear this village and that's exactly what we're going to do."

"They killed them?"

Scott nodded. "He ordered us to bury the bodies, then he filed a report saying the village was empty when we found it. And that was that. Or at least it would have been if I hadn't gone over his head and filed my own report. Guess whose version the Army preferred?"

"His, I assume."

He nodded again. "Especially when the other guys backed him up. I started sleeping with my gun, watching my back. When the investigators couldn't reconcile my story with theirs, they asked if I was on drugs again. I wasn't, but they discharged me anyway and sent me home for psychiatric treatment. My dad didn't believe my story either. So I left, came here, changed my name and started over."

"I'm so sorry," Jo said, at a loss. "Your parents, do they know where you are now, what you're doing?"

He shrugged. "They know I'm alive, that's all."

Jo thought about what he'd told her, but it didn't answer everything. "My dad and I noticed that whenever the press shows up, you disappear. Do you think you're in danger?"

"Threats were made. Not sure how serious they were, but I'd rather not find out by having my mug all over the news."

Jo smirked. "I can understand that. Every time I see Dawson in the firm's TV commercial, I get murderous thoughts."

Scott laughed. "That's different. In your case, it's totally justified. He's a dick. I hope you know Beverly hates working for him. She misses you."

"I know. I miss her, too. Even those sexy outfits of hers. You know she tried really hard to get your attention with that yellow one, cut down to here and up to there." Jo pointed midway down her chest and half-way up her thigh.

Scott snorted. "I noticed. I've been thinking I should introduce her to a friend of mine, Eddie, the P.I. who first hired me. Think they'd get along. Maybe I'll fix the two of them up when all of this blows over."

"Right. When it blows over," Jo said, but wondered when that would be, if ever, with her father being stalked by news-hounds and medical researchers looking for clues as to why he seemed to be growing younger and stronger each day. When would that stop? Jo remembered the story of Benjamin Button aging backwards in time until turning into a newborn. She shuddered at the idea and pulled her thoughts back to what Scott had just said, something about the private investigator he first worked for. "So why P.I. work anyway? What made you interested in that?"

"I don't know. Fate, I guess. I had no plan when I moved here, no idea what I wanted to do except that I didn't want to be locked up in a lab ever again. I just needed a job, so when I saw an ad for a process server, no experience necessary, I thought, 'Perfect. No experience is exactly what I've got.' Turned out tracking people down was a lot more interesting than I expected and it ticked off a lot of boxes for me. The work took me places I never would have gone otherwise and let me meet people in all walks of life. Eddie, the guy who hired and trained me, started giving me more and more challenging assignments. I started making good money and got a kick out of delving into people's deep dark secrets. Worked with law enforcement and helped put some bad guys away. It felt good putting my military skills to use in a positive way, so I guess it all kind of meshed."

"And now your background in lab work helped as well."

He laughed. "Yeah. Never saw that coming."

"Maybe your specialty should be investigating malpractice and pharmaceutical manufacturers. Not many people have your combination of expertise."

"Maybe we could partner up. You know, you do the court stuff, I do the legwork." He slid a hand over her thigh. "Get it?"

"Yeah, I get it." She didn't smile.

"Sorry." He removed his hand. "That was stupid, especially after I just dumped all that heavy stuff on you."

She let the silence hang.

"I should probably go. Thanks for listening. And not judging me." He got to his feet. "If you need anything, I'll be next door. Goodnight, Josephine."

It touched her the way he liked to use her full name. No one else bothered. She didn't want him to leave. "You're wrong about that. I'm definitely judging you. It took courage to share all that."

"Ha. Tell me about it. I'm still shaking." He held out a vibrating hand as proof, but the trembling was overblown and theatrical, covering up whatever tension was really there.

"Seriously, I'm glad you trusted me enough to tell me." She stood to face him. "Makes me think partnering up might not be such a bad idea."

"Oh, yeah?" He smiled, then paused. "Now are we talking professionally, personally or both?"

"Well, both possibly. But seeing as my career is a question mark at the moment, that just leaves the personal part for now."

"That makes sense."

They stood several feet apart staring at each other, tension building, neither one making a move.

"So, am I still leaving...?" he asked.

"I'd rather you didn't."

"That's a relief." He closed the gap and pulled her to him. Their lips met. His hands slipped under her clothing and she slipped free from her jacket and blouse, then started undressing him.

He broke off from kissing her but didn't pull away completely. "Wait, this isn't fair. I haven't told you everything yet."

Too eager to stop, she tugged his pants open. "Please. Tell me later. Not now."

"Okay." His hungry mouth and hands returned to her, and she didn't have to ask again.

CHAPTER TWENTY-SIX

A New Plan

The next morning Jo woke to bright sunlight and an empty bed. The door to the bathroom was closed, so she listened hoping to hear Scott moving about in there, but all was quiet. He was gone. She frowned, annoyed that he'd snuck out without telling her. Scenarios ran through her mind—maybe he went for a walk or back to his room for a change of clothes, or made himself scarce so as not to embarrass her by having her father see him leave her cabin—all perfectly plausible legitimate explanations. Still, he could have given her a heads-up. *Men.* She exhaled in disgust and threw the covers off her naked body just as the cabin door swung open.

"Ooh. Nice," Scott said. "Promise me you'll do that every time I enter a room."

She snatched the covers back self-consciously, silly considering the fact that he'd explored every inch of her last night. But that was in the flattering light of a flickering fire. This was ruthlessly honest daylight.

"Brought you some coffee," he said, brandishing a thermos as he closed the door.

She saw that he'd changed into a blue long-sleeved shirt and his hair was damp. "You could have showered here."

"I didn't want to wake you, plus I needed to talk to your dad."

"Why? Wait, what time is it?" she asked.

"A little after ten."

"Ten!" She bolted upright, clutching the blanket over her chest.

"It's all right. I kept you up pretty late, as I recall—no need to thank me."

Not really listening, she jumped out of bed, dragging the blanket with her. "I can be ready in ten minutes, fifteen max."

"There's no rush and you don't need that." He yanked the blanket away.

Exposed, she instinctively wanted to make a mad dash for the bathroom, but knew how ridiculous she'd look, so settled for crossing her arms over her chest. He shook his head and smiled.

"It's cold in here," she said.

"No, it's not." He wrapped her in his arms. "I don't want you to hide from me."

An embarrassed smile crept over her lips and she buried her hot face in his chest so he couldn't see it.

"Not sure you're getting the message." He tipped her chin up.

"Okay, okay. No hiding."

"I'm not just talking physically. You need to tell me what's going on in your head. I'm not a mind reader. When I opened that door, you were pissed. I saw it in your face, but instead of telling me off, you swallowed whatever was bothering you. If I'm in the doghouse, I want to know why."

"You're not. It was nothing. Really." She squirmed to free herself, but he held on.

"There you go again. Ever heard of radical honesty?"

"Sounds painful."

"A little, but in a good way. It eliminates misunderstandings and prevents that old relationship killer known as festering resentment."

Jo blinked up at him in surprise. "Just how much therapy have you had?"

"Enough to know better than to accept a non-answer. Last night was an example of radical honesty—I shared something painful with you because it's important that you know who I am and what you can expect from me. I need that same kind of honesty from you. So why don't you start by telling me why you were angry just now."

"I wasn't, I was just..." She stopped at seeing his raised eyebrow. "It's just that when I woke up alone, not knowing where you were or why you'd left, if I did something wrong or... you have no idea what runs through my head when there's a vacuum of information."

"Ah." He nodded, knitting his brows together. "Good to know. So, no vacuums."

"Right." She had to laugh at herself now. "No vacuums."

He stared off into the distance over her head, as if lost in thought, running his palms over her bare back.

"Um, Scott?"

His eyes refocused on her.

"Are you going to let me get dressed?"

"Seems a shame, but if you insist." He released her and stepped away. "I'll be outside."

Jo was good to her word—showered, dressed and out the door equipped with a steaming mug of coffee in under fifteen minutes. Scott was waiting outside, as promised, sitting in one of the bentwood chairs on the porch. He glanced at his watch. "I'm impressed."

"No make-up," she said.

"None needed." He waved at the other chair. "Come sit. I have more radical truths to share."

"Uh oh. I thought you were done with the deep dark confessions."

"Not quite. Afraid I got a little distracted last night."

She chuckled at that and sat down next to Scott, "As distractions go, it was a good one."

"I thought so, too."

As they shared flirtatious smiles she saw her father walking towards them down the stone path. Uncharacteristically dressed in jeans and a hunter green sweatshirt, he looked more casual and relaxed than she could remember seeing him in a long time. She leaned over and whispered in Scott's ear. "Should I get him to leave?"

Scott shook his head. "No, he's part of this and I already talked to him."

She didn't know what to think about that but waited.

Thomas stepped up onto the porch. "Have you told her yet?"

"I was just about to," Scott replied.

"Oh good. I didn't want to miss this," her father said with a knowing smirk. He leaned against one of the porch posts and crossed his arms.

Jo scowled at them both. "Okay, you two, what's going on?"

"I warned you he was hiding something," Thomas said, looking extremely pleased with himself.

Unfazed, Jo glared daggers at her father, then turned back to Scott, certain she could trust him. How could she not after his heartfelt confession last night, followed by hours of intense lovemaking? "Ignore him. What is it you need to say?" She held her coffee in both hands and waited for Scott to speak.

"Okay." Scott let out a breath and looked directly in her eyes. "I already told you about that burial site." She nodded. "What I didn't tell you is someone unearthed it a few weeks ago, corroborating my story, so now they want me to go back to D.C. and testify at a hearing. I've agreed, but if any of the guys I plan to testify against find me first, things could get ugly."

"Oh." She put a hand on Scott's knee. "So that's why we're up here? You're hiding from them?"

Scott grimaced. "Not exactly. The truth is we're here because I need your help and I wanted to get you to a secure location to explain."

Jo hesitated, trying to puzzle out what he was saying.

"Two nights ago, I received an anonymous call demanding that I deliver your father back to the Kessler Institute."

"What?" Jo shot an alarmed look at her father.

Scott sighed. "I refused, of course, but ..."

The sound of her father chuckling pulled her attention to him. She realized he was enjoying this, taking pleasure in her confusion. She gave him another angry scowl and turned back to Scott.

"But what?"

"But then he said, if I didn't do it, certain parties would be informed of my whereabouts and—"

"Oh no. That's terrible. How can we help? Do you have a plan?"

"Yes, actually I do."

"Good. Let's hear it." She took another sip of coffee, willing herself to be patient even as he and her father exchanged another annoying set of looks.

Scott let out a long breath and stared at his hands. "My plan is to make it look like I'm cooperating."

The sound of an approaching vehicle made Jo turn to look. A windowless black van was driving toward them down the dirt road.

"Crap. They're early. I wanted more time to explain," Scott said, frowning at the oncoming van.

"Explain what? Who are they?"

"Don't worry. They're friends of mine," Scott answered. "They'll be the ones taking you to Kessler. We need to stage a kidnapping, a fake one."

Jo spluttered a laugh, choking on her coffee. "Is this a joke?"

"I wish it were," Scott replied without an ounce of humor.

Jo looked at the oncoming van in alarm, her heart quickening. She jumped up and would have bolted, but for Scott standing and grabbing her arm.

"It's okay, Josephine. You're safe, I promise. No one's going to make you do anything you don't want to."

The doors of the van opened on either side and two men got out—two very large men. The taller one had a normal fit build, while the other bulged with muscle. He looked like he could mow down an entire football team on his own. Dressed head-to-toe in black, the pair walked toward them, ski masks hiding their faces. All she could see were their eyes.

"If they're friends of yours, why are they wearing masks?"

The men stopped and stood in front of the porch. "We're professionals, Ma'am," the taller one said, legs apart, clasping his hands in front like a soldier at-ease. "We need to protect our identities."

"Can you blame them?" Thomas asked.

"Yes. Yes, I can." Appalled, she looked at her father, expecting him to share her concern. To her surprise, he wore a grin.

"Come on, Josie," he said. "It'll be fun."

Jo gaped at him. "What are you talking about? Nothing about this is even remotely fun." A new worry formed in her mind. "Are you regressing?"

Thomas's impish grin vanished. "No, I'm not regressing. Is that what you're going to think every time I say something you disagree with?"

"Come on, Dad, even you have to know this is crazy. We have no idea who these people are."

"They're Scott's friends. Why do you have to be such a wet blanket?"

Scott waved his hands between them. "Okay, okay, stop it you two." He turned to the men. "Guys, what's with the masks? Are you trying to freak them out?"

The man who'd spoken unclasped his hands and shifted his weight. "Just getting into the role." He tugged the ski mask off and rubbed his short blond hair back.

Jo immediately recognized him. She pointed at his face. "I know you. You're that cop who pulled us over."

"Officer Frank Meadows, at your service," he said. He looked at his partner. "You going to take that off?"

The other man stood firm and crossed his arms. "Hadn't planned on it," he replied in a deep baritone.

"Seriously? You're going to keep that on the whole time?" Scott asked.

The man still wearing the mask let out a long breath. "Fine." He ripped it off, revealing a broad flat-nosed face and shaved head. He looked at Jo through narrowed eyes. "You don't know me, and I'd just as soon keep it that way."

She nodded, overwhelmed into silence for the moment. Adrenaline fading, she dropped back down into the chair lest her knees fail.

Scott kneeled before her, so their eyes were level. "I just need you to hear me out. Okay?"

She didn't know if it was okay or not.

"They need to think they've forced my hand. The man who called me said if I don't deliver you, he'll just send someone else, someone we don't know and have no control over. That's what I'm really worried about."

"He could have been bluffing," Jo said.

"It's possible, but I don't think so. And I sure wouldn't want to bet your lives on it."

"But you can't be certain."

Scott sighed, clearly reluctant to share this next bit of information. "I'm certain because he deposited $50,000 into my account and promised the other half when I delivered. That's serious money, which means he can get this done with or without me. This way, we're one step ahead of him. We can do this on our own terms. I have people I trust waiting for you on the inside, and we'll put a wire on you so we can listen in and record everything. We figure it's safest if you wear it, since it's your dad Kessler wants to examine."

"But if they only want my dad, how are they going to react when I show up? They already kicked me out of there once."

"You're pretty much inseparable and the most likely person to raise an alarm so it makes sense for us to deliver you both. Plus, I think Kessler might be glad you're there. You're Thomas's closest living relative and he'll probably want a blood sample, maybe a brain imaging scan."

She scowled at the concept of subjecting herself to examination, but how could she refuse after everything her father had already endured. "So you want us to pretend to be kidnapped?"

"Yes, but you won't be alone. The three of us here will be listening the whole time to make sure you're safe."

"Will we be?"

"I wouldn't do this if I didn't think so. Thomas is the most valuable patient Kessler's ever had, living proof that these injections of his can reverse Alzheimer's Disease. He might want to run more tests, but I can't imagine either of you would be in any real danger. You said you wanted to find out how many other people Kessler has experimented on. This is your chance to do that. You need to get him to talk, get him on record. And get his files. The private ones he keeps in his lab."

"How? I could only access one floor when I was there before."

"Don't worry. We have a workaround."

Jo shook her head. "You know this isn't anything close to what I had in mind. I was talking about getting the authorities to investigate, not me personally."

"I know, but they're not about to investigate anything until we convince them something is wrong. As far as everyone else is concerned, Kessler's a hero, a genius, the self-less doctor who's cured your father. Doesn't exactly make you look like the injured party."

"He's right, you know," Thomas interjected. "Remember how crazy you looked on the news the other day. You're the troublemaker, fired for lying to your employer."

"Hey!" she objected. "I never lied to anyone."

"By omission, you did. You failed to mention you were investigating a client. Face it, everyone thinks you've got a screw loose and that you're mean to your poor father to boot. That's probably why you haven't gotten any job offers. Scott might not be the only one in need of a new identity."

"Oh really, and what about you? Or maybe you enjoy seeing your face plastered all over the news."

Thomas grimaced. "I admit to relishing the attention at first. We all know I thrive in the limelight, something perfectly natural for —"

"A ham, a narcissist, an attention-seeking asshole?" Jo offered.

"An extrovert! The word is extrovert," Thomas said, glaring at her.

"Oh, well, thanks for clearing that up. You can understand my confusion."

"Wow." Scott said, his head turning between them. He sat back on his heels. "You two really have issues."

It took a moment to rein herself in. "Sorry," Jo said, embarrassed now.

"You sure this pair can work together?" asked the big man who had wanted to remain anonymous. "You didn't mention they were at war with each other."

"We're not," Jo turned her still simmering anger on him. "We're just unnerved by all of this. And who are you to be judging us?"

"Fair enough." He stepped onto the porch and dropped into Scott's vacated chair. Laying his ski mask on his thigh, he looked out at the rustling oak trees. "You can call me Jerome."

"Not your real name, I'm guessing,"

The edge of a black tattoo peaked out above his turtle-neck. He kept his face in profile to her, eyes scanning their surroundings. "You've never done anything like this before, which means we have a lot of ground to cover."

Jo looked at Scott for reassurance.

"He knows what he's doing. That's why I asked him to run this operation."

She laughed. "Operation? Is that what this is?"

Scott shrugged. "Call it what you like. Point is, we're the good guys, they're the bad guys, and this is how we prove it."

"And where will you all be while this is going on?"

"Close," Jerome said.

She struggled to wrap her mind around putting herself and her father at risk. But if what Scott said was true, they already were. Someone out there was ready to use any means necessary to get control of them, with or without Scott's cooperation. She had to admit Scott's plan held merit. By making it look as if he were complying, they might control the outcome. *Assuming he's telling the truth.* The possibility he might be lying was too horrifying to contemplate.

"I don't know," she said, stalling for time to think.

Her father let out an impatient grunt. "Well, I for one am not going to sit around waiting for some hired guns to show up when I least expect it. If I have to face Kessler, I'll do it under my own terms and with backup. That's what Scott's offering."

"Exactly." Scott nodded in confirmation. Down on his knees in front of her, he looked ready to propose, but there was nothing romantic about this offer. "So what do you say, Josephine?"

Jo examined the faces of the men surrounding her—Scott's worried frown, Frank's raised eyebrows, the impassive profile of 'Jerome', and finally the impatient scowl of her father. She narrowed her eyes back at them.

"Fine. Just tell me what I need to do."

CHAPTER TWENTY-SEVEN

Kidnapped

After several hours of instruction, Jo and Thomas climbed into the back of the windowless van. As they rode down the mountain, they sat in awkward silence each avoiding the other's gaze.

"Are you going to sulk the whole time?" Thomas asked at last.

She looked at him then. "I'm trying to avoid another argument. Plus, I'm going over the holes in this plan of ours," Jo said as she fingered the pin on her jacket. "Can't help wondering if we're making a mistake."

"The bigger mistake would be to do nothing. It's a good plan. Scott's watching out for us."

"I know why I trust him, but why do you?"

He shook his head. "Gut feeling I suppose. I've met a lot of con men and he doesn't fit the profile. People like that don't care who they hurt, and he obviously does. If it hadn't been for him, you might never have gotten me out of that Institute in the first place."

"You also wouldn't be going back there now."

"True. But I feel like I owe him and he's in trouble. I also agree with his logic. I don't want to be looking over my shoulder waiting for someone to grab me off the street."

"Wish Mom were here. She was always such a good judge of people."

"Was she? I don't recall her warning you not to marry a closet gay."

Jo's eyes widened in surprise. "How long have you known?"

"Right after you told your mother. She never could keep a secret from me. So my point is, you might consider me as good or better a judge as she was. While I may not have known Ethan's predilections before you married him, I was quite certain he wasn't the right man for you. Even told you as much. In retrospect, I should have kept my opinion to myself, or better yet, encouraged the marriage, then your knee-jerk reaction to do the opposite of whatever I say would have worked in your favor."

Jo couldn't deny that defying him had been a factor at the time, but she'd rather focus on what her father hadn't foreseen. "But the bottom line is that you didn't suspect it either. No one did, not even him. Guess that's the trouble with marrying young. You're still figuring out who you are."

"Surely there must have been warning signs—something off," Thomas said.

"If by off, you mean that he was kind and attentive and didn't judge me like you and every other man I've ever met, then yes, about as off as they come."

"I see. So you married your girlfriend. How did that work out? Still friends?"

"That's not fair." She glared at him. "And I don't hate him if that's what you're asking. Maybe if he hadn't moved to Seattle, we'd still have coffee occasionally."

"My. How magnanimous of you."

Jo frowned at his sarcastic tone and turned away. For the rest of the ride she sat with her arms crossed, relieved he didn't try to reanimate their dead conversation.

When the van came to a stop and the engine shut off, Jo's stomach fluttered. "Shit, we're here."

"Breathe," her father told her.

She nodded and took a breath, but her pulse quickened even more upon hearing the driver and passenger doors opening and closing. The backdoors swung open to reveal the dark parking lot behind the Kessler Institute. Frank and Jerome stood on either side of the doors, wearing their ski masks again, waving for them to get out. The same security guard she'd had the run-in with before waited beneath a red and white sign that said, Employee Entrance Only. Jo glared at him, but he kept his face blank, as if she were invisible. With Frank in the lead and Jerome behind, they followed the guard inside, down a hall, into a service elevator, up to the sixth floor, then finally to Kessler's office. The guard knocked, then walked away, never once having spoken or met her eyes.

Jerome rocked his chin up slightly and she activated the mic hidden in her jeweled pin. Then he opened the door for them to enter.

"Thomas!" Dr. Kessler exclaimed from behind his glass desk, opening his arms wide. "I'm so glad to see you."

Jo and her father shared a look, flummoxed by his evident cheer.

"Sit down, sit down," Kessler waved Thomas toward one of the upholstered chairs in front of his desk.

Jo took the other chair without being invited, while Jerome and Frank hovered at the back of the room. If Kessler was aware of anyone being present but Thomas, he made no indication. He sat again in his high-backed executive chair and leaned forward onto his elbows, smiling at Thomas, the only person in the room he seemed to see. "How extraordinary! Thomas, do you realize you are my first human subject to experience a sustained reversal of symptoms? This is exactly the breakthrough I've been waiting for." He laughed. "I can't tell you how delighted I am you chose to return."

"Chose?" Jo gestured over her shoulder. "These goons of yours threw us in the back of a van and drove us here."

Kessler's gaze moved to her, then to the men in the back of the room and he scowled as if noticing them for the first time. "Leave us!"

Frank and Jerome glanced at each other through the eyeholes in their ski masks, then walked out the door.

Kessler looked back at Jo. "You may go, as well."

Jo pointed from herself to her father. "Sorry, we're a package deal. I go where he goes. Nothing's happening here without my approval."

"You're the daughter."

"Yes, we've met. Remember?"

"Extraordinary achievements demand extraordinary sacrifice."

"So that makes it okay to kidnap us?" Jo asked, hoping to get his confession on record.

Kessler waved a hand as if to magically erase it all. "You need to understand how vital it is that I monitor his transformation. The last thing we want is for him to decline into senility again."

"You think that could happen?" Jo asked, alarmed by the suggestion.

Kessler scowled at her. "Yes, *entirely* possible. And if it happens it would be your fault. He needed to remain under my care, but you in all your medical wisdom dragged him out of here to be looked after by nurse's aides and a general physician." He spit out the titles as if they were insults. "It's a wonder he's still alive." Kessler turned back to her father and softened his expression. "Thomas, I've been extremely concerned about you. I need to keep a close eye on your progress."

"I spent enough time in this place already," Thomas said. "And what I remember wasn't pleasant."

Kessler erased the air again with his hand. "Yes, yes, I suppose but also remember why you came to me. You were dying—in the most humiliating way possible, slowly being robbed of your identity and any semblance of dignity. Without my intervention, that death would have been meaningless. Think of the millions of others out there with Alzheimer's. With you back here with me now, we can save them."

"That's all very noble," Thomas said, "but are you even certain that's what I had? Doctor Peterson thinks I may have been misdiagnosed."

"No. He has no idea what he's talking about. There's zero doubt. I'm certain you had Alzheimer's and it's vital that I preserve the evidence."

"It doesn't have to be here. He can get any tests you want done at any legitimate hospital," Jo said.

"Don't be a fool." Kessler glared at her again. "I, and I alone know what treatments were administered. Others may recognize he's undergone a transformation, but the reasons for it will be a complete mystery to them. He's my patient and must remain under my care."

"Why should we trust you after everything we've been through?" Jo asked. "Your administrator refused to even let me see him then she got me fired. That's the kind of *extraordinary*"—she did air quotes—"stuff going on around here. That's why I had to take *extraordinary* measures of my own, just to be sure he was safe. And he was. At home. With me.

Then you had the gall to sue for conservatorship, and when that failed, you brought us here by force. Maybe you're the one who needs a brain scan, Doctor."

Kessler pulled back and stared at her. The stare went on overlong until finally he blinked and cleared his throat. "Clearly, this has been badly mishandled." He picked up his phone and punched in a number. "Come to my office now." He set the phone down again and waited.

Jo watched the doctor as he sat with his lips pressed in a thin line, staring at his hands clasped on the desk with his thumbs bouncing off each other as if counting each second. It felt bizarre watching him sit there like that, but Jo was willing to wait to see what would happen next. After a few minutes, the door to Kessler's office opened and in walked Suzanne Sutton. Despite the late hour, she appeared as professional and polished as ever. Her blonde hair was swept up in a smooth roll and she wore a dark gray skirt and jacket over a simple white shell, adorned with pearls.

Jo narrowed her eyes at the woman.

Suzanne stiffened, then looked away to smile at Kessler. "You wanted to see me, Doctor?"

"Ms. Rinaldi here says she doesn't trust me and believes we had her fired from her job. Did you have anything to do with that?"

"I ...," Suzanne paused, then measured her words. "I mentioned to our attorney that one of his employees visited your office after hours, made some disrespectful comments and insinuated that we might be subject to a lawsuit. What he chose to do with that information was completely beyond my control."

"And did you bar her from visitation?"

"I did, yes. She was a disruptive influence."

"It appears then that you exceeded your authority."

"I'm sorry, Doctor, but it was my understanding that you—"

Kessler held up a palm to silence her. Seeing the flush in the other woman's cheeks, Jo reveled and hoped Kessler would fire her. *See how you like it.*

"We'll discuss this later," he said. "Call Matthew Dawson and see if there is any possibility of getting Ms. Rinaldi's job back for her. And as long as her father is here, she is to have free run of this facility. Understood?"

"But—"

"Is that understood?"

"Yes. Yes, of course," Suzanne replied, her cheeks a bright crimson now. She bit her lips together until they nearly disappeared.

"Good. You can go."

She nodded with her eyes cast downward and glistening, then hurried out the door.

Once again he waved his hand in the air like a magic eraser, then smiled at them. "My apologies. It appears in a moment of weakness, I may have shared some personal concerns with my administrator and she took it upon herself to solve those problems for me. Mrs. Sutton is a dedicated employee. Perhaps too much so."

"If by 'dedicated,' you mean pathological, I agree," Jo said, and meant it, not that she was buying this weak attempt of his to shift blame. Suzanne's guilt in no way absolved his own. Did he really think he was fooling anyone? He was a renowned medical researcher, a supposed genius. She tried to puzzle it out. How could he be that brilliant and this stupid at the same time?

"Now I can't promise Matthew will hire you back, but I can guarantee you unrestricted access to your father while he is here. See him whenever you like—or as often as he agrees to it. I'll let the two of you figure that out." He smirked as if he believed he'd said something amusing. "In the meantime, let's get him admitted." He lifted the handset from his desk phone.

"Wait, we haven't agreed to anything," Jo said.

Kessler narrowed his eyes at her.

Thomas put a hand on her arm. "Maybe he's right, Josie. He's the only one who knows what treatments I received. We need to figure this out."

"Thank you, Thomas, you're doing the right thing. It will just take me a few moments here to make the arrangements." Kessler turned his chair from them as he put the phone up to his ear. Jo listened to him ordering CT scans and a myriad of other lab tests in what sounded like a foreign language.

"Dad, it's not too late. We can get you out of here, right now," she whispered.

He glanced at the doctor who was facing away from them, then whispered back. "No, keep to the plan. We need to play our parts."

"It's too risky. He's acting odd. I think he's lost it."

"Trust me." He squeezed her hand. "This is going even better than we hoped. He's giving you access to the whole place. Use it."

Kessler hung up the phone and turned back to them. "One of our nurses is coming to get you and we'll start doing a complete work-up in the morning."

A soft knock came at the door, and in walked a woman pushing a wheelchair. Jo recognized her. Maggie's smile froze for an instant as their eyes met.

"This is Marguerite, one of our very best nurses," Kessler said. "I'm sure you remember Mr. Rinaldi."

"Of course." Maggie renewed her smile as she focused on Thomas. "Welcome back."

"I want him on the fourth floor this time."

"The fourth." Her dark eyes looked worried for a moment, then she focused on Thomas. "Can I help you into the wheelchair?"

"No need." Thomas bounced to his feet.

"Oh! Well, look at you," she exclaimed.

He strode ahead. "Race you down the hall." Then he disappeared out the door.

Eyes wide, she abandoned the wheelchair and ran after him.

"Remarkable. Absolutely remarkable," Kessler said, beaming.

"Yes, it is," Jo agreed. "I suppose a cure like that would be worth a lot of money."

"You think it's wealth I'm after? This isn't about *money*." His face twisted and his voice rose in volume. "It's never been about *money*. We're talking about a hateful disease killing millions. I've dedicated my entire life to this. To my work, the research. Finding a cure." He was practically yelling at her now, obsession written in every line of his face.

She wondered again if he were mentally unbalanced.

"I meant no offense," she replied in a low controlled voice, holding herself rigid to reveal no emotion. "I can only hope that you succeed, of course."

Kessler pulled back as if recognizing he'd gone too far. When he spoke again, his voice was equally controlled. "Yes. Well. Now that your father is back, I'm sure we will. Everything points to it. I'm glad you understand how vital it is that he remain here under my care."

"As long as I have unrestricted access as promised. I'll need a keycard like the one Mrs. Sutton has."

He nodded. "Yes. I'll make sure she gives you one."

"Thank you, I'll go see her and get it right now. Make sure she knows I'm on my way." When he nodded again, Jo stood eager to put his promise to the test. She exited Kessler's office and took the elevator down to the lobby, as of now, the only floor she could gain access to without the promised card.

When the elevator stopped on the ground floor, she held the door open as she stepped out. Suzanne Sutton stood at the end of the hall talking to a short heavy-set man dressed in a brown suit, white shirt, bolo tie, and a gigantic cowboy hat. The pair fell silent and looked back at her as the elevator door pinged in protest.

"I'd like that keycard now," Jo said.

Suzanne drew herself into a stiff pose, dug in her pocket, and walked toward Jo. Chin lifted, Suzanne stepped inside the elevator and inserted the card. Jo kept the doors open with one hand and punched the buttons for every upper floor with the other. All of them lit up. "Good. That's all I need. You can get out now."

"This is just a skirmish, dear." Suzanne stood in the open doorway to face her. "Don't for a moment think you've won."

"Guess we'll just have to see about that." Jo simultaneously released the door and shoved Suzanne out, making her stumble. "Bitch."

The door closed in Suzanne's furious face and up Jo rose, filled with victory. If there were any damning evidence in this place, she would find it, photograph it, and get it to the proper authorities. The question was, how much time would she have before Sutton tried to stop her? And by what means?

Scott promised he and the police would be listening and Jerome said they would be close. Are they just outside? Down the road? Miles away? Why didn't I ask?

"If I start screaming and no one shows up, I'm going to be really pissed," Jo said inside the empty elevator, hoping someone not too far away was actually listening.

When rudely shoved out of the elevator door, Suzanne Sutton hurried to take the next one up to Dr. Kessler's office. She needed to understand what was going on. That woman shouldn't be allowed to go wherever she pleased. And yet his order had been clear, and she had been the one subjected to a stern lecture. She walked through his open door and stood in front of his desk. Waiting for him to acknowledge her, Suzanne held her breath. Had she really overstepped her authority? After being dressed down in front of Josephine Rinaldi, the ground no longer felt solid under her feet.

He was busy making notations, so she remained respectfully silent, waiting. It wasn't until Reginald Howell stomped into the room that Kessler raised his head. Even then, he didn't look at her and his face registered no emotion. "Reggie, are you upset?"

Howell snatched off his cowboy hat and slapped it against his thigh. "Goddam right, I am. Lettin' that troublemakin' lawyer lady have free run of this place—have you lost your ever-lovin' pea-pickin' mind?"

"I'm keeping her occupied. While she's busy looking for something she has no ability to understand, I have her father in place. All I need now are tissue samples." He turned to Suzanne. "Get my surgical team in here ASAP."

Suzanne exhaled in relief. Clearly, he had a plan, and it didn't include firing her. "Yes, of course. Right away." As she exited Kessler's office to fulfill his request, Howell shook his head and followed her out.

He grabbed her arm. "Have you got this under control or not?"

"Yes." She gritted her teeth but didn't pull her arm free. "I'll keep an eye on the daughter and make sure Dr. Kessler has whatever he needs."

"Make sure you do, on both counts. I made plans for this evenin' and if I get interrupted, you won't like me very much."

Suzanne stopped herself from saying she'd *never* liked him.

When he let go and walked away, she once again exhaled in relief.

CHAPTER TWENTY-EIGHT

Evidence

Jo knew what she needed, proof that Kessler was performing illegal experiments on his patients. She'd start by locating records for the three she knew about—Johnson, Rubio, and Marks—whose families sued Kessler for wrongful death and medical malpractice. Discovery would normally have released those documents if the families hadn't settled out of court, under duress according to Mr. Johnson's off-the-record statement to Scott.

After first making sure the elevator would stop on every floor and that she could get off and on with no problem, she went back to the fourth floor to find her father's room. The cameras mounted in the ceiling glowed red, indicating her image was being transmitted. No doubt the guard down in the lobby was watching her every move. She found her father dressed in a hospital gown and lying in bed. His nurse—Jacob's girlfriend, Maggie—was bent over him, inserting an intravenous needle into the back of his hand.

"Is that really necessary?" Jo asked.

Maggie looked up. "Sorry. Doctor's orders. If I don't do it, it would be a red flag. I guess it's for all the tests they have him scheduled for in the morning... in case he needs medication."

"He won't need any medication."

"Don't make a fuss, Josie." Thomas waved his free hand in dismissal. "It's no big deal."

"You sure about that?" Jo looked at the other woman through narrowed eyes.

Maggie straightened and let out a sigh. "Look, I know we got off on the wrong foot the other night, but you ambushed me. I wasn't prepared."

"No, you were too busy running the other way."

"That was before I knew what was going on. I came here to help you, okay?"

"Yeah, okay." Jo nodded, knowing she needed her, then checked the time. "Two minutes," she informed them.

"I don't see why I can't go with you," Thomas grumbled. "What's the point of me lying here like a dead fish?"

"You know why," Jo answered. "They expect you to stay here in your room. Besides, you really want to be running around with your butt hanging out and a tube in your hand?"

He frowned, then the lights went out.

"Right on schedule," Jo said.

The overhead lights flickered back on, dimmer now. She'd been told that the building's emergency generators only provided enough power for lighting and vital medical equipment. The one elevator equipped with standby power would remain operational for emergency evacuation of bed-ridden patients if needed, while the others would lower to the ground floor where they would remain until full power returned.

Jo opened the door and looked up at the nearest security camera. The absence of the red light confirmed it was off. "All clear. Let's go."

She and Maggie went out the door. Entering the stairwell, they climbed one flight up to the fifth floor. Maggie led the way down the hall to a mesh-windowed door beside a security panel. "This is it, his private lab," she said. No lights showed on the panel, but she didn't reach for the door handle.

"Problem?" Jo asked.

"No, it's just always been off limits."

"Not to me." Jo pushed the handle down and thrust her way in. Maggie followed, wide-eyed and cautious. All the interior lights were off, but enough moonlight streamed in through the windows to outline the tables and equipment. Jo fished out her cell phone and activated its flashlight, throwing sharp angular shadows across the room. Devices she couldn't begin to identify loaded long steel-topped tables. "Any idea what all this stuff does?"

"Not really. I deal with patients, not specimens, but Jacob can probably tell you."

On cue, the outer door creaked open. Jo spun at the sound, heart racing as her phone lit up the man in front of her.

"Just me," Jacob said, squinting with one hand in front of his face. Jo lowered her phone to stop blinding him. Jacob smiled as he spun around. "I'd love to work in this lab. Kessler's got the coolest toys."

"Johnson, Rubio, and Marks," Jo reminded him.

"Right." He gestured at a bank of drawers built into the lower half of the far wall. "Should be in his files over there."

Jo walked over and started pulling drawers open, poring over labels on the hanging files within. "These are all coded. How are we supposed to identify them?"

"Initials followed by date of birth," Maggie replied. "Gladys Dawn Johnson would be GDJ19341020." She withdrew an inch-thick manila file and handed it to Jo, then pulled out two more. "And here are Marks and Rubio." She closed the drawers and gave the biggest file to Jacob.

They each started flipping pages and snapping pictures with their phones.

"You'd think this would all be digital by now," Jo said.

"Old habits," Jacob replied. "Takes a while to change over."

"How long before power kicks in?" Maggie asked.

"Scott said he'd keep it off for as long as we needed, but the security guard will be making a sweep, so we have to watch for him," Jo said.

"Yeah, this would be one of the first places I'd check," Jacob said.

Moments later, they all looked up at the sound of footsteps in the hall. "Speak of the devil."

"Hide!" Jo whispered. The three shut off their phones, grabbed their files and dropped to the floor behind desks just before the outer door opened and the beam of a flashlight swept the room.

Jo held her breath as the light moved past her, hit the outer window, and reflected into her eyes. She felt completely exposed, certain she'd been discovered, but then the light moved away leaving them all in darkness again. The outer door swung shut and footfalls faded into the distance.

She waited to be sure he'd left, then peered over at Jacob and Maggie. "I think he's gone."

It took another five minutes to finish photographing every page with Jacob finishing last. They returned the files to the drawers.

"Anything else we should be looking at?" Jo asked.

Jacob shrugged. "Hard to say. Lots of super expensive equipment in here, but there's no crime in that."

"How about a freezer full of brains?" Maggie asked, holding open the lid of a white chest. Icy fog billowed over the sides.

"She's kidding, right?'

"Nope." Jacob peered into the freezer. "These are human brains all right, but that's what he studies, so no surprise there. He's got an awful lot of them, though. Wonder where he's getting them all from."

"Are any from our three patients?" Jo asked.

"I'm looking," Maggie said, then paused. "Huh, that's weird. These numbers don't match our filing system— WA4234, BG1856, BA3221," she read. "And this one is 63457-098. I've no idea what they mean. Do you?"

Jacob shook his head. "Got me."

Jo thought there was something familiar sounding about those numbers but couldn't quite remember what.

Jacob lifted a slender package up to the light. "These are tissue slides, same as ones from the mouse labs. Course we have the advantage there. No waiting."

"What does that mean?" Jo asked.

"After brain death, changes occur that affect enzyme activity, nucleic acid integrity, oxidative modification, protein integrity, etc. ... all of which is a big problem, so the shorter the interval before fixation, the better."

"Fixation?"

"The immersion of the organ in a substance with tissue conservation properties."

"You mean like formaldehyde?"

"That's one of them. In the mouse labs, we use snap freezing with isopentane and liquid nitrogen. After fixation, the tissues can be sliced for analysis like these. The idea is to preserve—"

"Okay, okay," Jo interrupted the science lesson, "that's all really interesting if you're a lab rat, but how does it help prove Kessler's breaking the law?"

"Doesn't. I was just commenting that what Kessler's doing up here is pretty much the same as what we do in the mouse labs—collecting brain samples for analysis. The only difference is we don't have to wait for our test subjects to die."

"You mean you remove their brains while the mice are still alive?"

"We anesthetize them first. We're not monsters. But yes, technically they're still alive."

Jo remembered reading in the autopsy reports that the coroner questioned how long those three patients had been dead before their brains were removed. "You don't think Kessler would ever do that to a patient, do you?"

"No," Jacob and Maggie chorused together. "That's crazy. Yeah, crazy."

"I mean he's intense, but he's not insane." Maggie looked over at Jacob for confirmation.

Jo fingered the keycard in her pocket, thinking how oddly Kessler had behaved and how quickly he capitulated to her demands. "He gave me this for the elevator." She pulled it from her pocket.

"Wow. Way to go. Guess we won't need my janitor one then," Jacob said.

"But why would he do that? I mean, he must have known I'd go snooping." Jo stared at the card now, no longer trusting it. "What's he up to?"

Jacob hesitated and his face twitched. "It's probably nothing, but..."

"What?" Maggie and Jo asked simultaneously.

"Just before I came up here, I saw Jessica pulling into the parking lot. I wondered why she was coming in so late, but it never occurred to me that..." Jacob trailed off and shared a worried look with Maggie.

"No," she said. "He wouldn't."

"Wait, what's Jessica got to do with this?" Jo asked.

"She's on Kessler's surgical team," Maggie replied.

The image of the intravenous tube in her father's hand jumped into Jo's mind and fear blasted through her like a klaxon.

"We need to get to my dad. Now!"

CHAPTER TWENTY-NINE

Night Shift

Thomas lay in his hospital bed watching the hands on the black-framed clock on the wall, its numbers barely visible in the dim emergency lighting. His anxiety built with each click. *That's it. I'm not waiting here any longer.*

He retrieved his shoes and just as he was slipping them on, a voice interrupted.

"Naughty, naughty, Mr. Rinaldi. You're supposed to be in bed."

Thomas looked up to see a young female nurse wagging a finger at him. Tall, freckled, with long strawberry blonde hair, and dressed in pink-flowered scrubs, no one he recognized.

"Who are you?"

"I'm Jessica, your nurse tonight." She held a small container of syringes, alcohol wipes, and bandages.

"What happened to Maggie?"

She shrugged. "Gone home, I suppose. I hope the power outage didn't alarm you. You don't need to worry—our back-up generators keep everything going. Now let's get you back into bed, shall we?"

"Actually, I'd like to stretch my legs. Go for a walk."

"That's a nice idea, but I'm afraid it will have to wait." She kept smiling that same patronizing smile. "I need to administer your medication now. We need to stay on schedule, you know." She held up a filled syringe.

"What's that for? And what schedule are you talking about? I don't need any medication, and my immunizations are up-to-date."

"Doctor's orders." She came toward him with the syringe.

He jumped off the bed. "I said I don't need that."

"My, we are being difficult, aren't we?" Smile still intact, Jessica took a step back and picked up the phone on the bedside table. "Assistance, Room 423," she told whoever was on the other end, then hung up. She cocked her head at Thomas. "I'm so sorry. Your chart didn't say you were needle-phobic."

"More like doctor-phobic." He edged past her, aiming for the door. It opened before he got there, and two large men in orderly-white blocked his exit.

"Get out of my way," Thomas commanded.

Instead, they muscled him back to the bed, and held him down, pinning his arms flat on the mattress. Jessica came toward him with the syringe and her lips turned up in a patronizing smile.

"No, stop, stop."

"Now, now, Mr. Rinaldi, calm yourself. This won't hurt a bit." Instead of aiming the needle at his upper arm, she inserted it into the intravenous catheter protruding from the back of his hand. "Everything's going to be just fine."

Thomas's heart raced in desperation, adrenaline pumping hard as he tried to stay alert, but the drug invading his bloodstream soon countered any resistance. His muscles relaxed under the pressure of the orderlies' hands. Darkness crawled over his vision and her voice receded. Within seconds, his awareness faded to nothing.

Jo and her companions raced into her father's room. The bed lay empty, its bedsheets drooped to the floor, and a metal chair lay on its side.

"Looks like he put up a fight," Jacob said.

"Where would they have taken him?" Jo asked, turning to Maggie.

"The O.R.." Maggie ran ahead and Jo and Jacob sprinted after her down the halls only to find the operating room dark and empty.

"Where else could they be?" When Jo got only blank looks, she grabbed Maggie by the shoulders. "Think!"

"I... I'm not sure. There's a rumor Kessler has another operating room, somewhere near his lab, but I don't know exactly."

"Sutton would," Jacob said.

"It's not like she's going to tell us," Maggie replied.

"Then we'll have to make her. Come on." Jo took off for the stairs. Hoping Scott was listening, she yelled. "Scott, get ready to turn the power back on when I say."

"How is that a good idea?" Jacob asked.

"Trust me." Jo blew through the door for the fifth floor with Maggie and Jacob close behind and ran back inside Kessler's lab. "Okay, power it up now."

A second later, the security camera went red and the electronic door control panel on the other side clicked on, locking them in. She flipped on the switch by the door, flooding the room with light. "Get busy." She swept her arm across the nearest table sending everything on top of it flying. A rack of glass vials shattered on the tile. "Come on!" she yelled at their stunned faces and knocked a computer monitor over so that it crashed on the floor.

Jacob and Maggie jumped into action, destroying the lab's equipment with abandon. "I was going to quit anyway," Maggie said as she toppled a tall shelving system to the ground. More glass shattered.

"Yeah, what the heck, it's only our careers, right?" Jacob yelled as he slammed another computer to the floor. The three of them soon had even the heaviest equipment up-ended, file drawers emptied, and papers strewn across the room. Jo was about to pull the plug on the chest freezer, when the outer door flew open and Suzanne Sutton ran in yelling, "Stop! Stop!" Behind her came the armed guard and another large man dressed in white. Jo, Maggie, and Jacob froze and held up their hands.

"Are you insane?" Suzanne demanded.

"No, but I'm pretty sure Kessler is," Jo replied. "And we don't have much time."

Suzanne shook her head and pulled the door open. "Get them out of here."

The guard and orderly moved behind them to usher them out.

"Okay, okay, we're leaving," Jo said. She waited for Maggie and Jacob to go ahead. The orderly followed her with the armed guard right behind him. As Jo approached the exit, she spun and shoved the orderly into the guard, then yanked

Suzanne outside shutting the door before the two men could get back on their feet. Suzanne nearly fell as she stumbled into the hall. Jo had accomplished her goal. She and her friends were on the outside along with Suzanne, while the two men were locked inside the lab.

"What are you doing?" Suzanne tried to push past Jo to reach the door panel.

Jo shoved her back. "I don't think so."

With a snarl, Suzanne leaped at Jo, and they fell to the ground. Jo held onto Suzanne's wrists to stop her from clawing her face until Jacob pulled Suzanne off.

"You okay?" he asked.

"Yeah, I think so." Jo got to her feet and brushed herself off.

Suzanne struggled against Jacob's encircling arms and glared at them like an enraged puma. Strands of blonde hair hung loose. "You have no idea how much trouble you people are in."

"Vengeance later," Jo said. "Right now, we need your help."

"My help?" Suzanne scoffed. She looked at Jacob over her shoulder. "Let me go right now or you're fired." She tried to twist free, but he hung on.

"Yeah, like you'd let me stay after this. Anyway, I already quit," he said.

"Mrs. Sutton." Jo snapped her fingers. "Pay attention. Your precious Doctor Kessler is in serious trouble. If you don't intervene immediately, he's going to jail and this Institute will shut down for good."

Suzanne stopped struggling. "What are you talking about?"

"Her father. We think Kessler intends to operate on him," Maggie said.

"Yes, I know. He's taking some tissue samples. So what?"

It was Jacob's turn to scoff. "In our business, tissue refers to brain matter. You don't take samples while the patient is still alive."

"The head of your program here is about to commit murder," Jo said.

Suzanne shook her head. "No, you don't understand. All he's ever done, all he's ever wanted to do, is help the most people he can."

"Johnson, Rubio and Marks were still alive when he operated on them. How can you justify that?"

"They would have died, anyway."

"But my father isn't dying. He's fine."

"That's for Dr. Kessler to judge. You should be grateful for the extra time he gave him and be willing to help."

"By sacrificing my father's life? You know this isn't right. You have to take us to him. Please."

"No," Suzanne kept shaking her head. "No, I won't interfere."

Jo exchanged desperate looks with Maggie and Jacob, at a loss for what to do now.

Jacob gave her a half-smile as he held onto Suzanne. "If you don't, everyone in that room is going to die."

"What?" Jo asked, appalled, then stopped herself. It had to be a ruse.

"Mr. Rinaldi has a packet of anatoxin-a inserted under his scalp," Jacob announced as if it were a bomb threat.

"Ana-what?" Jo asked.

"Anatoxin-a, it's a potent neurotoxin. We use it in the lab on the mice. It causes VRPD—Very Rapid Death Syndrome—kills in minutes. If the seal were broken—say by a surgical instrument..."

"You're serious?" Jo asked, even though she couldn't figure out when something like that could have been accomplished.

Jacob wore a grim face. "I'm sorry, but your father was determined to end this if things went badly." He turned Suzanne around to face him. "Do you understand what I'm saying? If Kessler operates, everyone in that room will be exposed."

"No. I don't believe you. This is just some desperate story you're making up."

Jacob pulled out his phone and held it in front of her face. As she watched, her dubious expression changed to wide-eyed horror.

"Okay, okay." She shakily pointed back at Kessler's lab. "Fastest way is through the lab."

The guard glared at them through the thick meshed window, yelled something indecipherable and pounded on the door.

Jacob moved aside giving her access to the security panel.

"You're trusting her now?" Maggie asked.

"Like we have a choice?"

Suzanne entered a code and pushed the door open. The guard and the orderly charged forward, but she held up her hands. "It's all right, I've got this. You can go now."

The guard held his ground. "You sure?"

"Yes, Al, I'm fine. Return to your post," Suzanne said. Both men frowned, but finally walked away. Suzanne rushed inside with Jo, Maggie, and Jacob hurrying to follow.

The outer door automatically locked behind them with an ominous *clunk*.

CHAPTER THIRTY

Red-Handed

Thomas moaned and blinked, trying to focus.

"Watch it, he's waking up," someone said.

A pair of masked faces loomed over him. Startled, Thomas swung his arm up hitting the nearest one in the side of the head and rolled aside.

"Hold him!"

Thomas gasped as he fell from the table onto the floor. Blood sprayed and a sharp hot pain stabbed the back of his hand. He didn't know where he was, who these people were or what they wanted from him, so he flailed and kicked and scrambled away until trapped in a corner with the two masked people looking down at him.

"What's going on in here?" another surgically gowned man demanded as he entered the room. The two masked people turned to him.

"I'm sorry, Doctor." It was a man's voice. "I thought he was still under, but suddenly he started fighting us."

"Mr. Rinaldi, please, there's no need to panic." The other man pulled his surgical mask down under his chin to reveal his face.

Thomas recognized him. "Dr. Kessler. Where am I? Who are they? I don't understand what's happening."

"This is your nurse and your anesthesiologist. We were about to perform the procedure you and I discussed earlier, but it seems you've had a reaction to the anesthesia. It happens sometimes—nothing serious. Do you think you can stand?"

"I—I think so." This time he let them assist him to his feet. He felt disoriented and dizzy, but they steadied him. "What... what procedure? I can't remember."

"I'll explain it again, of course, but please lie down. We don't want you falling again, and we need to tend to that hand."

Thomas saw blood dripping down his fingertips and grimaced. "Okay."

He let them guide him toward the table, but as they turned him around to lie back, wisps of red hair peeked out beneath the masked nurse's cap and her green eyes met his, sparking a memory.

She drugged me.

"Wait! Stop! I didn't agree to any of this."

Their hands tightened, and Kessler approached with another hypo. Thomas feared if they got him back on that table, he was as good as dead. He kicked Kessler in the knee, twisted free of the anesthesiologist, and knocked the nurse aside. She crashed into a polished metal cart filled with surgical instruments, pulling it to the floor as she fell. Scalpels, retractors, and what looked like a small buzz-saw clattered across the tile. Bent over, Kessler cursed holding his right knee, while the anesthesiologist hesitated, seemingly torn between going to the aid of his colleagues and restraining their patient. Thomas took advantage of their momentary confusion and ran out the door.

"Stop him!" Kessler yelled.

Thomas half-ran, half-stumbled down the hall, sliding a bloody hand along the wall to stay upright. The door behind him banged open and running footfalls hit the floor. He looked back to see the masked anesthesiologist chasing after him. Thomas hurried around the corner, then stopped short. More people were coming the other way, but his eyes were too blurry to make out their faces.

"Dad!" Jo yelled and rushed toward him.

The anesthesiologist skidded to a halt, then ran back the way he'd come.

By then, Thomas was wrapped in his daughter's arms.

"It's okay. We've got you now," Jo said, hugging her father. He hugged her back and nodded.

"Looks like you ripped out your I.V. Keep pressure on it," Maggie lifted his hands, and put one over the other to stem the blood flow.

"Where's Kessler?" Jo asked him.

"Back there. I think he was about to operate on me, but I woke up. Luckily."

"Wasn't just luck," Jacob said. "Those injections Kessler gave you increase neuronal excitability, makes you more resistant to anesthesia."

"I'm sorry. I should never have left you alone," Jo said.

"No, you shouldn't have. You should have let me come along with you like I asked, but as usual, you wouldn't listen to me."

Jo stiffened at her father's rebuke. She'd admitted her mistake. *Why couldn't he leave it at that? Always has to have the last word, drive the nail in deeper.* None of which she said aloud.

"At least now we know how far Kessler's willing to go," Jacob said.

Jo nodded. "We need to confront him. Put an end to this."

"No," Suzanne said, stepping forward. "You have what you came for. Let me handle it."

Thomas narrowed his eyes at her. "Why is she here?"

"We never would have found you otherwise. None of us knew where Kessler's secret O.R. was," Jo said.

"It's not a secret. Merely a convenience," replied a male voice.

They turned to see Dr. Kessler standing in the hall, dressed in green surgical scrubs. A small dot of red spotted his chest. Behind him, still masked, was the man who'd been chasing Thomas.

Kessler focused on his administrator. "Mrs. Sutton, would you care to explain what you're doing here with these people?"

"I'm sorry, but they said you were in danger. They said Mr. Rinaldi here has a neurotoxin under his scalp and if you were exposed to it, it would have killed you."

Thomas scowled and a smile broke across Dr. Kessler's face. He pushed his black-rimmed eyeglasses higher with his forefinger. "And you believed them, a claim that absurd?"

"Not at first, but then he showed me a video of how they did it," Suzanne said.

A tall nurse laughed as she walked up to stand next to Dr. Kessler, her shoulder touching his. "Did they smear ketchup on someone's head and brandish a scalpel?"

Jo recognized her as Jessica.

"No, it..." Suzanne looked at Jacob. "Show them."

"Dyed corn syrup, actually," Jacob said. "A Halloween prank last year. Anatoxin-a's real enough though. Very lethal."

Kessler sighed. "Yes, but you'd have to either inject it or make me drink it. How were you going to accomplish that?"

"I wasn't. I don't kill people, not even in the name of medical progress."

"Good for you. But then you're just a lowly lab tech so hardly one to judge me."

"Is that a confession?" Jo asked.

"Of what?" Jessica asked hotly "That he's trying to save lives? What have any of you ever done?"

Kessler put his arm around her in a way that seemed too intimate to be casual, let alone professional. "It's all right. You don't need to defend me."

"Of course I do. They don't know you like I do."

Lovers, Jo realized. Suzanne was watching too.

"So this is the older boyfriend you've been so secretive about?" Maggie asked her roommate. The two women frowned at each other.

"You're sleeping together?" Suzanne's voice registered both dismay and anger.

"Not that it's any of your business," Jessica said.

Suzanne shook her head and her voice dropped to a near whisper. "All this time I thought.... But you've been running around with this whore."

"What did you say?" Jessica demanded in outrage, but then her mouth gradually widened into a smile. "Oh, my god, Adrian, I think she's in love with you."

Kessler looked from one woman to the other.

"That is so pathetic," Jessica continued. "Did you really think he'd be interested... in you? Ha! You do know what everyone calls you around here, don't you?

"Jessie, stop," Kessler cautioned.

"No. She should know. She can't go around here fantasizing there's something between the two of you. They call you the Iron Maiden, Mrs. Sutton, the *Frigid* Iron Maiden—ice cold and filled with spikes. Sometimes, we even get a chuckle out of it, don't we, Adri?"

"That's enough," Kessler said, but offered no denial.

Suzanne's face hardened into stone. "I see." She turned to Jo. "You won't be needing a confession from him. I'll tell you everything you want to know, and I have the documents to prove it."

"Suzie, no. You'll destroy everything I've accomplished here. All my work."

She smiled coldly at Kessler. "Yes, *your* work. I finally realize I was never really part of it." Suzanne spun on her one-inch heels and marched away.

"Think what you're doing," Kessler called to her and took a step as if to follow.

"Don't." Jacob pointed at him with an outstretched arm and he froze. "Face it, Doc. You messed up and it's over now."

"Yes, one must never underestimate a woman scorned," Thomas said, "and all that must follow."

Maggie nodded. "Yeah, what he said."

"Okay, this isn't helping. Let's go," Jo said. Following her lead, they turned away and trailed after Suzanne. What they failed to see was Dr. Kessler pulling his cell phone from his pocket.

❖ ❖ ❖

The sound of a croaking frog went off on the bedstand next to Howell. He read the time, 2 am, and the caller ID. With a heavy sigh, he reluctantly answered on the third croak. "You better have a good reason for calling."

"It's Suzanne," Kessler replied. "The daughter's turned her against me and taken my patient. I *need* him."

The wheels in Howell's head spun. Suzanne on the wrong side presented a tremendous danger to them all. "I'll handle it. Stay in your office and don't talk to anyone until you hear from me." He ended the call and sat up to dial Suzanne's number. When it immediately went to voice mail, he hung up.

"Everything okay?" asked the naked girl lying next to him.

"No." To his regret, the rest of the full-service experience he'd arranged for the night would have to go unfinished. "You need to leave."

She propped herself up on her elbows to peer at him through a tousle of bleached blonde hair. "But I thought you wanted me to—

"Out." He smacked her sharply on the ass. "Now."

"Ow!" She gasped, then got up, rubbing her bottom. "Okay, fine, but you still owe me for the whole night."

Howell nodded but vowed Suzanne would be the one paying.

CHAPTER THIRTY-ONE

A New Ally

Her father was safe, and with Kessler's administrator on their side now, Jo would soon have the prosecutable evidence she needed to put Kessler away. Jo felt like whooping in victory, but for Suzanne's sake, she remained quiet and kept her facial expression neutral as she watched Suzanne type furiously on her keyboard, eyes focused on the monitor screen, a determined outrage in progress. Jo offered no words of comfort. This was a righteous anger that needed stoking.

"Send it all to my email address," Jo told her.

Suzanne nodded wordlessly.

Jo turned to her father, keeping her voice low. "Once we have the documents, I'll file a complaint with the state medical board. What Kessler's doing here goes beyond malpractice, it's criminal. If these records she's sending me confirm our suspicions, I'm sure the state attorney will want to prosecute."

"No doubt," Thomas agreed quietly, then he cleared his throat and raised his voice. "I hate to be a bother, but could someone retrieve my clothing and get me a bandage?" He stood with his back to the wall holding one hand against the other to stop it from bleeding.

"I'll do it," Maggie said and Jo nodded, recognizing Maggie was the most likely member of their group to go unchallenged."

"Thank you," Thomas said.

"Wait. I don't like the idea of us separating," Jacob said.

"Don't make a fuss, I'll be right back." Maggie gave him a quick kiss then hurried away.

While Jacob scowled and watched through the one-way window until Maggie was out of sight, Jo walked over to her father. "Allow me." She pulled her father's gown together and retied the strings. "You know, for most people it's hard to look dignified in a hospital gown, yet somehow you manage it."

"It's a matter of one's comportment, not one's attire."

With Maggie gone, Jacob paced the room like a nervous cat. "How much longer is this going to take?"

Suzanne's flying fingers froze. "Oh, I'm sorry, am I going too slow for you? I suppose you think you could do better."

Jo realized that Suzanne's rage extended to the entire male gender. "Maybe you should wait out in the lobby."

Jacob rolled his eyes but left Suzanne's office. Rather than stare over her shoulder and risk annoying Suzanne further, Jo stared out her window, watching Jacob doing his pacing in the lobby now. The windows blackened by night reflected the lobby's interior, with only blurred white dots showing from lights in the parking lot beyond. A pair of headlights swept past, then the exterior view went black again. Probably someone on the graveyard shift going around to the staff entrance, Jo speculated.

While Suzanne focused on her task of typing and mouse clicks, Jo and her father remained respectfully silent.

Maggie soon returned with a bag in hand. "I'll show you where you can change, and we can fix that hand of yours," she said, then led him away.

Suzanne's staccato tapping and clicking continued. Jo remained with her arms crossed and her gaze focused on the lobby. The typing stopped.

"I suppose you think me a fool," Suzanne said.

Jo dropped her arms and turned. "No, I... I never thought that."

"No?" Suzanne's voice registered skepticism. "Then tell me, what do you think?"

"I think someone you trusted, someone in a position of authority, took advantage of that. Something we have in common."

"You think they do it because we're women?"

"Yes. And because we allow it."

Suzanne dropped her gaze and nodded. "No more. It stops here, and it stops now." She closed down her computer, the only light in the room. "I pulled everything you'll need to make any prosecutor sit up and take notice. Unfortunately, that prosecutor will also notice me."

"True, but coming forward like this should go a long way. It might also help that the District Attorney is a woman."

Suzanne smirked. "It might." Suzanne's eyes flashed wide and she jumped to her feet. Raising a finger to her lips, she hurried to her office door and locked it. "We can't let them see us," she whispered.

Jo looked back to see two men in dark clothing confronting Jacob, but the heavy wooden door of Suzanne's office muffled their voices. "Who are they?"

Suzanne shushed her again and pulled her down behind her desk. As they hid there, Suzanne quietly opened her desk drawer and slipped her hand inside. Jo heard a series of soft clicks, and when Suzanne withdrew her hand, there was a gun in it.

"What the hell?" Jo whispered in alarm.

Suzanne's only answer was a finger raised to her lips again.

"Go on, get out of here!" a man in the lobby yelled.

A moment later, the office door handle jiggled hard.

"Should I break it in?"

"Don't bother. Her car's not here. She must have gone home like that guy said. We'll check in with the doc first, then go find her. It's not like we don't know where she lives."

A low chuckle responded. As the men moved away from the door, Jo thought of Maggie and her father, hoping they were taking their time. *Don't come out, don't come out.* And, of course, they came out.

"Who are you?"

"Who am I? Who are you?" Thomas replied in his haughtiest professorial tone. "I'm certain we have more right to be here than either of you. Furthermore—"

"We work here," Maggie interrupted. "I'm one of the floor nurses and this is Dr. Rinaldi. We were just leaving."

"Rinaldi? That's the name of the guy we want."

"Yeah, and he matches the photo."

"Doctor, my ass. And you must be the daughter. Thanks for making this easy. Thought we'd have to hunt you down. Come on, you two, let's go see the doc."

"Unhand me!" Thomas yelled.

"Da—!" Jo started, but Suzanne slapped her hand over her mouth and hissed in her ear.

"Shh! You want to get us killed?"

Jo blinked at the word 'killed.' She was no superhero. Except for some half-forgotten kickboxing lessons, her only weapons were words and knowledge of the law, neither of which would hold sway with someone bent on violence.

CHAPTER THIRTY-TWO

A Necessary Procedure

Suzanne dropped her hand from Jo's mouth, then went to look out the window. "They're gone." She slipped the handgun into her jacket pocket and unlocked the door. "Time to go."

Jo's first thought was her father, so she ran out into the lobby to look at the security monitors to see where they were taking him. The screen for the sixth floor soon showed two men exiting the elevator while forcibly pushing Maggie and Thomas ahead of them. They were going back to Kessler's office. Rather than rely on the one-way communication of her pin, Jo pulled out her cell phone and called Scott. To her relief, he picked up immediately.

"Are you all right? What was all that whispering about?" he asked.

"Two thugs came in here just now and took Maggie and my dad back upstairs."

"Are they armed?"

Jo asked Suzanne who nodded back grimly. "Suzanne says yes."

"Don't go after them. Just stay out of sight until we get there with the police. Shouldn't be long."

"Okay." Jo ended the call and summarized for Suzanne.

She scoffed. "No one's coming. Howell will make sure of that."

"Who?"

"Reginald Howell. You saw him earlier—short, fat, wears this ridiculous cowboy hat." She held up her hands a foot from either side of her head. "Like he's ever been on a horse."

"The man I saw you with in the lobby. He's the same one I overheard arguing with Kessler. What's he got to do with all of this?"

"He represents our financial backers. Calls himself a lobbyist, but he's really a fixer by trade. Those men work for him—enforcement muscle. They've helped me protect Adrian when I've asked, but now it seems they're after me." She offered a smile. "Ironic, right?"

Jo thought the comment self-serving, but before launching into a tirade against this woman whose morals appeared anything but, she recognized Suzanne's sad smile for what it truly was—a broken heart. Jessica had been right. Suzanne was in love with Dr. Kessler, unrequited, perhaps even unrecognized. Apparently Kessler only thought of her as a once loyal employee who'd now chosen to betray him, and thus deserved elimination. Jo's anger faded and instead of a heated retribution, she said, "I'm sorry."

Suzanne and Jo's eyes met, and for a moment, they truly were on the same side, but the sympathetic connection passed as soon as Suzanne looked away. This was merely a temporary alliance lasting only so long as their interests coincided. Jo suspected Suzanne would have no qualms about turning against her should it prove strategic, speaking of which...

"Did you send those files to my email like I asked?"

"Not exactly," Suzanne replied coolly. "I'd have nothing left to bargain with then, would I? So, no, I uploaded them to my pass-protected cloud server. That way it stays in your interest to protect my interest."

Jo's anger flashed and died almost simultaneously. She sighed. "I suppose if I were in your position, I'd have done the same." She glanced at the clock. "Scott and the police should be here any minute."

"You're not listening. No one's coming. I'm sorry but your father's about to make the ultimate contribution to science, and if we don't get out of here so will we." Suzanne turned and headed for the exit. "My car's in the shop. We'll have to take yours."

Jo stood her ground. "No, I'm not leaving. And anyway, I don't have a car here either."

"Oh. Well, I suppose we could steal one. Do you know how to hotwire a car?"

"No, do you?"

Suzanne scowled and pulled out her cell phone. "Fine. I'll call an Uber."

Jo snatched her phone away.

"Give me that."

"This is as much your fault as Dr. Kessler's. You're his administrator. You were supposed to keep an eye on him."

"What was I supposed to do? I'm no scientist. I'm just a paper pusher. I did as he asked. That was my job."

"Try telling that to a jury."

"I'd love to, but to do that I have to stay alive. Your friend Jacob was smart to leave and we need to do the same."

"He must have gone to get help."

"Even if he did, it won't be in time. When those two discover they've grabbed one of our nurses instead of you, they'll be back."

"Then think of something. You're the administrator. We can't just leave Maggie and my Dad behind."

"Why do you care what happens to them? You barely know that woman, and I've seen what goes on between you and your father. All you two ever do is bicker. You don't owe him your loyalty any more than I owe mine to Adrian, not anymore. I say leave them to their fates."

For the briefest moment, Jo imagined a father-free future. The idea was both liberating and painful. "No. That's ... that's not what I want. I can't believe you do either. Not really."

"I don't see as we have a choice."

Jo scowled trying desperately to come up with one. "We could set off the fire alarm. That's how we got everyone out of here before."

"Adrian's not going to fall for that again. Unless..."

"What?"

"Unless it's real."

"What? No. That's way too dangerous. This building is full of old people. And you're right, if he thinks it's a false alarm, what would be the point?"

"He'll know it's real when he smells smoke. And my employees know what to do in an emergency. They may call me the iron maiden, but I've trained them well."

Jo didn't point out that she'd omitted the word frigid. "No, we're not setting a fire. You're the administrator here... can't you think of something?"

"I already have. Run."

The security monitor for the sixth floor showed the two men walking back down the hall toward the elevators. "They're coming back," Suzanne said.

"We can still get past them if we hurry."

"No, thank you. You can go running up there if you want, but I'm not risking my life for any of them."

"You're a real piece of work, you know that."

"And you're running out of time."

"Well, can't you do something at least? Like maybe shut down these monitors so they can't see me?"

Suzanne looked at the control station with its keyboard and a slow smile formed. "Why yes. Yes, I can." She sat down and began typing. "As you keep reminding me, I'm the Administrator and that means I can do whatever I want."

The two men entered the elevator.

"Okay, good. Where will you go?"

"None of your business."

"Fine. Whatever," Jo turned and ran for the stairs.

"No rush," Suzanne called out just as a high-pitched alarm rang through the lobby.

Confused, Jo stopped in mid-sprint. "What just happened?"

"Elevator two is offline, stopped between floors three and four," Suzanne said.

"Stopped? You mean you trapped them in the elevator?"

"I did. Like you said, I'm the Administrator."

"That's great! Now we just have to go up and make sure Kessler doesn't do anything crazy before the police get here."

Suzanne sighed. "Excellent plan except I keep telling you there won't *be* any police. But seeing as you won't listen to me, go right ahead. You can take one of the other elevators if you like."

"You're not coming?"

"No, but I think I'll stay here and watch. In fact, put me on speakerphone. I'd love to hear what excuses he makes."

Jo scowled but figured there was no point in arguing. "Fine." She started for the elevator, then hesitated. "You're not going to trap *me* between floors, are you?"

Suzanne smiled. "Now why would I do that? We're on the same side, remember?" As Jo turned away, she heard Suzanne add under her breath, "Not that I'll tell you when we're not anymore."

Jo frowned but continued on into the elevator. To her relief, it rose without interruption. Her phone rang. "Suzanne?"

"Still here. For now."

"Wonderful." Jo put her phone on speaker and slid it back into her pocket. When the elevator opened on the sixth floor, she ran to Kessler's office and threw open the door. To her dismay, the room was empty. "They're gone."

Suzanne's voice came from her pocket. "Oh. He must have taken his private elevator."

"He has his own elevator? You might have mentioned that before."

"It wasn't your business before."

"So where is it?"

"Hidden behind the bookcase, but it won't do you any good. The palm plate only works for Adrian. I'm guessing he took your father back to his O.R. You'll have to go back through his lab again. And I suggest you hurry."

Cursing now, Jo ran back to the elevator, rode it down to the fifth floor, and ran back to the same lab that she, Jacob and Maggie had trashed earlier. The red light on the security panel switched to green as she ran toward it. "Thanks for that," she said, realizing that Suzanne was not only listening and watching but also controlling things remotely.

Inside the lab, papers were still strewn about amid broken glass and upended equipment. If Kessler had seen the destruction, he was probably livid. Jo hurried through the mess to get to the door at the back. Its locked panel turned green and she ran through it and kept running, down the short hallway with its one sharp turn, and on to the operating room at the very end. The door panel clicked to green and she blasted through. The scene that greeted her was as before, two men in green scrubs and one red-haired nurse, but this time her father lay immobile on an operating table.

"Ah, Ms. Rinaldi, you decided to join us," Kessler said, as if she'd come for tea.

"What have you done to him?"

"Nothing as yet. You're just in time."

"Don't touch him," she said and strode towards them.

A large hand grabbed her arm from behind. She spun to face the same guard she remembered from before, and he looked as big and unfriendly as ever.

Almost before she realized what was happening, he pulled her arms behind her and secured them with hand-cuffs, then shoved her to the floor. "Quiet or I'll put a sock in it."

"Now, now, I'm sure that won't be necessary," Dr. Kessler said. "Ms. Rinaldi is an intelligent young woman, quite capable of listening to reason. Although, I was rather sad to see that she and her friends made quite a mess of my lab tonight."

"I hope it costs you a fortune."

"Oh, not to worry. Our insurance covers vandalism." Kessler looked to his assistants. "Shall we proceed?"

"Wait. What are you going to do?" Jo tried to catch Jessica's attention, but the other woman kept her gaze averted, and busied herself laying out surgical instruments on a chrome table.

"With her in here?" the anesthesiologist asked. "Are you sure?" He looked from Jo to Kessler as he held an oxygen mask poised above her father's face.

"Of course, I'm sure. This is a simple procedure. I've done it hundreds of times," Kessler answered. "And Albert is here to keep order."

"What procedure?" Jo asked, trying to get their attention. "Please, I'd really like to understand. Can't you just take a moment to explain it to me? He is my father, after all."

Kessler regarded her dispassionately for a moment. "Very well." He circled an area on the top of Thomas's partially shaved head with his forefinger. "I shall remove a section of the skull here and create a bone flap to access the brain underneath." He picked up an instrument which looked like a hand drill attached to a long tube. "This is a craniotome, a special saw with a footplate used for cutting skull bone without slicing into the dura mater."

"The *what* matter?" Jo asked, desperate to keep him engaged, anything to slow him down until help arrived.

"*Dura* mater, the outer protective covering of the brain. It needs to remain intact. This is all standard."

She chose her next words carefully. "But it's not really standard, not this time, is it? He's not like the others. He's not dying."

"No, your father is a special case. His brain contains a unique set of information I need to engineer a cure. This will make all the difference."

Jo saw the anesthesiologist and Jessica pause to share questioning looks with each other. Could it be that they were being duped?

"What about non-invasive tests like CT scans and x-rays?" she asked.

Kessler exhaled in dismissal. "Not helpful. I need to observe the changes on a cellular level."

"But if you kill him, you'll end up with nothing. You'll never know how long this cure of yours can last, or if there are any side-effects, or—"

His surgical team stood frozen now.

"You think I haven't thought of all that? You think I'm acting on a whim? This is the only option."

"But it isn't. It can't be. It's wrong." She addressed the others. "Please, you have to stop him."

"Get her out of here," Kessler growled.

The guard lifted her to her feet and dragged her out the door while she kept yelling at his assistants. "Stop him. He's lost his mind!" Neither of them moved. The door closed, shutting her out.

"That's enough out of you." Albert undid one cuff and slapped it over the railing along the wall. "There, that'll keep you put until the doc decides what to do with you." He crossed his arms and stood between her and the door, watching her intently as if she were about to perform a Houdini act.

"Can't you see what he's doing is insane? You need to stop him." Though no escape artist, she could argue a case convincingly. Unfortunately, she could also see immediately that in this juror's mind, she was the crazy one. She needed a new tactic. "Okay, okay, if he's really going through with this, then there's something he needs to know. Something that could affect the outcome."

"Yeah, right."

"I'm serious. It's Albert, right? It's about the meds my dad's been taking since he left here. Kessler doesn't know about them. He needs to know." She tried to look sincerely concerned, which wasn't a stretch. "You need to let me tell him, Albert. He'll be really upset with you if he finds out you knew about this, after it's too late."

He hesitated, scowling at her. "You better not be lying," he said, then cracked the door open. "Hey, Doc, she's probably just trying to mess with you, but she says there's something important about the meds he's been taking since he left here. You want to talk to her?"

Kessler came out, letting the door close behind him. "I hope you have something pertinent to share that justifies this interruption."

"Yes. Absolutely. I do. Like I told Albert here, it's about my dad's medication. You know, what Peterson prescribed for him that he's been taking ever since he left this place? she said, stalling, watching the electronic lock. "So, anyway, what you should know is that he... um..."

It turned red.

She blew out the air in her lungs and smiled. "Actually, what I really wanted to tell you is that you're locked out."

"What?" Kessler turned back. Seeing the red light, he grabbed the handle. It wouldn't move. He pulled out his keycard and slid it through the lock. The light stayed red. Kessler turned to Albert. "Try yours." The result was the same. Knocks came from the other side and the handle rattled.

"Suzanne," Kessler snarled the name. "It appears Mrs. Sutton is tampering with our security system. Go stop her."

Albert nodded and took off running. Jo hoped he was stupid enough to take the elevator.

Kessler waited with his arms crossed, wearing an annoyed expression. "This won't change anything. All you're doing is irritating me."

"And then what? Are you going to kill me, too?"

He looked puzzled. "Why would I bother? You're of no importance."

"What if I tell the police?"

He shrugged. "A far better use of your time would be to go home and plan a funeral befitting a man of your father's prestige. Something dignified, I think. I'll be sure to send flowers and my condolences."

"For a murder you will have committed."

He sighed. "You and your father agreed to donate his organs to this Institute. If anything you should be grateful for this additional time I gave him. Without me, he would have become a mere shell of himself, braindead for all intents and purposes, lingering uselessly until his vital organs finally failed. Is that the ending you would have preferred?"

"No, of course not, but that's not what's happening to him. He's not wasting away. He's thriving. And you're right. That is thanks to you, which means you should be just as eager as I am to keep him alive. He is living proof you've invented a cure. He would be the perfect spokesperson for you. Why would you waste that?"

Kessler shook his head vigorously. "No. No. I don't need a spokesperson. What I need is to look at his brain tissue. The more time that passes, the higher the likelihood is that he will regress. I have to do this now. This is the optimal time to harvest."

"This isn't a harvest, it's murder. First degree murder."

"You don't know what you're talking about."

"I'm a lawyer, remember? They won't let you get away with this."

"I don't see anyone here but you. Oh, were you expecting the police to swoop in and save the day? Trust me. They won't. They know the great public service I do here. The prison system needs me. I lighten their burden by taking their most problematic inmates off their hands."

At the word 'inmates' Jo flashed on the numbers Maggie read off the brain tissue samples in Kessler's lab, only now understanding why they had sounded so familiar. She knew them from when she had worked as a paralegal for a public defender. They were state and federal prisoner ID numbers. "You've been experimenting on prisoners?"

He didn't answer. She didn't need him to. Now she understood. Rather than deal with difficult seniors with dementia, prison officials were sending them to Kessler. Such an arrangement would require the complicity of the prison warden. And wardens had to file reports with their superiors.

"Just how far up the ladder does this go?" she asked.

"Quite a ways, I understand. I believe there's even a Senator involved. As usual, it comes down to the lowest common denominator, money. I need it to fund my work. My sponsors need it to pay their shareholders, and bribe their politicians, who in turn need it to run their campaigns to stay in office." He shrugged. "Sordid, I agree, but my purpose is a higher one. It goes beyond greed, beyond power-seeking, beyond sin even. Can you say the same, Ms. Rinaldi? Do you serve a higher purpose, or any purpose at all?"

The question took Jo aback, and she didn't know how to answer.

"How sad. I can think of little worse than a meaningless life." The light on the lock clicked to green, and Kessler smiled. "Ah. And so all your delay tactics come to nothing, just as I told you they would."

CHAPTER THIRTY-THREE

Blood Spilled

As Kessler took a step toward the door, Jo swung her foot forward, knocking his leg out from under him. He went flying and his head smacked against the door handle. Moaning he rolled over and sat with his back against the wall. Blood streamed down his face. He put a hand to his forehead and pulled it away, looking dazed as he regarded his reddened palm. Jo tried to kick him again, but the handcuff on her left wrist held her back and she couldn't reach him.

"Help!" she screamed, then ripped the pinned microphone from her lapel and yelled directly into it. "Where the hell is everyone?"

"Looks like I'm it," Suzanne said as she walked toward them. There was a gun in her hand, its barrel pointed at the ground. Jo remembered seeing all those shooting badges in Suzanne's office, which meant she must know how to use it.

"Suzie, thank heavens you're here," Kessler said. "Look what she did to me." He held out a red palm.

Suzanne stopped short and stared at him. Jo held her breath, uncertain which way this would go.

Kessler squinted his brows together. "Suzie?"

"You sicced Howell's men on me, then Al, my own guard." She looked at the pistol in her hand. "Were you hoping he would shoot me with this?"

"No, I just.... I just wanted..." Words seemed to fail him.

"To stop me? Whatever it took? And poor Al got caught in the middle." Tears streamed down her face. "What's happened to you, Adrian? It's like you're someone else."

"Nonsense. I haven't changed."

"You have. You were always dedicated to your work, I know, but not like this. Not to the exclusion of everything and everyone else. And never with me. I know you felt terrible about what happened to Ellen, but it was an accident and you wanted out that marriage, anyway. And I took care of it."

Kessler scowled. "Howell said he did that. He has pictures."

"Because I called him to help. I did it for you. And believe me, I've paid for it."

"Paid? Would that be with my money?" he asked.

She gaped at him. "Is that all you care about now? Money?"

"Well, I can hardly continue my work without it."

"Adrian, listen to yourself. This isn't you."

He frowned at her. "We're just wasting time here. I need to get back in and operate before it's too late. Come help me up."

The gun twitched in her hand. "I'm done helping you. I've been such a fool. Waiting for you all this time. Believing you'd come back to me. Did you ever even plan to? Was it all a lie?" Suzanne aimed the pistol. "Tell me the truth."

Alarmed, Jo interrupted, waving her one free hand at Suzanne. "Whoa! I'm sorry, Suzanne, were the two of you having an affair? You didn't tell me that."

She looked over at Jo and nodded. "Yes. Until his wife walked in on us one night. There was an accident and she died. He said he needed time to get over what happened, but it turns out he just wanted to be free of me so he could screw around with that... that child this whole time."

"Child?" Kessler said. "There's no child."

"She's means Jessica." Jo noticed a curious flatness in his voice.

"She's an adult," Kessler corrected.

"Barely. You're old enough to be her father." Suzanne's voice rose just short of shrill. "Why do you keep saying you need me when you want her?"

"I do need you."

"For what? Just to run this place and clean up your messes? I can't believe I put up with your excuses, while you let that cretin paw me, acting as if you didn't notice, but you knew Howell was bothering me, didn't you? You only pretended not to."

Kessler pursed his lips. "No, why would I? You never let on."

She leveled the gun at him again. "Stop lying. Just stop."

"Hey, hey!" Jo jiggled the handcuffs to regain Suzanne's attention. "Did you get the key from your guard for these handcuffs?"

Suzanne nodded, reached in her pocket, and threw the key to her.

Jo snatched it out of the air.

"Why free her? She's been nothing but trouble," Dr. Kessler said, strangely oblivious to the fact that he was looking down the barrel of a gun in the hands of a woman he'd wronged.

Jo thought she'd better keep them distracted before someone got hurt. "So what is it with this Howell guy, anyway? Why do you two let him get away with all this stuff?"

"He would have cut off our funding," Suzanne replied.

"Still might, unless I prove to everyone that I have a cure. I need to get back in there," Kessler said, then despite the gun still aimed at him, he pushed to his feet. Suzanne followed him with the muzzle of the pistol, but he didn't seem to care.

"I don't understand," Jo interrupted again as she struggled to get the cuffs unlocked. "If you want to convince people you have a cure, why would you want to destroy the evidence? How does that make any sense?"

"I'm not destroying it, I'm preserving it," Kessler said, then opened the door to the O.R.

"No!" Jo yelled. The handcuffs finally popped open releasing her. She scrambled to her feet to stop him, then saw she didn't have to. Jessica and the anesthesiologist stood in the doorway blocking his entrance.

"I'm done with this," the man said. "There's something wrong with you." He pointed at Kessler's face as he spoke, then shoved past and marched away.

Jessica hesitated, her eyes taking in all of them gathered there. Jo thought she looked shellshocked. "I'm so sorry. I didn't realize," she said, and then she ran.

"Wait! Where's Maggie?" Jo called after her, but Jessica was already gone.

"In here." Maggie's voice came from inside the operating room, "... with your dad. He's coming around."

"No, no, no!" Kessler hurried into the room. "You're ruining everything. I need to operate."

"The hell you do." Jo pushed him aside. He shoved her back, and she raised a clenched fist, ready to put it in his face—she didn't take those kickboxing lessons for nothing—but Suzanne grabbed her arm.

"Don't, please. I think something really is wrong with him. I should have seen it before."

Kessler glared at them both. "There's nothing the matter with me. You people are the problem."

Jo lowered her fist and took a step back. "No, I think she's right. None of this makes sense. Can't you see that?"

"No, I... this has to happen. How can I do my work if...?" He trailed off, seeming to lose focus. He rubbed his forehead, squinting his eyes as if in pain.

Suzanne slid the pistol into her jacket and took Kessler by the arm. "Adrian, please. It's over now. You need to come with me." He blinked at her, looking confused as she led him from the room.

Jo turned back to check on her father. "Is he okay?"

Maggie removed the tube from the new I.V. in his hand. "I think so."

"Where were you all this time?"

"Stuffed in a closet. Sorry I couldn't help earlier."

"I'm just glad you're all right." Jo watched as Maggie turned off the monitors. He was already opening his eyes. "Dad, can you hear me?"

He only stared around the room, wild-eyed.

"The ketamine stare. He'll come around in a bit," Maggie answered for him. "We should get him checked out as soon as possible, but I wouldn't trust anyone here at this point."

"Agreed." Jo pulled her phone out and called 911. After giving the emergency operator precise directions and being told an ambulance was on its way, she dialed Scott, only to get his voice mail. Furious, she hung up without leaving a message. "I can't believe he's not answering."

Maggie looked as appalled as Jo felt. "Where's Jacob? Is he okay?"

Jo shook her head. "I think so, but those two men chased him off just before they grabbed you. I assumed he went for help, but I don't know why it's taking him so long."

"I keep telling you. No one's coming," Suzanne said loudly from outside the room.

"Why would she say that?" Maggie asked.

"Apparently, Kessler has an *in* with the local authorities."

"You think we can trust her?" Maggie whispered.

"We have to. She has a gun," Jo whispered back.

Maggie's eyes widened "Oh great. She's as crazy as he is."

"She's only pointed it at Dr. Kessler so far."

Suzanne stuck her head in the room. "Hurry up. Those men will either figure a way out of that elevator or call for backup, if they haven't already. We need to go."

Jo turned to Maggie. "Can we move him?"

"Sure. This baby's got wheels." Maggie kicked off the locks on the table and rolled him forward.

Suzanne scowled at them both. "You know that's going to slow us down."

"I'm not leaving him behind," Jo said.

Suzanne's hand was inside the pocket with the gun, and Jo tensed with uncertainty, but then Suzanne nodded and said, "Okay. We'll take the service elevator."

CHAPTER THIRTY-FOUR

No Help

Kessler looked up from where he was sitting on the floor with his hand pressed to the wound on his head as they wheeled Thomas out of the operating room, "Where do you think you're going with my patient?"

Jo half-smiled in disbelief. "You really have lost it, haven't you?"

"He's my responsibility. I need to keep him under observation."

"Don't worry. You're coming, too," Suzanne said, then took his arm and helped him stand.

Jo didn't like having him along, but the gun in Suzanne's possession was a persuasive argument, so she kept her opinion to herself. Together, she and Maggie rolled Thomas through the hallways, following Suzanne and the doctor into a blanket-lined service elevator and down to the bottom floor. Suzanne led them through more halls, painted dull yellow, with side doors opening to kitchen, utility, and supply rooms, then finally out the back exit into the employee parking lot. Pole lamps offered the only light under a moonless sky clouded thickly enough to hide the stars. When the cold air blasted her, Jo sucked in a breath. She pulled her father's blanket up under his chin and he moaned in response.

"It's okay, Dad, I've got you. We're getting out of here."

He squinted up at her, but she wasn't sure he understood.

"Whose car are we taking?" Maggie asked.

Jo and Suzanne exchanged looks.

"Yours, we hoped," Jo said.

Maggie grimaced. "Sorry, Jacob drove."

Jo spoke to Kessler, "We'll need your car. Give me your keys. Where did you park?"

"In my reserved spot, of course, out front." He reached into his pocket.

"The Mercedes?" Suzanne asked.

"No, the Porsche," Kessler replied.

"A two-seater? Stick shift?" Jo asked.

"Yes, on both counts. You didn't plan this very well, did you?" Kessler pulled out a leather key fob.

Jo snatched it before Suzanne had a chance and handed the keys to Maggie. "Can you drive a stick?"

"Yeah, sure. Who's coming with?"

Jo wasn't about to let Suzanne drive away with Kessler and was certain Suzanne wouldn't let her do the same with her father.

"It's just you. Go get help."

Maggie hesitated for only a moment, then took off running.

"Be careful. That car's worth more than you," Kessler called after her.

After Maggie vanished around the corner, Jo listened for the sound of a car starting, hoping the squeal of tires making a speedy exit would soon follow. Instead, she heard a single high-pitched scream and men's voices.

Kessler giggled inappropriately.

Jo spun, looking for cover, but saw only the handful of cars in the lot, interspersed with planters of skinny trees.

"There's a trail down to the beach," Suzanne said and pointed behind Jo.

Jo turned to see scrub brush edged along the cliff with a small opening next to a posted sign. "You want to go down a dirt trail? In the dark? With a gurney?"

"You have a better idea?" Suzanne asked.

"I could yell for help," Kessler offered.

"Don't." Suzanne squeezed his arm hard and pulled him toward the trail.

"Ouch! It was merely a suggestion," Kessler said.

With no better alternative, Jo followed with the gurney, worried how it would handle once it hit dirt. She soon got her answer. The opening to the trail was wide and level enough to accommodate its width, but it bounced and jostled her father so roughly that he grabbed the rails and bolted upright.

"What the? What's going on? Where am I?"

Jo put her hand over his mouth. "Shh... it's me, Dad. Some people are after us and you have to be quiet, understand?" He sat there motionless for a long moment, eyes wide, digesting what she'd said. When he nodded, she removed her hand and whispered again. "We're right behind the Kessler Institute. Some men are coming, and we need to escape. Our only option is to go down this trail to the beach. Is there any way you can walk?"

"We're in danger, you say?" he whispered. She nodded. "And you want me to walk? Down to the ocean?"

"Yes, I'm sorry, but yes."

He inhaled slowly. "Very well, I shall try." He twisted and put his bare feet on the ground. She was glad they had left his underwear on, so he wasn't completely naked. Slowly he shifted his weight and stood, but would have fallen if not for Jo bracing him.

Finding his balance, he straightened. "I'm all right."

She grabbed the blanket and tied it over his shoulders to provide some protection. "We'll go slow." She took hold of his arm.

He gestured at the gurney parked in the middle of the path. "Kind of a red flag, wouldn't you say?"

"True." There was only one way to dispose of it. Making sure her father could stand without support, she aimed it toward the side of the cliff and gave it a hard shove. The gurney rolled forward, paused at a 45-degree angle for half a breath, then tumbled over the edge. Its metal rails banged and clattered as it fell and crashed below.

"Let's not do that," her father said, leaning back from the edge.

Jo nodded, equally spooked by the dramatic fall. "Hope no one heard that. Come on."

In the dim light, they cautiously wound down the switchback trail, squeezing through when the cliffs came together, and sliding their backs against the rocky wall when the path narrowed. The ocean below sounded like pulsing white noise.

"I'm almost glad it's too dark to see how far down it is," Thomas said, between making grunted sounds of pain with each barefooted step.

Jo could see the light of Suzanne's cell phone moving ahead of them.

"Who is that?" her father asked.

"Mrs. Sutton and Dr. Kessler. Be careful. She has a gun."

"This just gets better and better, doesn't it? And where is the cavalry that was supposed to come to our rescue?"

"Good question."

"Well, that's disheartening. I confess Scott had me fooled."

"You and me both," Jo said but didn't want to discuss it at the moment as she was too busy trying not to freeze up from sheer terror. Heights were one of her weaknesses. She concentrated on the uneven ground and tried not to think about how narrow that strip of earth beneath her feet was between the cliff on one side and the open air on the other. The ocean rumbled ever louder as they descended, its voice growing like a living entity as its waves whooshed in and out like heavy breathing. The switchback path steepened even more as they descended, the ocean's sounds swelled, and salt-laden air filled her nostrils. Somehow, she kept going, carrying part of her father's weight, and taking one sliding, downward step after another. Like a metaphor for her life, she decided.

"If I live through this, I swear things are going to be different."

Her father, breathing hard now and grunting from the pain of walking on the hard pebbled ground in bare feet, offered no comment.

When the dirt trail leveled out at last and Jo felt soft sand under her shoes, she might have dropped to her knees in gratitude, if not for the need to keep supporting her father. Ahead she saw Suzanne and Kessler waiting. With nearly the last of her strength, Jo helped her father over to a large flat rock and lowered him onto it.

"Oh my god," she gasped once relieved of his weight. "I can't believe we just did that." When no one responded, she looked back to see Kessler lying on his back, flopped on the sand, while Suzanne leaned back heavily against a large rock.

"You guys okay?" Jo asked.

Suzanne nodded and Kessler lifted one hand in response. Jo realized they were both at least a decade older than she was, neither of them athletic, and her own heart had yet to slow. Waiting for everyone to recover, she took in their surroundings. The dark waves foamed silver along the edges, rolling up onto the sand just a few yards away. *Must be high tide or near to it*, she thought. The hypnotic rhythm of the night ocean would have been soothing under the right circumstances. This was anything but that. She gestured toward a spattering of distant lights down the beach. "We should keep going. We'll be safer around other people."

No one moved. Jo waited, trying to be patient until pebbles rolled down the path above. Looking up, she saw flashes of light moving down the cliff. "They're coming. We need to go. Now!"

Suzanne shook her head. "Maybe you can outrun them, but I can't."

"Nor can I, daughter," her father said. "You should go. Get out of here while you still can."

"Huh," Kessler said, staring up at the sky from his prone position. "No stars. Just a sliver of moon—God's fingernail as my mother used to call it. How sad," Kessler said apropos of nothing.

Suzanne shook her head then removed the pistol from her pocket, flipped it around and held the handle out to Jo. "Here. Take this."

"No, you're the sharpshooter, not me, and you might need it."

"This was Al's. I prefer my own." She reached into the back of her waist band and pulled out another handgun. "Just point and squeeze. I'll do my best to stop them, but if I fail, they'll come after you next."

Reluctantly, Jo took the weapon, its deadly weight surprising her enough that she nearly dropped it. In the back of her mind hung the question, *So, what happened to Albert?* But this wasn't the time to ask.

Her father waved her away. "Go on. Hurry."

To save herself, all she had to do was leave them all behind and run.

CHAPTER THIRTY-FIVE

Into the Deep

Jo grabbed her father's arm and pulled him down with her behind the boulder.

"What are you doing? You need to go while there's still time," he said.

She shook her head and put a finger to her lips to shush him, then leaned out to see.

Suzanne crouched down beside Kessler who was lying on the sand. "Not one word," she told him in a stern voice.

Kessler sighed as if whatever might happen next held little interest.

Within minutes, two tall silhouettes emerged from the trail. Jo recognized their broad muscular shapes as belonging to the same pair of men Suzanne had trapped in the elevator.

"What took you so long?" Suzanne demanded of them. "I called Howell ages ago." She had one hand on the doctor's chest, the other hidden. "Dr. Kessler's injured. We need to get him to a hospital immediately."

One of the men came over to look down at Kessler. "His head's bleeding," he informed his companion then turned back to Suzanne. "Where are the other two?"

"They ran off down the beach when they heard you coming. I don't' think they could have gotten far but be careful—somehow she got hold of our security guard's gun."

Jo pulled back, feeling betrayed. If either of those men walked forward even a few feet, they would see them. She raised the pistol, ready to point and squeeze as instructed, wondering if she could do it. She'd fired a gun only a handful of times and only at paper targets on a shooting range. A lark with friends. She hadn't been particularly skilled at it nor found it much fun.

She flinched and gasped as two shots rang out, one sharp crack after the other, echoing off the cliffs. Trembling, Jo gripped the gun in both hands, pointed the muzzle and peered around the boulder, expecting the worst. To her surprise it was Suzanne standing upright, posed in a firing stance, while the two men lay on the sand. Kessler sat up and stared at the fallen men while Suzanne walked over and delivered two more shots, execution style. Jo flinched with each shot, horrified.

"You can come out now," Suzanne called. "I don't think anyone else has followed us. Howell will be waiting for word, but I doubt he'd show up personally. Even if he did, he'd never make it down that trail."

As Jo and her father emerged, neither of the men moved. She bent down next to the nearest one and felt for a pulse before realizing that part of the back of his head was missing. The distant lights reflected in his unblinking eyes. The other man lay twisted on his side with his open palm on the hilt of a handgun. Clearly he'd tried to defend himself—too late. The side of his face was a mass of unrecognizable flesh, while the one remaining eye stared ahead. Conflicting emotions filled her, revulsion at what she was seeing, relief to be alive, horror that lives had been taken, gratitude she hadn't caused it, guilt that she'd been ready to, and finally anger that she'd been put in this position. Jo raised her gaze to meet Suzanne's.

"Don't look at me like that. I was first on their hit list," Suzanne said as if Jo had demanded an explanation. "If they'd realized I knew it, I'd be the one lying there now."

Jo nodded. "It's just the way you went about it. Like you've done this kind of thing before."

"Only in war games and my imagination hundreds of times."

"Imagining it is one thing, doing it another. You okay?"

"I'll tell you later. Right now, I'm too pissed to fall apart. I'm only sorry Howell isn't with them."

"Stay angry then. Here," Jo said and offered the other gun back. "You'd better take this before I shoot myself in the foot."

Suzanne took the pistol, reset the safety, and stuck it in the back of her skirt's waistband. She stepped over to one of the prone men and pulled a pair of handcuffs from his waist.

"Put these on him." She pointed at Kessler. "He'll be easier to manage that way."

It sounded like a reasonable precaution, so Jo didn't argue. She took the handcuffs and walked toward him. "Put your hands out." He sighed and extended his wrists. "And please don't try anything. For both our sakes," she added. When he appeared compliant, she moved closer to fit the cuffs on his wrists.

A flash of silver glinted in his hand and he grabbed her. She felt the sharp edge of a scalpel pressed to her throat as he pinned her to his chest. Shielding himself from Suzanne with Jo's body, he got to his feet and backed away until they stood shin deep in the water. "I'll end her, Suzie, I will. I swear."

Pistol still pointed down at the sand, Suzanne took a step forward. "Adrian, stop. You're not thinking clearly. You need a doctor."

Kessler laughed. "I am a doctor. You're the crazy one. Can't you see we're running out of time? We'll lose everything. Why won't you listen to me?"

In his passion, Kessler gestured, freeing Jo from the blade. She elbowed him hard in the stomach and rolled aside, but he hung on and the scalpel shot upwards ready to plunge down on her. The sharp retort of Suzanne's gun froze his arm in midair. Kessler stumbled back, a look of shock on his face as a dark flower bloomed across his chest.

He turned to Suzanne whose face mirrored the same disbelief as on his. Then a wave hit him from behind and he collapsed into it.

"Adrian!" Suzanne dropped the gun and ran for him. Another wave came knocking Suzanne and Jo back towards the sand. As the water retreated, it pulled Kessler's floating body out with it. Suzanne rushed forward, sobbing as she threw herself into the deepening water, her hands clawing, trying to latch on. Jo stood momentarily frozen.

"Help me!" Suzanne screamed at her.

Jo's mind-numbing shock shattered, and she sprinted forward, reaching out to grab onto Kessler leg just as an even bigger wave crashed over her. She popped up again, hyperventilating from the sudden immersion and momentarily blinded. She blinked away the stinging salt water and spun round, searching for them. A few feet away, Suzanne was doing the same, then they both spotted Kessler even further out now, floating face down. Both women scrambled for him, reaching him barely in time to flip him over before the next wave hit. She and Suzanne held on to him, but now they were out over their heads treading water.

"Swim!" Jo yelled, seeing smooth water ahead. They struck out for shore, dragging Kessler between them. Jo kicked hard and pulled with her free arm, but soon realized they weren't getting any closer, just the opposite. The ocean was dragging them further and further out.

"Rip current," Jo gasped between breaths.

Suzanne nodded, and they changed direction. With Kessler between them, they swam parallel to the beach until the water stopped pulling, then re-aimed. The distance back to shore now looked immense. Jo's lungs heaved from the effort of swimming in street clothes while dragging an unconscious body. Despite their best efforts, Kessler's head kept bobbing under. Jo coughed and spluttered, and her lungs burned like fire, but she kept swimming and pulling. The cold black water seemed endless, and her body grew ever more tired, heavy, and numb. *Am I going to drown out here, trying to save someone who might already be dead?* Though tempted to let go, she hung on, sucking in as much air as she could, swimming hard for shore. Half-blinded by the water and the dark, she couldn't tell if they were making any progress or even if Suzanne was still there pulling with her. She was so tired of fighting.

So this is what it's like to drown. You just keep going until you can't anymore, until finally you give up and let the water have its way. It almost sounded pleasant. She thought of Tommy. *Is this how he felt?* Her head slipped under—once, twice. Her limbs finally stopped cooperating, and her world slowly darkened.

Unseen hands pressed her upward, lifting her to the surface, pushing her, moving her forward. Someone yelled her name, grabbed hold, and tugged her up onto the sand. She lay there coughing and shaking hard. Slowly, her eyes focused, and words made sense again. Her father was kneeling beside her.

"Josie, thank God. I thought I'd lost you."

He helped her sit up, and Jo squinted back at the dark water with its rushing whitecaps.

"What happened to S-s-suzanne and K-kessler?" she asked with chattering teeth.

"Not sure, nor do I care at this point."

"M-m-maybe we should," she said, thinking how Suzanne had saved them and about Kessler being ill.

"There are flashing lights up ahead. Maybe that's where they ended up. Come on, let's go before we freeze to death out here." He helped her to her feet and put his arm around her.

As they hobbled toward the lights, people came running toward them. One of them was Scott, calling her name. Three people in jackets marked FBI ran behind him including the mysterious Jerome.

"Looks like the cavalry finally arrived," her father said. "A bit late."

Scott grabbed hold of her. "Are you all right?"

"F-f-fine. N-no thanks to you."

"I know, I know, I'm so sorry. I was trying to get here, but..." He took a breath. "Never mind, I'll explain later. Right now, we need to get you some help." He waved his arm and called out, "We need a medic over here!"

A woman paramedic rushed up and guided them to an ambulance in the parking lot in front of the beach. Her male partner whipped heated blankets around their shoulders.

"Anyone injured? Trouble breathing?" he asked.

"J-just cold," she said through still chattering teeth. "B-but m-my dad here was given anesthesia."

He scowled at Thomas, then checked his eyes. "We better take you in." He helped them into the back of the ambulance and had Thomas lie down. Jo sat next to him, while the paramedic busied himself checking her father's vital signs. Out of the wind now with the warm blanket pulled snug around her shoulders, her teeth stopped chattering. Scott stood in front of the open ambulance door watching worriedly.

"Did you find Suzanne and Kessler?" she asked him.

"She's in custody, but we haven't found Kessler yet."

"She shot two men back there on the beach."

Scott nodded. "Yeah, she told us. The building guard, too. All in self-defense she claims."

Readying to close the back doors, the woman paramedic asked him, "You riding along?"

Scott opened his mouth, but Jo spoke first. "No, just me and my dad."

Scott raised his eyebrows. "Okay, I'll be right behind you then."

"Don't put yourself out," she snapped, but then saw his face revealed in the light from inside the ambulance. Not only did he look crestfallen, Scott had a split lip and nastily bruised left eye. "What happened to you?"

He touched his lip and flinched. "Like I said, I was trying to get here. The police chief and I had a difference of opinion about what constituted probable cause. It almost seemed like they were delaying things intentionally, but I couldn't imagine why until I heard Kessler tell you he was working with the local authorities."

"So, you were listening."

"Of course, I was listening," Scott answered hotly "What kind of man do you take me for?" He drew in a breath. "Look, I know I let you down, and I'm sorry. I trusted the local police and I shouldn't have. It must have seemed like I deserted you, but I didn't, I wouldn't. Ever. Honestly, I got here as soon as I could." He paused, waiting for her to say something.

She didn't.

He tried again. "Can't blame you, I guess. Good news is, thanks to you, we have Kessler's confession on record."

"For all the good that will do if he's dead. And according to Suzanne, he wasn't even in his right mind."

"Maybe not, but all the people who covered for him can't claim the same."

"No, they should be charged with conspiracy."

"You don't need to worry about any of that," Jerome interrupted. He'd been staying quiet in the background until then. "They crossed state lines shipping him prisoners to experiment on, so that gives the FBI jurisdiction."

"I want to be involved," Jo said.

"You'll be a witness, obviously."

"I'll be a lot more than that. I'm going to make sure his patients are represented. They can sue the Institute, his estate, his backers, and everyone else who enabled him. I want to find out just how high up this went. I can't wait to get a look at his correspondence and phone records. Suzanne already pulled a lot of it for me, so we can start there, but I'll need to get her password first."

"Whoa, slow down. I appreciate your enthusiasm," Jerome said, "but this is in the hands of the FBI now. Time for you to sit back and let us do our work."

A righteous anger in Jo exploded. "Don't you tell me to sit back. I did that way too long because I trusted that people in charge of keeping an eye on places like this were doing their job—people like you. Turns out, nobody was. But gee thanks for finally showing up." She stood and pulled the ambulance door shut in their faces.

"I guess we're leaving," the woman paramedic said, wearing a smirk. She walked over to the driver's side and got in.

"Wait, I'm coming with you." Scott said then ran around to the passenger side and jumped into the empty seat. As they drove away, Scott twisted to look back at Jo as she sat next to the paramedic tending to her father. She stared straight ahead, determined to ignore him.

"Did you mean all that?" he asked. "About representing Kessler's patients, taking on their cases?"

She was steaming mad and refused to look at him. "Of course, I meant it."

"Good. I think that's great. Means you'll be needing help though. Lots of investigative work involved."

"I suppose."

"Sounds like we've got a lot of work to do."

She turned her head to pin him through narrowed eyes. "I don't work with people I can't rely on."

He took a long breath. "Right. I deserved that. Look, I made a mistake, a really big one, I admit. All I can do now is ask you to give me another chance. Let me prove to you that this was a one-time thing. I'm not usually this gullible, believe me."

Jo looked away again, giving him the silent treatment.

"Josie," Thomas said from his prone position. "Aren't you being a little hard on him? Nobody suspected the authorities had a hand in all of this."

"I realize that, but he was listening the whole time. He knew we were in trouble. I was screaming my head off, for chrissake."

"Yeah, I heard you. That's when this happened." Scott pointed to his face. "I got out of there as fast as I could, grabbed Jerome, and drove straight here."

Jo frowned as she considered what he was saying, then suddenly realized she had no idea what had happened to their friends. "Wait, what about Maggie and Jacob?"

"They're fine. We found them tied up in a van in the parking lot. Jacob called me after those men locked him out of the building. I told him to lay low, but when he saw them grab Maggie he tried to stop them. I hate to think what they had in mind for the pair of them. Another staged accident probably."

"I guess we all had our share of trouble tonight." She fell silent for a long time, thinking it all over before speaking again. She felt a determined necessity to make her threats real, but how? She was just one inexperienced attorney, low on resources. How could she take on a major corporate entity?

"You're right about one thing. To do what I'm thinking— open up my own practice and follow up on all of this—I will need help. Trouble is, I can't even pay my bills let alone hire anyone."

"No problem. I recently got a windfall of $100,000."

"You're not actually thinking about keeping that money?"

"Absolutely not. But I would be willing to donate it to a worthy cause. This sounds like a good one to me. Should be enough to carry us for a while."

"Us?"

"Sure. If you'll have me. I want to be there, helping you. Hey, I'll even hang up your shingle." He smiled and swept his hand in an arc across the air. "Law Offices of Josephine Rinaldi and Associates... highly recommended."

As she stared at him, his grin faded, replaced by a sincere pleading look. "I know I messed up. You have no idea how bad I feel about how this went down, and you have every right to be furious. I should have punched that asshole in the face a lot sooner."

"Looks like he punched you back."

"Yeah, he did, and he had help." Scott touched his jaw gingerly. "Totally worth it, though."

Seeing the bruises on Scott's face and the guilt in his eyes, the last of Jo's anger dissipated. She wanted nothing more than to believe he'd done his best, that his intentions were pure, that he was someone she could trust. There was only one way to find out. She would have to take a risk.

"All right then. We'll give it a try and see how it goes. Just don't mess up again."

"I won't, I swear." He held up three fingers. "Scout's honor."

She smirked. "Don't tell me you were actually a Boy Scout."

"Eagle."

"Ha." She rolled her eyes. "I should have guessed."

CHAPTER THIRTY-SIX

Revelations

Despite the near miss of having his brain removed, then sliced and diced for inspection in a microscope, Thomas appeared to have suffered no ill effects, but three days later, the hospital still hadn't released him. More tests, they insisted, just a few more. This was a teaching hospital run by the local university. Jo supposed there was a lot to learn from someone who exhibited an unexplained recovery from an incurable disease. Dr. Peterson had rushed to the hospital the very night Thomas was admitted and had shown up every day since, looking a little too excited for Jo's comfort. There was a gleam in his eyes that Jo recognized, the same one she'd seen in Dr. Kessler's. Jo sat in the visitor's chair in her father's room and listened to Peterson's lighthearted banter as he examined her father.

"And how are we feeling today?" Peterson asked Thomas, giving Jo a quick smile to acknowledge her presence without actually interacting with her. The doctors and nurses all smiled encouragingly but basically ignored her unless she tried to run interference on her father's behalf, not that he seemed to need any help.

"*We* are feeling perfectly fine," Thomas replied, "And *we* would like to get out of here. All I do is lie here but I can't get any sleep for all the people coming and going, flipping on lights, taking blood. And the food's abominable."

"I understand, but we just need a few more days to run some additional tests. I'd like to schedule you for a functional near-infrared spectroscopy."

"A what? Never mind, I don't care what it is. I'm done with these tests of yours."

"I understand it's difficult, but this one is completely non-invasive. It measures the concentration changes of oxygenated and deoxygenated hemoglobin and oxygen saturation associated with your neural activity. It can also assess hemodynamic activity, all of which will give us additional information to work with."

"No, enough. I'm not your personal guinea pig."

"I understand how you must feel, but—"

"Stop telling me you understand when you obviously don't. Sign my release papers, or don't. Either way, I'm going home. Today."

"But—"

"He said he's had enough," Jo cut him off. "He's going home. Today."

Frowning, the doctor took a long breath. "Very well."

Unfortunately, home wasn't much quieter. The landline rang constantly even though Jo changed the number. By the end of the second day, she turned off the ringer and let the calls go to voicemail, most of which she erased, but when she stopped returning calls, people started showing up in person. Jo stopped answering the door. But that didn't prevent curiosity seekers from gathering outside to catch a glimpse of the walking miracle. Each day, it grew worse. Going anywhere required passage through a gauntlet of people—some polite, some not. The latter demanded answers and grew angry when none were forthcoming. An officer stationed outside their house tried to keep the more aggressive stalkers away. And then there was the mail—both electronic and snail. She changed email addresses, but people soon found them again. Each day, the postal service delivered overwhelming stacks of letters from drug companies, charitable organizations, medical researchers, news stations, talk shows, and countless individuals seeking advice or offering it.

Though neither she nor her father cooperated with the paparazzi, before and after photos of him kept showing up online and on gossipy television talk shows. Pictures of Thomas as a befuddled old man contrasted sharply with his recent ones. People were convinced he'd discovered the fountain of youth and weren't about to leave him alone until he shared his secret.

"This is ridiculous," Thomas said one afternoon, looking at another pile of unopened mail. "We should just throw it all out."

"Really? Your fan-mail? I thought you'd be eating up all this adoration." She let her sarcasm drip heavily.

"I want to be appreciated for my intellect, not as a freak of nature." He sighed and knocked the tower of mail over so that it slid across the table. "This is meaningless. I'm just the celebrity of the moment, anyway. I suppose if we're patient, people will eventually lose interest."

"I don't know. Have you looked at yourself in the mirror lately?"

He grunted. "Trying not to. Whatever Kessler did to me, clearly affected more than my brain function."

"Clearly. Your hair's even turning dark again." When he frowned, she added, "Seriously. Go look."

He hesitated for a moment, then got up and walked over to the mirror in the hallway and finger-parted his silver strands to reveal the beginnings of brown roots. "Jesus."

"Maybe it's true what they're saying—you're getting younger."

"Highly improbable." He turned his head from side-to-side scowling at his reflection.

"You don't have an aging portrait of yourself hidden away in a closet, do you?"

He turned his scowl in her direction. "This isn't a joking matter. No one knows what that charlatan did to me. I could drop dead any moment."

"Not according to Dr. Peterson." She sighed. "Maybe you should stop worrying about where this is all going and just enjoy how it feels, which according to you is a hell of a lot better than before. Seems to me you've been given the ulti-mate gift—a second chance."

"Hmmm... well, it's a nice thought, anyway." He smiled wistfully. "Assuming I don't screw it up as badly as I did the first one."

That surprised Jo. "You think you screwed up?"

"Of course. Doesn't everyone? I assumed you would be the first to agree, everything considered."

"Okay. Like what?"

"I'm sure you could come up with a long list."

"No, no. Don't put this on me. You're the one who said you screwed up. So how exactly? I want to know."

"You're not going to make this easy for me, are you?"

"No, I'm not. Maybe this is a second chance for both of us. If you have regrets, I want to hear them."

"I suppose this has been a long time coming." He walked back and sat on the sofa next to her. He took a few breaths without saying anything.

"I'm waiting."

"Don't rush me." He took another moment. "Okay. To begin with, I realize I wasn't the father you needed me to be. After Tommy died, I was so broken and angry I distanced myself from everyone, including you, maybe most especially you. It was a form of punishment, I suppose."

"Punishment?" She caught her breath and her chest constricted. "All this time, I thought it was my secret, but you knew." Her eyes stung. "I know I should have told you, but he made me promise."

"What promise? What are you saying?"

"I promised not to tell anyone, and he died. He died." The last came out in a choked sob.

Her father stared at her in horror.

Now she was crying in earnest, her long repressed guilt and shame exposed. "I knew where he was going, but I didn't say anything, and he died. He died because of me. It's my fault."

"Oh my god, Josie. No!" He reached for her and pulled her onto his lap. "My poor sweet girl." He squeezed her tight and rocked. "You mustn't think that, *ever*. You were just a child, and you adored him. If he told you to keep a secret, of course, you would. I can't believe all this time I thought you were blaming me when you were blaming yourself. I could barely look at you, I was so ashamed. You're not to blame. No. If anyone is, it's me."

She pulled away to look him in the face. "Why would it be your fault?"

"It was my job to keep him safe, not yours." He took a breath and shook his head. "I kept telling him he could do anything he wanted in life. I made him feel invincible when

I should have been warning him of the dangers. If anyone failed him, it was me."

She stared at him as the impact of his confession hit her and her tears dried with the shock of it. "That's bullshit."

He blinked at her. "I beg your pardon?"

"You heard me. This is all bullshit. But you're right about screwing up. We both have, blaming ourselves for something out of our control. Tommy chose to go surfing that day. You told him not to and so did I, but he did it anyway. The only thing you're guilty of is believing you could trust him, and the only thing I'm guilty of is keeping a promise. Tommy made his own decision and what happened to him was an accident, just a really rotten accident. No one planned it and no one's to blame, not you, not me, not even Tommy."

"Yes, you're right. Of course, you are." Thomas sniffed, and his eyes were red. "Still, there's no excuse for how I've behaved. I've been so hard on you and I'm not even sure why. Maybe it was some misguided attempt to protect you, or more likely, I was just trying to protect myself. Some flaw in my character, apparently. It certainly can't be explained by any in yours. I suppose all I can do now is apologize and try to do better."

"So, you think I'm an okay person then?"

His eyes widened. "Good lord, if not for you, I wouldn't even be alive, let alone getting a second chance. You're far more than just *okay*. You're amazing." He kissed her on the forehead, then looked in her eyes. "Josie, you are my greatest gift, my most precious daughter, and I need you to know in your heart that I love you every bit as much as I ever did him. I always have. I just haven't always known how to show it, and for that, I am deeply, deeply sorry."

Overwhelmed with emotion, she buried her face in his neck, breathing in the familiar spice of his cologne, the one Mother had bought for him every Christmas. "You don't know how much I needed to hear that."

He hugged her back, hanging on to her, until she was the one to pull away.

"Okay, okay, enough. Fences mended, water under the bridge and all that." Laughing to disguise her tears, she stood and swiped her face. "Now that we've got that settled, what are we going to do about all these admirers of yours?" She waved at the scattered pile of mail and the phone machine blinking with unheard messages.

His warm smile drooped as he looked where she pointed. "I've no idea, but I do know we can't go on living like prisoners in our own home. Maybe Scott has some suggestions. Where is he, by the way? I haven't seen him around lately."

"He had to go to Washington D.C. to testify at that hearing. He should be back tomorrow."

"Keeping his word then. Good. You're kind of stuck on him, aren't you?"

"A little. We're still figuring things out."

"Well, whatever you decide, you have my approval... as long as he treats you well, of course."

"Not really your business," Jo answered, but said it with a sardonic smile.

He raised an eyebrow. "Of course it's my business. I'm your father."

CHAPTER THIRTY-SEVEN

Ghosts

Jo called upstairs to her father. "Did you hear the news? The coroner report came back on Kessler's autopsy."

Thomas yelled back. "No, what did it say?" His voice came from deep inside his bedroom.

Rather than continue yelling, Jo walked up the stairs and entered his open door. He was standing in front of his bathroom mirror spraying something in his hair.

"Turns out Suzanne was right," she said. "He really was ill. They found evidence of something called Frontal Temporal Lobe Dementia. Seems the early signs of FTLD are poor judgement and lack of empathy. Sounds about right, doesn't it?"

He glanced at her and nodded. "That it does."

"Such a shame. A brilliant man like that. Destroyed by the very thing he was trying to cure."

"He was trying to cure Alzheimer's not FTLD."

"Okay, dementia then, whatever you want to call it. Seems to go by a lot of different names."

"Speaking of names, did you ever find out who was behind the San Diego Conservatorship Society?"

"Yes. It's a fiduciary owned by a woman in Los Angeles— pretty much a shell company Sutton used to run conservatorships through for the inmates transferred to the Kessler Institute. That way she had a legal basis for handling their finances, approving their treatments, and arranging their burials."

Thomas shook his head. "And to think I was almost caught up in that machine of theirs."

"Yeah, pretty diabolical. The more I read about how much abuse there is in the conservatorship system, the angrier I get. Some of these horror stories make what Sutton did look selfless in comparison."

"She turned a blind eye to a lot, and did worse herself to protect him. You might blame it on being in love, but it was never selfless."

"I suppose not." Jo thought back to that night. To the coldblooded way Suzanne had dispatched those two men, then shot Kessler when he'd held a blade to Jo's throat. She couldn't say what had motivated the woman. Self-preservation? Rage? She had no doubt though that Suzanne had immediately reacted with sincere shock and regret when Kessler fell, and she'd tried desperately to save him from being washed out to sea. They both had, and in trying to save him, Jo nearly drowned. How she survived that night still confused her and was hard to talk about, but the way it haunted her, she knew she needed to.

"Dad, I keep thinking about being out there in the ocean with him and Suzanne, the two of us trying to save him despite everything, but we just couldn't. It was so dark and cold, and I was exhausted from fighting everything and everyone, I just couldn't do it anymore."

He set the spray can down and looked at her. "What are you saying?"

"I'm saying I gave up. I stopped struggling to survive, stopped caring if I did. I was ready to drown, to join Tommy, but then something I can't explain happened. Someone or something pushed me to the surface and got me back to shore. I thought it was you, but you said it wasn't."

"Well, I did pull you out those last few feet."

She nodded. "No, I know, but I'm talking about before that, when I was still out there, past the breakwater, in way over my head. I was too tired to swim anymore and started sinking. I was blacking out when I felt myself being pushed to the surface."

Thomas furrowed his brows. "Well, I don't think it was Kessler, not with a bullet in his chest, and I'm told Suzanne was already out of the water by then. I suppose it could have been a friendly porpoise—I've heard of such things—or perhaps you imagined it. A surge of adrenaline when you think you're about to die can have strange effects on the mind."

"Maybe... but it seemed so real." She hesitated to go on but could see he was waiting for it. "You'll probably think I'm crazy, but... I felt like it was Tommy."

He took a long breath and nodded. "I don't think you're crazy. I feel him around me all the time. Your mother, as well. I just never talk about it.

"Don't tell me you believe in ghosts."

He shrugged a bit sheepishly. "Let's just say I'm open to the possibility. And it's not so farfetched, considering the improbable fact that I'm coloring my roots right now."

She walked over to take a closer look. The can held a silver dye. "Most people try to cover their gray, not add to it."

"I think you'll agree my situation is unique. I'm trying to look more like the prior me, the one in the before pictures. It's all part of a plan Scott and I came up with."

"Why wasn't I included?

"You are. I just hadn't gotten round to telling you yet. Step one is for me to return to my doddering old self. I need to convince the world I'm no example of everlasting youth, but they'll only believe it when they see a sickly old man lingering on death's door. Maybe when I'm dead and buried, they'll finally leave us alone."

Jo blinked in confusion. "What are you talking about? I thought you were fine."

"Don't be dense. I'm not actually dying. It's a ruse, part of the plan."

"You want to fake your own death?"

"Exactly. Do try to catch up."

She scowled at him. "You're doing it again. Using sarcasm to distance yourself."

He froze and looked at her. "I am, aren't I? I guess they're right. Old habits die hard. Apologies." He went back to examining his hair, parting it, and spraying.

"You're serious about this?"

"*Dead* serious," he said with a smirk. "I've made sure my will is up-to-date. I was thinking you might want to convert at least part of this house into law offices, but that's up to you, of course. Or sell it if you like. It's your decision. After the funeral, Scott will set me up with a new identity in a new location, sort of like a witness protection program. No one will know who I really am... or who I used to be, rather."

"What about the research? I thought you wanted to help."

"I'll continue to donate blood and get MRI's, and send the results to Jacob, no return address of course. He'll make sure the information gets to the right people."

"What about us? Will I get to see you?"

Thomas slowly set the spray can down again, but this time he focused on it rather than meet her eyes. "Probably not. To be honest, that's why I hadn't told you yet. If this is going to work, Scott says we'll have to cut ties."

She took a long deep breath, letting the idea sink in. "Well, if that's what you want."

"It's not, not at all." He turned toward her. "This has nothing to do with what I want, and everything to do with what's best. This is no kind of life for you, trapped in a fishbowl. You've done more for me than any father has a right to ask. It's high time I got out of your way. You say I've been given a second chance, but you deserve one, too. I need to do this, for both of us."

Jo nodded, then choked on a deep sob. She grimaced and wiped the tears away. "It's just that we were finally starting to get along, you know? I mean, really get along."

"I know, I know... I'm so sorry, I truly am." He put his arms around her and kissed her cheek before pulling back to look at her face. "But I'm so very grateful for it, too. And who knows—maybe now you'll be able to think of something nice to say at my funeral."

Jo smiled at his attempt at humor, but for her it was bitterly ironic. "I don't think I ever told you, but one of the last things Kessler said to me was that I should go home and plan your funeral."

"Well, that was in poor taste. But seeing as I'm still alive you won't have to." He let go and went back to looking at himself in the mirror, frowning as he turned his head from side-to-side. "No, I intend to plan it all myself. I'll even attend—in disguise, of course."

"You sure you want to?"

"Absolutely. How many people get a chance to hear their own eulogies? I expect it will be quite touching."

She barked a laugh. "Yeah, like a roast." She instantly regretted the unfiltered remark.

His eyebrows shot upwards. "Are you joking?"

She made a face. "Not really. Sorry."

He paused and pursed his lips. "I see. Well, in that case, I shall attempt to view it as a learning experience."

Epilogue

Jo sat in the airport, people-watching to pass the time while she waited for Scott's return. He'd dropped her off with their bags and gone to find long-term parking. Now that she was six months pregnant, he wasn't about to let her drag luggage around or do much of anything else.

"You're spoiling me," she frequently accused him, but enjoyed the extra attention.

As she waited, her half-worried, half-excited thoughts ran ahead to this planned trip to St. Louis where she would meet Scott's parents for the first time. She'd spoken to his mother, Julia, on the phone many times during these last three years, joining forces with her to smooth things over between Scott and his father. Despite her best efforts, the two men still hadn't been on speaking terms by the time their wedding date rolled round, so neither Julia nor Hector attended. The continued estrangement made Jo doubly sad in the absence of her own parents and drove her to repair the only parent-child relationship still salvageable.

"You need to fix this," she told Scott in a stern ultimatum when she discovered she was pregnant. "Our child is not growing up without grandparents."

She rested her hand on her swollen belly, now silently thanking their unborn child for being the impetus for this reunification. She hoped this face-to-face meeting would heal the last of the rift. She sighed, recalling how much resistance she'd encountered on both sides. Negotiating the maze of family history was always a thorny challenge. Her own had been no exception, but she took comfort knowing she and her father had resolved their differences before parting.

She didn't know where he'd gone or what name he went by now, nor did Scott, but the less they knew the better, seeing as reporters, investigators, and medical researchers still called, trying to pry information from them. Some asked about her father's symptoms, and the treatments he'd received. Others poked into the most lurid details surrounding Dr. Kessler. The gossipmongers she hung up on, but when genuine medical researchers called, she cooperated as much as she could, and they informed her of their progress in trying to reconstruct Kessler's treatments. Apparently his notes had become more and more erratic near the end until they made little sense. Scott's father, a medical researcher himself, was equally intrigued, but had no more insight than anyone else. It looked like it would be years before the answers were found, if ever.

On the plus side, their friend Jacob found himself in high demand for what he knew about Kessler's experiments in the mouse labs. She and Scott stayed in touch with Maggie and Jacob, and took part in each other's weddings.

As for Suzanne Sutton's fate, Jo had mixed feelings. While on the one hand she owed Suzanne her life, she and her father would never have needed saving if not for Suzanne's culpability. Nevertheless, Jo kept her word and helped work out a plea agreement reducing the charges against Suzanne in exchange for turning state's evidence. Suzanne testified against Reginald Howell, who'd been arrested at the airport trying to leave the country. The money trail led from Howell to his employers and on to a US Senator by the name of Randall Pike, who lost his bid for re-election due to all the negative publicity about illegal experimentation on prisoners. Meanwhile, Kessler's research facility closed, and its patients were moved elsewhere. Jo kept close tabs on them, many of whom became clients of hers. The federal investigation was still following the money and the wheels of justice were still turning, too slowly for Jo's liking, but they hadn't stopped. She and Scott stayed involved, determined to plug the holes in the penal system.

Their efforts resulted in Jo's private practice taking off, evolving in ways she never could have predicted. In advocating for the rights of seniors, and laws protecting vulnerable inmates from exploitation, she'd been drawn into representing other civil rights matters. Her client base covered a broad spectrum of age, race, ethnicity and gender orientation, and her case load had grown so much that she'd hired on three more attorneys. As her father had suggested, she converted the old family home into a law office, and Scott hung that shingle above the front door as promised. Both Carl and Bev came to work with Jo. Bev started out as her personal secretary, and evolved into the office adminis-trator, while Carl became a partner this last year. Thanks to a blind date Scott set up with his old boss, Bev had also ac-quired a live-in boyfriend. As the pair's relationship grew more serious, Bev's come-hither style turned into a more professional one, both to Jo's relief and amusement.

In the interim, Dawson's firm took a huge hit. After the Kessler Institute closed and stories came out about how Dawson helped with a cover-up, the other named partners split off, divesting themselves of the Dawson name. Word was that Dawson was under investigation, too, and stood a decent chance of being disbarred.

Such a shame, Jo smirked inwardly. She didn't mind in-dulging herself in a bit of schadenfreude at Dawson's expense.

As she sat there in the airport ruminating on all that had happened, people kept passing by her on their way here and there. A few caught her eye now and then, but she gave them little thought until a man came to a full stop before her. Her meandering thoughts jerked to a halt. He was dressed in a dark bespoke business suit and appeared to be in his prime—early forties perhaps. He gave her a puzzled look, changed direction, and approached, wearing an uncer-tain smile.

Startled, she stood abruptly.

"Excuse me, but—" he began, then stopped, seeing her protruding belly. "Oh my. Looks like congratulations are in order."

"Yes, yes...," she said, trying to pull her wits together.

"Boy or girl? Or is it a secret?"

"Boy," she blurted.

"Wonderful." He nodded and smiled. "I'm sorry, this is a bit embarrassing. Seems I'm drawing a blank here, but your face is so familiar, I'm sure we've met." He trailed off, scowl-ing as if angry with himself.

She hesitated, uncertain how to deal with this chance encounter, when he didn't even remember her name. "Yes, we have, definitely... but... it's okay if you don't remember."

"It isn't actually, though you're kind to say so. Please remind me—what was your name again?"

"Josephine or Josie."

"Josie." He repeated the name slowly as if tasting it. "Yes, that feels right. So how are you, Josie? Well, I hope."

"Yes, thank you, I am... I'm fine." She paused before continuing, trying to figure out how much to say. "I'm married now, and I started my own law practice. My husband, Scott... he's a private investigator for our firm. We specialize in elder law and civil rights cases."

"Impressive. Sounds like rewarding work. Speaking of which, I'm traveling on business myself. How about you? Off on vacation or are you working, too?"

"Yes, no, I mean, neither really." She took a steadying breath and tried to smile. "We're flying out to St. Louis to visit Scott's family. I wanted to meet them before the baby arrives—" She heard herself talking too fast, trying to act as if this were all perfectly normal. "To be honest, we need to mend some fences."

He raised his dark eyebrows, looking amused. "Family matters. Always a tricky business. Hope it goes well."

"Yes, thanks. So do I. So, um, what about you? How are... things?"

"Excellent. Truly. I recently remarried, you know. A widow with two young children, a boy and a girl, and my career's going gangbusters. Consultant work requires me to fly frequently. For some reason, people seem to think I'm wise for my age." He chuckled.

"I'm sure they're right."

"Thank you. I'm glad things are going so well for you. I hope you're happy for me, too," he added with sudden urgency, then turned red in the face.

"Of course. How could I not be?"

He furrowed his brow, looking perplexed, as if he wanted to say something more, but had no idea what. "Yes, well..." He looked down at the gold watch she remembered rescuing more than once. "Oops, better run. Good seeing you again. Do say hello to your husband for me."

She merely nodded, unable to speak as she struggled against an overwhelming desire to wrap him in her arms and hug him hard. It was only by sheer will that she held herself back, knowing it would only add to his confusion.

As he walked away, he raised a hand in farewell, and she waved back. When he turned from her to merge with the crowd, she slowly lowered her hand to her heart. Silent tears tracked down her cheeks, and the pain in her chest nearly stopped her from breathing. She wanted to run after him, tell him everything, make him remember. Instead, she stood very still and watched until he disappeared from view.

He had found a new family, a new life, free of regret, free of loss, free of guilt. And she had found hers.

"I am happy for you, Dad. I really am."

<u>Novels by Marla L. Anderson</u>

NanoMorphosis

The Cost of Living: A Life For A Life

Unethical: A Psychological Thriller

****

Dear Reader,

Thank you for reading UNETHICAL. If you enjoyed this book (or even if you didn't) please write a brief review on Amazon, Goodreads, or wherever you purchased it. Your feedback is important to me and will help fellow readers decide whether they would like to read this book too.

If you'd like to know more about this author, or be notified of new releases, please go to: https://www.mlandersonauthor.com

Marla Anderson, 2021

****

Printed in the USA
CPSIA information can be obtained
at www.ICGtesting.com
LVHW090925301223
767793LV00052B/1942